◆ALTERNATIVES *is a series under the general editorship of Eric S. Rabkin, Martin H. Greenberg, and Joseph D. Olander which has been established to serve the growing critical audience of science fiction, fantastic fiction, and speculative fiction.*

Other titles in this series are:

Bridges to Science Fiction, edited by George E. Slusser, George R. Guffey, and Mark Rose, 1980

The Science Fiction of Mark Clifton, edited by Barry N. Malzberg and Martin H. Greenberg, 1980

Fantastic Lives: Autobiographical Essays by Notable Science Fiction Writers, edited by Martin H. Greenberg, 1981

Astounding Science Fiction: July 1939, edited by Martin H. Greenberg, 1981

The Magazine of Fantasy and Science Fiction: April 1965, edited by Edward L. Ferman, 1981

The Fantastic Stories of Cornell Woolrich, edited by Charles G. Waugh and Martin H. Greenberg, 1981

The Best Science Fiction of Arthur Conan Doyle, edited by Charles G. Waugh and Martin H. Greenberg, 1981

Bridges to Fantasy, edited by George E. Slusser, Eric S. Rabkin, and Robert Scholes, 1982

Coordinates: Placing Science Fiction and Fantasy, edited by George E. Slusser, Eric S. Rabkin, and Robert Scholes, 1983.

No Place Else: Explorations in Utopian and Dystopian Fiction, edited by Eric S. Rabkin, Martin H. Greenberg, and Joseph D. Olander, 1983.

The End of the World

Edited by

Eric S. Rabkin
Martin H. Greenberg
Joseph D. Olander

Southern Illinois University Press
Carbondale and Edwardsville

Copyright © 1983 by the Board of Trustees, Southern Illinois
  University
All rights reserved
Printed in the United States of America
Production supervised by John DeBacher

Library of Congress Cataloging in Publication Data
Main entry under title:

The End of the world.

  (Alternatives)
  Bibliography: p.
  Includes index.
  Contents: Introduction / Eric S. Rabkin—The
remaking of zero / Gray K. Wolfe—The lone survivor /
Robert Plank—[etc.]
    1. Science fiction—History and criticism—
Addresses, essays, lectures. 2. End of the world in
literature—Addresses, essays, lectures. I. Rabkin,
Eric S. II. Greenberg, Martin Harry. III. Olander, Joseph D.
IV. Series.
PN3433.6.E6 1983   809.3′876   82–19365
ISBN 0–8093–1033–3

86 85 84 83 4 3 2 1

Contents

Introduction: Why Destroy the World?

Eric S. Rabkin

"This is the way the world ends," T. S. Eliot wrote in "The Hollow Men" (1925), "not with a bang but a whimper." But modern science fiction has it both ways: in one story worlds collide, in the next the degenerate remnants of humanity huddle in a cave. We are driven from our world by our exploding sun or killed upon our world by mutated monsters of both the gigantic and microscopic sorts. Aliens intervene to wipe us out or transform us into their livestock. Even in the blessed cases in which the real estate is neither disinfected nor thoroughly atomized, "the world as we know it" seems doomed. This is, of course, no better than we deserve: we who have sown the world with technologies that fairly seduce us into Armageddon should expect to reap the worldwind. The modern popular literature of the end of the world continues humanity's permanent questioning of its place and its permanent quest for a reason to exist. We forever reimagine the pilgrimage in and out of history, seeking the well at the world's end, to drink the knowledge the gods withheld from Adam.

> Behold, the man is become as one of us, to know good and evil: and now, lest he put forth his hand, and take also of the tree of life, and eat, and live forever: Therefore the Lord God sent him forth from the garden of Eden . . . and . . . placed . . . a flaming sword which turned every way, to keep the way of the tree of life. (Gen. 3:22–24)

One way or another, we have always wanted to know too much, have made our Father-Gods jealous, have risked changing the world and thereby, inevitably, changed it. Ending our world, we simultaneously create a new one, one sometimes fearful and one sometimes hopeful, but one that always depends for its emergence upon the destruction of the world that preceded it. No matter how indirectly, we always call destruction an act we regret and yet somehow cherish as our own. If paradise is lost by us, we who have scared the gods have it in us to create a paradise anew. The end of the world is a consequence of our Original Sin.

In the written tale of Noah (probably about 850 B.C.E.), God himself recognizes the inevitability of the sins for which He destroyed the world: "the Lord said in his heart, I will not again curse the ground any more for man's sake; for the imagination of man's heart is evil from his youth" (Gen. 8:21). Instead, having purged the world, he urges the remaining people and animals to be "fruitful and multiply" (Gen. 9:7) and promises a new world stability the sign of which is the rainbow, "a covenant between me and the earth" (Gen. 9:13). At Ragnarok, the "destruction of the powers" of Norse mythology, when the monsters slay the gods and our world is destroyed, Yggdrasil, the "world-tree" that is the universe, persists and, after fire and flood subside, opens to bear Líf and Lífthrasir, a new and perfect man and woman to found the next human race. Forever the world has ended and each time, in fact, it has in some way gone on. In Milton's telling, even when Adam and Eve's garden world ends, they have a new world before them and His concern:

> The world was all before them, where to choose
> Their place of rest, and Providence their guide.
> They, hand in hand, with wandering steps and slow,
> Through Eden took their solitary way. (Paradise Lost, 1667)

When the world ends, what really ends is not all of creation but—only—the world as we know it.

By understanding precisely how the world ends, or nearly ends, and by understanding the consequences of that ending, we come to understand the values inherent in the tales. In science fiction, the world ends by earthly plague or cosmic accident or nuclear war, and yet it goes on. Despite its often inhuman elements, it is still a very human literature, just what one might expect human beings to write. The last man on earth typically finds other survivors (George R. Stewart's Earth Abides, 1949) or a better world elsewhere (Ray Bradbury's The Martian Chronicles, 1950) or a successor race of non-humans on earth (Clifford D. Simak's City, 1952) or in heaven (Arthur C. Clarke's Childhood's End, 1953). Rare is the case in this romantic literature of the last man facing eternal damnation, though such cases do occur (Harlan Ellison's "I Have No Mouth And I Must Scream," 1967). Of somewhat more frequent occurrence and somewhat more interest are the cases in which the world's end is ambiguous. In H. G. Wells' *The War of the Worlds* (1898), the Martians look like they really will exterminate most humans and breed the survivors as cattle. But before the alien victory becomes complete, the Martians mercifully drop dead, killed not by any human intervention but

> Slain by the putrefactive and disease bacteria against which their systems were unprepared . . . by the humblest things that God, in his widsom, has put upon this earth.

In tales of the end of the world, the fact of the end of the world as we know it reflects the evil "imagination of man's heart"; in the Wells case, the Martians are to Earthmen as historical Englishmen were to Indians; the evil that prompts the destruction of our world is not eating the forbidden apple but racism. In these stories, the agency of the end of the world as we know it, the mechanism employed, indicates what we are to think of our own imaginings. Here the Martians are described as utterly cerebral, sexless, and blood-sucking; British colonialism then is seen as based on pursuing narrowly economic policies instead of the natural human promptings toward community. Yet there is no denying that the British held the upper hand in the Victorian era. In tales of the end of the world as we know it, crucial judgments arise by comparing the world destroyed with the world for which it makes room. The hope of the world under Noah's rainbow is brighter than that before the flood; God has repented for making man of evil imagination and offers him a fresh chance. Wells is not so sure. Thinking of his lucky Englishmen, freed from Martian domination, the narrator muses:

> Dim and wonderful is the vision I have conjured up in my mind of life spreading slowly from this little seed-bed . . . . But that is a remote dream. It may be, on the other hand, that the destruction of the Martians is only a reprieve. To them, and not to us, perhaps, is the future ordained.

"Perhaps" is a crucial word. In the world as we now know it, mankind must use all its wisdom and its fellow-feeling, as well as its brain, to successfully take its "solitary way."

There are virtually no tales of the end of the world in which all of creation ends. But there a few. In Arthur C. Clarke's "The Nine Billion Names of God" (1953), American computer engineers are employed by Himalayan monks to program a machine to enumerate in their special alphabet the nine billion possible names of God. They have been laboring at this task for centuries by hand; its completion, they believe, is the purpose of the universe. The unbelieving Westerners program the computer, de-bug it, set it running, and begin their mule ride down the mountainside, hoping to escape before the program reaches its conclusion and lets loose the monks' disappointed anger. As the Americans descend, twilight falls. The story ends:

> "Look," whispered Chuck, and George lifted his eyes to heaven. (There is always a last time for everything.)
> Overhead, without any fuss, the stars were going out.

Here, of course, the end of the world really is the end of the world. And yet, on second thought, "perhaps" it is not. The world ends, as always, because mankind has made it end, performing its little sins or minor tricks or, as in this case, silly rituals, and thereby seeming to *compel* the actions of God Himself, to *require* the attention and response of all creation. Western man may need to combine his technological skill with Eastern man's faith if we are to achieve a more perfect world, but having done that combining, even despite Western man's beliefs, the world is in fact perfected: the divine creation/order/being with its nine billion names obviously does care about human beings, obviously does respond to them, and obviously will persist. Who can doubt that humanity will not fulfill some unimaginably blessed—and doubtless crucial—role in the sequel, whatever that may be? The world as we know it, frankly, is often disappointing; here, the end of that world obviously grants some deep and important wish.

To end the world may be, simply, to break free from a mental cage, to supplant one point of view—say the strictures of Father or of God-the-Father—with another point of view—say the totalizing domination of the world by the self. In French, after all, "all the world," "tout le monde," is simply the phrase for "everybody." To those who are comfortable in, say, "the world of fashion," that world may seem spacious; but to those trapped by society's rules and driven by their "evil imagination of youth," by lust and adventurousness and rebellion, the world may seem much too small. In James Blish's "Surface Tension" (1952), microbial versions of humanity finally flee forever the world of their puddle to find a new world in the next drop over. In Poul Anderson's *Tau Zero* (1970) the human heroes, apparently trapped by technology in a dead-end journey through space, accelerate madly, bravely counting on relativity effects and crash right through the moment when the universe ends by collapsing into itself, emerging in the next universe, after the next big bang, as the free first inhabitants of a green and golden planet. Now the space voyagers, formerly trapped in their technology and doomed by natural law, stand free in the world after the world's end, breathing the clean air of the garden regained. The cage of viewpoint has been burst.

Often, deciding whether or not the world indeed has ended depends upon viewpoint. In H. G. Wells' "The Star" (1899), for example, a flaming planet from interstellar space hurtles through the solar system barely missing the Earth. In its passing, it creates tidal waves and earthquakes and permanently raises world temperatures, melting polar ice and washing away most of human civilization. In the last paragraph, a new voice is heard, that of a Martian astronomer who notes the "little damage the earth . . . has sustained. All the familiar continental markings and the masses of the seas remain intact" except for a shrinkage of the white "discoloration" around the poles. The narrator, whether human or Martian or other we do not know, concludes that the Martian observation "only shows how small the vastest of human catastrophes may seem, at a distance of a few million miles."

> *The world is too much with us; late and soon,*
> *Getting and spending, we lay waste our powers;*
> *Little we see in Nature that is ours . . .*

What Wordsworth would see in Nature is "Proteus rising from the sea . . . old Triton blow[ing] his wreathéd horn" (1807). Wordsworth's poetic speaker wants to share out the blame by aligning himself with others: "the world is too much with *us*," he says, but he means that in following the life of economic man he misses the life of imagination; he lets his practical needs—which after all are a matter of opinion, one can live less well—prevent his seeing the world full of shape-changers and music-gods. If this world of commerce would end, "*I* might . . . have glimpses that would make me less forlorn." But to end this world, what the speaker need do, he recognizes, is become "A Pagan suckled in a creed outworn." The world we see is the world we were raised to see; to have a world of our own we must destroy the world we inherit and project ourselves onto chaos. The world, which in daily life seems to be the other, in the imaginative life is in fact the self.

In *For A New Novel* (1963), Alain Robbe-Grillet concludes that

Belief in a *nature* thus reveals itself as the source of all humanism, in the habitual sense of the word. And it is no accident if Nature precisely—mineral, animal, vegetable Nature—is first of all clogged with an anthropomorphic vocabulary. This Nature—mountain, sea, forest, desert, valley—is simultaneously our model and our heart.

In reality, villages do not "nestle" on mountainsides and mountains do not "loom" over valleys. Clouds only darken the sky in the eyes of those who watch the heavens and the sun does not set at all except for those with a fixed point of view. The world is the world we see, each world a worldview, each a whole. One world must end for the next to be born.

The languages of literature—and of scripture and of science— create worlds, destroy worlds, and create worlds again. This process is one we have all lived through. In some fundamental way different from our formal learning there resides in us all a knowledge that the world began when we opened our eyes and will end when we shut them. This happens in a small way when we fall into and rise from sleep and seems inevitably to confront us when we contemplate falling into the grave and fear that we shall not rise from it. The world of Yahweh, to a believing Christian, ended when Jesus fell to Earth and the new world will come into being when we can all, like Christ, rise from the grave. We control God the Father through the Son of Man. In a smaller, less philosophical way, we mollify someone who has been deeply disappointed by saying, "It is not the end of the world." This phrase really promises a new chance; it means to say that the person may still through some other agency succeed in projecting himself to his own satisfaction and thus make *the* world into *his* world. Or *her* world. But not, please, someone else's world. Property rights are all. We must hang on to whatever we can for at bottom some part of us agrees with the inhabitants of Samuel Butler's *Erewhon* (1872) that "To be born . . . is a felony—it is a capital crime, for which sentence may be executed at any moment after the commission of the offence." It is the Original Sin and we want to deny it. We would even destroy the world to obliterate it.

Gaston Bachelard has observed that literature is someone else dreaming for us. In *The Interpretation of Dreams* (1900), Sigmund Freud observed that

> All dreams are absolutely egotistical; in every dream the beloved ego appears, even though in a disguised form. The wishes that are realized in dreams are invariably the wishes of this ego; it is only a deceptive appearance if interest in another person is believed to have evoked a dream.

The first moment of psychological development is the separation of the ego from the undifferentiated id, the stabilization of self in the grand fluctuation of psychic stimulus and release; where once there was only everything, now there is ego and everything else. One exists, but one is diminished. In literature we dream of undoing that diminishment by creating a world that is the self.

In "To His Coy Mistress" (1681), Andrew Marvell wants to speed up his wooing. He begins: "Had we but world enough, and time, / This coyness, lady, were no crime." But time does not wait and this young man's evil imaginings wish to make the world a place of carnal, beautiful knowledge. Although he would be slow, he says, he must be fast. He promises his desired that their love making will, like death, end time. He suggests that

> *now, like amorous birds of prey,*
> *Rather at once our time devour*
> *Than languish in his slow-chapped power.*
> *Let us roll all our strength and all*
> *Our sweetness up into one ball,*
> *And tear our pleasures with rough strife*
> *Through the iron gates of life:*
> *Thus, though we cannot make our sun*
> *Stand still, yet we will make him run.*

The ball they create will be a world of their own and, by changing point of view, that world will be one in which the very heavens are responsive to the urgings of the ego. The tales of the end of the world in science fiction typically involve great violence. And typically they involve sex. Adam and Eve, having eaten, knew their nakedness and were ashamed and were condemned to childbirth. The last man on Earth seeks the last woman. The new world, "tout le monde," cannot be made without the making of people; the urge to make people becomes the urge to make a new world. These are the last lines of *The War of the Worlds*:

> And strangest of all is it to hold my wife's hand again, and to think that I have counted her, and that she has counted me, among the dead.

The gun, the knife, the sword—even the flaming sword—may well function as sexual symbols. Orgasm, which the Victorians called "the little death," yields "the population bomb." The ending of one world and the subsequent creation of another is, like so many other projections of the self, a matter of sex and violence.

In "Sleeping Beauty," the heroine is a princess promised death, but the penalty for her father's rudeness is mitigated. On her fifteenth birthday, when she sees her first spindle, an obvious phallic symbol, "the maiden" took

> the spindle into her hand . . . but no sooner had she touched it than . . . she pricked her finger with it. In that very moment she fell back upon the bed that stood there, and lay in a deep sleep.

Her whole world sleeps with her, as it would in an infantile fantasy and as it should since she is a monarch and in some sense incarnates her world, as did Oedipus and Hamlet, other young would-be rulers. The classic heroes foundered in worlds where sexual urgings had broken the social order; they could not themselves bring a new world into being and had to be supplanted. We all die. But in the kinder world of science fiction and fairy tales, the outcome is more pleasant. The Sleeping Beauty is named "Rosamond," world-rose. A hedge of thorns grows around her world so that young men who would come to her "were caught by them, and not being able to get free, there died a lamentable death." But after a hundred years,

> When the prince drew near the hedge of thorns, it was changed into a hedge of beautiful large flowers [the sexual organs of plants], which parted and bent aside to let him pass, and then closed behind him in a thick hedge.

In this intimacy he approaches Rosamond, kisses her, she looks "very kindly on him," the world is reborn and they marry to live "very happily together." This is the ending of "Sleeping Beauty" and also of *Tau Zero*. In Kate Wilhelm's *Where Late the Sweet Birds Sang* (1976), the world ends for nearly everyone. A plague of sterility is nearly universal. We follow the fortunes of a lucky, gifted few who have withdrawn to a remote Pennsylvania valley. They go through generations by cloning rather than sexual reproduction while the remaining dregs of humanity exterminate each other. The products of this cloning are ever less successful but finally a new hero arises, born by an extraordinary sexual reproduction, and he finally leaves the valley, the world before him, to shape the earth in his image and by his children. It takes some violence to accomplish this return from asexuality, but the return is happy. Here in science fiction is "Sleeping Beauty" again, the common pattern of the world as a map of the self ending in order to be recreated, violence performed to make room for sex, the values of the elders thrown off to give freedom to the imagination of youth.

Mary Queen of Scots took as her motto, "In my end is my beginning." This referred to her struggle and uncannily predicted her martyrdom. In death, the motto now seems to say, she first achieved her true life. In "East Coker" (1940), T. S. Eliot uses this motto in its first form but he also reverses it: "In my beginning is my end." At first this seems to be an echo of the fatalism of *Erewhon*, but end has more than one meaning. The end of Mary Queen of Scots was doubtless her termination; but her end was also her goal, her struggle. In the last book of the Bible, the world is destroyed for its "fornication" with the whore of Babylon, yet John says,

> I saw a new heaven and a new earth: for the first heaven and the first earth were passed away; and there was no more sea. And I John saw the holy city, new Jerusalem, coming down from God out of heaven, prepared as a bride adorned for her husband. (Rev. 21:1–2)

At one level, stories of the end of the world display the consequences of our social values; at another, the meanings of our wishes. The end that the world meets it meets as its end: the goal of world destruction is world creation, pro-creation, and re-creation for the citizen, for the child, and, most important, for the self. In the story, the world may end; the story of the end of the world goes on.

The End of the World

I

The Remaking of Zero: Beginning at the End

Gary K. Wolfe

In Ray Bradbury's 1950 short story "The Highway," a poor Mexican farmer who has lived for years beside a highway from the United States, enjoying such odd fruits of this link to technology as sandals made from tire rubber and a bowl made from a hubcap, is startled one day by the sudden appearance of cars speeding northward in great numbers, all filled with apparently panic-stricken American tourists returning home. The farmer, Hernando, cannot account for this sudden flood of traffic. At the end of the flood, however, comes an aging Ford, topless and packed with young Americans who stop at Hernando's shack to ask for water for their failing radiator. The driver explains the reason for the exodus: "'The war!'" he shouts, "'It's come, the atom war, the end of the world!'"—and the tourists are all trying to return to their families. After the young people leave, Hernando prepares to resume his plowing. When his wife asks him what has happened, he replies, "'It's nothing,'" and sets out with burro and plow, pausing momentarily to muse to himself, "'What do they mean, "the world?"'"[1]

This little parable of holocaust raises, in Bradbury's best elliptical form, some of the most fundamental issues of stories that begin at or near the "end of the world." Bradbury suggests that Hernando's simple and apparently self-sufficient world will continue much as it has (though, one assumes, without the interruption of tourists), while the "world" that has been destroyed is the world of technology and profligate wealth represented by the highway to the north. As in most post-holocaust fiction, the "end of the world" means the end of a way of life, a configuration of attitudes, perhaps a system of beliefs—but not the actual destruction of the planet or its population (though this population may be severely reduced). For this reason, it is perhaps most enlightening to regard such stories as tales of cosmological displacement: the old *concept* of "world" is destroyed and a new one must be built in its place. The world—in the sense of economic and political systems, beliefs and behavior patterns—may be destroyed; but more often than not the earth abides—and so, at least in part, does humanity. This kind of "end of the world" has occurred fairly often in human history, most obviously in such dramatic holocausts as the destruction of American Indian civilizations or the Nazi death camps, but also, to some extent, in such broader historical movements as the Industrial Revolution. Often such holocausts are associated with new technologies or the introduction of technologically superior weaponry, and in fact many of the apocalyptic anxieties of the last few decades seem to arise from just such a technological innovation—nuclear weapons. But in the fiction of holocaust, the world is often transformed by a reversal of this historical process: available technologies are *removed* from the world, rather than new ones introduced. Much of the impact of such fiction arises from the speculations it offers about the effects of the loss of technology on machine-dependent populations—such as the population that Hernando in "The Highway" watches flowing past him.

Bradbury's story reveals a number of themes common to post-holocaust fiction. The highway represents the mobility of a society that contrasts sharply with Hernando's own deep relationship with his little plot of land by the river, but that will quickly have to learn the value of such a relationship. Technology appears in the story in four guises. First, the "big long black cars heading north" suggest a whole complex of industrial civilization: the availability of trained mechanics; the dependability of industries that produce petroleum products, rubber, metal, and plastic; the efficiency of governments in maintaining roads and bridges. After this initial flood of technological marvels has passed, a second, more ominous image of the same technology appears: the dilapidated Ford, its top gone and its radiator boiling over. While this machine is part of the same society that produced the earlier ones, dependence upon it is clearly a precarious matter. It has begun to wear out, it no longer offers full protection from such discomforts of the natural world as rain, and it must be repaired frequently by whatever means are available—in this case, well-water from a farm for the radiator. Significantly, the Ford is driven by young people, since it is the young who will have to make do with such machines in a post-holocaust world: the decaying detritus of a mechanical civilization that has lost the means to service and maintain its machines.

But there is a yet more ominous image of what is to come for these young people. At the bottom of the river that runs by Hernando's hut lie the remains of one of the big American cars that had crashed there years earlier. Sometimes the wreck is visible, and sometimes it is obscured by the muddy waters; in a few years the sediment of the river will cover it entirely. From this wreck Hernando has salvaged the tire from which he carved his rubber sandals, just as his hubcap-bowl has been salvaged from a hubcap that had flown off another car. These images suggest what may become of technology after even the old Fords are gone: the machines themselves turned into raw materials, their parts stripped for primitive implements and clothing before they are reclaimed by the natural world, covered by silt like the car in Hernando's river.

A fourth image of technology suggests what might happen still later, when even salvaging the remnants of technology is insufficient. This image, the last in the story, is essentially one of life and hope: Hernando sets his plow in the furrowed soil and begins tilling the land. It is at this point that he wonders, "'What do they mean, "the world?"'" and the question is an appropriate one, since Hernando's present world resembles closely the world that may come to pass after industrial technology has faded altogether and the survivors are forced to return to that most basic of all machines, the plow. In the end, Bradbury's story is optimistic in its suggestion of a return to a simpler, less complex life and the promise of a better world to come. Such a vision is presented also in Bradbury's *The Martian Chronicles* (1950), in which the Martian colonists, like the Americans in "The Highway," return home *en masse* at the outbreak of nuclear war on earth. One family, however, escapes *to* Mars, and there the father ceremonially burns such symbols of the old world as stocks and bonds.[2] This suggestion of starting a new world symbolically cleansed of the sins of the old is not only in keeping with earlier millenarian traditions, but is also common in literary works that begin at or near the world-ending holocaust. As we shall see later, one of the richest of such novels, George R. Stewart's *Earth Abides* (1949), conforms closely to the pattern implied by Bradbury's "The Highway."

Although in one sense the very notion of beginning a narrative with a climactic holocaust seems perverse, especially if the underlying tone of the novel is going to be optimistic, such a fantasy is very much in keeping with traditions of millenarian thought. As Mircea Eliade writes, "the idea of the destruction of the World is not, basically, pessimistic."[3] Norman Cohn has traced medieval millenarian movements to the unrest, disorientation, and anxiety of the rootless poor who sought to improve their lives but found little cause for hope in existing social and economic structures.[4] While modern fictional ver-

sions of the end of the world differ in key respects from these earlier
millenarianists—few involve supernatural agencies or clearly messianic leaders, for example—they often share the fundamental belief
that a new order can come about only through a complete destruction
of the old—that, in Eliade's terms, "life cannot be *repaired*, it can only
be *re-created* by a return to sources."[5] Or, in the words of J. G. Ballard,
one of science fiction's own master catastrophists, "I believe that the
catastrophe story, whoever may tell it, represents a constructive and
positive act by the imagination rather than a negative one, an attempt
to confront the terrifying void of a patently meaningless universe by
challenging it at its own game, to remake zero by provoking it in
every conceivable way."[6] "'Now we have finished with the past,'"
thinks the protagonist of Stewart's *Earth Abides* after surviving a
mysterious plague that all but wipes out humanity. "'This is the
Moment Zero, and we stand between two eras. Now the new life
begins. Now we commence the Year One.'"[7]

The promise inherent in the idea of "remaking zero" is certainly
one of the reasons this genre has survived as long as it has, and in so
many guises. On the simple level of narrative action, the prospect of a
depopulated world in which humanity is reduced to a more elemental
struggle with nature provides a convenient arena for the sort of heroic
action that is constrained in the corporate, technological world that we
know. The "true" values of individual effort and courage are allowed
to emerge once again, and power flows to those who possess these
attributes—to a "natural aristocracy" uninhibited by political and
economic complexities. (Perhaps, in this sense, the ancestry of the
modern disaster novel should include James Fenimore Cooper, whose
works also depict the emergence of a new aristocracy in the wilderness
of a new world where the conventions and constraints of the old have
been annihilated.) This simplification of relationships also permits a
simplification of the forces of good and evil, making it possible to
depict a world of easily discernible heroes and villains. Thus, merely in
terms of the action story, the notion of starting the world over is
appealing.

As science fiction, end-of-the-world stories provide a convenient
means of exploring at least two of the genre's favorite themes without
necessitating the sometimes cumbersome narrative apparatus usually
associated with these themes. One such theme, the impact of technology on human behavior, is most often dealt with through the
introduction of new technologies into fictional worlds—robots, time
machines, spacecraft, computers, etc. But the problems of developing

both the details of the new technology and the details of the fictional world create a rather complex dialectic for the reader, who must try to understand the impact of a fictional technology on a fictional world and draw from that some insights concerning our own world and our own technology. By *removing* familiar technology from a fictional world, however, the end-of-the-world story simplifies this dialectic considerably. Rather than introduce new machines, an author can remove or reduce the functioning of the familiar ones and still explore issues of technology and society. A number of science fiction stories—including E. M. Forster's "The Machine Stops" (1909), S. S. Held's "The Death of Iron" (1932), and Kit Pedler and Gerry Davis's *Mutant 59: The Plastic Eaters* (1972)—construct the entire holocaust around the failure of machines; the latter two stories concern worldwide plagues that affect only machine parts such as iron and plastic.

Another science fiction theme made accessible by the device of beginning at the end is that of humanity's relationship to its environment, or its alienation from that environment. Like new machines, new and strange environments are likely to require a great deal of narrative exposition concerning alien planets, climates, and the like. In the post-holocaust story, this problem can be circumvented by defamiliarizing familiar environments through the transformations wrought by the disaster. A city emptied of its people, whether through nuclear disaster or disease or environmental catastrophe, becomes a strange and alien place. Similarly, a pastoral landscape becomes a foreboding wasteland by the implied danger of holocaust survivors reduced to savagery, disfigured by radiation, or given to strange new beliefs. Leigh Brackett's *The Long Tomorow* (1955) and John Wyndham's *Re-Birth* (1955) depict wasteland journeys detailed with such geographical verisimilitude that they can be traced on current maps of North America; the territory is that familiar, and yet so alien that we can have no idea of what it may contain. Robert Merle's *Malevil* (1972) spends much time before the holocaust detailing the landscape surrounding the ancient fortress of Malevil, so that after the disaster we can better appreciate the devastating transformation this landscape has undergone. Generally, geography is an important recurrent element in post-holocaust narratives, and almost always it serves to establish a link between the strange new environment and the world we know.

Related to these familiar science fiction themes is what is probably the fundamental reason for the emotional power of post-holocaust narratives: the mythic power inherent in the very conception of a

remade world. The sources of mythic power in this genre are at least
threefold, for in most post-holocaust narratives we see the re-
emergence of chaos into the experiential world (and the attendant
opportunities this provides for ritualistic heroic action); the reinforcement of cultural values through the triumph of these values in a final,
decisive "battle of the Elect"; and the assurance of racial survival
despite the most overwhelming odds—a kind of "denial of death" on a
cultural rather than individual level.

By "the re-emergence of chaos" I mean the return of Nature as a
material adversary in the narrative. The appropriation of chaos and its
transformation into cosmos is a fundamental activity of technology,
and perhaps of culture. But as the arena for this confrontation moves
ever outward, the individual becomes ever more insulated from the
central adventure of cultural and technological growth. Much science
fiction follows this outward movement; once the natural environment
of earth has been subdued, Nature becomes outer space, or alien
planets. But the post-catastrophe tale brings this confrontation with
Nature closer to home; in these stories chaos may lie just beyond the
limits of the village, or outside the family circle, or—especially with
"last man on earth" stories—around the next corner. In M. P. Shiel's
The Purple Cloud (1901), the struggle is even internalized; the question is not merely whether Adam Jeffson, apparently the last man on
earth, can master the immense environment he inherits, but whether
what he calls the "White" forces of his own mind can master the
destructive and chaotic "Black" forces that cause him to deliberately
burn great cities and almost to kill the only surviving woman. Mythic
heroic action depends partly upon confrontation with chaos, and the
post-holocaust world repeatedly provides opportunities for such
confrontations.

But such confrontation is meaningful only if it can be associated
with a set of values, and the reinforcement of such values is another
mythic function of the post-holocaust tale. In fact, such tales oftenly
become openly didactic, pitting diametrically opposed value systems
against one another in a final battle for supremacy. Once the "evil"
antagonists are vanquished, such narratives seem to say, so will the evil
values they represent disappear, making it possible for the new world
to evolve toward greater perfection than the old. One of the most
didactic of such novels, Alfred Noyes's *No Other Man* (1940), pits the
devout Catholic protagonist against the mad scientist Marduk, only to
vanquish Marduk and thus somehow validate the superiority of religious over scientist thought. Only slightly less didactic is Alfred

Coppel's *Dark December* (1960), in which the opposed value systems are both military: the conscientious and professional but guilt-ridden (because of his role in the nuclear war as a missile officer) Gavin against the psychopathic, fascistic Collingwood, who sees the devastated environment as an opportunity for men like himself to rise to power. (Needless to say, Collingwood eventually falls off a bridge.) In Merle's *Malevil*, following the holocaust of nuclear chain-reactions, the rationalistic communal life of Malevil castle under the direction of Emmanuel Comte comes into conflict with an oppressive theocracy imposed on a neighboring village by the hypocritical false priest Fulbert le Naud. The ensuing struggle for supremacy not only validates the humanism of Malevil's system, but also indirectly validates the need for technology, since the struggle convinces the inhabitants of Malevil that they must begin research into the reinvention of weapons in order to protect their interests and values—despite their acute awareness of what the technology of weaponry can ultimately lead to.

A third mythic function of the fictional end of the world is that, ironically, it provides some reassurance of survival. In fact, most such fictions that we conveniently label "holocaust" or "end of the world" stories are in fact quite the opposite, and dwell on the *survival* of key representative types of individuals and in some cases the key institutions (such as the family) as well. It might be more accurate to label such fictions "*almost*-the-end-of-the-world" fictions, or "end-of-most-of-the-world" fictions, but works that describe a complete annihilation of the planet and all human life are comparatively rare. And even among this small group of works, such as Poe's "Conversation of Eiros and Charmion," there is some promise at least of spiritual survival. Eliade has suggested that old-fashioned millenialism has suffered under the threat of nuclear holocaust, that modern western thought does not hold out much hope for survival and regeneration. "In the thought of the West this End will be total and final; it will not be followed by a new Creation of the World."[8] But the fiction of holocaust belies this, and does provide some reassurance against nuclear anxiety. With the exception of a few works such as Mordecai Roshwald's *Level 7* (1959) and Nevil Shute's *On the Beach* (1957), most nuclear holocaust stories assure us that humanity can rebuild against the most staggering odds—and the same is true for other types of holocausts as well. This promise of survival redeems even the bleakest of post-holocaust fictions. Wilson Tucker's *The Long Loud Silence* (1952), for example, details the growing brutality of its protagonist in a shattered world. In terms of the survival of values we discussed earlier, there is nothing much promising about Corporal Russell Gary, who finally rejects all human companionship and—in the novel's unpublished original ending—even apparently resorts to cannibalism.[9] A similar bleakness and apparent destruction of values, leading again to cannibalism, characterizes Harlan Ellison's "A Boy and His Dog" (1969). But each of these fictions holds out the promise of survival, and Ellison's even perversely suggests that values, too, will survive, even if they are comparatively trivial and sentimental ones. After all, Ellison's protagonist says after making a meal of his lover to keep his pet dog from starving, "A boy loves his dog."[10]

Whether these stories aspire to simple adventure, to intellectual science fiction, or to cultural myth, stories that begin at the end of the world have, over the years, evolved a fairly characteristic narrative formula. The formula may be varied in many ways, with some elements expanded to fill nearly the whole narrative, others deleted, and new ones added, but there are commonly five large stages of action: (1) the experience or discovery of the cataclysm; (2) the journey through the wasteland created by the cataclysm; (3) settlement and establishment of a new community; (4) the re-emergence of the wilderness as antagonist; and (5) a final, decisive battle or struggle to determine which values shall prevail in the new world. While this formula describes specifically works which begin with the cataclysm itself, elements of it may also be found in narratives that begin before the holocaust or in ones that begin long after.

1. *Experience or discovery of the cataclysm.* Works that begin at the end of the world usually limit their viewpoint to that of one or two central characters, and the manner in which the cataclysm is revealed to these characters traditionally takes one of two forms: either the central character is isolated from others when the event occurs, and thus has no immediate knowledge of it, or the character witnesses the event indirectly from a relatively safe vantage point. The former case, in which part of the drama is the character's gradual discovery of the nature and extent of the disaster, includes Shiel's *The Purple Cloud* (and Ranald MacDougall's considerably different 1958 film from this novel, *The World, the Flesh, and the Devil*), Noyes's *No Other Man* (which coincidentally was also briefly considered for filming by Frank Capra), and Stewart's *Earth Abides*. Of these, only the Shiel novel attempts to forge a direct moral link between the protagonist's symbolic isolation from human society and the destruction of humanity. Adam Jeffson is off discovering the North Pole when the strange

volcanic gas kills all of humanity, but he achieves his goal only by committing a series of murders; furthermore, he describes himself from childhood as being "separate, special, marked for—something."[11] Jefferson sees his subsequent isolation alternately as a monumental punishment for his evil deeds and as a monumental reward for his being "special." He is cursed by loneliness and madness, but he also inherits the earth and founds a new race—resembling one of the Nietzschean supermen of Shiel's later fiction. Stewart and Noyes each provide some moral justification for the survival of their protagonists; in *Earth Abides*, Isherwood Williams is helplessly recovering from a snakebite while on an ecological expedition in the woods, and in *No Other Man* Mark Adams is trapped in a wrecked enemy submarine where he had been held captive. In each case, the character is relieved somewhat of the responsibility of being isolated, since the isolation is enforced by external circumstances. But in neither case is a direct moral link established between the actions of the survivors and the destruction of the rest of humanity.

Stories in which the survivors witness the cataclysm from a protracted vantage point are somewhat more common. The protagonists of both Roshwald's *Level 7* (1959) and Coppel's *Dark December* are military personnel stationed in underground bunkers. Philip Wylie's *The End of the Dream* (1972) and Kate Wilhelm's *Where Late the Sweet Birds Sang* (1976), both of which deal with complex series of ecological catastrophes, portray isolated strongholds specifically designed to withstand the impending cataclysms. The central characters of Merle's *Malevil* happen to be gathered in a deep wine cellar whose stone walls protect them from the holocaust of flame, and the collision of earth with another planet is witnessed from aboard a spaceship by characters in Philip Wylie and Edwin Balmer's *When Worlds Collide* (1933). In S. Fowler Wright's *Deluge* (1928) and John Bowen's *After the Rain* (1958), the good fortune of being on high ground or finding boats save the protagonists from worldwide floods. Geography also protects the survivors of nuclear war in Pat Frank's *Alas, Babylon* (1959) and Wilson Tucker's *The Long Loud Silence* (1952); both novels begin in small towns isolated from major target areas. And in one of the few openly comic treatments of this theme, Robert Lewis Taylor's *Adrift in a Boneyard* (1947), a mysterious thunderclap annihilates everyone except a family in their car on the way to the theatre—clearly suggesting the family was deliberately "chosen" for survival. (Though the two novels may seem odd bedfellows, *Adrift in a*

Boneyard shares with *The Purple Cloud* the implication that the end of the world is brought about largely to force moral choices upon the main characters of the novel.)

2. *Journey through the wasteland.* Perhaps because of its mythic aspect, this is often one of the most important elements in post-holocaust fiction; occasionally—as with Robert Crane's *Hero's Walk* (1954) or Roger Zelazny's *Damnation Alley* (1969)—it occupies virtually the whole of the novel. But extensive journeys also figure in the works mentioned by Noyes, Shiel, Wright, Coppel, Stewart, Taylor, Tucker, Brackett, and Wyndham. Such journeys serve two major functions: to provide an overview and confirmation of the disaster, and to serve as a kind of purgation of despair on the part of the central character. The longest such purgation, in Shiel's *The Purple Cloud*, takes Adam Jeffson through decades of madness and destruction. In the Noyes and Taylor novels, the journeys also serve to satirize the trivial aspects of pre-holocaust life by revealing people caught up in petty matters at the time of death. Stewart's protagonist sees on his cross-country journey the various ways people may relate to their environment, most poignantly observed in the contrast between a self-subsistent black farm family and a hopelessly technology-dependent Manhattan couple, trying to survive in an empty but still mostly functioning New York.

In Coppel's *Dark December* and Wright's *The Deluge*, the journey is motivated by the desire to reunite families separated by the cataclysm, with despair mitigated by the increasingly irrational hope that a wife or husband has somehow also survived. Such hope also motivates some of the survivors in Shute's *On the Beach* (1957) and Frank's *Alas, Babylon*. In Tucker's *The Long Loud Silence*, Brackett's *The Long Tomorrow*, and Wyndham's *Re-Birth*, rumors of a better society somewhere beyond the wasteland motivate the journey. And in nearly all these novels, the search for additional survivors with whom one might establish a new community is a central motivation for the journey.

But the journey has another aspect, too: the promise of new frontiers, of exploring a new or remade world. In Philip Wylie and Edwin Balmer's *After Worlds Collide*, which begins following the destruction of the earth, the world to be explored is literally a new planet where the survivors hope to settle (though the ruins of an ancient technological civilization make it seem curiously like the landscape of a future earth). But even earthbound disaster fictions suggest that the frontiers have been remade, especially if we remember that

the classical nineteenth-century definition of "frontier" was based on
low population density rather than simply whether an area had once
been explored. These new frontiers thus might include even urban
areas. Despair is once again mitigated, then, by the hope, restored by
cataclysm, of renewed patterns of growth and exploration, and by the
sense of immense freedom that comes from being able to choose
openly where and how one will live. Shiel's Adam Jeffson does not
hesitate to make himself at home in various palaces (the illustrations
accompanying the original appearance of *The Purple Cloud* in *The
Royal Magazine* even portray him as a sort of Oriental potentate), and
the family in Taylor's *Adrift in a Boneyard* quickly takes advantage of
the situation to move into the mansion of an eccentric millionaire,
enjoying the security that this provides against ravaging animals and
such luxuries as a fine wine cellar as well.

   3. *Settlement and establishment of a community.* Following the
confirmation of the cataclysm brought about by the wasteland journey
comes the establishment of a permanent settlement which will be the
basis of the new community and, by extension, of the new civilization.
In Shiel's *The Purple Cloud*, in which there are only two survivors, this
community has to be rather loosely defined, but the novel nonetheless
provides the archetype for post-disaster communities, which are frequently associated with the "marriage" of the protagonist, and hence
with the prospect of a new family and eventually a new community. Contrary to many readers' memories of *The Purple Cloud*, Jeffson's discovery of the sole surviving woman, Leda, occurs scarcely
more than two-thirds of the way through the narrative, and it is Leda
who causes him to cease his restless, destructive wandering and to
settle with her: at the end of the novel, when in despair he deliberately
abandons her to return to England, her telephone message that the
purple cloud has reappeared on the horizon causes him to flee back to
her and protect her. It is practically Jeffson's first motivated action
since the cataclysm, and the motivation is that of protectiveness and
preservation. Jeffson is clearly thinking of a good location for a settled
community by the end of the novel. Both Stewart's *Earth Abides* and
Wright's *Deluge* also associate the founding of the new community
with a woman; in the Stewart novel the new community accretes
around Isherwood Williams and his newly found wife Emily, while in
the Wright novel the community is associated with the simple values of
Mary Wittels, an almost archetypal "wise woman" who nurses the wife
of the protagonist back to health and is eventually instrumental in
reuniting them. Their reunion, we are led to believe throughout the

novel, is the single action most necessary to validate the stability of the new community. In Frank's *Alas, Babylon* and Merle's *Malevil*, both novels in which the symbolic journey is confined to short exploratory trips in the immediate neighborhood, the growing internal stability of the community occupies a proportionately larger role in the narrative. In *Alas, Babylon*, the journey motif is effectively replaced by a local ham radio operator who provides the necessary confirmation of the disaster by monitoring messages from other parts of the world. The narrative thus can focus on the problems the small Florida community of Fort Repose faces in defending itself from looters and obtaining necessary supplies. *Malevil*, perhaps the most determinedly localized of all post-holocaust novels, establishes at the outset the isolated, almost medieval aspect of the French countryside surrounding the small village of La Roque and focuses throughout on the problem of establishing a new social contract and the need for authority. It is interesting that both of these novels, with their paramount concern for the integrity of the village, end with the rediscovery of the necessity for military organizations and weapons, despite their demonstration of the dangers inherent in such institutions.

The novel that perhaps most clearly and thoughtfully explores the relationship between the outward journey and the community is Wilhelm's *Where Late the Sweet Birds Sang* (1976). In this novel, the integrity of the community is intensified by the presence of large numbers of human clones, who form social groups among those cloned from the same "donors." These "clone families" develop intense empathic relationships with one another, but when the necessity arises to make journeys to urban areas for supplies, they suffer a kind of separation anxiety experienced by ordinary humans during early child-hood. As a result, the journeys nearly fail, and the community is forced to turn for guidance to an "outsider," a normal child born without the genetic permission of the community who has learned the techniques of wilderness survival as a result of his isolation. The dangers of a community turned too much inward are emphasized even more strongly at the end of the novel when this outsider, Mark, establishes a community of normal "exiles" that survives long after the community of clones has failed. Mark's community, it is suggested, may mark a return to savagery compared with the protectiveness of the clone village, but it also represents the dynamic interaction with the environment that must take place in order to rebuild. Civilization cannot be preserved; it must be rebuilt.

4. *The re-emergence of the wilderness.* By "wilderness" I include not only the encroachments of the natural world on the community—the proliferation of rats, wild animals, disease, etc., and the erosion of such technological support systems as roads and electricity through the elemental forces of weather, fire, earthquakes, and vegetation growth—but also the challenges brought on by unorganized bands of fellow survivors, who commonly revert to savagery and thus threaten the stability of the frontier-type settlement. In many post-holocaust novels, the first great challenge to the survivors, once they have formed a community, lies in making the difficult transition from dependence on the detritus of the destroyed civilization—for example, raiding grocery stores for prepackaged foods—to reinventing an agricultural and mining economy that confronts the wilderness on its own terms. Hence, in *Alas, Babylon*, a major triumph of the survivors is discovering a natural source of salt to preserve meat following the loss of electrical refrigeration; in *Malevil*, a triumphant moment occurs with the successful raising of a small wheat crop. Stewart's *Earth Abides* details, through separate expository passages presented apart from the main narrative, the various ways in which natural forces over the years destroy the remnants of civilization upon which the survivors are initially dependent; and a continuing theme in Wilhelm's *Where Late the Sweet Birds Sang* is the growing inability of the isolated community to remain self-sufficient in the midst of growing wilderness.

Traditionally, with the wilderness comes the savage, and savagery in post-holocaust tales usually takes the form of individuals or groups who, rather than attempting to form stable communities of their own, roam in predatory bands across the countryside, threatening what stable communities have been established. Often, these roving bands are presented with some sympathy; one of the most traumatic moments in *Malevil* follows the massacre of such a starving band, whose pillaging of the wheat crop threatens the survival of the community at Malevil. Similarly, *Alas, Babylon* features the reluctant murder of outsiders; in both novels, the event teaches the community the necessity of military and police authority as an essential part of the social contract. Other kinds of "savages," though, are presented less sympathetically: these are often individuals who, fulfilling personal fantasies of power, represent a moral viewpoint antithetical to that of the novel's main characters. Wright, in *The Deluge*, goes to great pains to explain how weak or repressed individuals—accountants and government functionaries in the pre-holocaust world—find in the new world a chance to seize power by whatever means. Marxism, or anything that resembles it, does not generally fare well in these novels (*Malevil* in particular, which features a Marxist as one of the secondary characters, repeatedly demonstrates the failures of this character's schemes in reorganizing the new society). But novels in which the antagonists threatening the community represent a strong moral viewpoint usually do not associate such characters with the wilderness; such characters, instead, prepare us for the decisive moral battle discussed below.

    5. *The decisive battle of the Elect.* This phrase, borrowed from Norman Cohn (who sees it as an aspect of Marxist and National Socialist fantasies as well as of medieval millenarianism),[12] may seem a rather melodramatic description of the struggle between good and evil that concludes many post-holocaust narratives, but in some cases it is scarcely an exaggeration. Marduk in Noyes's *No Other Man*, Collingwood in Coppel's *Dark December*, Fulbert le Naud in Merle's *Malevil* are figures of almost consummate evil, direct descendants of the "Black powers" that threaten to overwhelm Jeffson in Shiel's *The Purple Cloud*. These are false prophets whose potential victory would transform not merely a community or an historical movement, but the entire future history of the human race—and in a few cases, such as Bowen's *After the Rain*, these prophets literally set themselves up as gods, as self-consciously supernatural figures in the mythology of the age to come. "'You had better begin by worshipping me,'" says the villainous Arthur to his subordinates in *After the Rain*. "'What is recorded of your behaviour will live on as revealed religion.'"[13] Stephen King's Randy Flagg in *The Stand* (1978), which begins with an influenza pandemic that nearly annihilates the human race, is a figure of consummate, archetypal evil, the "rough beast" of Yeats's "Second Coming"; and preparations for the final, cosmic battle against him make up the bulk of the very lengthy novel.

    Much of what is so threatening about these evil figures lies in the recognition on the part of the reader—and usually on the part of the protagonist as well—of how much they have in common with us. In Shiel, this identification of good and evil is internalized: the struggle for dominance takes place within the mind of Adam Jeffson himself. Coppel's *Dark December* is not far removed from this. "'I am you and you are me,'" says Collingwood to the protagonist Gavin. "'We're two sides of the same coin. . . . Yin and Yang, if you prefer.'"[14] Gavin realizes that such taunts from Collingwood nearly tempt Gavin to murder—which, of course, would be an ironic triumph for Collingwood's point of view. Gavin hates Collingwood most of all, he says, "for making me what I could feel myself becoming."[15] Similarly, the protagonist Martin in Wright's *Deluge* finds himself fearfully aware that he is learning to adopt the strategies and duplicities of the "savages" he is fighting; and in Merle's *Malevil*, Emmanuel Comte is compelled to imitate some of the actions of his rival Fulbert le Naud— such as making himself a false abbé in a religion he does not fully accept to counter the sway the false priest le Naud holds over the villagers. Clarke, the narrator of Bowen's *After the Rain*, is nearly swayed by Arthur's bizarre arguments, at least until Arthur's madness becomes undeniable.

But in each of these cases, a fatal ideological or moral flaw finally separates the protagonist from his opponent. In *Dark December*, Collingwood eventually reveals himself as nothing less than an agent of Chaos ("'Chaos is the natural condition of man,'" he claims[16]), his rationalism nothing more than a front for a vicious brand of fascism. Arthur's flaw in *After the Rain* is his obsession with natural selection and his reductive view of humans as nothing more than reasoning animals. "'Imagination,'" he says, "'is the enemy . . . when we have destroyed it, we shall have proved ourselves worthy of survival.'"[17] In both *Malevil* and *Deluge*, sadism and sexual excesses reveal that the actions of the villains are self-indulgent and wasteful, while sometimes apparently similar actions on the part of the hero are revealed to be part of a larger plan for the survival of the human race.

Other novels present this final struggle less as a moral confrontation than as a simple ideological argument. The culminating battle in Wylie and Balmer's *After Worlds Collide* turns out to be a struggle between democracy and communism after the survivors of a destroyed earth find themselves competing with another band of survivors, from communist nations, for dominance of the new planet. Larry Niven and Jerry Pournelle's *Lucifer's Hammer* (1977), Brackett's *The Long Tomorrow*, and a number of other works seek to validate the importance of science and technology in the face of post-holocaust neo-Luddite movements. Noyes's *No Other Man* may be the closest thing we have to the same story told from the neo-Luddites' point of view; in this novel, the apparently last surviving scientist, Marduk, is done in shortly before the two protagonists join a band of Franciscan monks. Wilhelm's *Where Late the Sweet Birds Sang*, seems, in the end, to be a validation of sexual reproduction over technological cloning—hardly a burning issue at this point in history—but in a larger sense, the novel also demonstrates the necessity of interacting with the environment rather than withdrawing from it protectively, as the community of clones attempts to do.

This five-part structure for post-holocaust tales might seem at first a bit mechanical, but it appears less so when regarded in terms of a representative novel of this kind. For this, there is probably no better candidate than George R. Stewart's *Earth Abides*, winner of the 1951 International Fantasy Award and one of the most fully realized accounts in all science fiction of a massive catastrophe and the evolution toward a new culture which follows. The novel has not received the attention it deserves among students of science fiction perhaps in part because it came from outside the genre; indeed, the sources of the novel seem to lie less in the tradition of science fiction catastrophes than in Stewart's own abiding concern with natural forces which seem almost consciously directed against human society. In two earlier novels, *Storm* (1941) and *Fire* (1948), Stewart presents these elemental forces as narrative protagonists. His studies of Western American history also often focus on natural catastrophes, while other anthropologically-oriented novels reveal his concern with the way societies evolve. But only in *Earth Abides*, freed from the constraints of historicism, was Stewart able to fully explore the themes of nature, myth, and society that his other works tended toward.

The title of the novel comes from Ecclesiastes 1:4—"one generation goeth, and another cometh, but the earth abideth forever"—and the action of the novel is in many ways a dramatization of the philosophy of that most oddly agnostic of the books of the Bible. Isherwood Williams, a young ecologist, suffers a rattlesnake bite while alone in the mountains and gradually recovers both from the snakebite and from another, inexplicable illness. Upon returning to a nearby village, he finds no other humans; but week-old newspapers tell him that a virulent new disease has attacked virtually the entire world population. Ish begins his wasteland journey by taking possession of a car and traveling to San Francisco, where he finds few survivors but observes that the automated processes of civilization, such as electric street lights and running water, continue to function, adding an eerie note of irony to the cataclysm. Still not certain of the extent of the catastrophe, Ish begins a transcontinental trek through the Southwest, the Plains, and the Midwest. In Arkansas, he finds a black farm family continuing much as they had before the disaster, figures reminiscent of the Mexican family in Bradbury's "The Highway." For them the world has not really ended at all. But at the end of Ish's journey, in New York, he meets a couple gamely trying to maintain a technology-dependent urban lifestyle amid the vast resources of an empty Manhattan. This couple, Ish realizes, provides a dramatic contrast to the black farmers and will probably be unable to survive once the automatic processes begin to break down and the wilderness begins to reassert itself. Having thus confirmed the range of the cataclysm, Ish returns to California "to establish his life" (p. 82). He adopts a dog named Princess—the first, slight indication of the new community—and locates himself in a place convenient to libaries and food supplies. In his despair, he seeks solace in books, but finds it only in the Bible and specifically in Ecclesiastes, with its "curious way of striking the naturalistic note, of sensing the problem of the individual against the universe" (p. 96). Only when he meets and falls in love with another survivor, however—a black woman named Em—does the third phase of the narrative, the establishment of a community, really begin. The nature and values of this future community are strongly hinted at by the interracial marriage which begins it.

Ish and Em begin to raise a family and take in other survivors, but the re-emergence of the wilderness—the fourth phase of our formula—threatens the budding community from the start. Plagues of ants are followed by plagues of rats from the nearby city and, in the years that follow, insects, crows, and even mountain lions reclaiming the territory they had lost to the advance of human civilization. Later elk, too, appear, balancing the threatening image of the mountain lions with a more uplifting image of wildness. Forest fires rage out of control with no one to fight them; a mild earthquake destroys many of the remaining human buildings, rotted with age; and diseases that might once have been easily dealt with—including the common cold— threaten the community, which nevertheless grows and begins to think of itself as a tribe.

Fighting the encroachments of the wilderness eventually ceases to be the aging Ish's main concern, however. "After twenty-one years . . . the world had fairly well adjusted itself, and further changes were too slow to call for day-to-day or even month-to-month observation. Now, however, the problem of society—its adjustment and reconstitution— had moved to the fore, and become his chief interest" (p. 159). The struggle to determine which values shall prevail in the new world occupies the entire second half of *Earth Abides*, and this struggle takes on a much more complex and ambivalent form than it does in such novels as Coppel's *Dark December* or Noyes's *No Other Man*. This struggle takes place on two fronts. The first, and more traditional, follows a second wasteland journey, undertaken by explorers of the

second generation sent out by the community to see how others have
fared in to the two decades since the catastrophe. Returning, the
young men bring with them Charlie, who comes as close as any
character in the novel to representing the kind of evil usually associated with the battle of the Elect. Charlie threatens to corrupt the youth
of the community and is described by one elder as "'rotten inside as a
ten-day fish'" (p. 242)—literally as well as figuratively, since Charlie is
a carrier of venereal disease. The elders of the community discuss
banishing Charlie, but decide the only safe route is to execute him. The
execution is reluctantly carried out, but not before Charlie's venereal
disesae spreads throughout the community killing, among others, Ish's
son and chosen successor Joey, the only child of the new generation
who has learned to read. The community thus assures its survival
against the kind of evil Charlie represents—but at the same time it
sacrifices, in the person of Joey, its only real link with the pre-
catastrophe culture and the values that culture represents.

   The other, more profound struggle of the last half of the novel is
involved with the death of Joey. Ish has struggled for years to transmit,
through education, the values and traditions of the pre-catastrophe
world, but early on he found his repeated imprecations about the need
for science and social institutions coming to be regarded as a kind of
eccentric obsession, much respected but little attended to by the youth
of the community—with the sole exception of Joey. Ish's attempts to
train the young people to become self-sufficient repeatedly fail, and he
has so strongly tried to inculcate the value of certain symbols of the old
world—such as the university library located nearby—that these symbols become totemic. Ish himself unwittingly evolves into a tribal
priest, venerated for the magical knowledge he possesses but brutally
pinched and tormented when this knowledge fails because the younger
members of the tribe no longer perceive the rationalistic basis for this
knowledge. Eventually, as an old man, Ish comes to realize that the
tribe is indeed becoming more self-sufficient, not because of his
teachings, but because of the "forces and pressures" that cause a
society to evolve in the first place. "'A tribe is like a child,'" an ancient
Ish says to his only surviving friend, Ezra. "'You can show it the way
by which it should grow up, and perhaps you can direct it a little, but in
the end the child will go his own way, and so will the tribe'" (p. 288).

   In an essay on *Earth Abides*, Willis E. McNelly has noted that the
names "Ish" and "Em" derive from Hebrew words meaning "man"
and "mother."[18] This and myriad other details invite a heavily mythic
interpretation of the novel, with Ish and Em standing not for a simplistic equivalent of Adam and Eve, as they might in lesser post-holocaust

novels, but for a broad range of human institutions. On the broadest level, Ish and Em are indeed Adam and Eve, and their adventure is the adventure of the human species. But they also stand for a culture, since despite their failure to deliberately inculcate codes of values, they nevertheless profoundly influence the behavior of generations to come. At increasingly narrower levels, they also stand for the tribe, for the family, and even for the individual, and the basic five-part structure we have used to explore this novel reveals new meanings when regarded in each of these separate contexts. And it may be that these complex levels of potential meaning account for the remarkable power and richness of all the best post-holocaust novels. Such novels are, in the broadest sense, epics of the power of humanity to remain dominant in the universe. Read this way, the cataclysm is literally a new creation or genesis, the period of exploration a dispersion or exodus, the establishing of a community the invention of a social contract, the emergence of the wilderness a testing of that social contract, and the final battle of the Elect a confirmation of permanence. At the tribal or family level, the five-part structure becomes the separation from existing family structures through cataclysm, the journey in search of new family members, the founding of the new family in a settled community, the struggle to maintain the family against the encroachments of disorder, and the final battle to preserve the sanctity and integrity of the family from "evil" forces that would pollute or destroy it. The story may even be viewed on a level of individual psychology, as an epic of individuation: the cataclysm becomes the birth trauma, the journey a period of growth and exploration leading toward ego development, the establishment of the community the growing awareness of the super-ego, the emerging wilderness the threat of the unconscious, and the final battle the triumph of the emerging personality over forces that would subsume or disintegrate it. To narrowly allegorize any of these novels according to such a system would of course be dangerously reductive, but to ignore such potential meanings altogether would be reductive in an entirely different way; *Earth Abides* supports each of these readings at least in part, as suggested by Ish's comparison, late in the novel, of the tribe both with human society in general and with the growth of an individual child. Perhaps, after all, the profoundest question we can ask of such novels is that simple question of Hernando's in Bradbury's "The Highway": " 'What do they mean, "the world?" ' " And perhaps it is for all these reasons that fictions which begin with cataclysm often include some of the most luminous visions of affirmation in the whole of fantastic literature.

2

The Lone Survivor

Robert Plank

I.

In the spring of 1945, racing through Germany toward victory, we often came upon barracks where the bunks were so to speak still warm. Some dorms were decorated, not with any pinup girls, but—reflecting, perhaps, a tendency to take play deadly seriously, or to make of the deadly serious a game—in a more solemn patriotic manner. A poem was painted on the wall of one room, in old-fashioned calligraphy, extolling the virtues of the current fighters for the greater glory of the fatherland: before them paled "die Not der Nibelungen und Tejas letzter Waffengang."

Having come to America only seven years before as a refugee from Vienna, I was my unit's undisputed expert on German language, history, and culture or absence thereof. The first use, incidentally, that the Army officially made of these talents of mine was a peculiar one. Our unit had captured a German general, he was invited to dine with our officers in their mess, and I was told to translate the menu into German. I hope the shades of Erich von Stroheim and his counterparts in *La Grande Illusion* will forgive me—I rendered the English into the spiciest Viennese vernacular that I could think up, so the German general might find the English original easier to read; or else, might he not pick the wrong food and choke on it?

The unofficial interest was more to my liking. There was a man in the unit, let's call him Huber, engaged in what now would be called search for roots. I was glad to comply when he asked me to translate the words on the wall; and then, when they yielded little beyond unfamiliar names, to interpret them. The first part proved easy. Like so many soldiers, Cpl. Huber was a reader of *Time, Life* and *Reader's Digest*, so he knew of Wagner operas and could imagine the plight of the Nibelungs. But who was that guy Teja with his "last feat of arms?"

Happily, I could enlighten him on this, too, to an extent: among the barbaric tribes that in the fifth century successively invaded and devastated Italy and destroyed the Western half of the Roman Empire were the Visigoths and Ostrogoths. The Germans tend to think of themselves, for reasons beyond me, as successors of the Goths, and, more astonishingly, to consider this an honor. Teja, last king of the Ostrogoths, was killed with all his men in a battle against the expeditionary forces sent by the Eastern Empire, as described in a novel by Felix Dahn which I had read as a boy (as had everybody who as a boy aspired to become educated in the German tradition).

Cpl. Huber let that sink in. Then he said: "Whatsa matter with them Krauts? Have they never had a victory?"

I am still not sure whether this remark was as profound as it sounded to me, or, which now seems likelier to me, more so.

I do not claim that Cpl. Huber and I were the only ones to have such thoughts: I am glad we were not. So I was gratified to read in that excellent German weekly *Die Zeit*, in its issue marking the fortieth anniversary of the outbreak of World War II, that Hitler "touched hidden emotional landscapes of the Germans: loyalty of the Nibelungs, death of the Goths, Goetterdaemmerung."

To pursue this would lead us away from our subject, which is not the end of the world ("Goetterdaemmerung"), but *stories* about that end. In giving us clues, though, on these, that poor poem on the wall of a deserted Army barracks is not without value. The works to which it refers envisage endings of somber grandeur, accompanied by deep if morbid emotion—quite incompatible with the occasional American view that the world may well come to an end but that it wouldn't necessarily matter that much—a concept embodied with mastery in my personal favorite among all of the end-of-the-world stories, E. B. White's *The Morning of the Day They Did It* (originally published in the *New Yorker*, now found in anthologies such as White's *The Second Tree from the Corner*, and elsewhere).

The anthropologist Loren Eiseley who in another context had spoken sharply of some modern men's disregard for other life forms, drove the point beyond its usual limits: "Sometimes of late years I find myself thinking the most beautiful sight in the world might be the birds taking over New York after the last man has run away to the hills."
And Emerson is reported to have replied, when a "Millerite" warned him that the Second Coming was near: "The end of the world does not affect me; I can live without it."

It is reasonable to see a correlation here with the fact that some of the best American (and British) tales of the end of the world are short stories. Many Anglo-Saxon authors have written long novels on the end of the world, but this is only seeming contradiction: they make actually little fuss about the end of a world and devote the bulk of the work with alacrity to the emergence of a new one. Brevity on the subject of the end of the world has a venerable tradition: The Great Flood (not including the subsiding of the waters and the aftermath) takes 42 verses in chapters 6 and 7 of Genesis (less than 3 columns in the edition I own, compared to 93 for Genesis as a whole, 1955 for the entire Bible).

This would be the point to widen the perspective and to review writers who are neither German nor Anglo-Saxon. What did Karel Čapek say about the end of the world (beyond *R.U.R*, where he said plenty)? Or Mishima? Should one reread Madách to see what there is in *The Tragedy of Man*? What about the immense literatures of Russia, China, Latin America, and so on?

It would not be impossible to answer all these questions, but it would require various facilities and a good-sized staff. If I were offered a million dollars, I would gladly undertake the job. Research grants have become scarce, though, and I think the problem is interesting, its study potentially fruitful; but I can't help thinking that there are many researchable problems more important and more urgent.

Would it be the honest thing to do, then, to stop here and to say, sorry, without that million dollars I can't give reliable answers, and I won't stoop to giving unreliable answers? I do not feel obliged to be quite that radical. As long as I do not claim to present scientific facts when I have hunches based on common sense, a reasonable amount of reading, and sensible impressions, I am not cheating. It will be unavoidable, though, that sometimes opinions which ought to be based on solid evidence will appear without such, like axioms. But I think that ever since non-Euclidian geometry was invented, the suspicion has grown that in fields less rigorous than mathematics examples will be used as such instead of as food for inductions and that sometimes postulates become axioms, not because they need no evidence but because there isn't any.

2.

Before proceeding to specifics, I'll have to present my terms. Our stated general subject is stories about the end of the world. Now what do I propose to mean by "story," by "end," by "world"?

"Story": A report (usually a printed narrative; but it could be a play, a film, etc.) of a series of events which have not taken place. We must distinguish between three modes, of which only one concerns us directly. Example: If a man tells us that flying saucers have hit London, somehow causing universal destruction, and that the British Isles have disappeared from the face of the Earth, we have to consider three possibilities (apart from the one we can discard both by definition and by easy checking—that the story might be true):

1. Though there is not a shred of evidence, the man believes what he says: This is delusion, we assume he is psychotic—if, that is, he is alone in his beliefs. If they are shared by millions, we shake our heads and wonder why we weren't born in a more rational age.

2. He does not believe what he says, but says it in the hope (for whatever purpose) that people will believe it: conclusion, he is a liar.

The first two possibilities are of interest to us for comparison only.

3. He does not believe it and does not expect or wish his readers to believe it, but tells his story for some such purpose as to entertain, instruct, edify, improve his readers. This is literature, and the philosophy and science of literature has spent the last twenty-three hundred years or so studying how literature works, and why. I am not going to solve these problems here and shall merely note that the key word is identification. Aristotle knew it. The story has its effect because (or to the extent that) the reader feels that the events described in it may happen to him, that he has acted or might act (or on the contrary, as the case might be, that he would never stoop so low as to act) like certain characters in the story, etc. Types of identification are manifold: some readers being contrary creatures, they do not identify quite as the author intended. Readers of Anthony Burgess's *A Clockwork Orange* (and viewers of the film) are surprised to learn, after they have come to know Alex, the protagonist, that he likes to read the Gospels. It turns out that he does so because he identifies with the tormentors of Jesus: every nail in the cross feels to Alex as though he had driven it in himself. Not what the Evangelists intended, but still identification.

Things are rarely that clearcut. The more sophisticated the work, the harder it may be to say with whom the author intended the reader to identify. Take *King Lear*: with the near-senile man whose folly brings disaster on himself and so many others? with Cordelia, almost too good to be true? with the shadowy gods that mete out punishment deserved and undeserved? Or, does it matter what sort of identification the author had in mind? A certain degree of ambiguity has long been considered a hallmark of good literature. Flaubert: "Ineptitude

consists in wanting to reach conclusions . . . . What mind worthy of the
name, beginning with Homer, ever reached a conclusion?" Wishing to
display a mind worthy of the name, I plan to stay away from conclusions in this essay as best I can. The study of stories about the end of the
world may have less value for conclusions that it might lead to make us
wiser than for the colorful variety it can demonstrate to make us
happier. Very systematic presentation would not advance that end;
happily I do not fear the proverbial "bugaboo of small minds,"
consistency.

"World": The word obviously has different meanings in geography, physics, philosophy, religion. The conventional usage that refers
to the third planet of our sun as "the world" may be objected to as too
provincial. Yet in psychology we may have to be even more generous
in bestowing the title "world" on small units. Making use of the
privilege I claimed of stating "axioms" I'll state two:

　　1. "World" is essentially a totality of human beings (the French
know this and use "monde" accordingly). Other living beings and the
entire non-living environment are secondary.

　　2. For a system to qualify as "world" it suffices that the individual
experiences it as such, that his life runs its course within its confines. So
we have the expressions "the new world" and "the old world." As
relatively small a system as the five boroughs of the City of New York
may be a world (doesn't everybody know some New Yorkers who
would indeed think that the end of New York would be the end of the
world?).

"End": In everyday life, when somebody tells of a series of
events, we are apt to ask how he knows it. In literature we don't. How
did Shakespeare know what Romeo and Juliet talked about to each
other? The question would be silly, and it is not asked. Stories of the
end of the world form an exception. If everybody dies, who is left to
tell? The question may still be silly, but it is sufficiently nagging
(probably because with other stories it is just improbable, but with
stories of the end of the world it is impossible that the author could
have learned what went on) so that authors have felt a need to answer
it; usually by making the end a bit less than complete, to let somebody
escape.

So a felt technical necessity of narrative opens a dichotomy—
which, however, will turn out to have deeper significance in another
context—the dichotomy between end-of-the-world stories with and
without survivors.

Now to sum up what we have so far—and perhaps, to do so more efficiently, to elaborate on a few points:

Where there is a boundary between phenomena in nature it is fluid. But to study them, we need lines of demarcation. We set them a bit arbitrarily—this is an essay rather than a scientific report; the state of the art does not permit more. Statements that would be more telling if supported by evidence obtained in extensive research come out in the guise of axioms, a venial sin perhaps, and in any case one often indulged in, e.g., by Dieter Wessels, the author of *Welt im Chaos*, the only book I have been able to find that is entirely devoted to our specific subject—the study of stories of the end of the world.

In defining "world," we speak of it in the sense of what is subjectively felt to be the individual's world. It makes no difference whether the story is told as straight narrative in the guise of history, or whether such narrative devices as dreams, etc. are used. "End" means essentially the dying out of mankind, or of that part of mankind that formed the significant characters' "world"; regardless of whether there is physical destruction beyond this. There are stories with and without survivors. Both types tend to be brief; longer stories are usually largely devoted to the later fate of the survivors, the re-creation of a world.

3.

Now we'll have to look for a method of cracking the nut of the question why stories of the end of the world are written, why they are written in the way they are, what their underlying meaning is, what they offer to their audience (readers, viewers, listeners).

One method that suggests itself is close textual analysis. Some "new criticism" went as far as to recommend doing nothing else: pay no attention to the author or to the work's background, treat it as though it had fallen from the sky. Let us try this on the following poem.

> *The Cry of the Jay*
> *I dreamt there was some poison gas.*
> *I dreamt they all were dead:*
> *The innocents in the meadow grass,*
> *The revelers in their bed.*
>
> *They did not have the time to ask:*
> *They lay as they had been hurled.*
> *And so the dream gave me the task*
> *To tell it to the world.*

Oh world, put on your mourning sash,
Put on your darkest veil,
And cover your head with sack and ash
To listen to my tale!

The world put on a shining garb
Of colors manifold,
Of cardinal and himmelfarb,
Of plastic and of gold . . .

I woke. There was no sign to guide
Me in the morning's grey;
No sound but from the mountain side
The mocking cry of a jay.

What do we have here? Two groups of indefinite size, the "inno-cents" and the "revelers" have been annihilated, though a larger "world" continues to exist. The agent of destruction is poison gas, but we are not told where it came from, or why. Perhaps punishment for what those people did "in the meadow grass" and "in their bed"? The world does not care one way or the other, and the narrator-dreamer's sense of mission is frustrated. The whole "dream" may be the resentful curse of one who is unable or unwilling to take part in others' enjoy-ment of sex and is unable to make effective literary use of it.

Valid, perhaps, but probably not capable of generalization. And we cannot see why some of the colors of the "shining garb" should be so peculiar: cardinal and gold may pass; but what is himmelfarb? And how is plastic a color? Are we perhaps better off if we try a second method, that of asking the author? Objections come to mind easily enough: it may be impossible to reach authors, they may not be frank, etc. We shall find weightier objections, but of those later. The first objection does not apply here: it is easy to reach the author—it so happens that I am the author. What good will that do?

I remember that I wrote the poem some twenty or twenty-five years ago, and I remember the circumstances, but I do not remember why I wrote it or what I meant by it. I was spending a happy vacation in the Adirondacks. I don't think I had such a dream, but I did hear the "mocking" (i.e., derisive; not imitating) cry of the jay, and there was dense morning fog. The lines just insinuated themselves. It used to be believed that the Muse whispered into the poet's ear; now we know that the "inspiration" comes from the writer's own unconscious.

I'll again postulate an axiom: There are two types of writers: the hack, who never fails to mix his formula just right to stimulate the reader's glands (tear glands, adrenals, gonads, whatever); he always knows what he is doing and why—and the other type, who works consciously to be sure, but on material rising from his unconscious. Neither of the two elements can be missing, as the surrealists found out: they started with "the programmatic suspension, in the act of writing or painting of all conscious control;" but the text used with a recent exhibition of the Cleveland Museum of Art makes clear that "Klee . . . would often let his pencil wander freely until he recognized the germ of an image which he then developed" and that Miró "used automatism as a catalyst for invention."

All this means that the hack's work tells us less of psychological interest than the other type's; it does not mean that the hack's work is bad, the other type's work good—my poem, for instance, I believe, isn't (which is the reason I never even tried to publish it).

The only literary quality I claim for my poem is that it is old-fashioned; and I am aware that this is not universally regarded as praiseworthy. It might, however, contain psychological treasures; but to dig them up the author may not be better equipped than anybody else. I can only add a few comments on details: I know, of course, that "himmelfarb" is not an English word (it isn't a German word either, properly speaking; I think I happened to read it somewhere, which made me glad because it seemed to have just the sound I wanted). And I know that "plastic" isn't a color; it came in handy because I couldn't think of a better word to express contempt (and the sound seemed right, too).

Colorful and pompous evocation of color and pomp was a characteristic of German baroque poetry. So were such apostrophes as "oh world." So was a taste for allegory, with leanings to skeletons and such. Characters in that type of poetry walk around as heavily hung with symbols as with brocade and baubles. Though written in the mountain air of the Adirondacks, my poem owes more to the atmosphere of Vienna, a city that peaked in the baroque and managed to retain much of the flavor of that era, blending it with nostalgia and decadence.

So this is what we get by asking the author—or, in this case, by the author asking himself. Was it worth the effort?

4.

Having now tried two methods with but limited success, let us turn to a third: the sociological-historical method. Wouldn't it seem most plausible that there should be stories of the end of the world when it is widely felt that such an end may be approaching? that the proliferation of such stories reflects the widespread anxiety about nuclear war? that the appeal of the theme to both writer and audience is intimately tied to its timeliness?

The trouble with this hypothesis is that if it is true then a corresponding change in the method of world destruction should equally show up in fiction. And this does not seem to be the case. Atoms were split in novels much earlier than in Los Alamos. Terrorists use them in Anatole France's *Penguin Island*, the British government in Harold Nicolson's *Public Faces*.

On the other side, tales of mankind being killed off by new epidemics (Mary Shelley's *The Last Men*, Jack London's *The Red Plague*) were hardly more numerous then, but became more frequent with H. G. Wells who blended the motif with that of invasion from outer space. The number of more recent such works is beyond counting, even though there is no reason to think that these special risks to mankind, if they exist at all, are any larger today than they were a hundred years ago.

A much greater difference than that between pre- and post-atomic fiction exists between the imagination of the end of the world as it prevailed in the Middle Ages, and even into times pretty close to ours, and on the other hand the stories of the end of the world as we have had them for about the last century. The former grew from the soil of faith and gave shape to the most sublime as well as the most terrible emotions. As if hypnotized by the expectation of that overwhelming moment when time would end and eternity begin, the Christian imagination of the end of the world brought forth great art (think of Michelangelo's "The Last Judgment" in the Sistine Chapel) and great poetry:

> *Dies irae, dies illa*
> *Solvet saeclum in favilla*
> *(The day of wrath*
> *Will dissolve worldly time into rubble.)*

No "survivors" here: all are to have eternal life, but some a life of eternal torment, others of eternal bliss.

We still possess these works, we have even added to their glory not so very long ago (the Dies Irae lives on principally in the requiem masses of the eighteenth and nineteenth century), but our own production is much less grand and more pedestrian: case histories, stories . . . and this is only part of the great change that has swept over the

Western world, and no historian and no psychologist has been really able to explain why it did so and why just then.

In any event, the image of the wrathful God, before whom you quake and tremble and who is yet also the loving father who will forgive and rescue you, has lost much of the hold it had on the hearts of our forefathers. Modern stories assume the end of the world to be decreed by much, much lesser powers. It is often a much less dramatic end: the phrase "not with a bang but with a whimper"—and even the word "bang" is a far cry from "tuba mirum spargit sonum" ("the tuba spreads the awesome sound")—has been much used to characterize modern stories of the end of the world.

Let us take an almost forgotten bestseller, *Mr. Adam* by Pat Frank. Written within two years after Hiroshima, it apparently was the first novel to utilize the colossal new theme. Annihilation here is slow: massive atomic explosions have had the effect of sterilizing all men in the world, except for one man—by symbolic chance his name is Mr. Adam—who happened to inspect the world's deepest lead mine and so was shielded. The extant generation would live out their lives, but no children will be born; mankind will die out unless something is done. Something *is* done: Mr. Adam is made a national treasure and a great project is set up to organize artificial insemination. The bulk of the novel is a satire on the bureaucracy that handles the project. It comes to naught, partly through mismanagement, partly because Mr. Adam is a very reluctant donor. When a certain female U.S. senator gets herself chosen as the first woman to be impregnated, he definitely balks; reading how she is characterized, you can hardly blame him. Meanwhile private research has found a drug to restore men's fertility, so mankind is once more saved.

Take for comparison a very short story by Damon Knight, "Not with a Bang," where suspense likewise depends on whether the population will be restored by procreation. Mankind has been nearly exterminated by the combined onslaught of bombs and of a new disease. A peculiar disease: it strikes without warning and causes instant and complete paralysis (no other symptom), which can be lifted equally fast by injecting a specific medication, which of course the victim can't do himself. One man of about thirty-five and one woman of about forty survive; she is immune to the disease, he is not. They meet. He feels nothing but utter contempt and loathing for her. But he needs her: to give him the injection if he should need it, and for the obvious other purpose. But the catastrophe has reinforced her attachment to her upbringing: she will not live with him in sin. He feels too weak to rape her. He finally persuades her to marry him (without benefit of clergy, there being no more clergy). She says yes, and he excuses himself to go to the restroom. The moment he enters he is paralyzed. He knows she could save him; but he also knows that she will never enter a room marked "Men."

Two conspicuous features are common to these two stories:

1. The fate of mankind depends on a man's sexual performance, but he is disgusted by the prospect.

2. Unless the author assumes that the end of the world will be brought about by God or a godlike power purposely annihilating everybody but one person or one clan (Noah is of course the paradigm), it is clearly likely that a global disaster, such as an epidemic, would spare either nobody or a scattered remnant; which is what happens in the more rational stories in our field, such as George R. Stewart's *Earth Abides*, Walter Miller's *A Canticle for Leibowitz*, Mordecai Roshwald's *Level 7*. For a disaster to strike blindly and to eliminate all but one person is defying probability; that two would be left, one male and one female, both of reproductive age, as happens in the shriller stories, would seem plausible only to those who have a more than ordinary willingness to suspend disbelief.

One curious chronological observation may be added here: *The Index of Psychoanalytic Writings*, the standard reference work in its field, lists four papers on fantasies about the end of the world published between 1907 and 1939, none since then (the book covers the period up to 1966). This does not tell us whether there were more such fantasies in that earlier period, or whether psychoanalysts paid more attention to them; either way it seems clear that the greater incidence or greater observation of these fantasies coincided with the period of special anxiety about the fate of our world. This was a strong element in the mental climate in the first half of the twentieth century in general, but not always of the same strength: Between 1939 and 1945 such anxiety would be diverted into action and did not need an outlet in fantasy, or at least was part of the lives of people sensitive to such feelings—comparable, perhaps, to forebodings preceding an earthquake—while the end of World War II ushered in an era of almost euphoria, now again past.

So our consideration of the historical method has inadvertently led us to our fourth and last method, the psychological exploration. Or rather, I might as well confess—especially since shrewd readers will long have suspected just this—that it was not inadvertent, but that it was where I wanted to be led all along.

5.

Before indulging this preference, though, we shall do well to review, briefly, our four types: Two, the straight truth and the straight lie, are of only indirect interest to us. The delusion is of interest for comparison. The fiction is our real material. There are, however, some works that do not fall clearly into any one of these categories: e.g., historical novels, blends of truth and fiction. There is a masterly description of the scene at the end of the year 999 A.D., when it was widely believed that the midnight bells would usher in the Second Coming, in August Strindberg's *Historical Miniatures*. There are also works that feature the end of the world without really narrating it; it serves rather as a parable or as the guise in which a certain religious-philosophical-political point is made. Some poems by the Swiss Nobel Laureate Carl Spitteler belong here. White's *The Morning of the Day They Did It*, mentioned above, comes at least close to this type, as does another *New Yorker* story, James Stevenson's splendidly brief and splendidly ambiguous *Notes from a Bottle*. Some authors have even treated the motif of the end of the world as a game to be played: so Stanislaw Lem in "How the World Was Saved" (in his collection *Cyberiad*), where a machine is invented that can be programmed to do or make anything beginning with a certain letter. Ordered to make things beginning with N, it may produce notebooks, nails, nematodes, navels. Given the word "nothing," it sits and does nothing; prodded, it begins to produce Nothing by eliminating one piece of the world after another—but is stopped in time. In a much more serious vein, Arthur C. Clarke's justly famous story "The Nine Billion Names of God" is somewhat similar. A third type of stories that, so to speak, place themselves outside of our purview is the story that mentions the end of the world as a sideline or as the preoccupation of one character; and we have a fourth type in works of scoffers, parodies of belief in the end of the world rather than stories about it.

Developments in other areas of intellectual history may affect the evolution of ideas about the end of the world and may transmute what seemed a terrible danger into a matter to scoff at. This is beautifully illustrated by the history of attitudes toward comets.

For long ages comets were widely and firmly believed to be portents of approaching disaster. Such belief in the "meaning" of comets seems to have been rampant in the Graeco-Roman world. It was not dislodged by Christianity, even though the scripture of the new religion contained the exhortation (Jer. 10:2) not to fear the signs of

Heaven, as the heathen do. This could be, and was, interpreted away as meaning that the heathen fear the signs, but Christians fear only God who sends the signs.

This didn't change much till the seventeenth century when the new scientific approach began to gain ground. The time when the scales were tipped to the new side can be fixed with a degree of accuracy that is rare in such matters (in this, as well as on other cometary affairs, I am largely following James H. Robinson's excellent monograph on the comet of 1680). The comet of 1665 caused such a panic in France that Louis XIV feared it would lower the productivity of the workers and peasants (who paid him the taxes and therefore interested him more than the comet per se), so he had a scientist in his service publish a popular book, explaining the true nature of comets as far as then known. Its immediate effect seems to have been slight; but by the time an even more impressive comet appeared in 1680, the opinions for and against the "meaning" of the phenomenon were in better balance. The forces of enlightenment had won the day—though perhaps only the day; not, as they may have thought, a battle decisive for all future. Such battles, it seems, have to be fought over and over.

Now that the comets were no longer signs but physical objects, a new malignity could be ascribed to them. Just as religion was used to attach to the flaming rod the fear of catastrophes *announced*, so now science could be held to teach that the intruders from space may actually themselves *wreak* destruction. The spirit that is greedy for news of the final cataclysm will not be satisfied unless one source of such news which is lost is at least replaced by another. Granted that comets didn't foretell mishaps; but if they were large bodies meaninglessly orbiting around the sun, they could blindly strike the Earth, couldn't they? The Reverend William Whiston, as early as 1696, computed the course of the comet of 1680 and found that it would return in 2255: by that time it would break the Earth to pieces for sure. Well, maybe so; we shall perhaps never find out, as we may succeed in destroying mankind, all by ourselves, without any help from any comet, long before that year. John Wesley also was among the preachers who admonished their flocks to repent in time, so as to avoid the risk of being still in a state of sin when the comet comes. And two centuries after the great comet of 1680, Ignatius Donnelly, a populist now best known as an early science fiction writer, wrote *Ragnarok*, not a work of fiction, but a presumably scientific work.

Donnelly collected material extensively from sciences, folklore, mythology, literature. He summoned as witnesses poets from Hesiod and Ovid to Milton and Byron. And so he "proved" that comets had struck the Earth many times, each time destroying mankind (which he assumed to have existed, even in a state of high civilization, in a much more remote past than is usually conceded) except for a small nucleus that would again and again rebuild civilization and repopulate the Earth. His pattern has been perpetuated by such more recent pseudo-scientists as Velikovsky, though by now comets are no longer thought suitable instruments of such large events; nothing less than at least a planet will do. Comets have been relegated to the humbler but perhaps more useful role of vehicles for poking fun at those who believed in their malignity.

Ridiculing the belief in the "meaning" of comets, Gamon, a French poet of the seventeenth century, had written:

Combien voit-on de fois que le Tout-Puissant jette
Les comètes sans maux et les maux sans comètes.
(How often has the Lord, of Earth and Heaven master,
Sent us disasters without comets, and comets without disaster!)

When the fashion in popular fears changed from comets *predicting* to comets *achieving* disaster, that new apprehension soon became a stock object of jokes and comedies, making the transition from the tragic to the comic, just as great spirits worshipped by druids had become the goblins of our Halloween. The comedy on comets was created by Fontenelle, notable pioneer of the Enlightenment. His *La Comète*, his immediate response to the debates about the comet of 1680, went on the Paris stage as early as January, 1681. His example was followed by Voltaire and by innumerable lesser lights. One of the more recent works in that line is a brilliant playlet, *Weltuntergang (End of the World)* by the Austrian playwright Jura Soyfer. It was staged in 1936. Soyfer died three years later, at the age of twenty-six, in a Nazi concentration camp.

6.

Having thus sorted out our material, we can readily see that those specimens that we do not exclude (we exclude those where the end is evoked rather than narrated) may be fictions, or delusions, or phenomena in between; and that both types of which I have spoken earlier are represented—there are ends of worlds with and without survivors.

A fatherless boy of fourteen, admitted to a hospital for unexplained hematuria, dictated this poem:

A Walk into Nothingness

It's just mostly like the end of the world.
With broken down buildings and torn up land
And you're the only one left
And you're all alone
Walking into nothingness. *

This illustrated a painting he had just made which shows, in rigid perspective and somber colors, a boy walking down a straight road lined with what looks more like deformed trees than like "broken down buildings." The boy is seen from the back. A member of the hospital staff noticed that the otherwise well-drawn figure had no hands. On a hunch, it was arranged for the patient, whose examinations had shown no disease to account for blood in his urine, to have a "man to man" talk with his medical student-doctor. The hunch proved correct: The boy had worried about masturbation. He returned from his interview relieved and elated. He expressed no more worry about his own fate or that of the world.

Among the spontaneous sayings of children collected by the Russian educator Kornei Chukovsky we find this from four-year-old Anka: "Mother, all the people will die, but someone will have to place somewhere the urn with the ashes of the last dead person, let me do it—all right?"

A poem by Hermann Hesse, "Small Boy," expresses a very similar idea, though it keeps it in the family:

Grownup people die,
Uncle, grandpapa.
But I, I shall remain
Ever, ever here.

And A. A. Milne, famous as the creator of Winnie the Pooh, relates in his *Autobiography* how he and his brother Ken spun out a fantasy that everybody else would die, perhaps from a plague or through a more direct act of God. The tangible benefit was to be "the freedom of the sweet-shops . . . to be able to step in confidently over the body of the dead proprietor—that was Heaven."

Adults may well present different motivations. There is Pascal's famous fragment (in his *Pensées*): "The eternal silence of these infinite

---

*Reprinted with permission of the copyright holder, Year Book Medical Publishers, Inc., Chicago, from Emma N. Plank, *Working with Children in Hospitals*.

spaces frightens me." Kant, perhaps equally frightened, did something about it. As a philosopher and scientist, he developed a theory about the origins of the planets. As a human, he speculated about their inhabitants. Beings on the outer planets may be too perfect to sin, those on the inner planets not smart enough to do so; leaving Earth as the only place where man could reach the full stature of responsibility, of being able to sin but also able to refrain from doing so.

People not quite as greatly endowed with philosophical vision have perhaps to lift themselves above the plane of others, though not necessarily as high up as other planets, to experience comparable feelings. The Swiss naturalist and pioneer of mountain climbing as a sport, de Saussure (he reached the summit of Mount Blanc in 1787), related that standing on an Alpine peak he had the feeling that everybody else was dead and that he was looking down on a land of corpses. It seems that there have been similar reports from later mountain climbers.

This type of material is not always found in professional literature; it is scattered. Psychiatrists have, naturally, concentrated on cases of the mentally ill. The most famous of these is that of Daniel Paul Schreber, a paranoiac. At the height of his illness he had a most original and complex system of delusions. Simplifying, they can be described as his believing thus: He had been transformed into a woman and impregnated by God (or one male divine person—instead of in the Trinity, Schreber believed in a Duality, a "Front God" and a "Rear God," somewhat along the lines of the beliefs of the Gnostics of early Christian days). Mankind would die out and he would give birth to a new human race. This might take thousands of years, but his God would see to it that he would live as long as needed.

A man of high intellectual and educational level (he was a judge on a high court), he explained his ideas in a book, *Memoirs of My Nervous Illness*, which he wrote while still confined in an institution. As in other classical cases of paranoia, his intelligence was unimpaired outside of the area of his delusions. He petitioned the courts for restitution of his civil rights—so he could validly contract for publication of his book—and won his case on appeal. Freud studied the book, was able to make sense of Schreber's delusions, and derived from it much of his theory on the causes of paranoia.

These are instances of fantasies of the end of the world with survivor. Those without survivor are apparently more frequent among schizophrenics, for whom it is not so unusual to take the first step toward realization of that special fantasy—suicide. Those lone survivors of comprehensive catastrophe do not always feel victorious

either, do not enjoy their status. The young hematuria patient saw
nothing before him but "nothingness." The only man who withstood
the strange paralyzing disease had to face the most harrowing death in
the men's room.

7.

One outstanding feature common to all those fantasies is ill will.
Sometimes it is open and may amount to rage, or it is barely concealed
in theory: Movements preaching the close approach of the end of the
world, like the Millerites of the 1830s, assumed that those not believing them were to go to hell. Sometimes it is subliminal. Kant added to
his speculations about extraterrestrial life a reference to a satirist who
had compared people to lice and commented that with regard to the
run of the mill of people the comparison was apt. Kant was ethnically
impartial, but Hitler is said to have referred to Russians and Poles as
the lice of the Earth. The motif returns in Soyfer's play, but with a
different twist: The planets have assembled to perform the harmony of
the spheres. Earth is absent, having called in sick. Inquiry reveals that
she "has humans"—and the messenger's gesture of scratching his head
with embarrassment leaves no doubt about the nature of the infesta-
tion. So a comet is sent out to destroy Earth; but returns with mission
unaccomplished: having seen the Earth close, he thought it too beautiful, its potential too great. Here ill will has been overruled by a
stronger force.

Where ill will prevails, it may be turned against the outside world
or against the creator of the fantasy himself. Which is primary? Well, is
suicide the wayward brother of murder, or vice versa, or are they both
the equally beloved children of their great and stern mother,
aggression?

For an answer we have to go to psychology. But which psychology? There are not only many schools, there are basically two
approaches, almost two different fields of reality selected for study
(though the demarcation line is, of course, not really sharp). There is
"dynamic psychology" or (perhaps a better term) "depth psychology," and there is what in contrast to it may be called surface psychology. The latter studies observable external phenomena and disre-
gards, as unsuited for scientific study, what goes on inside the person,
leaving that to depth psychology—not without some raising of eye-
brows, at times amounting to contempt, which is cordially recipro-
cated. Depth psychologists are apt to think that surface psychologists
can come up with nothing but trivia; surface psychologists tend to

think that depth psychologists can come up with nothing but figments of their own imagination, not capable of verification, even of rational formulation, not representing any reality. The questions of the one seem irrelevant to the other, the questions of the other unanswerable to the first; the answers of the one not worth having, of the other potentially important but meaningless.

Our basic question—why are stories of the end of the world written, and read, and why just that way? i.e., what goes on in authors' and audiences' minds?—is meaningless in the framework of surface psychology. This does not, however, mean that surface psychology could not contribute to its solution. It could, by establishing correlations between variables of observable behavior, such as producing and consuming such stories, and other observable bits or traits, such as scores on objective personality tests. But since the collection of even relatively simple data of this sort (say, age, sex, occupation, I.Q.) is a major task, this is where that million dollars would be needed; and until it comes, the question must remain moot. We'll have to turn to depth psychology.

If depth psychology were organized like the worship of Apollo of old, there would be an oracle, like the oracle of Delphi; we could go there with prepared questions (and if it were like Delphi was, here again a million dollars would come in handy), such as:

Why do people think of the end of the world?

Why does this become a belief with some, a fantasy or story with others?

Crosscutting this dichotomy, why is the end of the world sometimes envisaged as total, sometimes with a survivor or survivors?

Or, dividing the material in a third dimension, what determines the choice of the instrument of destruction: Collision with some other orbiting body? Invasion by "aliens" so superior to us in power and so inferior in morality that the mere rumors of their coming have driven people out of their wits? Or such more mundane influences as nuclear wars, epidemics, and the like?

8.

There is no New Delphi. We cannot simply ask for answers, we must search for them. Here we run into a similar dilemma as before: Which depth psychology? There are fairly well defined schools. I shall not attempt to outline their teachings beyond what is indispensable for our specific quest.

The key figure, of course, is the creator of psychoanalysis, Sigmund Freud. A nineteenth-century physician, he tried to anchor psychology on physiology. He thought that eventually a physical substrate would be found for every psychologic state or event. In the meantime psychological findings still should make sense—in the world view of his age, everything had to make sense. Much of people's conscious behavior didn't. His discovery of overriding importance was that of the role of the unconscious: by resorting to the unconscious, a rational explanation of the human mind became possible.

Freud's original concept was of the individual pushed into its directions by biologically based drives, notably two: those that have to be satisfied for the individual to exist ("ego drives"); and those aiming at pleasure (expanding the usual meaning of the word sex, he spoke of sexual drives, again a biologically based idea, since the sex drive maintains the species). The interaction of these drives with each other and with the givens and events of the external world cause the immense diversity of psychological development and behavior.

The ego drives are too compelling for their frustration to cause psychological changes: if a person's hunger and thirst are not stilled, he will not undergo psychological changes, he will die. This is not so when the sex drive is not gratified. The sex drive is of such psychologic importance not because it is more basic than the ego drives, but because it is less so.

The typical interaction of drives and external influences leads to a situation in early life characterized by the boy's love for his mother and hatred for his father. This is the celebrated Oedipus complex, so named for that hero of Greek myth who, without knowing what he was doing, killed his father and married his mother, thus realizing a wish that, while universal, normally remains unconscious and is not acted out.

The question may well be raised how such a complex could run through human history. This was one point where C. G. Jung—originally a collaborator of Freud and groomed to become his successor as leader of the psychoanalytic movement—developed his own system. Its special concept is the "collective unconscious": a deepest layer of the personality, congenital and indeed inherited from way back, that determines the most fundamental personality traits and behavior patterns.

Jung's aim was to find general laws of the human mind, to be able to show why people are so similar. Alfred Adler, another early collaborator of Freud who parted with him and established his own "school," "Individual Psychology," tried, rather, to find out why people are different. He postulated two basic forming forces: the "inferiority feeling"—here is where he anchors the mind on the body—and the supposedly universal "community feeling." The inferiority feeling is handled by various psychologic devices, chiefly "over-compensation," and these and the community feeling interact to shape personality traits and behavior.

How the application of the Freudian and the Adlerian theories lead to different views can be neatly shown by a controversy about an individual, which also demonstrates what Freud had in mind when he spoke of sex.

The Emperor Wilhelm II, better known in America by his German title, the Kaiser, became by his swashbuckling machismo, combined with his power as the head of one of the mightiest empires of the time, the bane of the early twentieth century. The question what made him so was naturally of wide public interest.

Now the emperor had been born with a "withered" (at least markedly underdeveloped) right arm. A German writer who specialized in best-selling biographies described his character (here borrowing from Adler's theory) as formed by the Kaiser's inferiority feeling. Not so, said Freud, at least not simply so: the birth defect may well have been fateful, but not directly and alone. Wilhelm had not only a withered arm, but also a proud mother who could not abide the idea of having borne a defective child. So he grew up without that mother love that is the natural endowment of millions who inherit much less than a throne.

As Freud lived to a ripe old age, always devoting himself to perfecting his theory, and as he also drew on a large group of disciples, many of them scientists and innovators of stature in their own right, even so-called orthodox psychoanalysis did not stand still. Hostility and aggression were at first largely explained through the vicissitudes of the Oedipus complex and aggression turned inward appeared as a result of inner conflict. Later Freud postulated another basic drive, the "death instinct" (it and the sex drive are also referred to by the name of the two corresponding Greek personifications, Eros and Thanatos), a tendency supposedly inherent in all life toward return to the inanimate state. This seemed to explain aggression both against others and against the self. The objection could obviously be made, though, that the law of parsimony, considered basic in the formation of scientific concepts, did not warrant postulating a death instinct: to explain how individuals and species (including the species *Homo sapiens*) are maintained may well require postulating drives which compel action that achieves these results, but the death of individuals and extinction of species are obviously sufficiently explained by external forces.

Later psychoanalysts developed a concept originated by Freud, but not given as great weight by him, narcissism. The term (derived from Narcissus of antique myth who fell in love with his reflection in water) refers to a very early state in which the child gains pleasure from his own body—including external sources of pleasure, especially the mother's breasts, which he has not learned to distinguish from himself. Frustration of narcissistic needs will lead to fixation on that stage, certain later frustrations to regression to it. One result may be narcissistic rage, either chronic (Wilhelm II may be a good example) or acute (outbursts of some people, often diagnosed as psychotic; we are apt to let it go at that, though the label doesn't really explain).

It may be noted that the proponents of these theoretical constructs, notably Heinz Kohut, by tracing personality traits further back than to the Oedipal phase, seem to effect a rapprochement to the system of Adler, though they may feel they are merely filling gaps in the system of Freud. It can similarly be said that the ethologists, again perhaps not intentionally, are forming a bridge between Jung's and Freud's thoughts, and indeed between depth psychology and surface psychology. Konrad Lorenz in particular, Nobel Prize winner and most eminent spokesman for ethology, expresses great respect for Freud and uses psychoanalytic thinking widely, but not vitally; his favorite term, when it comes to accounting for human behavior, is "genetically programmed," which is not so very far from "the collective unconscious," and his empirical consideration of humans is based on the method he uses with animals—external observation, though not entirely without experimentation, and with as much empathy as possible; but that hardly stretches to reading the mind of graylag geese.

We should now be ready to formulate the answers to the questions we posed at the end of section 7, or as ready as we can ever get, for it must be understood that in the narrow limits of this essay answers can only be offered with some diffidence and with a good deal of oversimplification.

9.

The "axiom" that it is basically ill will which is given body in the fantasies of the end of the world can be illustrated by considering Nietzsche. He, surely *the* philosopher of ill will if ever there was one, went out of his way to proclaim his delight in thinking of the destruction of the world:

That twilight of the gods, as the sun goes black, the earth sinks into the sea and whirlpools of fire uproot the all-nourishing cosmic tree, flames licking the heavens—it is the greatest idea human genius ever produced, unsurpassed in the literature of any period, infinitely bold and formidable, but melting into magic harmonies.

Many people might find other harmonies more magical and any glee about Goetterdaemmerung something other than harmonious. It was perhaps in the days of Nietzsche, perhaps a little later, that the concept of "Caesarian madness" came up: A sort of variant on Lord Acton's dictum that all power corrupts and absolute power corrupts absolutely, it assumed that intoxication with power led to the excesses that made Roman emperors notorious: like the one who reportedly wished that all mankind had but one head so he could cut it off with one stroke. Psychiatry has formulated many diagnostic entities since then, but "Caesarian madness" was not among them; however, the interest of those who established classifications was in clinical rather than in historical aspects.

A century after Nietzsche, the novelist and essayist Elias Canetti came up with a more comprehensive theory: That Roman emperor's desire would in its light appear, not as a deviation, but as an expression of universal feeling in special purity: Human emotions may be largely shaped by the need to come to terms with the inevitability of death. So to survive gives an intense feeling of happiness. In the lone survivor it becomes a passion, the passion for power. As with all pleasures, he who has experienced it strives to repeat it: to survive as many people as possible as often as possible becomes the aim of burning desire. If people will not die in sufficient numbers by themselves, they can be helped to do so. If the power is available . . . The most vicious circle rotates faster and faster: more tyranny—more power—more murders—more tyranny . . .[3]

Canetti was awarded the 1981 Nobel Prize for Literature, though not specially for this theory: its significance, which is great, is in the fields of psychology and philosophy rather than specifically in that of literature. It is perhaps interesting that another writer who was not widely known before he received the same Prize (in 1919), Carl Spitteler, to some of whose poems we have briefly referred above, presented an explanation of desire for mass destruction that shows some similarity with Canetti's: When Hera, in Spitteler's work the queen of the gods but mortal, sees her longing to become immortal totally thwarted, she finds her only solace in the thought that she can mete out death abundantly herself.

These speculations, of course, profess to explain why people want to be mass murderers, not why they write stories about mass murder; but one desire is clearly derived from the other. Masses of people identify with and admire the murderers of masses, which is what victorious war lords are. And they are so proud of their exploits: Shakespeare ("This England never did nor never shall / Lie at the proud foot of a conqueror") tells us that even their feet are proud.

The tendency toward mass murder was perhaps strongest in the cannibalistic empires. The word evokes the picture of Montezuma feasting on the bodies of Spanish prisoners. Some scholars have recently decided that the Aztecs resorted to cannibalism because they did not have enough other protein available. But the Romans had, and yet their empire was at least symbolically cannibalistic: their public life culminated in the *triumph*, the solemn pageant that the Senate granted to the *imperator* who returned home victoriously. No human flesh was eaten, but eminent prisoners were spared for the occasion; the triumph ended with a gorgeous meal, and while the imperator feasted, the prisoners were butchered. The institution of the triumph persisted throughout the several centuries of the aggressively expanding republic and through several centuries under the Caesars. The people jubilated just as nowadays millions will buy the books by authors like Hal Lindsey who has warned again and again that the end is near.

Ill will can be understood as inherent in the nature of man or as stemming from frustration of his natural drives. Since one is as universal as the other, ill will must be expected to exist in everybody; but quite possibly stronger in some than in others. This may not spell the answer, though, to the question why some are satisfied with lesser disasters than others. Mental life is best understood as conflict, and outward behavior (including opinions and feelings that are conscious, acknowledged and reasonably stable) as compromise of conflicting forces. The person who is hostile in acts, beliefs or fantasies is also under the pressure of forces that try to keep him from being so. Paradoxically, these forces may be assuaged by directing hostility to larger groups of victims, since this diffuses it. A soldier may find it easier to press a button and destroy a million people than to kill one man in hand-to-hand combat. Our stories of the end of the world reflect the same difference.

Freud conceptualized three main factors of the developed personality as the Id (the raw drives), the Superego (the internalized prohibitions, derived from parents, other authorities, society at large), and the Ego, i.e., the forces oriented to reality and striving to adjust to it, arbitrating between Id and Superego. Whether the taste for mass destruction is allowed to surface depends on the relative strength of the three. The balance between being "nice" and desiring large-scale destruction is not stable, it is a cybernetic process: the "nicer" the person, the more those desires will be submerged, relegated to dreams (Jane Addams, eminent social worker, mentioned in *Twenty Years at Hull House* that she "dreamed night after night that everyone in the world was dead except myself") or to remembered childhood fantasy (Milne); greater effort needed to keep forbidden wishes down will make the person "nicer."

If the Superego does not succeed in repressing those wishes, guilt becomes conscious and cries for atonement. Aggression is turned inward, becomes depression; the individual, looking for self-punishment, is no longer exempting himself from universal destruction—in fact or fantasy. Where the Id wants to go on merrily sinning, the Superego wants to punish and the Ego is too weak to mediate, the personality may break down, psychosis may result. Belief in ideas incompatible with reality becomes possible, indeed inevitable. In persons who are not psychotic, the idea persists as fantasy, not believed in like facts—usually unconscious or a conscious fantasy to which little attention is paid; in those who have the unusual gift (not yet explained, and perhaps never to be explained by psychology) of giving generally valid shape to their private fantasy so that others can partake in it, as works of literature or the other arts. That the writer thus draws from the same well as the psychotic, that their fantasies are morphologically alike must not be misinterpreted to mean that writers have psychotic traits. Shakespeare's Duke Theseus rightly stressed the parallels of "the lunatic, the lover, and the poet," but was equally right not to consider them identical.

Only in the rare morbid who turns aggression inward and at the same time gives it universal scope does the fantasy of the end of the world without survivor arise (and pass quickly if the underlying morbidity does, as in our adolescent poet). In others there may be a fantasy of an end with many survivors or with a new world to arise, or it may be the lone survivor, with the fantasizer seeing himself in that role: either overtly (all will die, I'll survive) as in fantasies of children (Chukovsky's Anka, Milne in his memory, Hesse's small boy) and in adults in their less controlled states (Jane Addams's recurrent dream) or covert. The overt fantasy is too crude for the more sophisticated adult: he can accept the fantasy, though, that some character will alone survive; but that he (and his audience) sees himself in this character is transparent.

Some of this may read as ambiguous and confusing as though it really came from Delphi. No wonder if scholars throw up their hands, claiming that peripheral questions may be answerable but that an irreducible core remains where we can merely say that things are as they are; a stance that has an exalted precedent in the Bible, where the Lord Himself is presented as despairing of ever really solving the problem: He decides that as the great flood hasn't quite achieved what He intended, He will not repeat the experiment, because "the imagination of man's heart is evil from his youth" (Gen. 8:21). For a modern reformulation I'll turn to Dame Rebecca West's *Black Lamb and Grey Falcon*:

> Only part of us is sane; only part of us loves pleasure and the longer days of happiness, wants to live to our nineties and die in peace in a house that we built, that shall shelter those who come after us. The other half of us is nearly mad. It prefers the disagreeable to the agreeable, loves pain and its darker night despair, and wants to die in a catastrophe that shall set life to its beginning and leave nothing of our house save the blackened foundations.

Not every writer can distinguish the forces struggling against each other within himself as clearly as Rebecca West. Bernard Crick in his biography of George Orwell points out how the protagonist of *Keep the Aspidistra Flying* longs for bombs to fall on London. He relates this to the "apocalyptic relish" which Bernard Bergonzi who had coined the term found in the literature of the thirties. Orwell did not mean to describe a momentary aberration: his next novel, *Coming Up for Air*, features the same motif.

This does not bode well for the future of mankind and of our world, but there is ironic solace in noting that our attitudes and actions may not have the effect we intend. It is a basic fact well established in biology (and as we have seen, it spills over into psychology) that hunger maintains the species (though the individual may have no more distant aim than to enjoy his food), and sex maintains the species though the individual may have quite different aims than progeny. Desire for catastrophe may fail to bring it, and some other desire may.

Ever since man became separate from the animal world, he has worked diligently and hard, though mostly unawares, toward the destruction of other species and eventually his own. Techniques have changed—alas, they have grown more efficient—and points of vulnerability have shifted. Freud believed half a century ago that mankind might die out due to excessive restraints on the sex drive. Orwell listed, during World War II, "philoprogenitiveness" as "one of the qualities by which any society that is to last longer than a generation actually has to be sustained." Today we know that on the contrary the excessive use of the sex drive for procreation threatens the safety of the world, and us with the rest, through the population explosion. What the prime danger will be fifty years hence even the oracle of Delphi would not know.

The thrust of *Mr. Adam*, the novel we discussed earlier, which depicts mankind's destiny as dependent on a man's sexual performance, seems in this light a bit outdated. It is helpful, though, to be reminded that basically the cement that holds human society together is erotic. The story "Not with a Bang," reinforcing this, adds that regression to other secretions will not do. It thus incidentally illustrates Freud's point that these indeed are different stages of one great drive. A visit to the toilet may still have greater emotional weight than polite society acknowledges.

10.

The twentieth century has trained us to expect catastrophes. If we are to expect an even greater one, can we guess how vast and how final it would be? Will the Earth be rendered lifeless for ever? Or will life only be "set back to its beginnings" and new life begin? Will a new flora spring from those "blackened foundations"? Why should we desire it? Why should we prefer, as we evidently do, that it be human life again?

A schizophrenic patient wrote to me to apologize for not having replied to a letter of mine more promptly: "The reason is that I was dead. However, I have been brought back to life by the grace of God and the United States Supreme Court." He did not tell me how it had felt to "be dead," and I do not think we find much about it in the professional literature. It is probably hard to describe. We can to an extent imagine it, though. The essential must be the utter cessation of relationships to the outside world. Concerning feeling, it may make little difference whether the patient feels he is dead and everybody else alive, or that he is alive and everyone else dead (a catatonic may to all appearances be "dead to the world" and suddenly break into an attempt to kill everybody around him). From the angle of his response, it does make a difference. The patient who wrote to me seems to have felt rehabilitated: since the unknown powers that had deadened him had done so in violation of the highest moral and legal rules, it took the highest powers in both these fields to reverse them and revive him.

His letter marks the limit to which a person can go and still communicate. Beyond it is silence, and if there are people there who think of the end of the world without survivors or rebirth, we do not hear of them. Where the fantasies are still communicable, they are of destruction with survivor or with restitution: if they were without either, there would be no point for the fantasizer in going on with them, as they could offer no screen against which to project anything, no target for either love or hate or any emotion.

No wonder then that Kant and Pascal were afraid of the uninhabited outer spaces; no wonder that the desire to fill them became the motive power of both the fantasy that populated space with flying saucers, etc., etc., and of the long effort to populate it from the Earth. Other public justifications of space travel (the military ones, which may be rational, are rarely exposed in public) amount to hardly more than rationalizations, especially when you consider how infinitely less money it costs to develop fantasies about spacemen than to become spacemen ourselves.

The empty infinite space is as bleak as the empty infinite time after the end of the world. But space can be filled in fantasy or by action, and the world after its end can be repopulated. The author or reader who projects himself into the lone survivor also sees himself as the future master and ancestor of a new race—and what greater glorification of the ego can there be? The world destroyed without survivor can— since to fantasy nothing is impossible—likewise somehow be rebuilt. Even Goetterdaemmerung does not have to be final: The *Edda* describes how Valhalla will be consumed by flames engulfing the universe, yet it also relates how a new world will arise from the ashes.

The imagined new world will always be the habitation—and, so to speak, the property—of humans, or of man-like beings who are clearly equal or superior to us. Eiseley, we noted, confessed to a daydream of birds taking over New York—a rather unorthodox idea since generally people think either of a real end, with nobody taking over, or of somehow our successors to be human again. The question is moot anyhow—experts have spoken of the insects as our more likely heirs. The idea hardly pleases us; neither would the prospect of inanimate or man-made future masters of the Earth, such as the robots in *R.U.R.* In that excellent novel by Nevil Shute, *On the Beach*, much of the Earth is depopulated, but faint new hope is raised by rhythmic knocking heard that may be a signal in Morse code. The scene where the rescue party finds that in reality it is a sound made by an empty bottle stuck in a shrub and brushing against dead branches is a poignant moment in the book (and especially in the film). The reason for our dismay at seeing the living supplanted by the lifelessly mechanic may not be immediately apparent; one concept possibly helpful in clarifying the issue is that of the *uncanny*. It was introduced by the psychologist Ernst Jentsch who laid down the rule that we are struck by the uncanny feeling especially when a situation leaves us in uncertainty as to whether we are witnessing something living or not living. Freud then studied the concept, elaborated on it, modified it, extended it—extended it, I would say, so far beyond the natural limits of this essay that the brief reference to his paper "The Uncanny" will have to do.

To be superseded by the inanimate is not part of the prospect seen when destruction and restitution are viewed as an endless chain, history as a repetition of cycles. They may, rather, be molded to the equally persistent need for hope by transforming them into a spiral: each cycle repeats the preceding one on a higher level, each new world is better than the old. In summer 1979 the eight-hundredth anniversary of Hildegarde of Bingen was celebrated—of a mystic who, though not officially canonized by the Catholic church, is widely venerated as a saint. Her description of the world after the destruction of ours is a classical expression of a vision of which our utopias, our hopes for the future are but secularized versions:

> The four elements shine in great clarity and beauty. The fire gleams golden as the glow of the dawn. The air is pure and radiant, the water tranquil, without overflowing or destructive power, the earth is even. Everything is in a state of calm and beauty. Sun, moon and stars are radiant with the light of clarity, like precious stones on golden ground. The circling that divided day from night has ended—it is a day never to cease.

II.

How this differs from the fate that many of our writers seem to have prepared for us in fantasy and that so many of us suspect our rulers are drifting into preparing for us in reality, a *night* never to cease!

Which perils we shall actually have to face is a question well beyond the bounds of this study, except insofar as it may help to enlighten us on perils that stories of the end of the world confront us with in the imagination—*if*, that is, these two lines of historical development are correlated.

Are they? Among the few who have declared themselves on this question is the Czech emigré writer Milos Kundera, who said: "If a fear has been present in the human mind for ages, there must be something to it."

Something, but what? Our survey has not shown a quantitative correlation: There is no evidence that the frequency of end-of-the-world stories has increased with the heightened actual risk of the extinction of mankind; or if there is such a correlation, it is small. Is there a qualitative correlation? Do changing preferences for one or the other agent of destruction reflect perils changing in reality? Or changing perceptions of perils? Or is there no connection?

The horsemen of Revelation may race each other for the Grand Prix of Armageddon: the rider who gets there first to wreak annihilation, the later comers finding nothing left to annihilate. Which riders are likely to win?

These seem to be the agents of destruction that now are, or recently have been, or soon will be, feared most:

1. *Nuclear War.* A generation has gone by since the Bomb was dropped on Hiroshima and Nagasaki. The shock has not worn off. Though to some extent we have learned to live with the mushroom cloud over our heads, and some may think that if nothing has happened until now, nothing probably will, the danger is on the other hand in some respects perceived as even greater: Those unhappy about the bomb could at first console themselves with the thought that the use of atomic energy for peaceful purposes would bring benefits that in a sense would make up for the dangers of future military use, if not for the deaths already inflicted, but it soon became clear that even the peaceful use involves terrible risks. For another thing, proliferation. The danger of the use of nuclear weapons in situations like World War II may be thought of as limited by the sense of responsibility of the leaders of major powers. Proliferation may put the awesome potential for destruction into the hands of the reckless, to say nothing of the plainly insane. This danger, now well known, appears aggravated by a recent change in international relations: What Thucydides thought of as an immutable rule—that the big powers do what they like and the small powers do what they must—seems no longer to hold, at least in the West.

2. *Human Reproduction.* Freud, as mentioned, thought (half a century ago) that mankind might be brought to the verge of extinction by persistent falling of the birth rate, due to the increasing restriction that civilization places on the sex drive. The only example of such a thought that I could find in present-day writing is in a book review by John Updike where he notes, in several recently published novels,

"characters with strikingly modest sex drives" and wonders "whether under conditions of dense metropolitan crowding this primeval social glue will tactfully dry up."

Today the very opposite looms as the greater danger. It is not as widely appreciated, though, as it would be if more people understood elementary mathematics well enough to perceive the pace of the "population explosion." The story of the inventor of chess and of his reward illustrates it. The king involved was perhaps not the last ruler of Persia to miscalculate, but the point relevant for us is that population growth follows the same mathematical formula—really a simple one: the summation of the powers of 2. The number of people on Earth has doubled in the last about thirty-five years. If the trend remains unchanged, by how much will world population increase in, say, the next 350 years? Most people's estimates lag far behind the truth: If the trend persists, then world population would grow, during a period equal to ten times its doubling time, by a factor equal to the tenth power of 2; i.e., by 1024. World population now being 4.5 billion, it would by the year 2330 reach some 4.5 trillion!

Some people respond with a shrug: Why bother? By that time we'll all be long dead. Well, I wouldn't be so sure. Progress of medical science is likewise self-accelerating. Medical men may develop devices to keep us alive that long.

Speaking in a more serious vein, I am not saying that world population *will* reach 4.5 trillion. This would happen only if the trend remained what it is, and I don't think it will because I don't think it can. It would take much less than 350 years for us to run out of resources, space, and patience.

Population growth can slow down, obviously, in two ways: through a lowering of the birth rate, and there indications now are that this will not happen radically enough and soon enough; or through rise of the death rate—meaning the apocalyptic riders again: famine, war, pestilence, all in dimensions to make the world wars and genocides of our happy age seem like tales of a lost paradise.

3. *Epidemics*. Diseases did not wipe out our species when it was younger and more vulnerable, so why would they now when medicine and public health shield us? However, innovations such as recombinant DNA research, or unforeseeable natural events, may release jinnis that will not let themselves be either forced or coaxed back into their bottles any more than the nuclear jinni did.

Still, any real fear of disease annihilating mankind would seem farfetched. The same is true of some of the more exotic agents of destruction, so beloved by science fiction authors—geological upheavals, attacks by extraterrestrial beings, etc.

4. *Dehumanization*. The end of the world, in the sense in which we talk of it (because the definition has to be that wide to catch the stories about the end) could also come—and could come without either a bang or a whimper—if the makeup of *Homo sapiens* were changed out of all recognition. This could conceivably be done by radical and massive attack on our genetic material (highly unlikely), or it could happen by mutation and natural selection (a *very* slow process), or by the less stable and permanent, but operationally equivalent effect of social and psychological deterioration.

Nobody who is now living and halfway attentive to what goes on around him needs examples of the stresses that very nearly tear the fabric of our society to pieces, and we have but seen the beginning. How will we live when most of the Earth will be plowed under or cemented over (chiefly the latter: farm land is being lost in the United States—not nearly the worst-off country—at a rate of twelve square miles *a day*); when the birds, far from taking over New York, will be extinct; when the last flower will be gone from the Alpine meadows of Europe and America? Several works of science fiction, notably John Brunner's *Stand on Zanzibar*, have explored this, but have hardly fathomed the depth of possible catastrophes.

Man does not live on bread alone (it would perhaps be worse if he did, for there won't be enough of it for 4.5 trillion of us). Many sages and many fools—not including a former governor of California who thought that when you have seen one redwood you have seen them all—have pointed out that man needs much of just what is now endangered or has already been destroyed, and needs it as badly as bread. Possible effects were predicted—to cite just one example—by Rudolf Brunngraber, a writer in the tradition of Utopian Socialism:

> It may be that in that most distant future in which we think of Earth as a chessboard of gardens and architecture, the violent will push the weaker ones around with a brutality that we can not even imagine. . . . It is thinkable that general leisure and affluence will but bring out the very lowest in man; that with drug-infested bodies, saturated to the point of nausea, and with pitiable craving—that then in utter despair everybody will massacre everybody.

When this was written five decades ago, people probably shook their heads over such wild ideas; today they would hardly be that sure. The prevailing American attitude toward much that could happen is perhaps still that "it can't happen here," but there is little support in facts for smugness. The world will not be able to continue long half affluent and half starving any more than six score years ago our country could continue half slave and half free. The present accelerating destruction of the tropical rainforests will threaten our climate and our economy, not merely that of the tropics. Recent waves of unplanned and undesired migration give us a foretaste of what may happen if the so-called developing countries stop developing and are ravaged by famine.

The United States is not an island; neither can small parcels of it be made into islands. There has recently been a curious case of nature (or rather, reality) imitating art ("art" here including fiction and not implying any judgment on value or quality): An old science fiction story, "The Sound of Breaking Glass," depicts how, as civilization collapses, an eminently gifted scientist converts a diner in the median strip of a toll road into his private fortress and what happens to his daughter after his death. News reports now tell us of "Survivalists" in Southern California with strikingly similar plans. They will not work.

Perhaps none of the "worst scenario" will ever happen. But to avoid it, to steer this ship of fools of ours into port before it is swept into the maelstrom that looms ahead, will require the highest degree of patience, wisdom, forbearance, and statesmanship, virtues that have been more praised than practiced. Can we confidently say that they will be forthcoming in the right place at the right time?

This question, being rhetorical, leads us back to the starting point of this section, to the question what correlation, if any, there is between the actual danger of an "end of the world" coming—i.e., to recapitulate, of the destruction of civilization, or of mankind itself, or of life on Earth, or of this very planet, or of unimaginable reaches of the universe beyond us—and stories about such an end.

As far as the evidence is before us, there is no quantitative correlation: it does not simply work this way that the greater the danger, the greater the volume of such stories. There is no simple qualitative correlation either: the agents of destruction chosen by writers of fiction are not particularly those most threatening in reality. What sense does it make then to enumerate and to try to weigh the factors that may actually loom as possibly bringing the end?

Simply this sense: Even if none of the actual risks were ominously large—and some of them may be so—the *perceived* risks are, or will soon become, large enough to matter, especially in cumulation. Such diverse risks as nuclear war, epidemics, invasion from outer space, may not be causally connected. But in their effect on the emotional and intellectual atmosphere we breathe they are synergetic. All of them together create that climate of anxiety and perceived pressure that chokes, alarms, stimulates escape. To live under the shadow of the nuclear bomb, the decline of living standards as resources dwindle, and the intolerable discomforts of crowding may become too much. The famous words, "it wasn't such a big deal," may come to be applied to mankind as a whole, not merely to a massacre in Viet Nam. It is the climate in which stories of the end flourish and eventually can be seen as describing a desirable event. E. B. White's story, "The Morning of the Day They Did It" in which two men on a satellite drop the bomb half out of boredom, half because the world seems no longer worth preserving, is a spoof; but also a warning.

We can expect to read many more stories of the end of the world—unless that end comes too soon for us to read anything (it may even come before this is printed). If we have a chance to read further, we'll read many embodiments of that double paradox that marks this branch of literature: we can especially expect to read more stories about an end with a lone survivor, or such variations of this theme as a couple surviving to become the Adam and Eve of a new mankind, or a small group of people surviving to be the nucleus of a new civilization. The probability of such a thing really happening is negligible. In fiction it looms large because psychological need makes it so. The unlikelihood of the event did not keep authors in the past from describing it, and there is no reason to think it will in the future. The best such fiction will be cautionary tales to be used wih great caution.

3
Ambiguous Apocalypse:
Transcendental Versions of the End
Robert Galbreath

We need *eternity*; for only eternity can provide space for our gestures. Yet we know that we live in narrow finiteness. Thus it is our task to create infinity within these boundaries, for we no longer believe in the unbounded.[1]

In *The Image of the Future*, Frederik Polak argues that the present age is historically unique in its lack of a positive, public conception of the future as either "utopian" (man-made) or "eschatological" (God-given).[2] Positive or not, contemporary thought is nevertheless rife with eschatological speculation about the End—the end of the world, the end of the human species, the end of the West, the end of the age. The pervasiveness of such speculation is beyond question, but the interpretation of its cultural and literary ramifications, including its frequent reliance upon transcendental imagery and themes disconnected from formal religious belief, is less certain. It is by no means clear that transcendental versions of the End in speculative literature collectively constitute "true myth" in Olaf Stapledon's sense.[3] Nor is it clear, adopting for the moment Mircea Eliade's thought that *littérature fantastique* is an instrument of knowledge, whether the cognitive function of literary transcendence is primarily to convey knowledge, disrupt reality, or project anxiety.[4] Yet it is noteworthy that secular literature finds imaginative resources in transcendence and feels the need to grapple with eschatology. Brian Stableford has caught the essence of the matter in writing of science fiction that it has been "forced to confront the age-old speculative issues associated with metaphysics and theology, in search of possible answers consonant with the discoveries of modern science—because of, rather than in spite of, the fact that science itself rules the questions unanswerable."[5]

With its suggestion of ultimacy and inherent meaning, the End is one such unanswerable question. Despite innumerable variations on the themes of human disaster, natural catastrophe, and entropy, speculative literature has shown no reluctance in also proposing transcendental versions of the End, whether or not they are in agreement with modern science. As "transcendental" fictions, most of them in fact go considerably beyond the present universe of science, but in this regard they are at least loosely consonant with the self-transcending nature of science itself. While works of literature must not be confused with metaphysical treatises, they can be read as responses—shaped and dramatized—to existential situations. The anxieties inherent in the contingency of being human in what Polak calls the "moment-bound now"[6] elicit varied responses, among them a preoccupation with transcendence and eschatology, but these terms no longer function in speculative fiction in quite the same manner as in formal theology or traditional metaphysics. In this regard, speculative fiction conforms to the general pattern in post-Newtonian thought of an immanentized transcendence or, as M. H. Abrams—borrowing from Carlyle—has characterized it for the Romantic period, a natural supernaturalism.[7] For those who cannot accept the transcendental in an ontological sense, yet who find the imaginative and emotional pull of transcendence still or even more powerful, the transcendental is displaced from the beyond and relocated within the cosmos, even within the human psyche. Thus immanentized or internalized, the transcendental is within nature, yet still beyond the known, still other (if not quite wholly), fully capable of eliciting awe, wonder, terror, but not truly a source of religious faith or an object of worship.

Natural supernaturalism is the point of Rilke's challenge and of speculative literature's preoccupation with metaphysical questions and transcendence. If we disbelieve in, yet still need, eternity, or infinity, or the transcendental, how can we create them within the boundaries of the temporal, the finite, and the natural? Broadly speaking, the creation of a credible natural supernaturalism is the focus of speculative fiction. Such fiction, including science fiction, fantasy, and occult or metaphysical fiction, is essentially characterized by a significant concern with presenting as objectively real various "radical discontinuities," "marvels," "novae," "crucial exceptions," and "impossible realities"—that is, with contradictions of the consensus view of reality presumably held by author and reader alike—which are made credible by virtue of rationales derived from science, philosophy, psychology, religion, mythology, the occult, and other thought-structures, actual or invented. The effect is to challenge the reader's conceptions of reality; the basic function is epistemological.[8] Science fiction, as the form of speculative fiction which seeks to establish credibility in relation to science and a scientific atmosphere, is especially suited to deal with Rilke's bounded infinite and to illustrate the ambiguities of natural supernaturalism. Science fiction has in fact been aptly characterized as a "developed oxymoron" for its concern with this-worldly transcendence and credible marvels.[9]

Transcendence is basic to science fiction. The nature of science fictional transcendence is partly captured by Donald Wollheim's eight-stage "cosmogony of the future" in twentieth-century Anglo-American science fiction. The final stage Wollheim calls "the Challenge to God":

> Galactic harmony and an undreamed-of high level of knowledge leads to experiments in creation, to harmony between galactic clusters, and possible exploration of the other dimensions of existence. The effort to match Creation and to solve the last secrets of the universe. Sometimes seeking out and confronting the Creative Force or Being or God itself, sometimes merging with that Creative First Premise. The end of the universe, the end of time, the beginning of a new universe or new time-space continuum.[10]

Wollheim depicts transcendence as human aspiration, striving, and evolution. At best, his picture corresponds to Polak's "man-made" or "utopian" image of the future. It entirely overlooks the opposite and equally powerful image of transcendence in speculative fiction, that of alien or supernatural intervention into human reality, the "God-given" or "eschatological" future. Here I am concerned with transcendence in speculative fiction only as it bears on the specific themes of the end of the world and the end of humanity. The transcendence in these fictions may be either man-made or God-given; but I differ from Polak in referring to both as eschatological transcendence.

Speculative fiction apparently cannot avoid ambiguity in dealing with transcendence, for its message is simultaneously that humanity can and must rise above its own limitations and that humanity deeply wishes for salvation by something greater than itself. It is a characteristic ambivalence of the times. But in placing transcendence of either kind within a naturalistic framework, speculative fiction does not always avoid a mechanical translation from one vocabulary into another, the supernatural into the natural, a linguistic alteration that is merely cosmetic.[11] Metaphorically, and often quite literally, we then have only "technological angels" (as Jung called flying saucers), not the "spaceships of the mind" (Nigel Calder's term for the big ideas of scientific speculation on colonizing the universe) which expand the imaginative universe virtually to the infinite, as Rilke sought.[12] The overall tone of these fictions, moreover, is that of a lack of confidence in any future. Taken collectively, they doubt both human potential and interventionist salvation. They offer no consensus on the nature of the End, the kind of transcendence involved, or its desirability. A few even doubt the finality of any End. They constitute, in short, an ambiguous apocalypse.

The ambiguities and variations of modern transcendental versions of the End can be readily appreciated by organizing a representative group of speculative fictions from the 1890s to the present according to their depiction of the interaction between the natural and the supernatural (the End/means relationship), then by examining in detail several points of ambiguity concerning transcendence and the human potential for achieving it. Thematic analysis of this sort unfortunately precludes consideration of texts as aesthetic wholes or of historical development. By referring to these texts as apocalyptic, for example, I wish only to draw attention to the attitudes of apocalyptic eschatology they express or imply, not to generic properties. I presume this to be the meaning also of the often-heard claim that science fiction is the contemporary form of apocalyptic literature.[13] Certainly it is not fortuitous that traditional apocalyptic and modern science fiction are both defined by the sense of radical discontinuity. But modern apocalyptic fictions do not in fact conform at all points to the generic characteristics of ancient apocalyptic, not least of all in their self-conscious status as fiction rather than divine revelation.[14] They are, however, apocalyptic in the broad sense of being purported "revelations" or "unveilings" (the literal meaning of "apocalypse") of eschatological matters, which are in some sense transcendental, which involve radical discontinuities in human and natural history, and which may—but not invariably—entail cosmic transformation and renewal.

Eschatological transcendence in speculative fiction refers to the End—the end of the world, the end of the age (*aion*), or the end of the human race—when that end is caused, characterized, or revealed by transcendental factors or transcendental analogues.[15] Traditional eschatological doctrines are conventionally divided into individual eschatology, concerning the end of each human life and the destiny that awaits it thereafter (death and afterlife), and cosmic or historical eschatology, encompassing the end of the world, the end of humanity, and the fulfilled goal of history.[16] The end of the world may be limited to the Earth or it may apply to the entire universe; speculative fiction will also occasionally describe the end of another planet or the end of a fantasy universe (e.g., C. S. Lewis's Narnia, Ursula K. Le Guin's Earthsea). Individual eschatology is beyond the scope of the present essay and will not be considered further.[17] Modern usage justifies the extension of cosmic or historical eschatology to mean the end of the present age without necessarily implying a final end to history.[18] By further extension, the end of humanity can refer simply to the end of the species as we now know it without necessarily denying future transformations through biological or psychical evolution or other processes of transhumanization. Both these extended meanings are accepted here.

Transcendence or the transcendental is that which from the human viewpoint lies beyond or goes beyond human limits as they are defined by spacetime, death, the biology of the species, and the cognitive norms of human understanding.[19] The transcendental is beyond this world, beyond this knowledge, beyond this life, beyond this humanity. Being beyond humanly known reality, the transcendental is literally metaphysical or supernatural, i.e., beyond nature. But unlike the Kantian "transcendent," the transcendental, although ordinarily unknown, is not intrinsically unknowable. Traditionally, its reality has been rationally deduced or inferred, as in the ontological and cosmological arguments for the existence of God. More to the point, since speculative literature gives far more emphasis to the transcendental as *experienced*, transcendence may be known through its own interventions into spacetime, through altered states of human consciousness (e.g., Platonic *epistēmē*, mystical consciousness, gnosis, visionary experience), or through the transhumanization of the human species itself into the transcendental (e.g., Teilhard de Chardin's hominization process leading to the Omega point).

To present the transcendental as an objectively real marvel, speculative fiction relies heavily on analogues which are textually presented or inferrable as existing within spacetime, yet so far exceed human understanding that they are functionally equivalent to the transcendental. Virtually any science fiction device may of course be a metaphor for transcendence; I restrict myself, however, to instances where the analogue is presented as actually transcending the known limits of the cosmos or the human condition. Even in this more restricted sense, the science fiction universe is filled with transcendental analogues in the guise of overminds, superaliens, godlike men, extraordinary powers, technological angels, and cosmic destinies which richly illustrate Arthur C. Clarke's Third Law that "any sufficiently advanced technology is indistinguishable from magic" and such variants as "any sufficiently advanced aliens or humans are indistinguishable from gods" and "any sufficiently advanced intelligence is indistinguishable from the godlike."[20]

Clarke's own fiction contains some of the best known examples of transcendental analogues in modern speculative literature. In both his novel *Childhood's End* (1953) and the screenplay of the film *2001: A Space Odyssey* (1968), which he co-authored, humanity possesses a hitherto unsuspected evolutionary potential for metamorphosis into the truly godlike. In *Childhood's End*, a collective apotheosis is described; in the film, it is Bowman's apotheosis into the Star Child—but his experience must be seen as paradigmatic for the human species as a whole. Humanity's evolutionary potential in *2001* is entirely manipulated by an unseen alien agency through the transformation (a parody of Nietzsche) from ape to man to superman. There is no indication that humanity would evolve on its own. The evolutionary metamorphosis in *Childhood's End*, however, is natural, if utterly discontinuous from all existing biological knowledge. Nevertheless, the risk of human self-destruction before the completion of metamorphosis is sufficiently great to require the presence of the Overlords who bring peace to the world, guard us against ourselves, and serve as midwives to the impending transformation. (The wish for protection from our own destructiveness is also expressed in Clarke's novel version of *2001: A Space Odyssey* [also 1968]. The first act of the Star Child is to destroy the nuclear weapons in orbit around Earth.) The "total breakthrough" takes place under the supervision of the Overlords: the emergence of the new children with physical abilities, their development into a group mind, their final collective upsurge from the Earth, destroying it in the process, to total mergence with the Overmind, an entity as far beyond the Overlords as the Overlords are beyond ordinary humanity. Overmind, Star Child, unseen manipulators—all are godlike, and the Overlords, who play the role of guardian angels, ironically look like demons. They, like the evolutionary and transformative processes at work, are transcendental, yet we are given no reason to believe that they do not somehow fit into the universe, even if they surpass our understanding.[21]

If eschatological transcendence signifies an End that is caused, characterized, or revealed by transcendental factors or analogues (the end of the world and the end of the human species as we know it are both transcendental in *Childhood's End*), then it can be formulated as the relationship between ends and means. The transcendental and the natural may interact in several ways in speculative fiction, depending on whether the End, the means, or both are transcendental, as the following chart indicates:

	End	Means
I.	Transcendental	Transcendental
II.	Transcendental	Natural
III.	Natural	Transcendental

"Transcendental" includes both the ontologically other and transcendental analogues, although in some fictions a clear distinction is not possible. Regardless of type, the End—of the world, of humanity, or of the age—may be represented variously as actual, impending, averted, or failed. The End may also be seen as desirable, undesirable, mixed, or even beyond such simplistic judgments. The means to the End are equally varied: intentional or accidental, personal or impersonal, interventionist or immanent.

Type I calls for ends and means that are both transcendental. Robert Hugh Benson's *Lord of the World* (1907) recounts the final struggle between Antichrist and Christ in the twenty-first century, culminating in Armageddon and the end of this world. The story is structured as the antithesis between the charismatic young American politician Julian (the Apostate?) Felsenburgh, who becomes President of Europe and through a chain of circumstances is even proclaimed Lord and God, and the modest young English priest, Father Percy Franklin, who becomes the last Pope, Silvester (perhaps referring to Sylvester II who was Pope in the millennial year 1000), and in whom the Word is again made flesh. Julian's ascendancy is described as the logical outcome of a century of progressive socialism, humanism, and religious decline. In the final confrontation at Megiddo (Armageddon), when Julian's air fleet attempts to exterminate Percy (now Pope Silvester) and the tiny remnant of the Catholic church, the drama becomes frankly supernatural. Signs and portents fill the sky, angelic Thrones and Powers manifest themselves, the Word enters Silvester, and the faithful few await the coming of Julian, whose identity is not left in doubt:

> He was coming now, swifter than ever, the heir of the temporal ages and the Exile of eternity, the final piteous Prince of rebels, the creature against God, blinder than the sun which paled and the earth that shook; and, as He came, passing even then through the last material stage to the thinness of a spirit-fabric, the floating circle [of airships] swirled behind Him, tossing like phantom birds in the wake of a phantom ship. . . . He was coming, and the earth, rent once again in its allegiance, shrank and reeled in the agony of divided homage.[22]

The world itself comes to an end with the final sentence of the book: "Then this world passed, and the glory of it."

In William Butler Yeats's story, "The Table of the Laws" (1896), the advent of the heterodox Joachimite Third Age of the Spirit is revealed, but ironically rejected by the convention-bound narrator as demonic. The advent of the White Bird of Kinship in the Fourth Millennium is left unexplained in Richard Cowper's *The Road to Corlay* (1978), but it seems fully transcendental and parallels both millennialism and the traditional image of the Holy Spirit as the dove descending. The destruction of the world is threatened in Charles Williams's *The Place of the Lion* (1931) by the Platonic Ideas which in the form of emblematic animals enter our world and gradually absorb it into their greater reality. To prevent the destructive commingling of the two realms of being and becoming, the hero must assume the role of Adam and by the theurgical act of the naming of the beasts restore them to their proper place and seal the breach, in much the same fashion as the Archmage Ged must close the door between the lands of life and death in Ursula K. Le Guin's *The Farthest Shore* (1972). The Last Trump sounds in "A Vision of Judgment" (1899) by H. G. Wells. Everyone comes before God for judgment and each is mortified to hear his actual record read aloud by the Recording Angel. When everyone is sufficiently chastened, God drops them all on a fresh planet revolving around Sirius and admonishes them, "Now that you understand me and each other a little better, . . . try again."[23]

Fictions of the first type of ends/means relationship tend to employ the transcendental directly. God, Christ, Antichrist, and the Millenium all appear in their own person. There are, however, well-known examples of transcendental analogues, such as the human apotheosis and this-worldly transcendence of Clarke's *Childhood's End*, in which End and means both exceed human comprehension. In other texts, such as Olaf Stapledon's *Star Maker* (1937), to which I will return later, and H. P. Lovecraft's Cthulhu stories, the ontological status of the Star Maker and the Great Old Ones shifts from this-worldly to other-worldly or even straddles both. In Lovecraft's case, the End is not apotheosis, but its opposite, the secular equivalent of the Antichrist's reign. His version of the apocalypse undermines human confidence:

> The most merciful thing in the world, I think, is the inability of the human mind to correlate all its contents. We live on a placid island of ignorance in the midst of black seas of infinity, and it was not meant that we should voyage far. The sciences, each straining in its own direction, have hith-

erto harmed us little; but some day the piecing together of dissociated knowledge will open up such terrifying vistas of reality, and of our frightful position therein, that we shall either go mad from the revelation or flee from the deadly light into the peace and safety of a new dark age.[24]

The revelations indicate that mankind once was and soon may again be at the mercy of the terrible Great Old Ones, entities Lovecraft sometimes describes as existing beyond spacetime, sometimes lurking within it. There is no doubt that their return marks the end of the world as we know it and the advent of "strange aeons." The recurring figure of Nyarlathotep, the messenger of the Great Old Ones, is explicitly connected in Lovecraft's fictions with the sense of an apocalyptic ending. He is first encountered in the dream sketch "Nyarlathotep" (1920, published 1931) coming out of Egypt, arising from the blackness of twenty-seven centuries, at a time of apocalyptic upheaval when "everyone felt that the world and perhaps the universe had passed from the control of known gods or forces to that of gods or forces which were unknown."[25] He makes nightmarish revelations about the ultimate gods and the End. In subsequent fictions, he serves as the messenger of the Great Old Ones and is associated with images of darkness, chaos, and the End. Robert Bloch gives him a major role in his Lovecraftian sequel, *Strange Eons* (1979), as the prophet of Great Cthulhu's ultimate victory.

Type II eschatological transcendence describes transcendental ends arising from explicitly natural causes or processes, such as technology, radiation, and evolution. Ontological status cannot always be clearly determined, however, as Arthur C. Clarke's classic short story, "The Nine Billion Names of God" (1953), indicates. The computer technology which drastically accelerates the Tibetan monks' task of counting God's names hastens but does not cause the transcendental end of the universe. According to their belief, God's purpose in creating humanity will be accomplished when all names have been compiled. Human counting, whether by hand or by human-created machinery, is merely God's instrument for achieving his inscrutable goal. On the other hand, humans apparently must choose to embark upon the laborious process (by hand, it will take fifteen thousand years); they are not being manipulated to undertake it. Human and divine wills must accord.

Another text that resists easy classification is the earliest one to be discussed here, Camille Flammarion's *Omega: The Last Days of the World* (*La Fin du monde*, 1893). The book's first and longest part takes the occasion of a threatened collision with a comet in the twenty-fifth century to review all that is known about the various natural ways in which the world may end. The second part moves ahead ten million years to the final days of the human race, when the Earth has cooled to the point where life can no longer be sustained. As the last man and woman, Omegar and Eva, collapse near the Great Pyramid to await death, the spirit of Cheops appears and reassures them that no one ever really dies. Time flows into eternity, world succeeds world: "All is eternal, and merges into the divine." When they die, their spirits ascend into the heavens like two flames, accompanying the spirit of the pharaoh. An epilogue traces the subsequent history of the solar system and the process by which new worlds and new universes will continue to appear throughout eternity. Flammarion thus presents a natural end succeeded by a transcendental end. The causal relationship is hazy, but he implies that human evolution progresses from the material to the spiritual plane of existence: "Mankind had passed by transmigration through the worlds to a new life with God, and freed from the burdens of matter, soared with an endless progress in eternal light."[26]

There is no ambiguity about cause and effect in the next two stories. An "ontological experiment" in Charles L. Harness's "The New Reality" (1950) destroys phenomenal reality and projects three human survivors into the noumenal realm of things-in-themselves.[27] Two of the survivors are identified as Adam and Eve, the third is the scientist who performed the experiment by splitting a photon of light, Professor Luce (Lucifer the light-bringer), and the new reality is the Garden of Eden. The story asserts, in what now seems like a satire of paradigmology, that perceived reality always corresponds to the human understanding of it. The expulsion from Eden is equated with the human need to interpret, so that things-in-themselves (Kant's *noumena*) are immediately obscured by human interpretations. As the interpretations change, so do the phenomena. The world thus was once literally flat. The Soviet science fiction novel *World Soul* (translated 1978) by Mikhail Emtsev and Eremei Parnov describes the result of an experiment gone wrong with a seaweed mutation as a "biotosis," an organic mass that perceives, stores, and manipulates potentially the entire conscious and unconscious mental life of humanity. Out of a divided humanity, it forges an average mental life most conducive to its own growth and proceeds to impose it at large. Somewhat confusingly, the biotosis is destroyed at the end by humans who unite to create a human future.

Psychic and biological evolution are frequently invoked to create a transcendental end for humanity. Psychic evolution produces *Homo Gestalt* in Theodore Sturgeon's *More Than Human* (1953). The book traces the painful maturation of a group mind comprising a handful of misfit children with psychical abilities to the time of its acceptance by those who have already evolved. Sturgeon leaves no doubt that the higher humanity is truly godlike, a humanity "sainted by the touch of its own great destiny," "the Guardian of Whom all humans knew—not an exterior force, nor an awesome Watcher in the sky, but a laughing thing with a human heart and a reverence for its human origins."[28] The transcendental implications of psychic evolution are no less clear in the dream of the "psi millennium" in Dan Morgan's *The Several Minds* (1969):

> ". . . consider fully the implications of Psi. Imagine, if you will, a world in which there are no secrets, a world where all the knowledge of humanity is freely available, a world where no one need ever be alone or afraid, where the touch of a loving, sympathetic mind is only a thought away." Becky stopped talking, her eyes shining with the brilliance of her inner vision.
> "A Psi millennium," Jerry said. "When Satan shall be bound, and Christ reign on Earth . . ."[29]

A variation on psychic evolution is found in Michael Murphy's *Jacob Atabet: A Speculative Fiction* (1977). The next development in humanity is described as a kind of body mysticism or somatic consciousness which fuses purely physical and meditative disciplines with control of biological evolution to produce the "glorified body" or "body of light" described in various religious traditions.

Biological transformations of humanity are central to H. G. Wells's *The Time Machine* (1895), George Bernard Shaw's *Back to Methuselah* (1921), and Olaf Stapledon's *Last and First Men* (1930). The latter traces eighteen major metamorphoses until the end of man two billion years hence. The first new species following us, the Second Men, do not appear for another ten million years. Beginning with his essay, "The Man of the Year Million" (1893), Wells popularized the image of the dome-headed, spindly-bodied future humans ("human tadpoles"). He may also have been the first to associate the devolution of humanity with the end of the world. If Eisenstein's interpretation is correct, mankind has devolved in *The Time Machine* into the tentacled football flopping about in the twilight of the world thirty million years from now.[30]

An unusual variant of the theme of evolutionary transcendence
depicts the replacement of humanity by artificial people and machines.
Karel Čapek's play, *R.U.R.* (1921), has humanity exterminated by its
own chemically created "robots." Originally created as a cheap, non-
human labor supply, some of them have been modified by a human
scientist to make them more human, chiefly by giving them a "physi-
ological correlate" to the soul. The meaning becomes clear at the end
of the play when two of the modified robots feel tenderness and love
for one another, and are told by the last man: "Go, Adam, go, Eve.
The world is yours." John W. Campbell's early short story, "The Last
Evolution" (1932), traces the evolution of ever more efficient forms of
existence as Human Beings are replaced by their creation, Beings of
Metal (machines), and they in turn by their creations, the godlike
Beings of Force, "eternal, and omniscient." More recently, cyborg
stories have become popular. The cyborg as the symbiosis of human
and machine certainly indicates a transcendence of the human condition and points toward the eventual loss of distinction between metal
and flesh, but these developments are not usually linked in the fictions
with the end of the human species.[31]

The third type of End/means relationship in eschatological transcendence envisions the possibility of a transcendental cause or means
connected to a natural end. The connection between the two may be
causal or synchronistic. In the synchronistic story the narrator or
protagonist employs (or is subject to) transcendental states of consciousness and modes of cognition—visions, dreams, precognition,
out-of-the-body experiences—to become an eyewitness of the evolution of the world or cosmos to its ultimate, natural end. The transcendental means (altered states of consciousness) have no causal relationship with the end at all.[32] Wells in *The Time Machine* provides
technological rather than transcendental means for the traveller to
witness the End. Although the machine itself is described so sketchily
that it is difficult to think of it as a mechanism, the lengthy discussion of
time as the fourth dimension establishes a naturalistic framework. By
contrast, the narrator of Stapledon's *Last and First Men* is directly
inspired—indeed, his "docile but scarcely adequate brain" has been
"seized"—by one of the Last Men from two billion years in the
future;[33] the narrator of *Star Maker* soars up in disembodied form to
begin a visionary, Dantesque journey through ever-expanding degrees
of consciousness until he encompasses the cosmos and beholds the Star
Maker itself; and in *Darkness and the Light* (1942) the narrator's twin
visions of the future fate of humanity take place in a sort of post-

mortem state assisted (apparently) by one of the Last Men. The narrator of William Hope Hodgson's *The House on the Borderland* (1908) dwells in a strange house in Ireland on the bring of a pit which, perhaps like the unconscious mind, is linked in some metaphysical fashion with evil (monstrous swine-things climb out of it to attack him) and with transcendence. In some unexplained manner, the narrator experiences an incredible speeding-up of time while he stands at his window. Days and centuries hurtle past him; his furniture and his body crumble into dust; millions of years pass at blinding speed, the sun dies, the Earth is captured by a Green Star, then it too is destroyed. Still the narrator goes on, encountering cosmic marvels, psychic experiences, a godlike star, and various horrors until he returns to the present.

Unlike the synchronistic stories, transcendence causes the natural end of humanity or the world in the following works. It should be noted that stories of transcendental causality in this category are often concerned with human shortcomings. The tone can be cynical; humans are occasionally likened to garden pests and small animals. Wells has God's Trumpet accidentally fall to Earth, in "The Story of the Last Trump" (1915), where it is blown. A hand of flame snatches it back, but the sound of the Trump is heard worldwide. For just that instant, everyone sees the transcendental reality according to each person's predilections: a glimpse of God, a vision of angels or watchers, a sudden sensation of happiness and freedom. "They saw Him," Wells writes, "as one sees by a flash of lightning in the darkness, and then instantly the world was opaque again, limited, petty, habitual." After a series of vignettes showing the mundane reactions of several characters, the story concludes that "if a thing is sufficiently strange and great, no one will perceive it. Men will go on in their own ways . . . as rabbits will go on feeding in their hutches within a hundred yards of a battery of artillery." Both are creatures of habit.[34] Thomas M. Disch's *The Genocides* (1966) portrays an Earth mysteriously seeded with alien trees whose rapid growth wrecks human civilization and destroys nearly all indigenous life forms within a few years. A handful of human survivors witness the first harvesting of the trees by their alien gardeners and the seeding of the next crop. Humans are apparently only garden pests to be exterminated whenever found. The aliens have no interest whatsoever in establishing contact. Sir Arthur Conan Doyle's *The Poison Belt* (1913) offers a similar explanation but also gives humanity a second chance. Professor Challenger propounds the proposition that the poisonous ether which threatens the existence of humanity is the work of the Great Gardener who bathes his fruit in a disinfectant to remove the mold, i.e., humanity.[35]

In "The Story of the Last Trump," Wells showed humanity resolutely ignoring the implications of its momentary glimpse of God. Robert Silverberg's "Thomas the Proclaimer" (1972) provides not a glimpse of God, but a full-blown miracle. In response to worldwide prayer for a sign, the Earth stands still for exactly twenty-four hours on June 6 at 6:00 A.M. (the date and time of the birth of Damien the Antichrist in David Seltzer's *The Omen* [1976], and the number—666—of the Great Beast of the Apocalypse). Although Silverberg states that he regards the miracle as pure "fantasy,"[36] the consequences are realistically given. No one doubts that the world has stopped, and without physical destruction of any kind, but a bewildering and utterly plausible babble of interpretations immediately arises—was it caused by God? Satan? extraterrestrials? does it mean the beginning or the end? The chaos of cults and competing interpretations brings increasing disorder. The cult of the Apocalypticists claims the world will end on January 1, 2000. By the end of the story, as that date approaches, the collapse of civilization seems certain. The End is the human but inadvertent consequence of supernatural intervention.

These examples give sufficient indication of the variations within the three types of ends/means relationships in the speculative literature of eschatological transcendence. Variation is equally evident in attitudes and judgments. One especially sensitive source of anxiety concerns human progeny. The physical end of the world and the eventual death of humanity seem abstract compared to the immediate fate of our own children. The prospect of a new and superior species of humanity emerging from our children is common in these fictions, but whether it occurs through evolution or outside intervention, it is counted, so to speak, as a mixed blessing. In *Childhood's End* humanity simultaneously ends its childhood and loses its children. The new children, those of the total breakthrough, withdraw in just a few years from their parents. No contact or communication is possible thereafter. With the loss of the children, the will to survive is also lost: "For reasons which the Overlords could not explain, but which Jan [the last man] suspected were largely psychological, there had been no children to replace those who had gone. *Homo sapiens* was extinct."[37] The hope normally invested in the next generation is totally frustrated. The new children and the Overmind they join are no longer human by any recognizable standard. If godhood is the destiny of humankind, it is at the cost of humanity, so that the gulf between man and god remains as deep as before. *Homo Gestalt* in Sturgeon's *More Than Human* also represents the next stage in evolution, a psychic evolution into a collective mind which, as we have seen, is described in frankly religious terms. The children, however, are shown as misfits and outsiders. The mutant children of John Wyndham's *The Chrysalids* (1955; U.S. title: *Re-Birth*) are presented sympathetically to the reader, but they are persecuted by their post-holocaust society in Labrador as "blasphemies" against God's will that man must always be in his image, complete with five fingers on each hand, five toes on each foot, and no telepathic abilities. As in *More Than Human*, the chrysalid children must learn that they are not random freaks but part of the New People, and that life and evolution mean change, not stasis. In this story, the "normal" people reflect our own fear of mutation and change, but they are seen as a dying species. In the same author's *The Midwich Cuckoos* (1957), the new children are unequivocal threats to the survival of humanity. Born of an alien experiment that makes surrogate mothers of the entire child-bearing population of a small English village, their collective abilities give them every advantage in the struggle for survival. One human even wonders if the children were placed on Earth by some Outside Power that is using the planet as a testing-ground for competing species. The new children in these four novels from the 1950s are all described as gods, freaks, mutations, enemies, saviors. The thought that our children can be radically different—the horror story equivalent is surely Ira Levin's *Rosemary's Baby* (1967)—is not reassuring, even when it is treated sympathetically. We fear our own destiny if it means the loss of our humanity and our children.

There is a similar lack of confidence in Christianity as the traditional framework of apocalyptic transcendence. Religious orthodoxy is scarcely to be expected in a literature of natural supernaturalism and transcendental analogues, but Christianity does appear overtly with surprising frequency, although seldom in an unambiguous way. Benson's *Lord of the World* is an exception. More commonly, Christian elements are disconnected from the total belief-system and used to further the sense of doubt, ambiguity, or cynicism (see the Type III stories of causality, discussed earlier) or to create other effects. Seltzer's *The Omen* puts the advent of the Antichrist not in the traditional Christian framework of a prelude to the Millennium and the New Jerusalem, but in a fictionalized context of spurious astrology and invented history, simply for the sake of creating an atmosphere of horror. Gore Vidal's *Messiah* (1954, revised 1965) establishes a transcendental context of messianic expectation complete with signs in the skies in the guise of flying saucers. But the new Messiah, John Cave, is much less impressive than the life story and gospel that are tailored by his associates to conform to the needs of the time. Vidal invites the reader to reflect on the probably similar process by which the Christian gospel was formed.[38] The hope of Christian redemption is transformed imaginatively by Walter M. Miller, Jr.'s *A Canticle for Leibowitz* (1959) into the two-headed mutant Mrs. Grayles/Rachel. The awakening of the entirely innocent Rachel-head as nuclear holocaust once again engulfs humanity is effective, affecting, and hopeful, but it is not orthodox, not even by the standards of the Church of that future time. *A Case of Conscience* (1958) by James Blish is not primarily about the end of the world, although in it a world does end. The planet Lithia, in the judgment of the Jesuit Father Ruiz-Sanchez, is the work of the Devil, a seemingly innocent world designed to confuse the faithful and snare the unwary. The novel's ending, when the planet explodes as a miscalculated human experiment goes wrong and Father Ruiz-Sanchez performs a rite of exorcism, allows both natural and supernatural explanations. It is the end of a world, but we cannot be certain if it is nature or supernature that is ending. George Zebrowski's *The Omega Point* (1972) derives its inspiration, as the title indicates, from the unorthodox theology of Teilhard de Chardin. Zebrowski's far future story of the development of a lone survivor of a war against imperial Earth from isolated ego to participant in a galactic mind at the inner essence of the cosmos is a concretized version of Teilhard's concept of the "planetarization of Mankind," the process of metamorphosis by which humanity evolves toward collective, disembodied consciousness culminating in fusion with the universal center and supreme synthesis, the Omega point. These examples of unorthodox Messiahs, gospels, theologies, and Antichrists, together with those discussed earlier, indicate a fundamental ambivalence. On the one hand, there is a fascination with traditional images of the End, both for their continuing power and for their accessibility as a familiar structure of otherworldliness and radical discontinuity; on the other, there is a tendency to disconnect these images from formal belief and, indeed, to place them in contexts of ambiguity, skepticism, or heterodoxy.

The internalization of apocalyptic eschatology is a further source of ambiguity in these fictions. In his *Natural Supernaturalism*, Abrams interprets Wordsworth's "high argument" as an internalization of apocalyptic eschatology, in which the marriage between the human mind (in a state of unaided visionary experience) and nature will create the restored paradise predicted in Revelation. What can be accomplished now by the single mind, Wordsworth believes, may in time become universal for humanity. For the present, however, the visionary poet's revelation of this human possibility will awaken some of those who hear him from their deathlike sleep and open them to a spiritual apocalypse or resurrection. In this view, external or historical apocalypse is internalized into the spiritual awakening of, first, the individual, then the species.[39] An example of this process from outside speculative literature is Hermann Hesse's *Demian* (1919). Emil Sinclair's quest for his own higher self or daimon (personified as Max Demian) combines personal and historical apocalypse in his battlefield vision of the Woman Clothed with the Sun/Great Mother giving birth to the new humanity, followed by his discovery of his personal savior, Demian, within himself. The novel depicts an internal or psychic process of awakening, incorporating Nietzschean, Christian, Jungian, and Gnostic elements.

Speculative fiction must present its marvels as objectively real, but it too gives evidence of concern with the internalization of apocalypse. In a fashion similar to *Demian*'s preoccupation with the reconciliation of opposites and the overcoming of conventional thinking, speculative fictions of eschatological transcendence may combine the end of the world or the species with internal awakening. The visions afforded by catastrophe (Doyle's *The Poison Belt*), expanded consciousness (Stapledon's *Star Maker*), or science (Flammarion's *Omega*) constitute awakenings to new understanding. Following a lengthy review of scientific evidence for belief in the unending duration of physical reality, Flammarion concludes his novel in an uplifting manner: "And these universes passed away in their turn. But infinite space remained, peopled with worlds, and stars, and souls, and suns; and time went on forever. For there can be neither end nor beginning."[40]

In other fictions, e.g., stories by Wells, Vidal, and Silverberg previously discussed, skepticism or uncertainty over humanity's potential for transcendence is dominant. Ambiguity about humankind's awakening is manifested most interestingly in works which paradoxically combine optimism with doubt, e.g., *Childhood's End*, Stapledon's fictions, Ursula K. Le Guin's *The Lathe of Heaven* (1971), and Doris Lessing's *Briefing for a Descent into Hell* (1971). Clarke and Stapledon clearly wish to enlarge human vistas, but they are not free from doubt concerning our unaided ability to achieve transcendence. Le Guin and Lessing focus more on the problem of distinguishing reality from illusion. In their novels, they seem to be saying that we should not push too hard to understand reality technologically, that the end of illusion comes, if it comes at all, through an internal process. The compact sequence of apocalyptic revelations in *Childhood's End* may be read as a deliberate challenge to human confidence in its ability to understand reality, but the challenge operates on two levels. On one Clarke obviously wishes to puncture naive anthropocentrism and the illusion that science in its present form can potentially encompass reality. The U.N. Secretary-General's confident assertion to the still unseen Overlords in chapter 3 that their physical appearance can make no difference, that to an enlightened people biological form does not matter, is stunningly upset by the revelation of the Overlords's actual demonic appearance. Many years later at Karellen's last news conference, he explains the ban on human space flight by likening it to the situation of cave men in a modern city. A reporter challenges this view. To a humanity in possession of science, alien things might seem strange, but not magical. Karellen's reply, "Are you quite sure of that?" recalls Clarke's Third Law and is confirmed not only by the experiences of the stowaway Jan on the planet of the Overlords but by the evolutionary drama that begins to unfold. That the metamorphosis is incomprehensible certainly wounds the human ego. But on another level, it expresses a lack of confidence in the human ability to understand transcendence, to achieve it unaided, or to solve its own problems.[41]

The multiple evolutions and alternative histories in Stapledon's fictions betray a similar ambivalence. They are not, I believe, to be read as linear narratives but as variations on the theme of human potentiality. We are what we can be, and in Stapledon's writings that nearly fills up eternity and infinity, a science fictional equivalent of the principle of plenitude: eighteen major transformations of humanity over two billion years in *Last and First Men*, the movement from individual consciousness to world-mind to galactic mind to cosmic mind to the visions of the Star Maker itself in *Star Maker*, the double fates of humanity in *Darkness and the Light* which are necessary complements to one another. These visions constitute awakenings to infinite potentiality and thus are encouraging, as they are meant to be; yet the encouragement derives from the content of the visions, not from the experience of visionary transcendence. Visionary experience is not paradigmatic for humanity as a whole. The narrators are privileged by virtue of their experiences. We have no reason to assume that we may duplicate their experiences. In two of the novels, in fact, the visionary experiences are made possible only by the intervention of Last Men, while in *Star Maker* the cosmic vision is left unexplained. Although one leaves Stapledon's books convinced of the need to transcend human pettiness, this resolution is to some extent undercut by the device of outside intervention and inexplicable transcendence.

In Le Guin's *The Lathe of Heaven*, George Orr's transcendental power of "effective dreaming" (a kind of magical psychokinesis) causes reality to mutate with each dream. That we exist at all is due to Orr, who claims that the world was destroyed by nuclear warfare in 1998 and that all that remains is what his dreams create. This variation on the Taoist parable of Chuang Tzu dreaming he is a butterfly or the butterfly dreaming it is Chuang Tzu poses the insoluble problem of reality and illusion, but it does so by suggesting that illusion is the attempt to mold reality to fit one's wishes. Dr. Haber demonstrates this point with his zealous efforts at social engineering through a mechanistic control of Orr's talent. Despite his well-meaning liberal goals, his every attempt worsens matters and threatens ultimate chaos, until Orr can stabilize matters by learning to accept instead of manipulate his talent and to see reality as an infinity that eludes understanding but not acceptance. The message is obviously an important one. It is embodied in an end-of-the-world story that is far more concerned with the end of mental worlds or mental prisons. Nevertheless, Le Guin's use of a truly "wild" talent that resists direction and operates magically seems to imply that awakening or understanding depends upon some extraordinary intrusion into our reality.

Briefing for a Descent into Hell also concerns illusion and reality and the end of the world. The novel focuses on Charles Watkins, a professor of Classics, whose unusual mental experiences may be either psychotic delusions (he is being treated at a psychiatric hospital) or genuine wisps of memory, the residue of a celestial briefing he received before descending, much like a Gnostic messenger, into the poisonous atmosphere of Earth (Hell) in a perhaps vain effort to awaken humanity to an impending planetary catastrophe. Lessing's skill in alternating viewpoints constantly upsets the reader's certainty about Watkins's mental health. Watkins's struggle to grasp fleeting thoughts and images, thwarted at nearly every step by the doctors' insistence on drugging him into tranquillity, becomes urgent. Part of his apparent delusion is the warning given him during his briefing that in Earth's atmosphere celestial messengers lose awareness of their true identity and may even be regarded as mentally troubled. This thought allows Lessing to turn the novel into a struggle also between competing psychiatries, one seeing only mental illness, the other—similar to R. D. Laing's—interpreting the schizophrenic's apparent delusions as a healing journey to understanding. Watkins's final decision to submit to electric shock treatment to force the issue is critical. The treatment destroys his visionary/delusionary capability and restores him to what is commonly regarded as normality. He is now either sane or trapped irrevocably in our collective delusion of reality.

No spiritual awakening or apocalypse takes place in Lessing's novel. Humanity cannot begin to comprehend the Overmind and the evolutionary process in *Childhood's End*. Stapledon's visions rely on privileged experiences often initiated by cosmic helpers, the Last Men. George Orr's effective dreaming can only be accepted, not controlled. The injection of unexplained or inexplicable transcendental analogues into these texts creates an ambiguous effect. The novels seek to destroy illusion and to awaken understanding, yet they convey also a certain lack of confidence in humanity's unaided ability to transcend its limitations or to understand transcendence. There is, however, another way of interpreting this ambiguity. Each author attempts to awaken the reader through the shared vision of the text. The vision, however arrived at, is not actually one of transcendence in the sense of a revealed answer or an ultimate solution. These texts tell us that transcendence can only be a further question, not a final answer. From this perspective, ambivalence about human powers of understanding and transcendence may be seen as doubt about overconfident reliance upon seemingly magical solutions, but also as fear that we may persist in sleeping. In this light, the ambiguity of these transcendental versions of the End is less significant for its uncertainty about the End than for its certainty that no End is final and unquestionable. It is only fitting, therefore, to end with a question. It is the question Carlyle asks about philosophy in his chapter on "Natural Supernaturalism" in *Sartor Resartus*, but it applies to speculative fiction with equal appropriateness: "Nay, what is Philosophy throughout but a continual battle against Custom; an ever-renewed effort to *transcend* the sphere of blind custom, and so become Transcendental?"[42]

4
Round Trips to Doomsday
W. Warren Wagar

1. The Circles of Time

The end of the world is seldom the end. With the exception of a few modern men of science, writes Mircea Eliade, "humanity has never believed in a definitive end of the Universe." Always the cataclysm is followed "by a new creation, by a new humanity, unsoiled by sin."[1] For David Ketterer, "The fulfillment of the apocalyptic imagination demands that the destructive chaos give way finally to a new order."[2] Eliade's anthropology of ideas and Ketterer's critique of the apocalyptic in literature do not exhaust the perspectives available to students of terminal visions in science fiction, but they furnish convenient epigraphs for this chapter. Our task is to explore the relationship between cyclical conceptions of time and literary doomsdays. On the whole, we shall not find the task arduous. Ends that lead to fresh beginnings and further ends appear regularly in science fiction, reflecting some of the most characteristic anxieties and ideological paradigms of late industrial culture.

Not that every end imaged in speculative literature necessarily entails or implies a cyclical theory of history. There are catastrophic ends that leave no grain of hope, and neo-Epicurean ends spun out through millennia of irreversible decline. Other literary eschatologies follow the Christian kerygma more or less literally, and supply a post-disaster paradise that ends the tribulations of time altogether, giving man his long-dreamed rest, as in William Morris's seraphic *News from Nowhere*. Some ends turn out to be mere interruptions, warnings from nature or history that civilization enjoys no absolute guarantee of its survival. H. G. Wells's *The War of the Worlds* and Arthur Conan Doyle's *The Poison Belt* are examples of such cautionary near-catastrophes.

But the life-force does not take readily to the thought of the extinction of consciousness and the cessation of effort. Although many

73

religions offer as the ultimate reward for piety the frozen delights of eternity, the greater part of humankind for the greater part of its history has limited its concern to the realm of time, conceived as a sacred circle of birth and rebirth. Nor, as Kryzsztof Pomian notes, has the emergence in modern times of a chronosophy of linear and cumulative progress by any means brought with it the disappearance of earlier chronosophies, including the cyclical.[3] In all the sciences, as well as in fiction, cyclicism thrives, unadulterated or in combination with other chronosophies.

The purest cyclicism in imaginative literature, typically the expression of a conservative, neo-romantic, or sometimes merely cynical world view, comes close to what might be called the traditional pagan consciousness. For such a consciousness, authentic novelty is unthinkable. *Plus ça change, plus c'est la même chose.* Or, in the words of Thucydides, the study of history matters because, "human nature being what it is," the events that happened in the past "will, at some time or other and in much the same ways, be repeated in the future."[4] Cyclicism also has its place in orthodox Jewish and Christian faith. Of the two cities in Augustine's reading of world history, only the city of God moves forward unrelentingly. The earthly city (*civitas terrena*) turns in endless circles, bedazzled by pride and greed.

A portion of eschatological science fiction is the work of writers in whom one or another of these cyclical views of history still prevails. Camille Flammarion, in *The End of the World*, and M. P. Shiel, in *The Purple Cloud*, were such writers. Among more recent figures, René Barjavel, Walter M. Miller, Jr., and James Blish come to mind; all five will be examined more closely below.

But the cyclicism in eschatological fiction is not always pure and unadulterated.[5] When science-fiction writers adopt cyclical conceptions of history, their strategy is often to combine elements of cyclicism with the dominant world view of modern industrial man, a positivist faith in science, technology, and human effort, culminating in an affirmation of progress. The paradigms of the cycle and linear progress are thus joined together, sometimes awkwardly and unconvincingly, with linear progress enjoying the last word. Nations, worlds, galaxies rise and fall, but when all is weighed and tallied, humanity has recorded net gain, by the criteria of good and evil of the writers themselves. For our purposes, it goes without saying, no other criteria need be mentioned.

Of this imperfect cyclicism, overlaid with ideas of progress, the unrivalled master in science fiction was surely Olaf Stapledon, in *Last*

and First Men and again, on a scale still grander, in *Star Maker.* Isaac
Asimov, Brian Aldiss, Michael Moorcock, George Zebrowski, and
several others have continued Stapledon's quest, although no one has
quite equalled the vaulting audacity of his vision. To all these, and
more, we shall also return.

But the opportunity should not be missed to emphasize once more
that the cyclical element in modern science fiction grows out of world-
conceptions as old as human thought itself. With or without admix-
tures of rationalist progressivism, the cyclical romance harks back to
archaic modes of structuring human experience that have never entirely lost their imaginative power. Presumably, they never will, as
long as human beings remain bound to the cycles of nature and mortality. Night and day, the lunar month and the solar year, the tides, the
round from birth to death, seedtime and harvest: everything in archaic
life suggests a pattern of eternal return. Even calamities, such as floods
and storms and famines, alternate with "normal" times in a roughly
predictable fashion, as if they, too, were ticks of the cosmic clock. To
attribute to the time of history the cyclical cadence of the time of
nature was entirely logical, for minds accustomed to axiomatic belief
in the correspondence of universal and human values.

Cyclicist mythology in its earliest forms can only be guessed at,
but surviving texts, and references in those to others more ancient,
argue that it flourished in most of the civilizations of antiquity. A lost
Greek translation of Babylonian texts made in the third century B.C. by
Berossus of Chaldaea is cited frequently by Greek and Roman authorities as a principal source of the cyclicism of the ancient Near East. In
these writings appeared the doctrine of the "Great Year." According
to Berossus, the world was periodically destroyed and restored again:
destroyed by fire when the seven planets were gathered in the sign of
Capricorn, and by flood when they were gathered in Cancer. The time
of fire was the "Great Summer" of the cosmic year, the time of flood its
"Great Winter." A more elaborate and better documented cyclical
myth is found in Indian texts, where each Great Year (*Mahāyuga*) was
said to last 4,320,000 years, ending in a degenerate age known as the
Kali Yuga, the time at which mankind had now, unhappily, arrived.
Babylonian and Indian cyclical teaching no doubt descended from
common sources in the thought-world of ancient Mesopotamia. Parallel, but historically unrelated doctrines of cyclical rise and fall
flourished in traditional Chinese historiography and in the cosmologies of the Aztecs and Mayans.

In the classical West, cyclicism was taught by most of the leading schools of natural philosophy. The pre-Socratics, Plato and Aristotle, the Stoics, and the Neoplatonists all had their versions of it, not to overlook the cyclical historiography of Polybius. A representative source is the Roman Stoic Seneca, in whose textbook *Quaestiones Naturales* the idea of periodic cosmic downfall is presented as a matter of fact. In a single hour, he wrote, the whole world would be consumed in fire or submerged in water, and then reborn, innocent and pure, to start the long travail of rise and fall once again.

The absorption of pagan thought into the world view of medieval Christianity resulted in a blending of cyclical conceptions with the predominantly linear cosmology of Jewish and Christian tradition. The biblical tradition was linear in the all-important sense that it required a single creation and a single end of time. God made heaven and earth, man and woman, once and once only; God came into history as Jesus of Nazareth, was crucified, and rose from the dead, once and once only. He would come again, to be sure, but not as a Palestinian carpenter. His second appearance would be a return in glory, as Christ the King, to rule and judge, and preside over the annihilation of time itself.

Nevertheless, the Christian world view retained certain features of archaic cyclicism. The procession from Genesis to Revelation was not actually a straight line, as in modern theories of progress from savagery to civilized utopia; rather, it constituted a single grand cycle originating and culminating in holy bliss. In the beginning, man and woman lived in purity, a state they shared with God's other creatures, the angels. As certain prideful angels had fallen before history began, so man and woman later fell from divine grace, and suffered expulsion from Paradise. The eternal joy promised to the elect after time's end would, in one sense, merely restore the joy of Paradise, and thus bring mankind full circle. The Neoplatonist doctrine of the "Great Circle" of procession and epistrophe was easily taken over by Christian philosophers like John Scotus Erigena and interpreted as a pagan prevision of Christian truth. All that needed to be excised was the Neoplatonist belief that the Great Circle turned endlessly. For Christians, as applied to universal history, it could turn only once.

Medieval thinkers also pointed to the biblical record as evidence of cycles in the purely secular affairs of mankind. The rise and fall of pagan states, and the constantly repeated transgressions even of God's Chosen People, showed with mournful clarity the powerlessness of man to achieve lasting good without divine help. All ventures purely human, all towers of Babel, collapsed upon themselves in chaos and ruin. Such was the message of Paulus Orosius, disciple of St. Augustine, in his *Seven Books of History Against the Pagans*, the treatise on profane history best known to medieval scholars. Some philosophers, chiefly apologists for kings and emperors, imputed to Christian states the same transcendent and eternal dignity enjoyed by the Church. But orthodox Christian teaching insisted on a sharp distinction between the linear time of God's City and the cyclical time of that other City described by Augustine, whose origins were traceable to the rebellion of Satan and whose end was everlasting Hell-fire. Although orthodox belief did not equate existing polities with Augustine's other City, the *civitas terrena*, any more than it claimed the literal identity of the visible Church with his *civitas Dei*, it saw no hope of stability in the secular affairs of sinful mankind, which were played out in earthly time, and were therefore subject to corruption and decay.

In the Renaissance, a reawakened interest in secular history and the more distinguishably secular aspects of classical literature and thought helped lead to an expanded view of the contours of universal history. Cyclicism was often applied now to history as a whole, and even the arts and letters were seen as rising and falling. For Machiavelli, nature herself decreed the cycles of history. "The nature of mundane things not allowing [provinces] to continue in an even course, when they have arrived at their greatest perfection, they soon begin to decline." It was equally fitting that, having sunk to their lowest point, they reascend. "Thus from good they gradually decline to evil, and from evil again return to good."[6] No ancient historian or cosmologist could have put the matter more succinctly.

But with the unprecedented upsurge of Western civilization in the sixteenth to eighteenth centuries, it became increasingly difficult to adhere to the traditional cyclical view of history. Scorn for medievalism soon extended well beyond the sphere of the arts and letters. Critics of the medieval heritage saw the period between the fifth and the fifteenth centuries as a time of darkness and superstition, even of barbarism. Reflecting on the rise of classical civilization from its rude beginnings, and the still greater achievements of modern man, some contended that the shape of universal history was not so much cyclical as progressive. Enemies of the Church, such as the *philosophes* of the French Enlightenment, rejected or reversed the dualism of the Augustinian paradigm of the Two Cities. It was the earthly city, the city of man and man's science and power, that in the vision of the *philosophes* moved in a more or less straight line toward its own millennium of earthly perfection. By contrast the so-called city of God—or at least the Christian Church—was trapped in a vicious circle of greed, ignorance, and cruelty.

The evolution of a belief in general human progress, which became the dominant chronosophy of Western culture in the springtime of capitalism and the new age of sovereign nation-states, is a major theme, perhaps the master-theme, in the intellectual history of Europe and America in the eighteenth and nineteenth centuries. It seemed to sweep everything before it, a point underscored by close study of the only powerful cyclical theory of history of the eighteenth century, the theory expounded by Giovanni Battista Vico in his *New Science* in 1725. The most memorable feature of Vico's philosophy of history, for twentieth-century readers, is its cyclicism. He proposed a three-stage model for the history of nations, which traced their inexorable passage from theocratic monarchy to heroic aristocracy to democracy and finally dissolution and return to a new theocratic age, a model based on Aristotle's cyclical theory of politics. But the Jewish and Christian nations, Vico added, did not experience the simple empty repetitiveness of pagan societies. Aided by God, these nations achieved cumulative progress in spite of their equal vulnerability to cyclical change. What looked like circular movement was actually spiraliform, and mankind as a whole progressed. Like many science-fiction writers attracted to the cyclical hypothesis, Vico by no means played cynic or relativist or world-weary Stoic. He hoped that mankind could learn to avoid the vices and errors that led to the downfall of nations; and he saw some progress in human affairs, in spite of everything.

During the one hundred years between Vico's death in 1744 and the rash of revolutions in Europe in 1848–49, doctrines of linear progress came forward in great numbers, and went largely unchallenged except by conservative Christian apologists. Turgot, Condorcet, Adam Smith, Kant, and Comte were among its most articulate exponents, and their chronosophies continued to shape thought, and gave rise to others of a similar bent, well into the twentieth century.[7]

Yet as the nineteenth century wore on, grounds for doubting the validity of the progressivist paradigm multiplied. Cyclical theory, still bearing the marks of its ancient and medieval origins, returned in a myriad of new forms, and it is from these modern cyclical conceptions of historical change that imaginative literature in our time draws its chief inspiration. The new varieties of cyclicism appeared in the natural sciences, reviving the ancient idea of cosmic cycles; they also appeared in philosophy, speculative historiography, and the social sciences, arising in large measure from well-grounded anxiety about the future of a civilization threatened by increasingly lethal internecine warfare and massive world-economic malaise.

Ironically, the germ of modern self-doubt was planted by a Prussian philosopher whose faith in human progress and satisfaction with his own times bordered on smugness. Hegel proclaimed a chronosophy of progress, but he eschewed the simplistic linear formulas of many of his French and British forerunners. As M. H. Abrams points out, Hegel's thought amounted to a secularization of Christian Neoplatonism, viewing time as a single Great Circle that proceeded from primordial unity to division to the future restoration of unity, as spirit worked out all its potentialities in the dialectic of world history, and became one again with itself.[8] The key idea in Hegel, which forced his world-historical time-line to curve, was the dialectic. Change occurred not through rectilinear progress, but through the collision and integration of opposing forces. In the cunning of history, conflict was productive, and indeed essential. Hegel's well-known division of human experience into four great ages from Asian tyranny to Germanic freedom is therefore both meliorist and cyclical, yielding as in Vico a spiraliform theory of progress. But its greatest influence in later generations was its emphasis on the dialectical character of world-historical change.

Hegel's faith in the dialectic no doubt reflects his own experience as a German living through the high drama of the French Revolution and later observing, and participating in, the fierce German response to French political and cultural hegemony in the age of Napoleon. Revolutions, struggles for national liberation and unification, and periodic economic crises became almost normal events in the course of the nineteenth century. Hegel himself lived long enough to see the liberation of Greece in the 1820s and a second French Revolution in 1830. Much more was to follow.

Western cultural fatigue took various forms, in response to the stresses of the century. The romantic pessimism of Schopenhauer and his intellectual progeny was one. In Nietzsche, who came under Schopenhauer's posthumous influence, a sophisticated revival of pagan cyclicism is apparent, although Nietzsche shunned anything like a systematic or dogmatic chronosophy. His one-time colleague at Basel, the great historian Jacob Burckhardt, expressed similar, yet more despairing, views in a series of melancholy lectures on the meaning of history, published after his death.[9]

For others, only a thoroughgoing and explicit resurrection of cyclicism could express the full tragedy of modern times and give modern man a clear view of the disaster awaiting him.[10] Several Russian thinkers, notably Nikolai Danilevsky, adopted a cyclical philosophy of history as a strategy for instilling expectations of national glory in their compatriots, whose "turn" it was to replace a decadent and failing West. Danilevsky's *Russia and Europe* (1869) marks one of the first significant attempts in the nineteenth century to rehabilitate cyclicism in historiography. It was followed by several others, such as Brooks Adams's *The Law of Civilization and Decay* (1895), Karl Lamprecht's works on cultural history, Vilfredo Pareto's *Treatise on General Sociology* (1916), and, in 1918–22, Oswald Spengler's *The Decline of the West.*

Spengler began writing his *magnum opus* several years before the outbreak of World War I, but the publication of its first volume near the end of the war could not have occurred at a more propitious time. To a Germany shattered by defeat, and an Atlantic world appalled by the costs of victory, Spengler offered a grim, but curiously consoling explanation of all that had gone wrong with Western civilization. There was no need to gnash one's teeth, or feel guilt or humiliation. All was happening according to plan. The West, victors as well as vanquished, had simply entered upon an inexorable decline, similar to the declines of all past societies, and as unavoidable as the daily setting of the sun or the coming of winter in December.

The impact of Spengler on the public consciousness of Europe and America in the 1920s and 1930s is incalculable. *The Decline of the West* served up a pure cyclicism, almost untouched by ideas of progress, utopia, or transcendence, and deeply scored with forebodings of the end-time of modern man and all his works. Its richness of imagery and its wealth of hypothesis for social scientists in every field raise it above all its successors.[11] And successors were not long in appearing. The historian Arnold J. Toynbee published his more elaborate (and ultimately spiraliform) version of Spengler, *A Study of History*, in 1933–54. The sociologist Pitirim A. Sorokin adhered closely to Spengler's cyclicism in his *Social and Cultural Dynamics* (1937–41). The anthropologists Alfred L. Kroeber, in *Configurations of Culture Growth* (1944), and Philip Bagby, in *Culture and History* (1963), adapted Spenglerism to the theoretical needs of their discipline.[12] Out of all these efforts, and others, emerged a promising interdisciplinary movement for the comparative study of civilizations, which tends nowadays to be far less eschatological and also less cyclicist than its founding fathers.

Indeed, the success of cyclicist philosophies of history and sociocultural change in the academic arena has never been what one would call overpowering. Largely ignored or ridiculed by scholars in the nineteenth century, they have enjoyed at best a marginal acceptance in the twentieth. For the professional academician, they smell too ripely of dogmatism and metaphysical passion, neither of which suits the odorless analytical style of contemporary philosophical and social-scientific scholarship. It is among the non-specialists—politicians, clergymen, journalists, literary folk, and the like—that full-blown cyclical theory has no doubt wielded its most potent influence.

The only exception occurs in a branch of social science not yet mentioned: political economy. In its eighteenth-century origins, political economy was resolutely progressivist, contributing much more than its share to the emergence of the belief in the general progress of humankind. But the maturation of the capitalist world economy brought in its train profoundly disturbing cyclical phenomena that no amount of Enlightenment optimism could argue away. Even if economists maintained that the overall trend was progressive, toward greater production, higher real personal and national incomes, and the industrialization of the non-Western world, they had to reckon as well with recurrent periods of negative growth, declining incomes, unemployment, and business failure. In some countries, during especially severe downward swings of the pendulum, the political and psychological effects have been as great as those of any war or revolution. Socialist critics of capitalism were among the first to call attention to the business cycle. Even orthodox liberal economists eventually had no choice but to admit its existence, not as something extraordinary, but as a regular and more or less predictable feature of the capitalist system. The periodicity of crises in capitalism became a well-established subject for analysis by political economy from the 1860s on. In the twentieth century, the most celebrated treatments of the business cycle are perhaps those of N. D. Kondratieff and Joseph Schumpeter.

Long before Kondratieff and Schumpeter, one socialist critic, Karl Marx, had already put forward a powerful theory of cyclical phenomena in capitalism that incorporated a secular eschatology. The heart of Marxist social science is its detailed analysis of capitalism as a system of relations of production that must inevitably fail because of the cyclical recurrence of business crises of ever worsening severity. Each crisis, by the very means employed to resolve it, generates its successor, until the whole system collapses once and for all, ushering in a new civilization.

As many students of Marx have commented, his philosophy of
history, with its segmentation of the human past into five stages
connected in each case by a massive world-crisis transforming the
social relations of production fundamentally, and its assumption that
the first and final stages will both be characterized by public ownership
of capital (primitive and industrial communism, respectively),
amounts to a reworking of the cosmology of Hegel. Like Hegel, it
views history as single grand cycle punctuated by dialectical metamorphoses of the social order, in which the highest stage represents in
one sense a return to the lowest. By such a reckoning Marx is simply
one more exponent of the spiraliform model of the idea of progress,
with an unacknowledged debt (through Hegel, if in no other way) to
the cosmology of the Bible.[13]

Be this as it may, political economy both Marxist and non-Marxist
is a considerable source of cyclical ideas of world history in the modern
era. At the same time, at least in its Marxist dress, it bears a clearly
eschatological import. In Marxist prophecy, the end of the capitalist
world will be a catastrophic event, a time of vast upheaval and a clean
break with the past. Moreover, it is a world's end dictated by empir-
ically verifiable laws of social science.

In the natural sciences, theoretical progress no less authoritative
than anything happening in economics or the other social sciences has
given cyclicism further encouragement. This progress might have been
ignored by writers of science fiction in happier times, but, in times such
as they are, the natural sciences have helped stoke the cyclicist imagination, and stoked it well. From astrophysics have come stupendous
theories of universal cycles of creation, entropy, and re-creation re-
quiring billions of years each. Geology offers theories less skull-
cracking, but more immediately threatening, of cycles of vulcanism,
floods, sunspots, or glaciation that afflict the planet periodically and
could bring civilization to a natural doom within centuries or even a
few years from our own present. Evolutionary biology has contributed
its scenarios of the rise and fall of species now extinct, suggesting to the
popular imagination a pageant of successive "lords of the earth,"
analogous to the Hegelian notion of the passing of the torch of high
civilization from Asia to the classical world to modern Germany. If the
dinosaurs once "ruled" the world as Rome once ruled the West, and if
the dinosaurs became extinct, just as Rome and other great ancient
empires fell and vanished, what guarantees the perpetual ascendancy
on earth of *Homo sapiens*, or occidental civilization, or the white race?
The question is illogical, if not positively silly, but the research of

paleontologists has played its part in stirring the imagination of writers of cyclicist science fiction.

Other sources of cyclicism in modern thought and experience could be discussed, but we need not continue. Let us only repeat that cyclicism is not the whole story. Visions of doomsday that lead, purely and simply, to other doomsdays by whatever mechanisms, and without net gain for mankind or the universe, represent only one use of cyclical theory by science-fiction writers. The belief in progress also powerfully grips the modern mind, and is still the stronger of the two paradigms by which world history is measured. In imaginative literature cyclicism is often pure, reflecting a kind of cultural despair that one may expect to see grow in coming decades; but it has also been introduced to add dramatic complexity or cautionary wisdom to an image of the future that remains, at bottom, progressive.

2. Chained to the Pendulum of Our Own Mad Clockwork

The time is 3781 A.D. World War III had reduced modern civilization to cinders and forced the survivors to build a social order much like that of Western Europe in the sixth and seventh centuries. Now civilization has risen to "modernity" once again, and World War IV is imminent. Abbot Dom Zerchi, from whose ancient monastery the Church of New Rome will launch a starship to transfer the authority of St. Peter from earth to Alpha Centauri, ponders the tides of history.

> Listen, are we helpless? Are we doomed to do it again and again and again? Have we no choice but to play the Phoenix, in an unending sequence of rise and fall? Assyria, Babylon, Egypt, Greece, Carthage, Rome, the Empires of Charlemagne and the Turk. Ground to dust and plowed with salt. Spain, France, Britain, America—burned into the oblivion of the centuries. And again and again and again.
>
> *Are we doomed to it, Lord, chained to the pendulum of our own mad clockwork, helpless to halt its swing?*[14]

These reflections from near the end of *A Canticle for Leibowitz* (1960), by Walter M. Miller, Jr., belong as much to Miller as to his Reverend Father Abbot. The answer to each rhetorical question is yes. Mankind is chained to its pendulum, cursed by original sin, and destined to repeat the same crimes over and over again. The Church, too, is immortal, charged with its holy mission until the last trump. Life remains what it has always been: good and evil locked in relentless combat. The dispatch of the ecclesiastical starship to Alpha Centauri

was not an act of utopian hubris, therefore, but simply a continuation
of the ancient struggle. "Too much hope for Earth had led men to try
to make it Eden, and of that they might well despair until the time
toward the consumption of the world."[15]

A Canticle for Leibowitz is a critic's dream-book, rich with symbols and metaphors, open to many conflicting interpretations. The
novel teems with hints of man's coming redemption, and perhaps even
progress of a sort. Robert Scholes and Eric S. Rabkin compare its
closing pages with Arthur C. Clarke's Childhood's End, a much less
ambiguous forecast of good things to come.[16] But on balance Miller's
message seems to be essentially the same as that of C. S. Lewis or, for
that matter, St. Augustine. The promises of redemption refer to the
time beyond time, not to a higher life under any sun known to astronomers. Miller's world view is the cyclicism of orthodox Christianity,
neither hostile nor friendly to science as such, but contemptuous of all
utopism. As he writes in the opening paragraph of Part III, "Fiat
Voluntas Tua," it is inevitable that man should conquer the stars and
make after-dinner speeches celebrating his victory. "But, too, it was
inevitable that the race succumb again to the old maladies on new
worlds, even as on Earth before . . . Versicles by Adam, Rejoinders by
the Crucified."[17]

Not all thoroughgoing cyclicists in modern speculative literature
share Miller's Christian perspectives. In fact such perspectives are
quite rare in science fiction. But a number of Miller's fellow writers do
share his fundamentally negative assessment of the complex of hopes
and values associated with the belief in progress. It is all part of a much
larger struggle that has raged for centuries between two families of
world views in Western civilization. The one family, which includes
rationalism, positivism, and materialism, and both liberal and radical
social philosophies, puts its trust in human effort, and applauds all
strivings to "modernize" the world. For this family, general human
progress is possible, and perhaps inevitable. Its adherents, as a matter
of course, are drawn from social classes in the self-perceived vanguard
of mankind's evolution. The other family of world views, which includes romanticism, irrationalism, and idealism, and inclines to more
conservative social philosophies than its great rival, has limited faith or
none at all in human effort, and regards the modernizing process with
suspicion, if not positive scorn and loathing. The first family embraces
such odd bedfellows as technocrats, tycoons, and prophets of red
revolution; to the second family belong fascists, aesthetes, and gurus
of the "counterculture." Our lists of family members are facetious; or,

rather, woefully incomplete. But the duality itself is no joke. Although many thinkers profess values drawn from both camps, or shift allegiances back and forth throughout their lives, it is not difficult to see where the lines of battle are drawn, and to hear the din of combat in every department of Western culture, science fiction included.

In the next several pages, our attention will center on examples of cyclicism in science fiction's right wing, the cyclicism that affords little or no hope of progress. In one way, the fiction of this right wing is anti-science; but more often it is simply ranged against what it thinks are false hopes about man himself. Since so many twentieth-century mainstream writers offer the same low valuation of human possibility, it may be tempting to regard these right-wingers as more "literary" than their competitors on the left, but this is a temptation worth resisting. At least in the relatively small group of science-fiction stories and novels under consideration in this chapter, works that explicitly combine cyclicism and eschatology, neither the so-called right wing nor the so-called left wing enjoys artistic superiority.

Miller's novel, like most cyclical science fiction right or left, is placed in the relatively far future. A few cyclical romances, not the least interesting, occur in imaginary remote pasts. In this sense, and often in their ideology as well, they resemble the historical novels that became so popular in the nineteenth century, dealing with the decadence or downfall of Egypt, Rome, medieval Christendom, the Indian empires of pre-Columbian America, and the like.

The favorite site for cyclical romances of the past is of course Atlantis. The Atlantis myth has its roots in ancient Greek legend, where it served to help illustrate cyclical chronosophy. Plato refers to it in two famous dialogues, recalling the story of how, in "one grievous day and night," the whole great island of Atlantis, with all its people, vanished beneath the waves. The ruins of Atlantis were identified by Jules Verne's Captain Nemo in *Twenty Thousand Leagues under the Sea* (1870), and her civilization has been brought back to life again and again by modern writers, always with the same lugubrious finale. A classic example is C. J. Cutcliffe Hyne's *The Lost Continent* (1899), with its romance of two survivors, man and woman, fleeing by ark as Atlantis slips into briny oblivion.

The best contemporary tale of a lost civilization in the Atlantis tradition is set in 900,000 B.C. René Barjavel's *La Nuit des temps* (1968, in English as *The Ice People*) begins in the near future, as French scientists testing a new sub-glacial geological probe in Antarctica uncover evidence of a city buried deep in the polar ice cap. An international team of experts thaws out the last Antarcticans, a man and a woman preserved at absolute zero in a golden sphere full of scientific marvels suggesting a civilization higher than that of the twentieth century. Using a device that projects the woman's memories on to a television screen, the scientists are able to watch the last days of her utopian homeland, Gondawa.

Utopian or not, Gondawa was totally destroyed by something far from mysterious to the woman's twentieth-century rescuers. A series of four world wars (the same number as in *A Canticle for Leibowitz*) fought between the superpowers of 900,000 B.C., Gondawa and Enisor, left the planet all but lifeless. The third, a nuclear exchange prompted by Enisorian aggression against Gondawan lunar bases, had killed eight hundred million people alone. In the fourth, Gondawa used a doomsday weapon that obliterated Enisor, sinking much of it under the Atlantic Ocean, and tilting the earth's axis so drastically that Gondawa, also wasted, was now located at the South Pole, where its ruins soon disappeared under thousands of feet of ice. Despite vehement peace demonstrations led by students, Gondawa (an advanced version of the modern West) was prepared to risk world annihilation rather than submit to the ruthless collectivism of Enisor (a parody of modern Soviet Russia or Maoist China). "They're us!" cries the American scientist Hoover after he witnesses the final hours of Gondawan history. The few dozen survivors of the fourth war had somehow scratched their way back up to civilization in nine hundred millennia. "They've repopulated the world, and now they've achieved the same state of idiocy they were in before, ready to blow themselves up all over again. Great, isn't it? That's the human race!"[18]

As the novel ends, the Antarctic expedition no longer dominates the world's headlines, thanks to the sabotage of all its secrets by a scientist who had plotted to sell them to parties unknown. Elsewhere, it is business as usual. Crises roil Asia, South Africa, the Middle East, Berlin. Student protesters shout in the streets, demanding peace. The world dangles on the brink of war. The distant heirs of Gondawa and Enisor gird themselves for yet another cataclysm. Barjavel has made his point, skillfully if not with any excess of subtlety, that *Homo belligerans* is doomed to repeat his follies as long as he lives.

The "sword-and-sorcery" tale, usually situated in a legendary past freely adapted from the history of archaic Northern Europe or the Middle Ages, also gives the imaginative writer an opportunity to introduce cyclical themes. The several volumes of Michael Moorcock's "Elric Saga" and the "Warlock" series written by Larry Niven reveal this not otherwise cerebral genre at its least absurd. In Niven's final Warlock novel, *The Magic Goes Away* (1978), an astonishing mélange of legendary and mythical material is assembled to the accompaniment of cyclicist themes and musings. The premise of the story is the death of the gods and the subsequent gradual disappearance of magic some twelve thousand years before the time of Christ. In the course of events the last of the great sorcerers, the Warlock, dies in the attempt to restore to earth the psychic energy or "mana" that permits the practice of his art. One of his fellow adventurers is a Greek survivor of the sinking of Atlantis, which would have drowned centuries earlier but for the spells of its wizard-kings. The replacement of gods and magicians by barbarians is in the end viewed stoically by the Warlock and his comrades. "Animals die," the Warlock admits. "Classes of animals die. Civilizations die. New things come to take their places. . . . The strong ones adapt."[19] At this point Niven owes more to Darwin than to the *Nibelungenlied* or the Icelandic *Eddas*, but the cyclical message is plain enough.

To return to future time, where writers of science fiction feel much more secure, the prototypical cyclicist novel is perhaps *La Fin du monde* (1893, in English as *Omega: The Last Days of the World*), by the French astronomer and popularizer of science, Camille Flammarion. The novel is a compendium of most of the theories of disaster current in the astronomy of the nineteenth century. Where it suited his purposes, Flammarion abandoned fiction altogether and reverted to the usual style of his scientific journalism.[20]

La Fin du monde is a work of intimidating scope, linking the first of all the great world's end novels, J.-B. Cousin de Grainville's *Le Dernier homme* (1805) with such later eschatological classics as Wells's *The Time Machine* (1895) and Stapledon's *Last and First Men* (1930). With all these works it shares the long view and, with Stapledon, a profound sense of the circularity of time. The first and less ambitious half of the novel concerns a calamity occurring in the twenty-fifth century, when a comet strikes Europe, killing millions and almost wiping out (anticlerical comic touch!) the college of cardinals at St. Peter's just as it was celebrating the new dogma of papal divinity. But the Vatican is spared, and "humanity continued to rise toward higher destinies."[21]

The second half is of much greater interest. Flammarion takes us on a journey through ten million years of future history. Races and civilizations rise and fall, but ultimately the planet becomes a single *patrie*, ruled by reason and science as in the loftiest dreams of the *philosophes* of the Enlightenment. Then the laws of nature intervene to strike down proud humanity. On the worn and cooling surface of the globe the waters gradually dissipate. The population shrinks, until only two inhabitable spots remain at the bottom of long-evaporated equatorial seas. Flammarion borrows Grainville's idea of a last Adam and a last Eve,[22] one from each of the last two outposts of civilization, who meet, fall in love, and die when no drop of water remains on earth. A new and even higher humanity arises on Jupiter and Saturn, but "for them too the days of old age arrived, and they too descended into the night of the grave."[23] Throughout the universe, Flammarion reflects, as stars turn black, others flame into brilliance, planets rotate, and new races of men flourish, wane, and pass. Our own small epoch is "an imperceptible wave on the immense ocean of the ages."[24]

Flammarion's novel is not entirely innocent of the belief in progress, since for long stretches of time on earth and later on other planets, progress does surely occur. But the last word always belongs to nature, which decrees for stars and planets, and for all species no matter how intelligent or amiable, the same decay and ultimate extinction that lays low the individual man and woman. Nature is not mocked, and the grave is not cheated. One is left with a sense of the marvelous richness of life, but also with a sense of its iron limits. The message of modern natural science for Flammarion, as for T. H. Huxley and many others of his time,[25] is that man should fight the good fight, but conform his expectations to the measure of achievement permitted by nature, whose time is cyclical, not linear.

The great Jules Verne, who did as much as anyone to attract late nineteenth-century readers to the romance of science and engineering, revealed at the close of his career another facet of his thought that could have been inspired by Flammarion's *La Fin du monde*. In *L'Eternel Adam*, a novella written shortly before his death in 1905, Verne tells the story of a monster earthquake causing floods that engulf the whole world in the twenty-first century. All islands and continents are submerged, but Captain Nemo's Atlantis miraculously returns from the deeps, the only dry land available to the single shipload of human survivors. From their offspring, who at first degenerate into savages, arises a new human race that restores civilization after thousands of years of struggle. Verne's protagonist, a savant of the new Atlantis, considers the evidence available to him, including a just-discovered memoir of one of the few survivors of the twenty-first-century world deluge and the archeological remains of ancient Atlantis, and brings the novella to a close with a world-weary meditation on the cycles of history. "Bending under the weight of those vain efforts piled high in the infinity of time, the Zartog Sofr-Aï-Sr acquired, slowly, grievously, an intimate conviction of the eternal return of all things."[26] Sofr's last thoughts may well have been Verne's, too, but they are scarcely consistent with the boyish exuberance of the "Extraordinary Voyages." A fin-de-siècle mood had finally overtaken even Jules Verne.

Fin-de-siècle fascination with death, sin, and world-cycles pervades a good many science-fiction novels from the turn of the century that make little or no use of the pessimistic implications of modern science drawn by Flammarion. *The Time Machine*, for all its Huxleyan biological philosophy, partakes now and again of the purely literary conventions of *la Décadence* of the 1880s and 1890s.[27] More literary still are such minor masterworks as M. P. Shiel's *The Purple Cloud* (a title that doubles as an unkind tag for Shiel's prose style), first published in 1901, and William Hope Hodgson's *The Night Land* (1912). Both novels are laborious morality plays linking the end of the world to a grand cosmic struggle between the forces of good and evil. Both involve natural disaster, but their central interest is humanistic and ethical. In Shiel's story, after long domination by the "black powers," the last male survivor of a world cataclysm, Adam Jeffson, embraces the "white." Inverting the biblical myth, the last woman tempts him to do good, rather than evil. The terminal Adam abandons the delicious, fin-de-siècle wickedness of his former self (a solitary mad arsonist who had burned more than three hundred cities to the ground), and agrees to become the father of a new race. The world will rise again, and the cycle, one presumes, will repeat itself. In the Hodgson tale the victory of good can only be short-lived, since earth has entered its final years, but the joy of his terminal lovers is no less sweet; indeed, much more so.

The science fiction of recent decades includes several first-rate specimens of a relatively pure cyclicism that depict future doomsdays in the spirit of Flammarion and Shiel. The best of the lot, in the judgment of the present writer and many professional critics of science fiction, is Miller's *A Canticle for Leibowitz*, discussed above. René Barjavel's *Ravage* (1943 and 1949, in English as *Ashes, Ashes*) and *Le Diable l'emporte* (1948) also deal grimly with the prospects for a renewal of technological civilization after catastrophic wars. George R. Stewart's well-regarded *Earth Abides* (1949) breaks off before civilization can rise again, but the reversion to a new Paleolithic age at the end of the novel leaves little doubt as to what will happen next. In the words of the Last American, quoting the cyclical wisdom of Ecclesiastes, "Men go and come, but earth abides."[28]

The extensive literature of galactic colonization and galactic empires pioneered in the Gernsback era of science-fiction history has generated its own cyclicist classics. Some, like the novels of Olaf Stapledon, are considered later in this essay. But one at least deserves attention here: the remarkable tetralogy *Cities in Flight* (1955–62), by James Blish. Like his contemporary, Walter M. Miller, Jr., Blish was something of a religious philosopher and amateur historian as well as a writer of superb science fiction. His other work includes *Doctor Mirabilis* (1964), based on the life of Roger Bacon, and *A Case of Conscience* (1958), whose Jesuit hero struggled with the theological implications of the future at just about the same time as the stories from which Miller drew *A Canticle for Leibowitz* were appearing in *The Magazine of Fantasy and Science Fiction*.

Cities in Flight began its publishing history as the "Okie" stories in the pages of *Astounding Science-Fiction* in 1950. The first of the four novels to be published as a book was *Earthman, Come Home*, in 1955, which became the third volume in the tetralogy. The others appeared between 1957 and 1962, rounding out a galactic history twenty-one centuries in length. Richard D. Mullen has shown in some detail the close correspondence between Blish's history of the future and the cyclical pattern of the past laid bare by Spengler in *The Decline of the West*.[29] Blish cites Spengler in the work itself, and also mentions other cyclical philosophers of history.[30]

Blish's account of the rise, fall, and rise again of human civilization in outer space, together with brief allusions to earlier and later non-human empires, is unambiguously Spenglerian. At the same time, Blish cannot resist the rather Asimovian touch of building into his future the heroic, quintessentially modern Western theme of men who are affected but not dominated by the cyclical rhythm of galactic history and who, ultimately, transcend it. For Isaac Asimov in *The Foundation Trilogy*, the heroes are the master-minds of the First and Second Foundations; for Blish in *Cities in Flight*, the flying cities themselves, and above all Mayor John Amalfi and his peripatetic Manhattan. Strong traces of the paradigm of cumulative progress mark the millennial career of Amalfi and his city, although nothing so forthright as the progressivism in the Asimov novels.

But the cyclical paradigm returns in triumph in the last volume of the tetralogy, when the cosmos comes to an abrupt end in 4104 A.D. as the result of a stupendous collision of the realms of matter and anti-

matter, at the exact midpoint of the cyclical histories of both. Our
champions, the leading citizens of Manhattan, fly a planet to the hub of
the universe, where the bodies of each will ingeniously survive the
cataclysm to become the world-stuff of new universes. At the very
moment of the Big Bang, "Creation began."[31] Blish's combination of
almost Wild Western titanism and Spenglerian fatalism is unique, held
in balance only by the imaginative energy, no less unique, of this
distinguished novelist.

Of one thing there can be no doubt. Whatever will happen to the
atoms and molecules of John Amalfi in the next universe, he and his
comrades belong very much to the human race. A variant on the
cyclicist theme, generally a more pessimistic one, envisages the replacement of humankind by some other species, which may then
proceed to make (or avoid) the same mistakes as *Homo sapiens*. Blish
touches on this idea in *Cities in Flight*, by reporting in his last volume
the rise of an alien empire known as the Web of Hercules, whose
conquest of the universe is halted only by the doomsday of 4104. One
of the earliest examples of a successful supersedure of *Homo sapiens* is
the victory of the inscrutable ferromagnets in J.-H. Rosny's grisly
novel *La Mort de la terre* (1912). The ferromagnets are living minerals,
which can grow only from iron once used in man's industries; naturally
occurring iron repels them. Karel Čapek twice replaced mankind, by
robots in his play *R.U.R.* (1921) and by giant salamanders in his novel
War with the Newts (1936), although it seems clear that both surrogate
species are only symbols, in the one instance cautiously hopeful, in the
second wry and bitter, of modern industrial man himself. Clifford D.
Simak vented his frustrations in *City* (1952) by replacing mankind with
an ethically superior race of peace-loving dogs. More recently, Doris
Piserchia has given us her ironic imitation of humanity by rats in *A
Billion Days of Earth* (1976) and Gore Vidal his dark prophecy of a
world-cycle of monkeys in *Kalki* (1978).

Whether the lords of creation are men or monkeys, the point in
cyclicist fiction of this first, or "pure" variety, is always that life is
constrained by the circular shape of time to repeat itself. The writer of
such fictions may be angry, resigned, or enthralled. In any event he
borrows an ancient wisdom, most often for the sake of expressing
present-day anxieties.

No one has summed up that ancient wisdom more poignantly than
James Thurber in his cartoon history of the future, *The Last Flower*
(1939). The story begins with World War XII, which, "as everybody
knows, brought about the collapse of civilization." A young woman

restores love to the world, by her tender care of its last surviving
flower. From such simple beginnings, the race regenerates. Towns
grow, troubadours sing, workmen toil. Demagogues return, too, fan-
ning the fires of discontent, until mankind goes to war once again.
"This time the destruction was so complete . . . that nothing at all was
left in the world . . . except one man . . . and one woman . . . and one
flower."[32]
Which was probably enough.

3. When the Giants Died and Time Began Afresh

The vision of a new Middle Ages, which for many latter-day romantics
and ecological neo-Luddites is not such a bad idea, has become a cliché
of modern apocalyptic science fiction. We have seen it put to work with
a touch of genius in *A Canticle for Leibowitz*. In *The Chalk Giants*, a
novel by Keith Roberts published in 1974, the Middle Ages have come
round again, too, and again in the aftermath of a nuclear holocaust. A
seer tells of the old times, when the Giants fought in iron warboats.
Forests grew on their decks, and "others sailed beneath the water,
hurling javelins that scorched the earth." The crops were withered, the
hills shaken, the cities of the Giants destroyed. But little by little, the
ways of the Giants return. A king of kings unifies the warring lands,
vowing to make them one people. They will worship the one true God,
who had lately descended to earth as a man, was broken on the Wheel,
and then rose again from the dead to bring eternal life. Arriving with a
fabulous army equipped with "war engines of every shape and size,"
including "the legendary firetubes . . . that spit out thunder and bring
the lightning down," the great king charges his provincial vassal to
consult the old books. "Build me a Hall of stone, such as the Giants
knew . . . proof against arrows and the firetube darts." It is Christianity and the Middle Ages and the Renaissance all over again, as a new
world emerges from kingdoms founded "when the Giants died and
Time began afresh."[33]
    Roberts is better known as the author of *Pavane* (1968), the
magnificent story of an alternative Renaissance, in which the Spanish
Armada conquers England in 1588, delaying the Industrial Revolution
by two centuries, and producing in the end a more humane, more
unified Western world that misses the horrors of the twentieth century
of our own time-stream. The cyclicism in Robert's work is apparent.
Yet the upshot of both *The Chalk Giants* and *Pavane* is the inevitability
of progress, regarded as a good thing. From disaster comes victory.

Roberts speaks for many science-fiction writers who have blended cyclical, dialectical, and eschatological themes in a celebration of human progress. The line between them and some of the novelists examined in the preceding section is thin, but the distinction matters, at least for the historian. In modern (and perhaps only in modern) society, pure cyclicism is an index to cultural fatigue and despair. The more one finds of it, and other forms of disbelief in progress, the more one may conclude that the society itself is in grave trouble, since artists and intellectuals do somehow pick up vibrations from the public mind. The more one finds progress reaffirmed, even in a literary genre that specializes in the imagination of disaster, the stronger the morale of the society is likely to be, and the greater its willingness to tolerate danger and suffering.

The two supreme classics of dialectical progressivism in science fiction are Olaf Stapledon's *Last and First Men* and *Star Maker*. As all his aficionados well know, Stapledon was a historian and philosopher, by credentials as well as interests. He held degrees from Oxford and Liverpool, and taught philosophy professionally. The influence of Spinoza, Hegel, and Marx, and of Bergson, Shaw, and Wells, is everywhere to be seen in his work, and yet it also stands on its own authority as an original contribution to modern speculative cosmology, a counterpart in fiction to the thought of Pierre Teilhard de Chardin. For the sake of argument, at least, it is tempting to suggest that Stapledon was the more attractive thinker, and Teilhard the more authentic artist.[34]

In any event, one must agree with Thomas D. Clareson that although Stapledon did not quite qualify as a utopographer, he saw progress in the vast cycles of man's future history.[35] *Last and First Men* (1930) is a journey through eighteen successive species of humankind, each the natural or man-bred descendant of its predecessor, a journey of two billion years in duration. Doomsday comes many times: great wars involving the major powers, until the building of the World State in the twenty-third century; a long dark age of savagery after world supplies of energy fail some forty centuries later; a second, far longer dark age following an accident at an atomic power plant that reduces the human race to only thirty-five individuals; and scores of other disasters, too many for even Stapledon to count. Again and again, humanity reverts to barbarism or worse, and then climbs back. The general direction is upward, to enhanced intelligence, more powerful science, expanded consciousness and extra-sensory faculties, improved sociality, longer life-spans, culminating in the Eighteenth

Men, the best and final species, who live on Neptune, one million million strong, in what is almost Paradise. They will soon be wiped out by the radiation from a supernova in a nearby star system. But they have raised consciousness to its highest point in human history, and elsewhere in the universe their goal of bringing "the full potentiality of the Real" to expression will be pursued by other, more fortunate races.[36]

A sequel, *Last Men in London* (1932), added the discovery that a civilization of intelligent lemurs, "the only truly Christian race that ever existed," had flourished long before the coming of *Homo sapiens*; the lemurs had been slaughtered to the last individual by man's anthropoid ancestors.[37] In a further sequel, *Star Maker* (1937), Stapledon took up the other threads of the story cut short for mankind by interstellar disaster in *Last and First Men*. He roams in imagination through the whole universe, encountering a plethora of higher civilizations, now and in the future. Although most races never break through the vicious circles of war and calamity that still afflict modern man, some do succeed in "wakening." In the remote future, there will be an intergalactic community of telepathically linked and "wakened" worlds, until the cosmos itself cools and dies. But even the death of the cosmos is not the end: God, the Star Maker, will start the whole process over again, creating a new cosmos, and another and another, in an order of ascending maturity of spirit, until the ultimate cosmos is born, and the creative mind outside of time achieves perfect union with its perfected creation. The similarity of Stapledon's vision to Teilhard de Chardin's Omega Point, when God as transcendence will meet his fully evolved hyper-personal counterpart within time, is striking. Stapledon's cosmology is even more comprehensive, since it also offers a metaphysical explanation of the cosmic cycles postulated by modern physics. At the same time, it is in every sense (like the cosmology of Teilhard de Chardin) a philosophy of progress. For Stapledon the cyclical process is not an end or meaning of things in itself, but rather an instrument of creative evolution.

No one has outreached Stapledon among the writers of the years since his death in 1950, but his metaphysical cast of mind still has its place in science fiction. Arthur C. Clarke is one of the chief heirs of Stapledon's interest in evolution and the superman. The theme of progress through both historical and cosmic cycles recurs in Brian Aldiss's *Galaxies like Grains of Sand* (1959), and again in Michael Moorcock's trilogy, *The Dancers at the End of Time* (1972–76).

Aldiss's novel, published in his own country as *The Canopy of Time*, is actually a group of eight short stories from the author's early

years stitched together by prologues written for the occasion, but the
stratagem works well. The result is a chronologically arranged series of
episodes in the history of the future, from a global war early in the
twenty-first century that almost annihilates the human race to the
rebirth of the cosmos in "the ultimate millennia." As in Stapledon, the
future conceived by Aldiss is full of disasters. At one point humankind
is reduced to a few cave-dwellers, and the planet swarms with master-
less robots looking for someone to obey. Cultures ebb and flow, and
yet in the long run humanity prospers. A galactic federation brings
order and harmony to its scattered children. As the universe finally
grinds down to extinction, a godlike superman mysteriously appears to
explain that he will survive into the next cycle, to continue the cosmic
experiment at a higher level. More advanced than man, the superman
will be the lowest life-form, the amoeba of the next galaxy. In an
epilogue addressed to the superman, "we who have already superseded you" note that they have recorded these scenes in his honor, as
he once paid his respects to his human precursors.[38]

No greater contrast in style to the Sunday morning sobriety of
Stapledon can be imagined than the novels of the *Dancers* trilogy
written by another of his countrymen, Michael Moorcock. The trilogy
is a glorious mix of the comedic Wells of *Kipps* and *The History of Mr.
Polly*, the cinema of Mack Sennett, and the television of Monty
Python. Many readers and critics have so far refused to see it as
anything more than a bit of froth on science fiction's New Wave, but
Moorcock is a serious and profoundly joyful writer, and his tales from
"The End of Time"—like all superior comedy—have much more to
offer than light entertainment. They also transcend their veneer of
sophisticated amoralism, in itself a brilliant burlesque of the British
Decadents of the 1890s.

The premise of the trilogy is soon told. After millions of years of
the rise and fall of every kind of social and cultural order, humanity has
deliberately dwindled to a handful of innocent immortals who draw
freely on the energy of the dying universe to indulge in fantasies,
games, and distractions. "If they had a philosophy, then it was a
philosophy of taste, of sensuality."[39] But as the adventures multiply,
including trips back and forth to the nineteenth century, attention
comes to center on the romance of the hero of the trilogy, Jherek
Carnelian, and his late Victorian inamorata, Mrs. Amelia Under-
wood. Gradually Amelia converts Jherek, natural son of the godlike
Lord Jagged, to her own seriousness of purpose. As the cosmos ends,
Jagged arranges everyone's salvation: a loop in time fabricated by
Jagged allows the Dancers to pursue their pleasures forever, and

Jherek and Amelia, transformed into the new Adam and Eve as
Jagged had planned, elect to travel forward in time to the next world-
cycle, where they will rebuild civilization in the next Lower Devonian.
Mankind will take up life from the point where it had left off (but
without the immortality or cosmic powers of the Dancers), will start
much earlier in the geological time-scale, and presumably will reach
even higher peaks than before. Despite calamities, decadence, and
cosmic doom, the message of *The Dancers at the End of Time* is hopeful. Even the idlest of the Dancers are treated without scorn. Moorcock rejoices in their essentially innocent fun, and he rejoices still
more in the earnest striving of Jherek and Amelia. As he writes of
the Jerry Cornelius family, heroes of other novels by Moorcock, so he
might have written of Jherek Carnelian (whose name is after all nearly
the same, and suspiciously like that of the Christian Messiah, to boot):
"The Cornelius family survives to seek again because, like me, it is
essential optimistic. I believe that eventually we shall find a way to be
ourselves while serving the needs of our society."[40]

The same optimism infects the latest major example of progressivist cyclicism in science fiction, George Zebrowski's prodigious
novel *Macrolife* (1979). Most of the book deals with the replacement
of planets by mobile space habitats as the future homes of man,
extrapolating from the prophecies of space colonization in the writings
of Dandridge Cole and others. But in Part III, "The Dream of Time,"
Zebrowski addresses the concerns of Olaf Stapledon in *Star Maker*. At
the end of the cosmic cycle, after aeons of scientific and cultural
progress, much of life manages to survive the implosion of the universe
by lodging in a black hole at its center. It reaches the next cycle,
meeting and fusing with a still higher form of collective being from
earlier cycles. Together, the old and new minds will continue life's
exploration of a reality that has no end.[41]

Fortunately, chapters do have an end. Ours has now used up its
allotted share of the world's timber supply. Zebrowski's *Macrolife*
shows the continuing grip of both cyclicism and progressivism on the
literary imagination. It also brings us back to the point made at the
beginning of this chapter. In science fiction, as in mythology and
cosmology, the end of the world is seldom the end. It may usher in the
millennium, set stages for the romantic exploits of last men and
women, or inaugurate a new cycle of rise and fall. Whatever the
aftermath, fictions of the endtime feed our hopes for fresh beginnings.

5
Man-Made Catastrophes
Brian Stableford

All human life, everywhere, is haunted by the possibility of catastrophe. The degree of anxiety manifest in a particular society or felt by a particular individual may vary greatly, but there is no human situation which is free of it. A great deal of literary and dramatic art has, throughout history, been preoccupied with the possibilities of general or personal disaster. No culture lacks illustrations of disaster or prescriptions determining the appropriate attitudes and responses to disaster. Much imaginative endeavour has also gone into the attempt to provide reassurances that it is, after all, possible to avoid or survive catastrophe, if only we behave in an appropriate manner.

That this should be so is by no means surprising. Human existence depends on the ability to reason and the ability to foresee the possible future outcomes of the situations which confront us. If we could not anticipate disasters we could not avoid them, and it makes perfect pragmatic sense to be perpetually on the lookout for the possibility of disaster. When disaster threatens from without, we must be prepared to ward it off, or take evasive action—and we must, of course, be doubly cautious that our own actions do not precipitate disaster.

There is, however, no culture which is really objective in its attitudes to misfortune. All societies—and perhaps all individuals—sanction the belief that some people *deserve* to suffer, and that when catastrophe strikes the guilty the moral order of the universe is being conserved. Here, of course, human ideas about what ought to be the case frequently come into conflict with observations of what actually is the case, for (as St. Matthew and everyone else has observed) Heaven "sendeth rain on the just and on the unjust." The sense of satisfaction which we feel when the wicked are punished is bought at the price of a sense of confusion which we tend to feel when the innocent also suffer. We tend, in such cases, to seek special explanations—both history and cultural anthropology bear eloquent witness to the ingenuity which characteristically goes into the search. The scientific world-view which some members of modern Western culture have adopted is virtually unique in holding all such special explanations to be invalid, and holding fast to the logic of chance, which presumes that where natural catastrophes are concerned there is no earthly reason why the just should have any particular advantage over the unjust. Only where catastrophes are man-made does the scientific world-view leave room for a moral order. For this reason the characteristic attitudes displayed in science fiction stories about man-made catastrophes are markedly different from those displayed in stories of natural disaster.

Ours is perhaps the only culture where it is possible (because of the sacredness of the scientific world-view) for individuals and groups to suffer catastrophes without seeking to debit the moral responsibility for the misfortune from themselves or from others. It is *possible*—but it is not easy. The most-asked unanswerable question is still: "Why did it have to happen to *me*?"

The tribal societies which we are pleased to call "primitive" are never at a loss when called upon to preserve faith in the moral order of the universe in the face of disaster. For such societies, *all* catastrophes are man-made. If I fall ill, it is because the ancestral spirits have been angered by some failure of duty, or because I have broken a taboo. If I really am completely innocent of any such transgression, then witches are at work. Some tribesmen are more given to guilt than others— many societies allow witchcraft only as a rare and exceptional explana- tion, while others use it habitually. The beliefs of the Azande, who find witchcraft everywhere, have been extracted from their context as an exemplary illustration of how unreasonable savages can be. *We* know that when a man sickens and dies he has been carried off by cancer or trypanosomes, and *we* know that the fact this man and no other was crossing the bridge when it collapsed is a coincidence of no significance.

What we often fail to realise, though, is that we have paid a price for our entitlement to this intellectual snobbery. The pseudotheory of witchcraft functions in Azande society not so much as an explanation extending an understanding of the way the world works, but as an imaginative instrument which allows people confronted with misfor- tune to *do* something about it. It enables the tribesman to respond to catastrophe in a *meaningful* way, so that even in the absence of medical knowledge he can pit himself against the ravages of sickness and need not feel helpless or that the universe has suffered a fall of moral parity.

It is an awkward question for modern Western man to face when he asks himself who is better equipped—in purely pragmatic terms—to deal with the experience of grief and the horror of helplessness: the tribesman who hunts witches; the religious man who prays to God; or the rationalist who understands the workings of chance.

In the context of these observations we may, perhaps, be able to see one of the reasons why contemporary science fiction writers are so fascinated by disasters which come about not through the workings of blind cosmic chance but as a result of our own actions. There is a certain irony in the fact that science, which destroyed the moral order implicit in our traditional frames of reference, should also have given us the power to bring destruction upon ourselves on such a vast scale. The mythology of man-made catastrophe which we are in the process of building is replacing the taboos whose violation would once have angered our ancestors with a new set, whose violation will overpopulate and spoil the earth. The witches whose innate evil threatened the security of traditional communities are being replaced by different kinds of evil men, whose threat is certainly no less. The analysis of stories of man-made catastrophe will reveal them to be propaganda for new codes of social behaviour, embodying new concepts of sin—or perhaps refurbishing old ones.

At first glance, in fact, it appears that modern catastrophist fiction relies heavily for moral inspiration and implication on traditional catastrophist fantasy. There are few modern stories of flood or plague which do not refer back explicitly and metaphorically to the incidents in Genesis and Exodus when God instigated reprisals against human wickedness and pharaonic intransigence. Closer inspection, however, will reveal that where we are dealing with writers whose allegiance is to the world-view of modern science rather than the presuppositions of religious doctrine the parallels are drawn specifically to be broken. Even in the works of twentieth-century writers whose commitment to Christianity is wholehearted we very often find an attitude to catastrophe which does not at all reflect the story of Noah. (An excellent example is provided by Alfred Noyes, author of the atomic holocaust story *The Last Man* and the holocaust-threat story *The Devil Takes a Holiday*. The latter story, in trying to come to terms with modern man's apparent predilection for self-destruction, breaks new theological ground in redefining the role of the devil.)

It is not too difficult to find stories which provide crucial turning points in the imaginative attribution of significance to catastrophe. In John Beresford's "A Negligible Experiment" the impending doom of the Earth is taken (by a scientist) to imply not that God has tired of human wickedness for once and for all but that God has grown tired of a trivial experiment and is moving on to new fields. In such a scheme there is no room for Noah and the Ark. The personal catastrophe which strikes down the hero of H. G. Wells's *The Undying Fire* becomes an exemplary visitation developed in parallel with the story of Job. The moral of the tale is similar: what is called for is a massive reinforcement of faith; but it is also crucially different in the important matter of what the new Job is required to believe *in*. Later in his career, Wells was also to recast the story of Noah to hold a related moral: the hero of *All Aboard for Ararat* accepts his commission only on condition that God steps down from his exalted position to let man and science adopt the crucial role of moral guide and guardian.

The tendency for modern practitioners of exemplary catastrophism to borrow metaphors from older traditions has been greatly encouraged by the fact that our cultural heritage is particularly rich in imaginative strategies for dealing with the question of moral responsibility for misfortune. The scapegoat strategy of the Azande is amply represented in the history of medieval Christendom by the slaughter of the Jews in the wake of the Black Death and by the witch-craze which attended the decay of the Roman Catholic Empire of Faith, and has also been echoed in more recent times. The notion of divine retribution occasioned by the breaking of taboos is amply represented by that fraction of our religious imagination which derives from the Old Testament. In addition to these strategies we also have (again courtesy of the Old Testament) the story of Job, which cunningly suggests that the misfortunes of the innocent might be a test of their faith. This notion is particularly ingenious in that it removes altogether the notion of guilt, and it may perhaps be something of a tragedy that the Christian world much preferred its own imaginative *tour de force*, the concept of original sin, which abolished instead the notion of innocence. This unusual versatility of the Western religious imagination permits catastrophists to draw morals from their stories in several different ways, and not all of them are out of keeping with a rationalistic world-view. The Darwinian theory of natural selection has (for social Darwinists, at least) put a new gloss on the notion of the catastrophe-as-test; while the science of genetics, especially when its implications are misconstrued, has injected new meaning into the notion of original sin.

Another thing to remember when we find modern tales of disaster drawing metaphors from the literature of the ancient world is that ours is not the first Western culture to have coped with the rise of rationalism. The Greeks invented science, and *their* exemplary literature quite frequently exposes genuine parallels with our own style of thought, with the one important difference that we have taken rationalism and science somewhat further than they. *We* live in a *post*-Promethean age.

The scientific imagination, in providing a new mythology of catastrophe, has to overturn the old mythologies provided by the religious imagination. It has no option but to reflect them even as it transfigures them. In so doing, however, it is subject to a curious restraint, in that much of the vocabulary we have built up in order to talk about possible catastrophes is derived directly from particular religious myths. The words, in consequence, cannot help but carry implications which are antipathetic to the new meanings which the scientific imagination wishes to impose upon them. The words which we use to talk about the possibility of impending doom are coloured with echoes of religious mythology, and none more so than the word *apocalypse*, which carries with it a whole host of imagistic associations. From the same source, of course, we acquire *Armageddon* and the *Millennium*. The very use of the words confers ambiguity upon modern fantasies in which they feature strongly, and they recall metaphors whose mesmeric power is obvious even when they are used ironically (as, for instance, in Norman Spinrad's story "The Big Flash"). The main consequence of this fact is that we can see in twentieth-century catastrophist fiction a curious kind of ideative resonance, by which the apparatus of the religious imagination echoes in the literature of the scientific imagination as a series of apparitions. Look, if you will, at the illustrations in the pulp magazine *Famous Fantastic Mysteries*, which was for a long time filled by stories of the end of the world, and see how frequently religious symbolism is employed to capture the mood of such stories.

In the discussion of literary works which follows, I shall make abundant use of such loaded words as "apocalypse" and "Armageddon." I shall also refer back frequently to ancient myths whose function was to allocate moral responsibility and to define different kinds of misconduct. This should not be allowed to distract attention from the fact that what is really under scrutiny is the construction of a *new* mythology of moral responsibility, and we are concerned not with the reaffirmation but with the metamorphosis of our concepts of sin.

The Advent of the Age of Anxiety

It might be argued that what it has become fashionable to call "the Age of Anxiety" began when people realised that they were not, in fact, responsible for catastrophes, and that an entirely arbitrary disaster (a plague or a cometary collision) might wipe out mankind at any time. The rationalists of the Enlightenment could stop worrying that God might send another deluge to punish their apostasy, but they also had to stop believing in a divine protective power that would make sure nothing happened to the chosen people. The Age of Anxiety is therefore correlated in its rise with a developing awareness of man's vulnerability to *natural* catastrophe.

If we follow this line of argument, however, we are constrained to point out that there arose in the wake of *this* feeling of apprehension a different sense of threat which redoubled our sense of existential insecurity, for the rediscovery of the possibility of *man-made* catastrophe created a feeling rather different from the one men had when all misfortunes were punishments or sorceries. The new mythology of man-made catastrophe—the essentially *science fictional* mythology—stressed that the mundane activities of ordinary human beings might set in train sequences of cause and effect which could destroy civilization. This was a new idea. It surfaced less than a hundred years ago, and perhaps correlates better with the application of the label "Age of Anxiety."Being at the mercy of Nature caused us only mild concern; being at one another's mercy was quite another matter.

There are actually very few nineteenth-century stories which invite description as tales of man-made catastrophes, though there is a certain touch of foreboding in many stories of personal tragedy. It is not too difficult today to read Mary Shelley's *Frankenstein* (1818) as a kind of parable in which the unlucky scientist represents modern man in his totality, threatened with destruction at the hands of the monsters of his own creation. This interpretation certainly helped Brian Aldiss to find in *Frankenstein* not only the first but also the *archetypal* science fiction novel, but its force would not have been appreciated by Mary Shelley. The same is true of some other mid-century parables, including Herman Melville's Renaissance fantasy "The Bell-Tower," which has been annexed by some recent science fiction historians. This theme does appear once in nineteenth-century imaginative fiction, in the section of Samuel Butler's "Erewhon" (1872) which is entitled "The Book of the Machines," but there it is only the ghost of an idea. Butler certainly refrains from lending wholehearted endorsement to the Erewhonians' reasons for abandoning machinery. Butler had first put forward the idea that man might be overtaken and enslaved by his machines in the article "Darwin among the Machines" (1863) which he signed "Cellarius," but he replied to his own article with an opposing argument in 1865, his tone throughout being ironic. "The Book of the

Machines" anticipates an important twentieth-century argument, but the anticipation does not really testify to considerable foresight on Butler's part. A much more realistic—and certainly sincere—fear of the effect machines might have on human life was that expressed in William Morris's *News from Nowhere* (1890), which is by no means a catastrophist work.

In fact, of course, nineteenth-century attitudes to technology were overwhelmingly optimistic. The fruits of the steam engine were welcomed far and wide; it represented in the eyes of most visionaries a way to free men from drudgery and to increase the productive capacity of society so much that every man might become wealthy. There were plenty of people who observed the unpleasant consequences of industrialisation, who abhorred the growth of filthy cities and the creation of the new urban poor, but they were far more ready to blame poor social institutions for this kind of misery than the machines themselves. We see in nineteenth-century English literature many eloquent pleas for political reform but hardly any sympathy for the Luddites. The one striking exception is Richard Jefferies' *After London* (1885), which looks forward to the day when the ruins of the great cities are no more than poisonous sores in a rural landscape. Though the reversion to barbarism of England's populace is described in the first part of the novel, the nature of the catastrophe is deliberately unspecified, and is perhaps to be regarded as the working of an ironic Fate rather than either a natural or man-made disaster.

Most nineteenth-century writers concerned with anticipating future technological developments regarded the industrial revolution as a prelude to Utopia. The archetypal expression of this view was Edward Bellamy's best-selling *Looking Backward* (1888). There were plenty of objectors to Bellamy's view of the socialist Utopia, including William Morris, but most of the replies to his novel are alternative Utopias few of which dispute the necessity or desirability of mechanisation. The one major catastrophist reply—Ignatius Donnelly's *Caesar's Column*—objects only to Bellamy's premise regarding the direction of socioeconomic "evolution." Technology provides Donnelly's world-destroyers with the means, but the *cause* of the holocaust is the nature of the capitalist system.

In *Caesar's Column* the catastrophe is twice man-made: it is revolution led by the "Brotherhood of Destruction," but made necessary by the greed of the capitalists who control the world's wealth and keep the working class in conditions of grinding poverty. Donnelly's assumptions differ very little from those of Marx, but what sets him apart from most quasi-Marxist socialists is precisely his catastrophism: most Marxists looked forward to the revolution as a means of liberation. Marx did, of course, anticipate that the revolution might be bloody, but he did not consider that this blood was on anyone's hands—according to this economic thesis the revolution was inevitable, and the role of the Marxists was to lessen the birth-pangs of the new world by acting as "midwives." In the view of orthodox Marxists, the catastrophic aspects of the revolution wre to be classed as a *natural* disaster—only its positive aspects were to be regarded as man-made. Donnelly dissented from this, believing that the revolution could and should be avoided if only men would commit themselves to Christian values in their economic transactions.

Not everyone, of course, saw revolution in the same way. For Marx, it was both inevitable and desirable, so that it was neither man-made nor a catastrophe. For Donnelly, it was clearly undesirable, but was only inevitable if men declined to act. For others—especially those who felt threatened by the possibility of a rebellion of the lower classes—there was no doubt at all that revolution constituted a man-made catastrophe, and it is in connection with such political anxieties that we can identify nineteenth-century imaginative fictions which most nearly approach the subject matter of this essay. The exploits of the Revolutionary Tribunal in Paris in 1793 created anxiety in Britain, and the history of the ill-fated Paris Commune of 1871 seemed to provide a further moral lesson. Accounts of such imaginary uprisings were, however, limited by the presumption that no really effective destructive power would be available to the revolutionaries. Anarchists armed with airships did not appear until 1893, when E. Douglas Fawcett produced *Hartmann and Anarchist; or, the Doom of the Great City*. The scale of violence in that book is not quite parochial, but it is hardly apocalyptic. Destruction on a far vaster scale was featured in another novel of Terrorist uprising published the same year—George Griffith's *The Angel of the Revolution*—but here the Terrorists are the heroes and the world is being liberated rather than raped.

The prospect of a socialist revolution, however, was not the most important cause for political concern in late nineteenth-century Britain. Much more attention was paid to the possibility of international war, and it was this prospect which exercised the most powerful influence over futuristic fiction. From 1871, when Sir George Chesney published his imaginary account of "The Battle of Dorking" as a piece of propaganda for rearmament, until 1914, when the Great War at last broke out, war-anticipation stories were the most prolific species of futuristic fiction in Europe.

It would be a mistake to consider all the future war stories of this period as catastrophist fictions. The prospect of *losing* a war was, of course, a prospect which no one could tolerate, but the prospect of a successful war was something else. To many of the writers who participated in the debate aroused by Chesney's fictional essay, war was still a great adventure, not to be commenced for the sheer fun of it but by no means to be shirked. There are many British stories of possible invasion which recognise the truly disastrous nature of that prospect, but the authors almost invariably relished the opportunity which such scenarios offered for tales of heroism and glorious derring-do. There were very few writers who displayed the least trace of the attitude which became commonplace in future war stories written *after* the Great War: the view that involvement in war is a catastrophe for *everyone*, winners and losers alike.

Before 1914, war could still be regarded as a game, especially by those whose attitudes had been fixed by a knowledge of history. The horrors of war had been made known to the British by reportage of the war in the Crimea in 1854–56, but this was a war fought on foreign soil, in which only soliders were involved (on the British side, at least). The weapons used there were extremely limited in their destructive capabilities. It was this kind of contest which was imaginatively associated with the notion of a future war by the majority of nineteenth-century writers. Only a very small number of men realised the extent to which technology could and must remake war. Some of these were among the European observers in the American Civil War, who had seen glimpses of the future in the use of breech-loading rifled guns, machine-guns, ironclad ships, observation balloons, flame-throwers, poison gas and submarines. Few of these things had made any significant impact on the actual fighting, but their existence was sufficient to create an awareness of threat in the minds of those with sufficient imagination. This awareness grew steadily through the half century which separated the end of the Civil War from the beginning of the Great War, but before 1900 there were really only three writers of futuristic romance who foresaw the possible nature of a new war. These three were George Griffith, author of *The Angel of the Revolution*; M. P. Shiel, author of *The Yellow Danger* (1898); and H. G. Wells, author of *When the Sleeper Wakes* (1899). None of these novels, however, can be regarded as catastrophist fantasies. *When the Sleeper*

Wakes is, like *The Angel of the Revolution*, a story of a liberating
revolution whose inevitability has been assured by socieconomic factors. *The Yellow Danger*, which involves the annihilation of the entire
populations of Asia and the European mainland by means of bacterial
warfare, excuses its excesses by means of the logic of social Darwinism. Of the three, only Wells went on to cultivate an attitude to war
which was much more in keeping with the wholehearted catastrophist
view that became commonplace in the 1920s.

One striking aspect of the war-anticipation stories of the nineteenth century, including those cited above, is the dominance of the
notion of a "war to end war." Those writers who did foresee death and
destruction on a vast scale believed to a man that such horrors could be
justified as the necessary prelude to a new way of life. The greater the
wars envisaged by these stories, the stronger was the commitment to
the notion that they would represent a final settlement of all accounts.
This combination of ideas helps to explain the essential moral ambiguity of the attitude to war manifest in these stories. No one before 1900
used speculative fiction in order to stigmatise the impulse to make war
as a species of original sin.

The notion of using new and extremely powerful weapons to put
an end to war forever was one which cropped up regularly in
nineteenth-century imaginative fiction, when the logic of ultimate
deterrents seems to have been very widely accepted. Examples include
The Vril Staff (1891) by "X.Y.Z." and *His Wisdom the Defender*
(1900) by Simon Newcomb, where single individuals put crucial inventions into the hands of a benevolent few. Many future war novels gave
a crucial role in deciding the course of such conflicts to inventions
made by lone scientific geniuses. There was, however, an unpleasant
corollary to this line of thought. If lone inventors could discover
weapons so dreadful that they might terrify the world into peace, what
of such inventions in the wrong hands? It is in connection with this
notion that we discover the few wholeheartedly catastrophist stories of
the nineteenth century which focus directly on *man-made* catastrophes. They are fantasies of evil scientists—frequently mad scientists—who threaten the world with destruction. An early example is
The Crack of Doom (1895) by Robert Cromie. In virtually all stories of
this type, the would-be world-wreckers are thwarted, but the plot
nevertheless shows a developing awareness of the *vulnerability* of
society to the destructive power of new inventions.

The principal limitation placed on both the future war story and
the mad scientist story was, of course, the kind of weapons which the

contending forces could be imagined to possess. The main reason why the stories of these kinds produced in the last years of the nineteenth century differ so markedly from those produced even in the early years of the twentieth century is that in the space of a few years, from 1895 to 1898, a great deal of new imaginative fuel was added to speculation about future weaponry by certain unexpected discoveries in science. Before 1895 it was easy enough to imagine battles fought by airships and submarines, but these were primarily important in modifying the way that battles might be fought rather than adding to the destructive power of the opposing armies. That submarines might make sea travel extremely dangerous, and that the advent of the aeroplane would make the aerial bombing of cities possible, were realised by some writers—notably Griffith—but even these possibilities seemed inadequate as a recipe for Armageddon.

In 1895, though, Roentgen discovered X-rays and Becquerel described the property of "radioactivity" in uranium. Both discoveries were widely publicised, and the following year saw publication by Marconi of his work on wireless telegraphy. So dawned, in the popular imagination, the age of miraculous rays and no-longer-unsplittable atoms. These discoveries provided an imaginative *carte blanche* for technological fantasies of all kinds, including stories involving weapons of miraculous potency. It was the notions of death-rays and disintegrator-rays which fed the new apocalyptic imagination, together with the less popular but more prophetic notion of atomic bombs. By 1900 it was a great deal easier to imagine that the power to annihilate mankind might one day rest in human hands than it had been in 1894, and it was this expansion of imaginative power which made the year 1900 a genuine *fin de siécle*. The discoveries of Roentgen and Becquerel gave speculative fiction the imaginative ammunition needed to take technological fantasies far beyond the boundaries which had previously confined them, to perceive many new wonders and to see for the first time those unfortunate possibilities which lurked just beyond the imaginative horizon.

The Lotus Eaters

In 1930 Geoffrey Dennis published a painstaking study of the apocalyptic mythology of modern science, *The End of the World*. The book discusses the various possible ends of the earth revealed by contemporary knowledge, and considers the relative likelihood of each one. It considers also the possibility that man might become extinct before the

death of the earth, and the possibility that men might actually outlive
their home world by migrating to others. Concerning man's possible
contribution to the end of the world, however, Dennis has little to say.
The possibility of a war so destructive as to wipe out the race is not
even mentioned *en passant* (though it figures large, for obvious
reasons, in Kenneth Heuer's identically titled study published in
1953). There is, however, one possible route to human extinction that
he does consider in detail, and that is the notion that man might doom
himself to extinction by choosing a way of life that leads the species to
gradual degeneration. Indeed, he summarises—though he is reluctant
to endorse it—a common contemporary argument to the effect that
this is already happening:

> Civilization is sapping man's vigour, blunting his senses, always reduc-
> ing the scope for his endeavour. He no longer needs strong right arm nor
> mental resource, no longer need fend for himself, the super-State is his
> protector, his poisoner, according him cheap survival for an ever smaller
> expenditure of brain and brawn. State and faculty have joined their
> murderous hands. Medicine, while saving the individual, enfeebles the
> race; the proportion of weaklings is mounting like a tide of death. . . .
> Tools do our "manual" work for us; the hand is losing its cunning, and
> with it a rich area of the brain its cunning also. When tools for mental
> work soon appear, the brain's brightest regions will follow little toe and
> little finger into atrophy.

Dennis was by no means alone in regarding this process of degeneration as the chief threat facing human life. The magazine *Today and
Tomorrow* published in its first issue (October 1930) an article by
C. E. M. Joad called "Is Civilization Doomed?" in which the author
advanced a similar argument. Joad, too, is reluctant to endorse it as a
true vision of the future, stating that he considers it his duty to be as
pessimistic as possible in the hope of alerting his fellow men to the
dangers which face them in time for them to take the appropriate
action.

This kind of attitude takes its inspiration from the Darwinian
theory of evolution, and in particular from the notion of "the survival
of the fittest" in "the struggle for existence." If this were the key to
evolutionary ascendancy, it could easily be argued that by exempting
himself from the struggle for existence man might suffer a drastic loss
of biological "fitness." In point of fact, the argument is based on a
misunderstanding of the nature of genetic inheritance, but it retained
its influence in the popular imagination long after the rediscovery of
Mendelian theory. The line of argument is particularly obvious in the

work of the early Wells—in the portrayal of the society of the Eloi in *The Time Machine* (1895), and in the careful attempt to preserve the biological fitness of the Samurai, masters of the new world in *A Modern Utopia* (1905). It was, of course, an argument very effectively deployed against technological Utopianism by E. M. Forster in "The Machine Stops" (1909).

Forster's version of the case is particularly strong in that it avoids the use of spurious pseudo-biology. He simply imagines a society where all needs are mechanically supplied, and where people in consequence have become idle, impotent and depersonalised. They have neither the knowledge nor the spirit necessary to cope with the disaster that follows the failure of their machines. Other writers were prepared to suggest that such a dispirited society might not need the *coup de grace* of disaster: James Elroy Flecker's story of "The Last Generation" (1908) is an account of the mass resignation of the human race from the business of living, which has come to seem rather pointless. A much more elaborate explication of the same idea was provided by S. Fowler Wright a generation later in *The Adventure of Wyndham Smith* (1938). The sentiments expressed in these stories are genuinely anti-Utopian, arguing that if society should ever reach the point where all men can live in harmony, with all their desires gratified without effort, then life itself becomes literally purposeless.

In his book on *The English Utopia* (1952), A. L. Morton points out that Utopian speculation, though it may represent the social aspirations of different classes and different individuals in particular sets of historical circumstances, is rooted in a fundamental "image of desire" which he terms "the Utopia of the folk." His archetypal example is the fourteenth-century poem *The Land of Cokaygne*, which describes "an earthly and earthy paradise, an island of magical abundance, of eternal youth and eternal summer, of joy, fellowship and peace." It is a land where no one has to do any work, where everything is free, and where there are no duties of religious observance. The last point is of cardinal importance, for the poem is an anti-clerical satire as well as a wish-fulfilment dream, and it serves to remind us that this Utopia of the folk stood to be condemned as depraved, immoral and degenerate. The notion that a life of ease and comfort is both extremely attractive and utterly reprehensible is much older than the myth of Cokaygne: it is embodied in the myth of the lotus eaters who were briefly visited by Odysseus and whose way of life ws recorded by Herodotus and Pliny. In this form, and in the fourteenth-century poem, it is a myth of a miraculous ecology, but in its twentieth-century version it becomes a myth of miraculous technology.

The alternate world of Cokaygne becomes a technological reality in "The City of the Living Dead" (1930) by Laurence Manning and Fletcher Pratt, in which most of the inhabitants of Earth's cities elect to have their sensory organs removed and replaced with wires piping synthetic experience directly into their brains. The cities die as everyone retreats to live in his dreams. The people are helpless before the possibility of a malfunction, but it is not so much the prospect of their dying which is represented horrifically as their predicament in life; in particular, the way that they have blinded themselves in order to control exactly what they may see.

The condemnation of the city dwellers in this story (which is offered, in fact, by one of their number) has two principal components. On the one hand, the wonderful lives which they lead are not *real*, and the acceptance of ersatz experience is seen to be a kind of moral failure. On the other hand, the universality of the practice has led society into a blind alley—it has put an end to *progress*. This double indictment recurs frequently in stories published during the last half-century, particularly those concerned with the invention of new media of communication. When James Olds discovered that direct stimulation of a particular area in the hind-brain of a rat had an effect so powerful that a rat given the means to self-stimulation would repeat the appropriate action until it dropped from exhaustion, tolerating no distractions, the implications fit readily enough into our suspicions about human psychology.

The most comprehensive science fictional account of the fate of a society equipped with the technological means to take the philosophy of hedonism to its logical extreme is to be found in James E. Gunn's *The Joy Makers* (1961). The last part of the story—originally published as "The Naked Sky" in 1955—features a more sophisticated version of the same imagery that was displayed in "City of the Living Dead." In Mack Reynolds's *After Utopia* (1977) a high-technology society which has solved all the social problems of today faces the spread of "dream machines" which threaten the same eventuality. A political radical brought forward out of our own time is set the problem of saving the world from stagnation, and accepts it willingly, inventing an external threat which convinces the people that they cannot yet retreat into themselves secure in the knowledge that they will be left in peace. (The solution seems, at best, to be temporary.)

The value-judgments expressed in these stories are taken so completely for granted that the moral philosophy behind them rarely becomes wholly explicit. It is not too difficult to see what the clergy of the fourteenth century had against the land of Cokaygne. In their view, men did have duties of religious observance which they must not shirk, and the means of production available to the society of the day were such that it could support very few idlers. Neither of these arguments can be held to apply to the futuristic states imagined in these modern stories. Though condemnation is no less strong, the nature of the moral complaints has altered.

The fact that a preference for ersatz experience over real is seen as a moral failure has much to do with a conviction that lies at the heart of the rationalistic, scientific world-view: that subjective experiences are worthless by comparison with "public" experience of the external world. This judgment is, of course, crucial to the ascent of empiricism to its privileged position in modern philosophy, and to its total dominance of the philosophy of knowledge. The worthlessness of experience which is private and cannot be corroborated by objective evidence is central to the contemporary philosophy of science. The advancement of this claim is held to provide the foundation-stone of a value-free science, but this should not obscure the fact that the claim itself is a value-judgment. It implies that dalliance with subjective experience is a kind of self-betrayal, a wicked preference for ignorance and illusion over the true path of enlightenment. It is this line of argument which has made the term "escapism" into an inherently pejorative one. (There is a certain irony in the fact that imaginative fiction, which is frequently charged with being pure escapism, often adopts a moral stance which is harshly critical of escapism.)

Positivism—the most radical form of empiricism—has declined in popularity in the last two decades, partly because of new fashions in the philosophy of the social sciences and because of the exploits of sociologists of knowledge, who have exposed allegedly fraudulent aspects of the orthodox representation of scientific method. It might be expected that this will soon be reflected in science fiction by the appearance of apologists who will defend the city of the living dead against the well-meaning Luddites, but to date there is not much sign of this. It is, however, noticeable that a more tolerant attitude occasionally crops up. In the *Star Trek* episode "The Menagerie" the crippled starship captain, totally helpless in the real world, is allowed to retreat (along with his aged and enfeebled female companion) into a world of pleasant illusion, taking with him the good wishes of the entire *dramatis personae*. Perhaps more significantly, the concluding volume of Michael Moorcock's *Dancers at the End of Time* trilogy, *The End of All Songs* (1976), allows the decadent immortals to continue their theatrical existence in a bubble of eternity sealed against the ravages of entropy, while a few of their number set off to create the universe anew. The creative few still have the moral advantage, but there is a sympathy for the lotus eaters which finds no echo in *The Joy Makers*.

The second charge levelled at lotus eater societies—that they have forsaken progress—is perhaps easier to understand. The advance of technology, in the popular imagination, *is* progress, and the notion that it should someday lead to the death of progress almost smacks of paradox. The worthiness of progress has been doubted far more widely than the unworthiness of subjective experience, but this doubt has affected the science fiction community less than most, and in science fiction progress is often elevated to the status of the greatest good. In Mack Reynolds's "United Planets" series the sole criterion for the evaluation of a political system is whether or not it permits progress (i.e., innovation and the growth of scientific understanding). The growth of anti-technological movements in society has sometimes been subject to scathing criticism in science fiction—a good example is the examination of near-future prospects presented in "Spirals" (1979) by Larry Niven and Jerry Pournelle. One of the reasons why science fiction writers are so prolific in their presentation of primitive societies (whether post-holocaust cultures or colonies on other worlds) is that it is easy enough in the context of such societies to see *what counts* as progress, and therefore what goals each society has. Considering the nature of the genre it is astonishing how shy contemporary science fiction writers are of imagining societies in which the problems of the present day have been adequately solved. Again, as the myth of progress declines in the real world, we may begin to see science fiction stories presenting apologies for non-progressive worlds, but what seems more likely to happen is that our definitions of progress will change. In its original meaning, the word "progress" had little to do with technology and much to do with the notion of moral perfectibility, and science fiction already gives evidence of the return swing of the pendulum in the prolific post-war mythology of future human evolution.

In the light of this characteristic emphasis on progress it is ironic that most stories criticising lotus eater societies can find no solution to the problem except smashing the machines and starting all over again. The irony is revealed for appreciation in Isaac Asimov's "The Life and

Times of Multivac" (1975), which takes a fresh look at the question of what happens when the machine stops.

The fact that there is no such solution to be found shows up the real heart of the problem, which is a lack of faith in ourselves. The whole issue would seem quite unproblematic if we were not so ready to see in ourselves this predilection for degeneracy. We tend to see the society of the technologically-assisted lotus eaters as a "no win" situation: in itself it constitutes a catastrophe of one kind, whereas the way out of the predicament involves a catastrophic return to primitive circumstances. We see no other alternatives because the ideative seed from which these images grow is so deeply implanted; it is the notion that human beings are, in their fundamental psychological nature, fatally flawed. No one believes that a significant fraction of the human race could actually withstand the temptation of the dream machines; we conceive of ourselves as being helpless in the face of addiction to pleasure-seeking. It is, of course, highly significant that we chose to label the addictive circuit in the brain discovered by Olds "the pleasure centre."

It is this notion of basic flaws in human nature which lies at the heart of the mythology of man-made catastrophe. We no longer think of these supposed flaws as "original sin," except in metaphor, but their role has not changed. Science fiction writers, in particular, conceive of them as the legacy of our evolutionary biology: primitive "drives" and "urges" which, for all our piety and wit, we cannot overcome, the moving finger of evolution having written indelibly upon our being. The notion has been bandied about abundantly in recent popular science and pseudoscience, notably in the works of Robert Ardrey and Desmond Morris, and perhaps most dramatically in Carl Sagan's exposition of the myth of the triple-brain, *The Dragons of Eden*.

The myth of the dream machine—of the technologically-supported society of lotus eaters—is only one facet of this image of flawed humanity. Several others exist, and all are associated with particular traditions of catastrophist fiction. All of them are interlinked, but some of them are in conflict, and come to the verge of contradicting one another. Before we pass on, however, to look at some of the other fatal flaws which are popularly considered to mar human nature, it is necessary to point out one particular variant of the myth of the lotus eaters notable for the extremism of its imagery. This is the line of thought which develops from Butler's "Book of the Machines" and which construes "degeneracy" not in a moral sense but in a physical sense as well.

Butler, commenting on the Erewhonian treatise on machines, offers the following summary of the case:

> The one serious danger which this writer apprehended was that the machines would so equalize men's powers, and so lessen the severity of competition, that many persons of inferior physique would escape detection and transmit their inferiority to their descendants. He feared that the removal of the present pressure might cause a degeneracy of the human race, and indeed that the whole body might become rudimentary, the man himself being nothing but soul and mechanism, an intelligent but passionless principle of mechanical action."

Wells, of course, was to follow up an identical line of argument in developing his image of "The Man of the Year Million"—a creature with a massive head and withered body, incapable even of supporting himself. We find this image repeated in many early pulp science fiction stories, most notably in "Twilight" (1934) and "Night" (1935) by John W. Campbell, Jr. (writing as "Don A. Stuart") and in "Alas, All Thinking!" (1935) by Harry Bates. Several early stories by David H. Keller, including "The Revolt of the Pedestrians" and "Stenographers' Hands" (both 1928) feature more specific accounts of physical degeneration occasioned by unnatural selection.

The most significant thing about *this* line of argument (as opposed to that followed by "City of the Living Dead," *The Joy Makers*, etc.) is that it is entirely false, having its basis in a pseudo-Lamarckian notion of inheritance. The fact that unused muscles will atrophy and become useless is irrelevant to any consideration of genetic deterioration, in that acquired characteristics are not transmitted from one generation to the next. It may be true that civilization—and modern medicine in particular—preserves within the gene pool certain genotypes which would otherwise be eliminated, but such an increase in the "genetic load" carried by a species does not set in train a degenerative process affecting all the individuals within the population. Even though the selection operating against deleterious genes is muted in its effects, it will still work in favour of more useful genes, and certainly not in such a way as to exclude them from the gene pool, however gradually.

Fictions such as "Twilight," in fact, are not extrapolative fictions at all, and have much more in common with the Victorian myths concerning the effects of masturbation: they represent an urgent call for moral rearmament, whose propagandistic priorities override the question of fidelity to empirical realism. Their plea is that we should not, and must not, relax and be satisfied, and their fear is that a representation of the actual effects of succumbing to the fruits of the technological lotus is an insufficient deterrent. In that the fundamental assumption of this line of argument is that the temptation is virtually irresistible, they are very probably right.

Epimetheus Unbound

The fear that machines might make us all too comfortable is, of course, by no means the only anxiety which we feel concerning the advance of technology. Indeed, the danger that we all might retreat into private worlds of synthetic experience exists in parallel with the suspicion that our developing technology might ultimately destroy the very possibility of private experience. If machines have the power to give us all perfect freedom (albeit within the limits of an artificial solipsism) then they also have the power to take away our freedom altogether—to make us subject to manipulation and oppression and the most absolute of tyrannies.

There are two versions of this mythology. In the first, the development of new technology gives the ruling elite within society the power to perpetuate its rule indefinitely, and to refine progressively the extent of its command over the lives and thoughts of the underdogs. All the most striking images in twentieth-century dystopian fiction derive from this line of thought: the watchful mechanical eyes of *1984*; the entire apparatus of social control in Huxley's *Brave New World*; etc., etc. In the second version the power elite have become redundant, and the machines themselves are the manipulators and oppressors, and sometimes the destroyers of humankind.

Like the story of the physical degeneration of the species, the story of the revolt of the machines is primarily of figurative significance. Many such stories make no pretence of realism, and invite a straightforward allegorical reading: Robert Bloch's "It Happened Tomorrow" (1943), Clifford Simak's "Bathe Your Bearings in Blood!" (1950, also known as "Skirmish") and Lord Dunsany's *The Last Revolution* (1950) are examples. There are, however, versions of the myth which are better rationalised, and since World War II we have made such vast strides in the development of machine intelligence that a good many fantasies of the pre-war period have been re-endorsed with frightening plausibility.

The anxiety, in its simplest form, has been dubbed by Isaac Asimov "the Frankenstein Syndrome," and it is displayed with particular moral clarity in Karel Čapek's work, particularly the play

R.U.R. (1921). In this work the "robots" produced by man to do his work for him eventually become so perfectly adapted to the task that they replace him altogether, going to war to remove him once he has made himself quite redundant. In another of his works, the novel *The Absolute at Large* (1922), Čapek describes a worldwide catastrophe precipitated by the development of an atomic engine, the karburator, which annihilates matter and releases the spirit bound up within it—a spirit with which man is ill-equipped to cope.

These stories represent the inventor not as Prometheus (a common nineteenth-century metaphor) but as Epimetheus, unwisely accepting "gifts" from the gods, so that his curiosity may release a plague of troubles upon mankind.

Parables following up this line of thought ask not "what happens when the machine stops?" or "what will happen to us if it works as intended?" but "what happens when the machine malfunctions, or when our discoveries turn out to have unfortunate corollaries?" Mechanical brains in science fiction show a distinct tendency to go mad, or to have no sense of social responsibility in carrying out their instructions. While science fictional machines quite frequently defy such trivial constraints as the law of conservation of energy, they hardly ever defy Sod's Law—the principle that if something can go wrong, it will.

Hugo Gernsback founded *Amazing Stories* in order to inspire young readers with magnificent dreams of the wonderful future that science would create. He himself was a Utopian optimist of indomitable naiveté, but the great majority of the stories which were written for his magazines actually featured technology gone wrong: the marvellous machines fell more frequently into the wrong hands than the right ones, and very often they were troublesome entirely on their own account. The world was almost invariably saved, but the significant thing is the fact that it was constantly in need of saving. A particularly eloquent early example of mechanisation-anxiety of this kind is Miles J. Breuer's *Paradise and Iron* (1930), in which the inhabitants of a Utopian island find themselves suddenly under threat when the artificial brain coordinating its advanced domestic and agricultural machinery begins to malfunction. Similar plots have remained a part of the staple diet of magazine science fiction, more modern variants being Philip K. Dick's "Autofac" (1955) and John Sladek's *The Reproductive System* (1968, also known as *Mechasm*). In contemporary science fiction computers frequently aspire not only to emulate man but even to emulate God. Asimov, the arch-apologist for technology in general and artificial intelligence in particular, has written numerous stories in which the usurpation of human privileges by robots is seen as being by no means catastrophic, and in "The Last Question" (1956) he was quite sympathetic to the godly ambitions of a computer. Other writers, however, have taken a rather darker view of these prospects—examples include Philip K. Dick's *Vulcan's Hammer* (1960), *Larger than Life* (1960) by Dino Buzzati, *Colossus* (1966) by D. F. Jones and the surreal "I Have No Mouth and I Must Scream" (1967) by Harlan Ellison. The computer's view of the situation is amply represented by the satirical moral fable *The Tale of the Big Computer* (1966, also known as *The Great Computer*) by the Nobel Prize winner Hannes Alfven, writing as "Olof Johannesson."

An important aspect of this kind of story is that very often the artificial intelligences involved are not malicious. Sometimes they go mad because they are "too human"—as in several ridiculous stories in which robots or computers fall in love with their creators and subsequently suffer awful frustration and jealousy—but more often they cause trouble simply by trying to do their best. Machines which are *too* helpful are featured in several stories, including Murray Leinster's "A Logic Named Joe" (1946) and Jack Williamson's classic "With Folded Hands" (1947). Those stories which describe the logic by which computers come to consider themselves superior to man normally concede that there is some justification in the decision, and that the machines have an adequate warrant for their belief.

As time has gone by we have become more and more concerned about the *side-effects* of technology—the unintended consequences of discovery. Industrial waste has been with us for a long time, but it is only recently that we have begun to fear that the negative effects of industry upon the environment may outweigh the positive effects of its products on the quality of our lives. In recent years, too, we have become much more sensitive to the prospect of a major accident involving some product of our technology—the escape of a new bacillus or an explosion at a nuclear power station. Catastrophist fantasies associated with these anxieties generally promote the allegation that we are downright irresponsible, and will be discussed further in a later section of this essay, but the indictment levelled by stories of the revolt of the machines and technological oppression are not primarily criticisms of human irresponsibility. Rather they serve to put the argument that knowledge and wisdom are not identical, and that we have far more of the former than the latter.

Curiosity, it is said, kills cats, and this proverb extends its implications into imaginative fiction in two ways. First, there is the story whose moral is that "there are things man was not meant to know"— stories where the truth is awful and enlightenment fatal. Archetypal examples are the fantasies of H. P. Lovecraft. Science fiction has little room for this kind of story, which is implicitly anti-scientific. There is also, however, the story whose moral is that in matters of scientific discovery one has to take the rough with the smooth—there is no guarantee that the technological possibilities revealed by the advancement of science will necessarily be edifying. This is a lesson that we have learned well enough by courtesy of the atom bomb.

Stories of disasters which come about because of new inventions usually stress that the real root cause of the disaster is the element in human nature which drives us to seek advantage over our fellow men. In stories of technological oppression the men who already have those advantages are given greater power to indulge them and greater power to secure them. In stories where machines take over the world they are merely reflecting (often innocently) this basic tendency of their makers. Perhaps the most revealing stories of technologically-induced social collapse are those which steer a middle course between these two versions of the myth. In George O. Smith's "Pandora's Millions" (1945) and Damon Knight's *A for Anything* (1959) the invention of matter-duplicators destroys the social order by blasting apart the economic relations which bind it. In the former story civilization is "saved" by the development of a non-duplicatable substance which can function as a medium of exchange and hence restore capitalism. In the latter, however, there is no such *deus ex machina*, and the social order is reconstituted, with possessors of the machines establishing themselves as an upper class dominating the lower orders whose sole function is to provide services. The point being made here is that no machine, whatever it does, is likely to be used in a way that benefits all men equally. Machine-power is an instrument in social intercourse, and is always likely to be used to create or support inequalities rather than to erode them.

Perhaps the most perfect ironic fantasy in this vein is "E for Effort" (1947) by T. L. Sherred, in which the invention of a device which can "see" through time and space threatens to destroy forever the very possibility of secrecy. No one who enjoys any kind of privilege at all can face this prospect, and immediately the news of the discovery breaks there begins a war of all against all as every power-group makes its desperate attempt to corner the use of the machine. By trying to keep it out of the hands of any particular power-group, the heroes of the story precipitate a war that will destroy mankind.

Stories of this kind are essentially ironic, not simply because (as with the lotus eater stories) they focus on our inability to withstand fateful temptations, but also because they habitually retain something else from the myth of Epimetheus: the notion that the Pandora's box of invention contains, as well as a host of troubles, such hope as we may legitimately entertain for our future prospects. The machine-power which may turn against us also offers us the promise of a better life. The fact that the promise might be so easily betrayed (whether after the fashion of *Paradise and Iron* or "E for Effort") cannot affect the fact that it has been made.

The feeling that underlies these Epimethean fantasies is that machines, one way or another, are getting out of control. We build them to be our servants, and somehow they seem to be threatening to enslave *us*. Even if we leave aside the potential exploits of artificial intelligence, this feeling is not entirely unrealistic. In the final analysis, political and economic power is dependent upon and shaped by the means of production available to society. It would be over-deterministic to say with Marx that the hand-mill will inevitably generate a feudal system while the steam-mill will generate capitalism, but it is nevertheless true that machines, by making available new means of production, can destroy certain kinds of social structures and greatly encourage others. It is by no means easy to see *what* kind of new social order might emerge from the ultimate triumph of machine-production, and very different opinions are offered by various science fiction stories. Knight's *A for Anything*, which envisages a new feudal-ism, contrasts sharply with Jack Williamson's "The Equalizer" (1947), which foresees an anarchist Utopia emerging from the harnessing of free energy. The major difference between the premises used in the two stories is the simplicity of the machines; in Williamson's story the key to unlimited abundance is available to everyone, but in Knight's novel it is complicated enough to be cornered by the fortunate few. Neither author doubts, though, that it is the nature of the machine, constrained by the happenstance of scientific possibility, which will determine the form of the society which discovers it: the desires of men are impotent.

How impotent the desires and political philosophies of men really are remains open to dispute. There is no doubt, however, that there is sufficient cause for anxiety. It is, indeed, possible that the advancement of technology will bring about great changes in the social order to which we are accustomed, and that we cannot hope to steer a course through those changes exactly as we would wish. Machines *do* control, at least to some degree, the range of possibilities expressed in our contemporary social evolution, and there can be no guarantee that they will not drive us into an upheaval so great that virtually all of us may consider it catastrophic.

It might be argued that the great failing of twentieth-century science fiction in respect of its dealings with future invention is that it is not *sufficiently* catastrophist. The Epimethean fantasies considered here are, after all, a tiny minority of stories compared with the flood which foresee hardly any changes in the social, political and economic matrix which surrounds their inventions. On the other hand, it might be argued by some that when writers do foresee sweeping changes in social behaviour ordained by new technologies they are too enthusiastic in condemning them as evil by reference to our own transient and artificial value-system. After all, leaving aside those fairly unambiguous cases where humanity is wiped out, catastrophe is in the eye of the beholder. The point at which progress becomes too costly remains a matter for subjective judgment, and there is much lively debate in today's world between those who would place it in the future and those who would place it in the past. The debate has become urgent ever since 1945, when it became clear that technology could and would provide nations with the means to bring about that most unambiguous of catastrophes—a war which might annihilate the human race.

Weapons Too Dreadful to Use

The war-anticipation stories of the period 1871–1914 were, on the whole, quite cheerful and optimistic. War, even fought with airships and submarines, could be seen as a great adventure, and even where it was regarded as an unmitigated evil there was the commonplace assumption that in order to put an end to it one more final war would have to be fought. The one future war story written before the outbreak of the *real* war which attempts to show in full measure the horrific extent of the misery and destruction that a high-technology war must bring in its train was *The War in the Air* (1908) by H. G. Wells, and even that did not represent the outlook of a wholehearted catastrophist. Wells feared the next war, but felt that it might do some good in tearing down the fabric of the old social order so that the construction of a new and better one might begin. It is by no means insignificant that his other major future-war novel, featuring the destruction of the world's major cities by atomic bombs, was written on the very eve of the Great War and was titled *The World Set Free* (1914). As the real war began Wells wrote a series of newspaper articles commending it as a marvellous opportunity—these were subsequently collected in the pamphlet "The War That Will End War" (1914). In 1916 he wrote *M. Britling Sees It Through*, a novel providing a moral justification for the war, and produced non-fiction works dealing with the reconstruction of civilization which would follow it. That reconstruction, however, failed to make any headway after 1918, and *The Salvaging of Civilization* (1921) heralded a decline into pessimism that was only occasionally to be alleviated during the remainder of Wells's career. The hope that perhaps the Great War really *had* ended war was steadfastly maintained by a few optimists, but it was really a very feeble hope. Many speculative writers took the view that not only did war remain a possibility, but that it was well-nigh inevitable that it would break out again, and that the only way war would put an end to itself would be in reducing mankind to such a primitive state that he would no longer be capable of waging it.

Before the war there had appeared several novels in which scientific supercriminals blackmailed cities, or even the whole world. There had been others in which mad scientists embarked upon careers of spectacular vengeance. Now there was a new fear to set beside these: the fear that by following behaviour-patterns that were already well-established and quite normal the politicians of the world might duplicate or surpass the worst that any supercriminal or mad genius might do. It was appreciated that no one would go to war with the deliberate intention of exterminating the human race, but writers now became aware of the possibility of *escalation* which haunted restrained and local conflicts, and they also became suspicious of the logic of defensive deterrents.

At least one of the contributors to the war-anticipation story repented of what he had done. Erskine Childers, author of *The Riddle of the Sands* (1903), had espoused in that novel the notion that by being prepared for war Britain might actually preserve herself from war. Later, apparently, he recanted this view. Childers himself was executed in 1922 in consequence of his activities supporting the Irish Republican Army, but his nephew added the following note to the 1931 edition of the novel:

"In *Riddle of the Sands*, first published in 1903, Erskine Childers advocated preparedness for war as being the best preventive for war. During the years that followed, he fundamentally altered his opinion. His profound study of military history, of politics, and later of the causes of the Great War convinced him that preparedness induced war. It was not only that to the vast numbers of people engaged in the fostered war services and armament industries, war meant the exercise of their professions and trades and the advancement of their interests; preparedness also led to international armament rivalries, and bred in the minds of the nations concerned fears, antagonisms, and ambitions, that were destructive to peace."

This perspective, coupled with the knowledge that armaments had already increased in power sufficiently to make the destruction of nations practicable, caused the growth of a new kind of war-anticipation story which was genuinely apocalyptic in its mood.

Edward Shanks's *People of the Ruins* (1920) shows the survivors of a series of crippling wars scratching out a living as scavengers amid the wreckage of civilization, still involved in a constant war of "all against all." *The Collapse of Homo Sapiens* (1923) by P. Anderson Graham follows the career of a group of refugees hiding from the next war in a shebeen, and goes on to describe the barbarian science-fearing culture that grows up along the banks of the Thames in a desolated England. In *Ragnarok* (1926) by Shaw Desmond the survivors of the war live in sewers and caves, fighting against the rats for the means of subsistence while the surface of the world is devastated by bombs and poison gases. The use of poison gas—the most unselective of weapons—also figures large in the scenes of appalling destruction featured in Neil Bell's *The Gas War of 1940* (1931 as by "Miles," subsequently retitled *Valiant Clay*), Ladbroke Black's *The Poison War* (1933) and Francis Sibson's *Unthinkable* (1933). New and more powerful explosives were also featured extensively: aerial bombing destroys Britain's cities in *The Black Death* (1934) by M. Dalton and in *Day of Wrath* (1936) by Joseph O'Neill.

The scale of the destruction envisaged by these stories grew steadily as World War II approached. Alfred Noyes's *The Last Man* (1940) imagines the nations locked in war having simultaneous recourse to the ultimate weapon, with the result that only a handful of survivors are left to haunt the empty world. The same year saw the first publication of L. Ron Hubbard's *Final Blackout*, a frenetic political fantasy set in a Europe laid waste by the fury of war. In Alfred Bester's "Adam and No Eve" (1941) the destruction is so complete that the only hope for a new beginning lies in the bacteria which multiply in the body of the new "Adam" after his death, and which may perhaps commence the evolutionary story afresh.

The notion that war is too high a price to pay for any political aim or ideology was common in imaginative fiction during the twenties and early thirties. Numerous science fiction stories represented it as the ultimate irrationality—examples include "The Gostak and the Doshes" (1930) by Miles J. Breuer and *In Caverns Below* (1935, also known as *Hidden World*) by Stanton A. Coblentz. A particularly sharp black comedy is John Gloag's *Tomorrow's Yesterday* (1932), in which a theatre company presents a play depicting various stages in the decline and fall of man as a result of war. The play is greeted with hostility and derision and forced to close just as the next war begins. As the thirties proceeded, however, the element of black comedy was eliminated and the notion that no price was too dear to pay for the avoidance of war became much less respectable. The Spanish Civil War of 1936 and Hitler's invasion of Czechoslovakia reopened the question of the moral justification of waging war even in the shadow of Armageddon. For this reason, the war-anticipation stories of the late thirties frequently recaptured something of the crusading fervour of those that appeared before the Great War.

The weapon too dreadful to use made its debut on the stage of history in August 1945, its use justified in that it put an end to World War II, literally at a stroke. The relief brought by the atom bomb was, however, short-lived, for it endorsed in no uncertain terms all the apocalyptic anxieties which had built up in the twenties and thirties. It left no room for doubt that a third world war would be quite capable of destroying the world. Though it was not until 1953, following the advent of the H-bomb, that the United States Secretary of Defence announced officially that the United States and the USSR each had the ability to exterminate the human race, that prospect had been inevitable since 1945. Tales of atomic Armageddon followed in great profusion, the most notable being *Shadow on the Hearth* (1950) by Judith Merril, *The Long Loud Silence* (1952) by Wilson Tucker, *On the Beach* (1957) by Nevil Shute, *Level 7* (1959) by Mordecai Roshwald and *A Canticle for Leibowitz* (1960) by Walter M. Miller.

The element of black comedy first featured in *Tomorrow's Yesterday* returned in full force in several extraordinarily embittered stories, ranging from Aldous Huxley's *Ape and Essence* (1949) to Peter George's *Dr. Strangelove* (1963). These stories spoke most eloquently to the notion that if the world was bound to end, it was no more than our just desserts. L. Sprague de Camp's "Judgment Day" (1955) provides a biography of a scientific genius whose childhood is a catalogue of miseries. Despite being bullied, harassed and vilified he survives to become a brilliant physicist and discovers the secret of the doomsday weapon. He knows that his political masters will use it, but he has no hesitation at all in giving it to them. *A Canticle for Leibowitz* is an account of how civilization is put back together after being bombed back into the dark ages, and shows the inexorable process which leads to its bombing itself right back again. Norman Spinrad's "The Big Flash" (1969) recounts the story of a rock band called the Four Horsemen who embody the spirit of their age, and whose climactic concert coincides with the countdown to World War III. The same author, in *The Iron Dream* (1972), features a science fiction novel written in an alternate universe by a German immigrant to the United States named Adolf Hitler, in which a heroic superman destroys Earth in "saving" it from domination by mutants but succeeds in sending the seed of his Aryan super-race to the stars. Here science fiction recoils upon itself, striking out at its own mythology and imaginative instruments.

The science fiction community was exultant in 1945, following Hiroshima. The events of history had provided editors, writers and fans with a golden opportunity to shout "I told you so!" The same exultancy is obvious in *Ape and Essence*, written by the man whose vision of *Brave New World* had provided a vocabulary of symbols for the adherents of anti-progressive pessimism in the thirties. It was not long before the followers of John Campbell realised in a similar fashion that their prophetic victory was in some ways a very bitter one. The pleasure which prophets obtain from being proved right tends to be a rather perverse pleasure when their prophesies carry implications of doom. The prophets of the Christian Millennium had always avoided this perversity well enough by assuming that the end of the old world would be the beginning of the new—salvation for the chosen few, while only the wicked must go to the devil. The prophets of atomic apocalypse, however, had no such escape-clause. Radioactive fallout could not be expected to discriminate between the just and the unjust.

It has been argued that our consciousness of the world changed in a fundamental way after 1945—Gunther Anders has claimed that the dictum "all men are mortal" was converted into "all men are exterminable," and that the change was not without consequence in terms of everyday social relationships and political calculations. Whether that is true or not, it is certain that science fiction changed dramatically in its characteristic attitudes, concerns and methods. Scathing satire and black comedy became common, there was much interest in religious themes which had previously been rigorously excluded, and there was an upsurge of misanthropy which worked wonders for the fortunes of aliens and supermen (who had previously been subject to consistent chauvinistic discrimination). James Blish, in his essay "Cathedrals in Space" (1953), noted that the genre seemed to have become the showcase for a "chiliastic panic" whose like had not been seen since the year 999. In fact, the new situation was rather worse, in that it was now so difficult to believe that disaster might be tempered by the mercy of God. The view of modern man's existence embodied in T. S. Eliot's "The Hollow Men" (1925) persisted, even though it seemed that the world was to end with a bang and not a whimper after all.

Stories of atomic holocaust and its effects are so many and so various that it is difficult to extract from them a consistent opinion regarding the essential flaws in human nature which tend to launch man toward self-destruction. There are, of course, numerous stories which make overt moral points—a notable early example is Theodore Sturgeon's "Thunder and Roses" (1948), which insists that men armed with atom bombs cannot afford the luxury of retaliation—but there are several opinions as to which element in human nature warrants most criticism. More often than not, it is not any *positive* trait in human nature which is stigmatised, but rather a negative one. There are attacks on militarism, on aggression in general, and on spitefulness. In the final analysis, what these stories have in common as their fundamental assumption is the argument that we do not—and perhaps cannot—care enough about one another. We are all estranged, and even when we do not find it all too easy to hate one another we still find it far too difficult to care much one way or the other what happens to people. This is not exactly a new discovery, but only in recent times has it come to be seen as a recipe for catastrophe.

What is perhaps most remarkable about science fiction of the fifties is neither its conviction that the future would be catastrophic nor its continual recourse to scathing black comedy in its manifold images of unpleasant futures, but rather the nature of the escape route which it found to allow its favoured few back to the tollpath to Utopia. It was in the fifties that the mythology of the spaceship really came into its own in science fiction. It was no longer the means to a new and more exciting kind of tourism but a vital and necessary method of outrunning the terrible destiny of Earthly civilization. If it could blast off for a new Eden, all well and good, but even if it was heading for a hell planet like the Venus of *The Space Merchants* (1953) it was still necessary to get aboard. The reclamation of Earthly society came to be seen, characteristically, as an impossible task. Genre science fiction packed up the future in its kitbag and set off for the stars, while futuristic fiction outside the labelled enclave set about mapping the utter dereliction of our Utopian aspirations. Since 1960 there has been some remission of this condition as speculative writers have grown more accustomed to the everpresence of the H-bomb, but so far the forces of moral rearmament visible in the activities of various futurologists and the more technophilic science fiction writers have made little headway in displacing the conviction that every day, in every way, things are getting just a little bit worse.

Looking back on the history of the last hundred years it is not very difficult to convince ourselves that the tide of progress somehow turned against us during that time. Most people, by inclination if not by nature, are optimists, and in the real world there has been no massive upsurge of despair. The nightmares of popular fiction—and those of not-so-popular fiction even more so—have little more effect on our mundane lives than the haphazard nightmares which visit us in sleep. No matter how seriously one takes stories of atomic holocaust, the effect that they will have on one's everyday life is likely to be slight. The exceptions remain exceptional. Nevertheless, the fact that the future now seems threatening to most of us *has* had its effects—notably in refocussing determined optimism on those aspects of life and future possibility which seem least threatened. In the terms suggested by Frank Manuel, faith in "euchronia"—the better future for society—has evaporated, and has been replaced by faith in "eupsychia"—the possibility that we may (individually or in small groups) achieve a better state of mind. Mysticism has advanced its cause remarkably. So has psychotherapy. So has sex. We are more preoccupied than we have ever been with the problem of getting ourselves straightened out, and the reason is that we have lost all faith in the world getting *itself* straightened out. We have been set on this path since 1945, and it is not easy to see whether we can get off it again in the foreseeable future.

The point of all this is that the advent of atomic weapons did more than confirm a growing suspicion that the modern world possessed the means to bring about a man-made catastrophe of awesome dimensions. It helped bring about a consciousness of the future as a kind of *continuing* catastrophe—a mess which we had already made and would have to take special measures to escape. The lesson of Hiroshima was that *it was already too late* to avoid the dark and hostile future which had earlier been feared; the world was locked on course and only individuals might avoid disaster by locating and occupying boltholes of various kinds. In pursuing this new view of things, the science fictional imagination has for the last twenty years and more, with the active collaboration of many futurologists, discovered a whole host of man-made catastrophes which are already happening.

Catastrophe à la mode

Unlike Dr. Strangelove, most survivors of World War II did not learn to stop worrying and love the bomb. What *has* happened, however, is that the prospect of atomic war has faded from immediate consciousness into the background of the imagination. There it has merged with a whole series of spectral bugbears which lurk in the shadows of the contemporary image of the future, waiting to devour us as the march of time carries us inexorably into their jaws. We have rediscovered the Malthusian logic of population explosion; we have become painfully aware of the extent to which the wastes of industrial society are poisoning the environment; we have realised how rapidly we are consuming non-renewable resources. In brief, we have begun to come to terms with the built-in obsolescence of the way of life which is followed in the "developed" countries.

When Malthus first published his *Essay on the Principle of Population* in 1798 he was an isolated cynic in an intellectual regime dominated by Enlightenment humanism and an optimistic mythology of progress. His thesis was severely criticised by William Godwin, who felt that human beings could surely rise above the "natural" tendency of populations to increase beyond the limits of their means of subsistence. Malthus was led by this criticism to modify his case, and added to the list of population checks which he had compiled (war, famine and plague) the notion of conscious population control by "moral restraint."

There is no doubt that Malthus's second thoughts offered a better analysis of the situation than his first. We live today in a world in which strategic action to cope with population growth, on an individual and on a political level, has dramatically changed the pattern of population increase in the developed countries. The means by which this has been achieved are not quite "moral restraint" in the Malthusian sense, but there can be no doubt that the intervention of cultural factors has robbed the tendencies of nature of their deterministic power. It is now obvious that the rate of population increase depends on human choice rather than the tyranny of "natural law." The trouble is that we have come to doubt whether we (or, more usually, other people) are making the right choices, or are *capable* of making the right choices. A few science fiction stories of the fifties played with images of an overcrowded world. Cyril Kornbluth's "The Marching Morons" (1951) is a black comedy displaying the eventual consequences of the "negative eugenic" trend by which the stupid consistently outbreed the wise. Kurt Vonnegut's "The Big Trip Up Yonder" (1954; also known as "Tomorrow and Tomorrow and Tomorrow") envisages the world becoming hopelessly overcrowded because longevity has reduced the death-rate, forcing the return of the extended family to Western culture. Frederik Pohl's "The Census Takers" (1956) is a sardonic story of the time when those keeping tally of the population will be required to adjust the actuality to their envisaged ideal. Heavily ironic fables in this vein continued to be produced for another twenty years, until the fashionability of the population explosion began to wane, but they were soon complemented by alarmist stories which took the central Malthusian thesis very much more seriously.

Robert Silverberg's *Master of Life and Death* (1957) follows a critical period in the career of the man responsible for the eugenic decisions which enforce the moral restraint which people are reluctant to supply on their own account. This was written in a period when it was still possible to imagine people submitting to laws embodying "scientific rationality." A decade later it was more usual for writers to take a bitter view of the likely outcomes of the democratic process insofar as the politics of population limitation were concerned. The most notable alarmist novels of this period are *Make Room! Make Room!* (1966) by Harry Harrison, *The Wind Obeys Lama Toru* (1967) by Lee Tung and *Stand on Zanzibar* (1968) by John Brunner. The extremes to which the world might be driven if required to contain a population several orders of magnitude higher than the present one are given detailed consideration in *A Torrent of Faces* (1968) by James Blish and Norman L. Knight and *The World Inside* (1972) by Robert Silverberg. Draconian alternatives in the matter of population controls administered without the benefit of democratic approval are envisaged in *The Quality of Mercy* (1963) by D. G. Compton, *Logan's Run* (1967) by William Nolan and George Clayton Johnson and "The Pre-Persons" (1974) by Philip K. Dick. The decade within which all of these stories were written was the one in which the population explosion was seen as the principal menace to the future well-being of mankind, though for the latter part of the decade it vied for primacy with the menace which subsequently replaced it: the bugbear of pollution.

Though the fundamental analogy which inspired the new alarmism was taken from science—the fate of yeast-cells confined in a test-tube with an unlimited food supply and their own toxic wastes—the term itself has religious connotations which are by no means out of context when one considers the upsurge of "ecological mysticism" to which this species of alarmism eventually gave birth. The moral tone of the crusades launched in the real world against industrial pollution (which quickly spread to the condemnation of other "ecological sins") has always implied that there are more than mere pragmatic concerns at stake.

In terms of the actual amount of waste materials produced, nineteenth-century factories were frequently far worse than modern ones, and horses rather more profligate than motor cars. The fact that it was not quantity that mattered was first made clear to the world by the publication in 1962 of Rachel Carson's *Silent Spring*. Carson pointed out that new organic compounds synthesized for various specific uses were introducing new components into the biosphere. Unlike the poisons manufactured by nature the new compounds were not biodegradable, and once released into the ecosystem they persisted in living tissues, gradually accumulating in concentration until they reached toxic levels in species at different points in the food-chain. Thus, chlorinated hydrocarbons used as insecticides, like DDT, were gradually being redistributed within the biosphere, threatening fish, birds and mammals (including man) with a kind of biological time-bomb. Once present, these compounds could not be eradicated—and, by an unfortunate stroke of irony, soon lost their effectiveness as pesticides because the insects they attacked, subject to a ruthless regime of natural selection, quickly developed immunity. Heavy metal pollution, especially involving lead and mercury, also became a special cause for anxiety—where these elements had previously been locked up safely in their inert ores, technological usage was slowly releasing them into the biosphere, where their effects could be deadly.

As with overpopulation scare-stories, it is possible to find isolated examples of eco-doom stories in the science fiction of the fifties—Cyril Kornbluth's "Shark Ship" (1958) is a notable example. The boom in this species of alarmism, however, followed close on the heels of the peak in Malthusian alarmism. The most striking stories of this kind include "We All Die Naked" (1969) by James Blish, "The Lost Continent" (1970) by Norman Spinrad, *The Sheep Look Up* (1972) by John Brunner, *The End of the Dream* (1972) by Philip Wylie, "To Walk With Thunder" (1973) by Dean McLaughlin and *Brainrack* (1974) by Kit Pedler and Gerry Davis.

As with overpopulation stories, a dominant premise in these extrapolative fantasies is that nothing will be done to prevent disaster until it is too late. Two of the listed stories are apocalyptic in character, while two others look back with ironic approval at the self-destruction of the gluttonous West. McLaughlin's story is a particularly subtle political fantasy which suggests that as long as we have technological facilities to combat the direct personal effects of pollution we will be prepared to put up with it—he is frighteningly plausible in offering an account of the political circumstances which encourage people to permit the poisoning of the atmosphere while the wonders of technology can purify the air supplies to their own homes. The basic argument is that we are insatiable in demanding short-term gratification of even the most puerile of our whims, even if the ultimate consequences will include the suffering of future generations and the death of the earth.

By the time that the new Malthusian crisis and the destruction of the environment had taken their place alongside atomic weapons as seeds of the new apocalypse, other anxieties could fill only a peripheral role. The problem of dwindling resources never became the principal focus of any temporary glut of alarmist science fiction stories, but simply joined the list. So, too, did the gathering anxiety about our psychological and neurological fitness to cope with the pace of change, dubbed "future shock" by Alvin Toffler. Fears of a new economic depression of the kind experienced in the thirties could add no more than a few new drops to an ocean of anticipatory tears.

As pollution ceased to be the primary focus of near-future hysteria in science fiction, its place was taken by a much more generalised anxiety. The combined effect of overpopulation and pollution had been given a new name by Paul Ehrlich, who sketched a brief scenario for a nightmare future in "Ecocatastrophe!" (1969), and the notion of a chain-reaction disaster precipitated by a combination of evil circumstances became common. John Brunner's novel *The Shockwave Rider* (1975), which completed a curious "apocalyptic trilogy," makes use of Toffler's notion of future shock, but the nature of the problematic morass into which its future America is sinking is actually much more elaborate and complex than those featured in *Stand on Zanzibar* and *The Sheep Look Up.*

Science fiction became, in the period when these stories were written, the principal medium by which this pessimistic image of the future was disseminated. Indeed, "non-fictional" speculation and science fiction began to overlap when those engaged in what has come to be known as "futurology" or "futures research" began manufacturing "scenarios" after the fashion of Herman Kahn and Alvin Toffler, and computer simulations of the future after the fashion of the Club of Rome's study of *The Limits to Growth* (1972). The non-fiction, by and large, attempts to make as much use of the sense of tragedy and of hypothetical moral predicaments as does the fiction. ZPG—a movement advocating Zero Population Growth as a political policy for the United States—published a science fiction anthology, *Voyages: Scenarios for a Ship Called Earth* in association with Ballantine Books in 1971, which was intended as propaganda. Several futures researchers have produced apologias for science fiction which put a strong case for its use in education. Meanwhile, science fiction writers and editors have been ready enough to accept a didactic role in this connection— other science fiction anthologies which are overtly propagandistic in their alarmism include *Nightmare Age* (1970) edited by Frederik Pohl, *The Ruins of Earth* (1971) edited by Thomas M. Disch and *Saving Worlds* (1973, also known as *The Wounded Planet*) edited by Roger Elwood and Virginia Kidd.

Whether science fiction is really effective as an *agent provocateur* inciting the development of a better social conscience is, of course, debatable. It might be suggested that by banishing contemporary (and quite real) social problems to the realms of imaginative fiction, where they take their place alongside invading Martians, giant insects, galactic empires, time travel and E.S.P., science fiction is defusing anxieties rather than amplifying them. Final settlement of this question remains a matter for empirical enquiry, but the correlation between the growth of science fictional concern with ecocatastrophe and the growth of concern in the real world does not suggest that the feedback from image to political strategy has been negative. It is much easier to argue the case for a positive feedback.

Some commentators have found it difficult to reconcile the argument that these visions of man-made catastrophe have a constructive role to play with the fact that so many of them are characterised by black despair and a conviction of utter hopelessness. (The same, incidentally, is true of many futurological speculations, which claim that it is already too late for any action to be really effective—a cardinal example is the recent *Delivrez Promethée* (1979) by Jerome Deshusses.) In reply, the immediate temptation is to recover the argument used by Joad in his essay of 1930, to the effect that speculators have a duty to be as pessimistic as possible in order that they "may hope to irritate . . . readers sufficiently to provoke them to make the efforts necessary to prove [their] predictions false." Often, however, the arguments used in these stories are so completely nihilistic that it is difficult to construe them as anything other than exhortations to complete passivity. This is especially true of those science fiction stories which contain an element usually missing from futurological speculations—the element of jeering black comedy. Robert Silverberg's story of imaginary tourist trips to colourful apocalypses, lauched from a near future which is dying its own sordid death, "When We Went to See the End of the World" (1972) is one of the more subtle examples; Kurt Vonnegut's "The Big Space Fuck" (1972) is surely the most bitterly hysterical. In their account of the "human nature" which precipitates catastrophe these stories not only leave no room for hope but suggest that if hope *did* exist it would be a violation of common justice. In so many science fictional catastrophe stories of the last two decades we are urged to believe that we deserve every last moment of the suffering that we are bringing upon ourselves. It will, it is presumed, constitute an adequate payment for our sins, even though it will not constitute an expiation. Only a tiny minority of stories actually carry this "message" in manifest form, and many more reject it insistently, but the very fact that it exists at all is a matter of considerable significance, and it is, indeed, no more than the logical extreme of the line of argument taken by all the fiction which accepts the image of an ecologically sick future.

The true measure of the despair which has begun to gnaw at the heart of the image of the future contained within science fiction is not so much to be found in the violence of its images of destruction, but in the way that the accusing finger which seeks to allocate blame so frequently leaves no exceptions. In stories written before 1945, whether they deal with lotus eater societies or future wars, the allocation of responsibility is usually selective. For the most part, the clear-sighted middle-class intelligentsia are absolved of blame—it is the power-groups above them or the lower orders below whose greedy short-sightedness precipitates disaster. As most of the writers of these stories were members of the middle-class intelligentsia who saw their work as an attempt to send out warning signals, this exemption is not altogether surprising. After the war, however, attitudes changed markedly. The supposed moral neutrality of scientists came under suspicion, and the scientists had always seemed to represent the ideological spearhead of the intelligentsia. When the pollution crisis became dominant among the anxieties of the period, the culpability of the intelligentsia as a whole could no longer be doubted, for it was in maintaining the standard of living expected by the middle classes that industrialism was threatening to run riot and poison the earth. To some extent, therefore, the absolutism of the note of despair sounded in some of these stories represents a kind of self-abuse on the part of speculators who have come to see themselves as active participants in the catastrophe they anticipate. Andrew J. Offutt, in his ecocatastrophe story *The Castle Keeps* (1972), quotes with approval the words of the comic-strip character Pogo: "We have met the enemy, and he is us!"—a comment which is highly pertinent in both a general and a special sense.

When we bear this fact in mind, it becomes easier to see why the note of despair sounded by the more extreme apocalyptic fantasies does not destroy the possibility of their filling a constructive role. As evangelical rabble-rousers discovered a long time ago, it pays to reduce your audience to despair by convincing them of their personal damnation before attempting to win them to the cause with conditional promises of salvation. It is a tried-and-true recipe for making converts (though the treatment has periodically to be renewed lest they lapse). The whole point about the eclectic catastrophism which is so prominent in contemporary science fiction is that it is not a warning about what *they* might do to us if we let them, but a warning about what we are doing to ourselves. The scapegoat-strategy by which we try to pin blame to other individuals or groups, to other people's ideas, or to facets of "human nature" which we have risen above while others cannot, seems (at long last) to be going out of fashion.

"What is sin?"

The question "What is sin?" is asked by Felix Hoenikker in Kurt Vonnegut's *Cat's Cradle* (1963), when one of his colleagues wonders (after the fashion of J. Robert Oppenheimer) whether the invention of the atom bomb constitutes a scientists' sin. Hoenikker is a scientist through and through, and all his concepts are scientific ones. The concept of sin is not among them. For him, all problems are theoretical, and have no moral dimension. Thus, when he is asked to find a way to freeze battlefields so that soldiers will not have to fight in mud, he does so. His invention, ice-nine, will also freeze the entire world if a single drop ever escapes into the environment, but that is a problem which he leaves for his children—and, indeed, all the world's children—to cope with. In the end—which, of course, really *is* the end—they *can't* cope.

Cat's Cradle is exceptional among modern stories of man-made catastrophe because it sets against the hopelessness of our envisaged situation a very powerful note of pity. The irony of our impending self-destruction is allowed full rein; there is no doubt expressed within the story that we are getting pretty much what we deserve. Nevertheless, argues Vonnegut, we are to be pitied in our plight. It is this element of pity, also strongly expressed in *Mother Night*, *God Bless You, Mr. Rosewater* and *Slaughterhouse-Five*, which makes Vonnegut a unique figure in modern American literature. Those who recognise that the hopelessness of his stories is a kind of self-abuse are apt to construe the pity as self-pity, and are generally antipathetic in consequence, but it is not difficult to see why his attitude has seemed so attractive to those who have made Vonnegut a cult-figure. In Vonnegut's books we are all *responsible* for the coming catastrophe, but there remains a special sense in which we are nevertheless innocent. We are victims of "samaritrophia" (chronic degeneration of the conscience) but it is not really our fault—we are embarked upon a curious kind of "children's crusade."

The ideology opposed to Hoenikker's morally-blind scientific rationalism in *Cat's Cradle* is Bokononism, a mock religion which boasts of its falseness but claims that belief in its tenets is pragmatically essential because life is otherwise intolerable. Vonnegut echoes Voltaire in observing that since God does not exist it is necessary for us to invent him, and adds that we should not let the manifest absurdity of the project deter us in the least. Ice-9 will get us anyway, but there is a chance that some of us, at least, can go out thumbing our noses at the utterly indifferent universe which has sealed our fate.

This kind of catastrophist comedy re-emphasizes the message transmitted by catastrophist tragedy. (This is not surprising, in that the common subject-matter of comedy and tragedy is failure—they merely represent different attitudes to human fallibility.) The argument is that we have failed our children and our children's children, and in so doing we have failed ourselves. We are no longer required to believe that death will deliver us into purgatory or hell for our due punishment, but there remains a special sense in which we can be, and are, damned.

It could be argued that the sins which figure large in modern stories of man-made catastrophism are not so very different from the sins identified by our remote ancestors. Pride, covetousness, sloth and gluttony still make convenient labels to use in connection with Epimethean fantasies, the modern version of the lotus eater mythology, and anticipations of drowning in our own wastes. Mythical parallels are not only easy to draw but rather difficult to avoid. However, there is one vital, and perhaps all-important, difference between the concept of sin which is revealed and propagandised by modern accounts of man-made catastrophe and the concept which figures in the Bible and other ancient mythologies. The character of the sins, insofar as they reveal human propensities for antisocial behaviour, has not changed, but the essential nature of sin itself has.

Our ancestors saw sin in the context of a static order of nature. They conceived of it as a violation of that order—a rebellion against order which would (or, at least, should) call down retribution. Because it was seen as a violation of some kind of rigid framework, sin was held to be *unnatural*. The tendency to sin might be universal—and, indeed, all men might be tainted by it even if they never actually *committed* any sins of their own—but sin was nevertheless a flaw in human nature from which men could (or, at least, should) be redeemed. The Christian mythology of sin is particularly clear in this respect, but this kind of attitude is one of the things which is common to all religious systems.

We no longer see sin as a violation of a natural order, but as part of it. The human propensities which seem to propel individuals and societies toward disaster are now seen to be a *part* of human nature rather than a flaw distorting it. This change of perspective, of course, became inevitable once we realised that we are the product of evolution rather than special creation. We are what circumstances have made us, and what is common to us all must be accepted as a part of what we *are*, not as an accidental deterioration which we suffered after our essential nature was determined. This recognition does not, of course, rule out the possibility of redemption, for if we are the product of past evolution then future evolution might remake us more as we would like to imagine ourselves, but it makes the process of redemption a much more difficult business than we had ever suspected.

The rationalistic philosophy of science claims that knowledge itself is morally neutral, and that the question of what *is* must be separated from the question of what *ought to be*. However, we must observe that even if science does not actually *contain* a moral philosophy, it nevertheless determines what kind of moral philosophy *can* exist. It denies validity to any moral philosophy which seeks to validate its commandments by embedding them in empirical claims, whether such empirical claims are true or false. It catches religious mythologies in a double stranglehold, making their claims false in the simple sense where they are genuine empirical claims, and falsely empirical where they are metaphysical in nature.

The result of this is that the only kind of morality which can genuinely co-exist with and complement systematic scientific knowledge is a pragmatic one, which makes the desirability of ends the sole criterion for the assessment of means. The true beauty of this is that the instrument by which we seek to calculate the outcomes of our present policies in order to discover the ends which we must weigh up, and by which we also seek to extend the repertoire of our available actions in order to widen the range of our possible ends, is scientific knowledge itself. Thus, though a pragmatic moral philosophy can make no claim to *be* science, it nevertheless depends for its potency entirely upon the competence of science. It is no use trying to evaluate an action by its consequences unless you actually have the means of calculating its consequences. Pragmatism cannot exist without science, and science is useful (and hence attractive) only in a pragmatic sense.

The essence of sin, in the age of science, is to be a bad scientist—which is to say, to fail to calculate correctly (and hence to realise fully) the consequences of one's actions. This becomes, in fact, the very nature of sin in a wholly pragmatic world. It seems at first to be a rather harsh and simple-minded doctrine, in that the cardinal sin then becomes stupidity, and the register of deadly sins then becomes a list of different kinds of stupidity. The true situation is, however, more complicated than this, though we have perhaps only recently begun to realise the fact.

In the pre-war mythology of man-made catastrophe investigated in this essay, it is true that the ultimate crime, however it is characterised, is a form of stupidity. The stories of lotus eater societies are perhaps the best example, for what those societies are seen to have abandoned is progress, foresight, and the use of intelligence. What has atrophied in such societies is precisely the capacity to make plans and to set up new goals. In the anti-war stories war is very frequently represented explicitly as a kind of stupidity or a kind of irrationality. If one studies the impassioned speeches made by the sympathetic characters in these stories, while they survey the wreckage of civilization or watch it collapsing about them, there can be no mistaking the consistent indictment of stupidity, and the taken-for-granted belief that if only the world were run intelligently and rationally everything would be all right. In catastrophist stories written outside the science fiction magazine community, the intelligentsia were generally held immune from criticism, though the characterisation of the class differs somewhat between, say, H. G. Wells and Aldous Huxley. In labelled science fiction, there was greater consensus on this matter in that the intelligentsia were more exclusively those educated *in science*.

As we have seen, however, this exemption is made far less frequently in post-war catastrophe stories. There are few people today who could commit themselves to the Wellsian ideal of a state run by technocrats. Stupidity may still be the essence of sin, but we have lost faith in rationality as the overriding virtue.

The reason for this is simple enough. It is all very well for scientific knowledge to function (through technology) as the means of extending our repertoire of actions, and hence of options, and to be the instrument by which we may calculate the consequences of our proposed actions. The trouble is that none of this will help us to decide exactly which ends *are* desirable and which are not. The nineteenth-century rationalists would have been unable to perceive a problem here—man, as the product of evolution, was considered to have his desires "built in" to his nature, and the Utilitarians were quite confident of their ability to add up social equations in terms of "hedonic units" of one kind or another. Even the Utilitarians, however, began to find practical difficulties when they began to weigh up immediate personal gratifications against long-term policies which would generate hedonic satisfactions only for future generations.

Obviously, it would be oversimplifying the case to say that post-war catastrophists discovered this problem, or even that they rediscovered it. What they *have* done, however, is to realise its immediate and urgent significance. For what they are saying, in its essence, is that *our* sin consists of gambling with the happiness of future generations in the pursuit of immediate gratification for ourselves. They say further—and quite rightly—that the intelligent are more to blame in this sense than the stupid, for it is they that have the means to do it. Thus, sin is balanced against sin, and there *is* a curious sense in which, though we are all responsible, we are each in our different ways innocent.

It can readily be seen that this *new* sin, though it is different from the sin of stupidity, is still a sin in the pragmatic sense of the word. It is still a sin of *consequences*, not of violation of nature. It reveals the unanswered question which underlies all pragmatic philosophy: how far must I take my calculation of consequences before pausing to evaluate their desirability? In a crude sense, it has always been known to moral and political philosophers as the question of how much I can take into account benefits which accrue to me if the actions which generate them cause hardship to others. The fact that in cases of man-made catastrophe the others I am forced to worry about include my own children adds a measure of poignancy to the question, but does not alter its character to any great extent.

The main reason why the question seems to be renewed and reinvigorated in these contemporary versions is precisely because the advance of science—the instrument of pragmatism—has ensured that the consequences of our present-day collective actions are so much greater, and that we are better able to calculate them. Along with a greater ability to make disasters has come a greater ability to foresee them. It is this second ability which has generated the immense wealth of recent catastrophist nightmares, but the fact that the stories themselves are "science fiction," making use of techniques of extrapolation in order to make predictions which (we fear) it may be too late to overturn, should not be allowed to distract us from the fact that the problem which they pose for us is not a technical problem but a moral one. In a way, this is a shame, because technical problems have solutions which are "already there," waiting only to be found. If moral problems have "solutions" at all, they have to be created, not merely discovered.

Whether we are "naturally" incapable of such collective creative effort is open to doubt, but one thing is certain: we haven't had much practice.

If we really are going to fail the examination to which circumstances are currently subjecting the human race, that will be the reason.

6

The Rebellion of Nature*

W. Warren Wagar

1. The Red Mother

The improbable scene for one of mankind's numerous last stands against world disaster in science fiction is the quiet agricultural county of Rutland in the English Midlands. New breeds of animals with enhanced intelligence lay siege to villages and small towns. Few people remain in the cities, as supplies of food run low. The new animals, the "paggets," have collaborated to disrupt systems of transport and communications, and the human race is quickly dying out, except for pockets of resistance in places like Nether Saxham, in Rutland, at the country redoubt of Mil Lambert and her brother Don. Mil and Don are principal characters in *The Fittest* (1955) by the Scottish writer J. T. McIntosh; it is neither a great novel, nor a poor one, but wholly representative of that remarkable sub-genre of modern speculative literature, the story of the world's end. *The Fittest* also illustrates the subject of this essay, the fictive end of the world produced by nature: not the nature of Newton or Wordsworth, but the blood-stained nature of Darwin and Clausius, the mother red in tooth and claw who kills her own children or lets them freeze, burn, starve, or drown with perfect indifference.

In Rutland, the paggets attack in waves. Packs of abnormally clever dogs and swarms of voracious rats threaten every stronghold of man. As civil order disintegrates, man himself becomes an enemy to be feared—in particular a gang of half-breeds, drifters, and gypsies who have occupied the abandoned village of Greetham under the rule of a brutal performer from a travelling circus. "But men had fought all

*The author wishes to thank the National Endowment for the Humanities for its award of a Senior Fellowship, during which part of the research for this chapter and its companion, "Round Trips to Doomsday," was completed.

139

through history," as McIntosh notes. "This was the first time men had faced something bigger, more serious than any struggle with their own kind."[1] Of fifty million Britons, barely two-fifths have survived, and their numbers dwindle every day. The rest of the world faces the same fate. No peace is possible between human beings and paggets. Each side "wanted the whole world and will never be satisfied with anything less."[2] Two final battles—since "armageddons" are nearly as obligatory in world's end fiction as grand climactic orgy scenes in pornography—bring the action of the novel to a resounding close. The first features the massacre of the Greetham gang by the triumphantly virtuous forces of Mil and Don, and is closely followed by the even more decisive repulse of a monster raid by pagget-dogs. The battles are turning points. Henceforth, the Rutland community and others like it throughout the world will start man's long climb back to civilization.

But only by beating nature at her own game. McIntosh stresses over and over again the importance for human survival of military discipline and toughness of character. Don finds himself almost happy when his beloved but purely ornamental wife Gloria is killed by paggets in the opening pages of the novel. She could never have made it in the jungle-world created by the paggets, and would have proved a dangerous encumbrance to her husband. Later, he blunders into a similar liaison with a young Rutland woman, Eva. But after her death at the hands of the Greethamite boss, he marries sensibly, choosing a strong-willed born survivor not unlike his own sister, a woman who has learned to kill as dispassionately as any man when she must. The weaklings of the world, Don realizes, are obsolete.

> Because all such people, male and female, young and old, were going to die. Most of them were dead already; any that were left would soon follow. It was the survival of the fittest, and only the fittest. The weak, the stupid, the timorous had gone, were going, and would go the way of Gloria and Eva.[3]

Speaking strictly, *The Fittest* is a story of man-made disaster. The paggets are the unintended outcome of experiments conducted by an American scientist, to test the effects of "different vibrations and radiations on animal tissue and nerve cells."[4] The radical improvement of memory and intelligence that results, the genetic transmission of the improvements to subsequent generations, and the escape of some of the animals from their cages were unforeseen, and perhaps unforeseeable, events. Although the world blames the scientist, McIntosh views him with sympathy. Don and Mil turn out to be the scientist's own children; two others were killed by an angry mob in America. The only villains in the piece are the paggets, whose ferocity is demonic, and the few human beings, like the Greetham gang, who have sunk to their level. Intelligent or not, the paggets are true animals, "with animal motivations, savagery, tradition, and temperament. As such they're automatically enemies of any other creatures which threaten their own survival, particularly men." Human science had merely accelerated a natural process. "They're animals whose brains have been forced a few million years further along the evolutionary highway."[5] In short, despite the role of human carelessness, the ultimate responsibility for the disaster falls on nature. The superior intelligence, stronger will power, and higher moral values of humankind will prevail, in the end, but nature will exact a heavy price, including compliance with the Darwinian laws governing the survival of any species.

Although there are not a few apocalyptic stories like *The Fittest* in which the critic must probe beneath the surface to find where the blame, if any, for the catastrophe properly rests, the great majority do not pose a problem. In some, the fault lies entirely with man himself. In others, nature is clearly to blame. In still others, best illustrated by absurdist science fiction of the "New Wave," responsibility is shared, or of little importance, or beside the point altogether. As one might expect, the catastrophe caused by man predominates in world's end fictions written since 1914. In an inventory of two hundred and fifty literary doomsdays, the present writer has found a two-to-one ratio of man-made to natural catastrophes in stories written since the outbreak of World War I. Before 1914, the ratio is just the opposite: one-to-two. Man's fears of himself have obviously multiplied in this century of total wars and total states, of genocide and ecocide.

But no less obviously, nature has remained a major source of anxiety for writers and readers of science fiction down to the present day. In many quite recent novels, such as *The Sixth Winter* (1979) by Douglas Orgill and John Gribbin—a vivid evocation of a new Ice Age caused by diminished solar radiation and increased volcanic activity— civilized mankind emerges wholly innocent of wrong-doing. To be sure, there is always much more in apocalyptic literature than the apocalypse itself, and its ostensible causes. The contents of the bowls of wrath or the identity of the angels who spill them over the land do not exhaust the significance of our secular books of revelation, any more than they exhaust the significance of the original text, by St. John the Divine. But catastrophes are seldom chosen casually. They tell us a great deal about the value-structures of the modern mind, and they may point to anxieties for which the catastrophe itself serves only a symbolic function.

The psychic estrangement of modern Western man from nature, deplored by romantic critics since Blake, is a central concern of intellectual history. One could write a fairly comprehensive history of modern Western thought hinged on changing ideas of nature, and in particular on the civil war within the intelligentsia between what might be called the naturists and the Promethean humanists. Science fiction is only another battleground of that war, with the Aldous Huxleys and Ray Bradburys on one side, the H. G. Wellses and Isaac Asimovs on the other. It is not surprising to find that most scenarios of world disaster produced by the operation of blind natural forces are the work of writers who tilt toward Promethean (or even absurdist) humanism.

As historians measure time, let us note, this civil war is of comparatively recent origin. In traditional Christian thought, man was the divinely appointed steward of a natural order created for his use and guidance, and no basic conflict between the two was conceivable, except when man rashly abused his stewardship or willfully disobeyed natural law. The Scentific Revolution of the seventeenth and eighteenth centuries made drastic alterations in the man-nature equation, but retained belief in an underlying harmony between the two realms. Both were created by a reasonable Supreme Being, and functioned in accordance with the same mathematically precise laws, which reason—a faculty natural in mankind—fully disclosed without supernatural aid. Once again, it was only when man ignorantly or willfully defied nature and nature's reason that he got himself into trouble.

But the logical and historical paradoxes of the postulated harmony of man and nature proved overwhelming to many of the most original minds of the late eighteenth and early nineteenth centuries. David Hume and Immanuel Kant exposed the fallacy of confusing the empirical "is" with the ethical "ought," destroying the rational foundations of natural law ethics and the concept of natural rights. They also set severe limits on the power of human science and pure reason to know the world as it really is. At the same time, moralists began asking why, in a presumably harmonious world, the study of history revealed so much folly, ignorance, crime, and suffering. The great Lisbon earthquake of 1755, which took sixty thousand lives, prompted questions about the rationality and essential goodness of nature, and nature's God. Voltaire's philosophical poem "The Disaster of Lisbon" (1756) and his inimitable story of *Candide* (1759), as everyone knows, were expressions of the growing uneasiness of the European mind with the claims of rationalism early in the second half of the eighteenth century. In retrospect they seem to mark a turning point, the beginning of a massive disillusionment that did not reach its apogee until the next century, or perhaps our own.

Another sign of things to come was the debate in moral philosophy between those who agreed with the somewhat scandalous Bernard de Mandeville and those who agreed with the third Earl of Shaftesbury, on the question of the relationship between self-interest and the public good. Mandeville had argued in *The Fable of the Bees* (1714) that the foundation of a commercial society was the rigorous pursuit by individuals of their own self-interest. Private vice, as it were, led to public virtue. Shaftesbury and his followers, such as Francis Hutcheson, postulated a moral sense deeply embedded in man that inclined him to acts of selfless good. At the often unseen heart of the debate lay the problem of whether man was good by nature, and whether nature herself was good. The whole issue was recapitulated in French thought in the controversy between the rational egoism of Helvétius and the romantic altruism of Diderot. Mandeville's perspectives ultimately triumphed in the political economy of Adam Smith and Parson Malthus, which held that the relentless search for private gain was, indeed, the mainspring of national well-being. The good Parson, of course, added some sobering thoughts about the balance of nature not to be found in the romantic poets who were his contemporaries. At about the same time, in an ingenious defense of criminal psychopathology, the Marquis de Sade put forth his own vision of the balance that made war, famine, plague, and sexual murder invaluable games in nature's colosseum show, to keep populations under control.

What makes Sade especially interesting is the way he pushed his arguments to outrageous (but never illogical) extremes that, in the end, disgusted even Sade himself. Anyone who takes the trouble to toil through the interminable dialogues of his pornographic novels will find a loathing for the immorality of nature, and (for that matter) the immorality of the Creator of nature, that carries the implications of the case against the innate goodness of nature much further than any other thinker of his time dared to go. For Sade, private vice led only to public vice, a drama of wolves and lambs tht kept the show open at a price which no amount of moralizing humbug could conceal from the enlightened philosopher.

As the natural sciences continued their progress in the late eighteenth and early nineteenth centuries, they arrived at views of the ways of nature in close consonance with the most radical thoughts of the most impudent moralists, metaphysicians, and political economists of the Enlightenment. The world-model of Newtonian science had stressed mathematical order, harmony, uniformity, and stability. Much of the newer science found a place for struggle and disaster. As efforts were made to reconstruct the natural history of the earth and its life forms, it became necessary to account for the accumulating evidence of geology and paleontology that the earth was not always as it appeared today. For example, how could one explain fossils of marine creatures found on high ground, creatures that in some instances had no living descendants? Such evidence pointed to great disasters in the earth's history, disasters that had resulted in the extinction of species, and the creation of new ones. Even the planets themselves might, in the speculations of the Comte de Buffon, have resulted from a tremendous catastrophe, the near-collision of the sun with a comet, causing the ejection of solar material that had in turn condensed into planetary bodies. Buffon's ideas became unfashionable for a time, but were revived in the late nineteenth century by A. W. Bickerton and others, and dominated astronomical thought for generations.

Meanwhile, catastrophism grew rapidly into a new orthodoxy in geology, with the chief controversies centering only on whether the great world-cataclysms that had produced the geological eras of the past were floods, earthquakes, volcanic eruptions, or some combination of these. Georges Cuvier, the major geologist of the first third of the nineteenth century, effected a synthesis of catastrophist thinking that collapsed after his death but left an indelible impression on the public and scientific mind. Even when geologists no longer accepted catastrophism as a universal causal explanation, the fact of relatively sudden changes in the climate, topography, and flora and fauna of the earth at various points in natural history remained well established. Other formidable discoveries, such as those of Cuvier's pupil Louis Agassiz, gave us the idea of successive eras of glaciation, or "ice ages."

The second half of the nineteenth century brought to light fresh horrors: Rudolf Clausius's second law of thermodynamics, the "heat-death" of the universe, along with the prediction by Hermann von Helmholtz of the inevitable cooling of the sun in a matter of hundreds of thousands, or, in later revised estimates, ten million years; Charles Darwin's picture of the origin of species through the ruthless natural selection of random variations; and the discovery by Louis Pasteur and others of the microbiological jungle that spawns disease and pestilence. Fuller knowledge of comets, meteors, stellar novae, and other deadly wonders of outer space fed the imagination of disaster as well. Any writer of fiction could draw the obvious moral: nature was not the anthropomorphic mother of romantic myth or the mighty whirling mechanism of Newtonian physics, but a stage of endless slaughter and catastrophe. Anything that had happened before could happen again, here and now; and at best the whole universe was sinking by degrees into the cool calamity of heat-death.

Yet it is arguable that none of the theories and discoveries of science between, say, 1750 and 1900, would have caused more than brief alarm if not for one other event: the event that Friedrich Nietzsche billed in *The Joyful Wisdom* as the death of God. The steady decay of Jewish and Christian faith after the middle of the eighteenth century deprived nature of her divine origins and purposes. Natural disasters could no longer be viewed in any literal sense as "acts of God," as punishments or tests of man imposed by an ultimately loving Father for his own ultimately good ends. Except for those whose faith remained intact or who subscribed to any of the various idealist or vitalist cosmologies that in effect turned nature herself into a god, the disasters of the natural order were simply disasters, the blind and brutal doings of an intrinsically pointless universe.

Thomas Henry Huxley—agnostic, humanist, man of science—crystallized the thoughts of thousands of his contemporaries in 1894 when he declared war on the "cosmic process." Nature's ways, he wrote, should never be man's. What lay before the human race was "a constant struggle to maintain and improve, in opposition to the State of Nature, the State of Art of an organized polity." The natural instinct of "unlimited self-assertion" disclosed by Darwin, the biological equivalent of original sin, had to be replaced by morality, the love of the common good, "until the evolution of our globe shall have entered so far upon its downward course that the cosmic process resumes its sway; and once more, the State of Nature prevails over the surface of our planet."[6] In that same year, 1894, Huxley's one-time biology student H. G. Wells was preaching a similar sermon in his own way, in *The Time Machine*. Their views on the relationship between man and nature in a godless cosmos were nearly identical.

The twentieth century, for all its incredible proliferation of science and scientists, has not yielded any fundamental reconstruction of the world-picture assembled by Darwin and Helmholtz and all the other luminaries of science from the period just discussed. Or rather, it has yielded no fundamental reconstruction of the empirical basis for Huxley's concept of man's distance from nature. Nor has what Basil

Willey once described as "the secular drift" slowed appreciably, in spite of all sorts of ingenious theological contortions and seasons of revived religiosity. The majority of thinking men and women in the Western world throughout this century, as in the latter part of the preceding century, have been agnostics, atheists, or believers so passive and confused that their belief counts for little.

In biology the Darwinian synthesis has held firm in its essentials, notwithstanding great progress in genetics, and a considerable broadening and deepening of the fossil record. Such apocalyptic events as the sudden disappearance of the dinosaurs at the end of the Cretaceous period or the glaciation of the Pleistocene epoch are better known, but still not definitively explained. Astronomers have extended the life of the sun by several billion years, showing that it will grow much hotter (in its "red giant" phase) before it eventually cools, but it remains mortal all the same, along with its brood of planets. New cosmic catastrophes such as supernovae, black holes, and the "Big Bang" that is plausibly theorized to have created our universe some fifteen billion years ago and may launch the next universe after entropy has done its inevitable worst, supply the eschatological imagination with all sorts of nourishment, beyond what nineteenth-century astronomers had to offer. Yet the new theories and data have not appreciably altered the values of the man-nature equations. The tension between the two remains as before, a point reinforced by the psychology of Sigmund Freud, with its disturbing analysis of the unconscious as a treacherous swamp of raw natural energies that poisons our dreams and demands relentless monitoring and control by society, or by the reasoning ego, or both.

The tension between man and nature is seldom a central theme of twentieth-century philosophy, but only because most modern philosophers have learned to despair of finding useable truth in the natural order. Twentieth-century positivism has expressly proscribed the grounding of ethical, metaphysical, or aesthetic values in scientific knowledge. The existentialist rebellion of the middle decades of the century, at least in the version promulgated by Jean-Paul Sartre, turned away from nature in almost the same measure as the positivists. For Sartre nature belongs to the realm of *l'en-soi*, being in itself, being that exists without will or freedom, being that is opaque, silent, sickening. The art and literature produced under the influence of existentialism adds its own voice. *The Plague* (1947), Albert Camus's masterpiece, uses an outbreak of bubonic plague as a symbol of all the evil and adversity in the world of experience, natural and man-made alike, which must be fought tirelessly in battles that are always followed by yet more battles. The same treatment of nature as emblematic of the massive dehumanizing stupidity of *l'en-soi* appears in Eugène Ionesco's absurdist play *Rhinoceros* (1960). As Percy Shelley's skylark, in the familiar ode, supplies an example of man's efforts to bring the human and the natural together, so Ionesco's pachyderm is a grotesquely apt symbol of their estrangement.

But the summing-up must be left to the twentieth century's greatest English-speaking philosopher, Bertrand Russell. The world that science offers us, Russell wrote in "A Free Man's Worship," is a world without purpose or meaning. Man is an accident, and all the noonday brightness of his genius is "destined to extinction in the vast death of the solar system. . . . Blind to good and evil, reckless of destruction, omnipotent matter rolls on its relentless way." Man's only recourse is proud defiance. He must keep his mind free "from the wanton tyranny that rules his outward life" and, certain of no help from gods, he must sustain alone, "a weary but unyielding Atlas, the world that his own ideals have fashioned despite the trampling march of unconscious power."[7] The prose is a shade too purple and the sense of disillusionment a little too sharp, but Russell's words still reach us, and they help define the frame of thought responsible for many of the century's literary apocalypses.

2. The End of Time

The largest public disaster available to the literary imagination, or any other, is cataclysm in the heavens. When the sun no longer shines or the sky falls, we are well and truly lost. In Revelation, many of the afflictions visited on man in the last days are cosmic, including flaming stars that strike the earth, the darkening of one-third of the sun and the moon and the stars, solar flares hot enough to burn men, and a rain of hailstones like boulders. The final disaster occurs on the Day of Judgment, when "earth and heaven vanished away, and no place was left for them" (20:11). The end comes, as in Fritz Leiber's vignette "Last" (1957), with the extinction of space and time themselves. But in the Biblical end, as opposed to Leiber's, disaster is followed at once by renewal. A new heaven and a new earth appear in glory, and man passes from time into eternity, saved or damned.

One of the first attempts to envisage a secular end of the world in modern literature is a curious poem by Lord Byron. His "Darkness" (1816) is steeped in a fine romantic melancholy far removed in mood and substance from any book of the Bible. Anticipating the worst fears of nineteenth-century astronomy, Byron dreams of a future age of eternal night. The sun has burned out, the moon has disappeared, and men have set fire to their cities and forests in a crazed lust for light. Famine soon arrives, so acute that "even dogs assailed their masters," except one paragon of canine loyalty, who guards the corpse of his owner, moaning and licking its unresponsive hand. Transformed into skeletons, the last men shriek at the sight of one another and die "of their mutual hideousness." Finally, no one remains. The earth is a lifeless lump. The seas, without tides, waves, winds, or sailors, stand still, and the whole universe is devoured by Darkness.

The theme of the end of the world and the "last man" became a minor cliché of romantic literature in the years after Byron's poem, culminating in Mary Shelley's turgid novel, *The Last Man* (1826).[8] As art, none of the works concerned deserves more than passing notice, but the daring of their implicit rejection (in most instances) of a cardinal tenet of Christian belief, indeed the greater part of Christian eschatology, is something else again. Also notable is their attitude toward nature. Whether the end comes through disorders of heaven and earth, or through pestilence, it is a doom pronounced by nature, in which man has no responsibility. The last men, metaphors for the loneliness, alienation, and world-weariness that belonged as much to romanticism as the sweet striving pantheism for which its is better remembered today, are victims, not villains. Disaster strikes in Shelley's novel at just the time when mankind has never been so well ruled, and never so happy, with every reasonable expectation of further progress. In Byron's poem, the sun dies more or less suddenly, without warning. Mankind is stripped of all its dignity and hope by a sequence of disasters so pitiless that the sympathetic reader can feel only anger against the universe.

Even in the prototypical tale of the world's end by a romantic writer, J.-B. Cousin de Grainville's *Le Dernier homme* (*The Last Man*, 1805), the work of a priest who clung to the bare essentials of Christian eschatology, it is nature rather than man that fails in earth's declining years. Byron may well have read Grainville's novel, published in England in 1806. The Frenchman's sun does not die altogether, but it grows pale and weak. Crops no longer flourish and mankind itself gradually becomes sterile. Personified as *le génie terrestre*, nature fights back, using trickery to encourage earth's last fertile couple to reproduce, but it is no use. When the last man resists temptation, reversing the original sin of Adam, God lets the world come to a merciful end. The final pages of Grainville's romance safeguard the core of the Biblical message, but most of the novel wears a quite different face. After foolish wars and a time when earth's resources were consumed too rapidly, mankind has settled down to a wise maturity. What spoils everything is the fading, truculent, senile natural order, which cannot even manage to die gracefully.

The theme of the death of the sun was revived, with closer attention to what astrophysics had to say on the subject, in many scientific romances of the 1890s and 1900s. By this time, entropy was an established and familiar principle, and understanding of the phases of stellar evolution was well enough advanced to lend the authority of science to stories of the world's end by natural causes. Essayists also harped on earth's inevitable doom, notably Anatole France in the now forgotten pages of his fin-de-siècle classic, *Le Jardin d'Épicure (The Garden of Epicurus,* 1894), where he paints with a few sure strokes the picture of a cold earth and its wretched human survivors, fallen into savagery. Again, nature is to blame. Men think they can progress forever, but the quality of their lives, not to mention survival itself, depends on a delicate balance of sunlight and moisture.

> One day the last of them, beyond hatred or love, will expel the last human breath into the hostile air. And the Earth will continue to roll, bearing through silent space the ashes of humanity, the poems of Homer and the august remains of the marbles of Greece, clinging to her frozen flanks.[9]

In fiction the one passage that sticks in everyone's memory appears near the end of Wells's *The Time Machine,* where the Time Traveller leaves the degenerate future society of the Eloi and Morlocks to visit the last days of earth. The planet no longer rotates, and the sun is red and cool, motionless on the western horizon. In this eternal twilight, man no longer exists. The Time Traveller watches giant crabs crawling across a lurid beach, beside a still sea, until—thousands of years later—even the crabs have disappeared, the thin air is bitter cold, and the only motion he detects is that of a black thing with tentacles, "hopping fitfully about." All the images are of death and dying: the blood-red color of the sun, its position low in the western sky, the terminal symbolism of the beach, the chilling silence, the "evil" eyes and hungry mouth of the crab-monster as it moves to attack our hero, the blackness of a total solar eclipse that takes place during the last moments of his journey. Wells also discussed the demise of the solar system in a sketch entitled "The Man of the Year Million" (1893). Here, a global brotherhood of enlightened supermen with enormous brains puts up a brave fight against the encroaching cold from its strongholds deep in the earth. The surface of the planet is thickly mantled with ice and all life there is extinct. As the Utopian spokesman Urthred remarks in Wells's *Men Like Gods* (1923), responding to the criticism that Utopia is too "artificial,"

> These Earthlings do not yet dare to see what our Mother Nature is. . . .
> They do not see that except for our eyes and wills, she is purposeless and
> blind. She is not awful, she is horrible. . . . She made us by accident; all
> her children are bastards—undesired; she will cherish or expose them,
> pet or starve or torment without rhyme or reason. She does not heed, she
> does not care.[10]

All of Wells's writing, from the earliest stories and essays to the dark reflections in *Mind at the End of Its Tether* (1946), was only a set of variations on this basic Huxleyan theme. Life consisted of a deadly struggle against nature, and against the residues of nature in man. Extinction always waited just around the corner.[11]

The device of the terminal redoubt, the last home of man in a dying universe, with its inevitable suggestion of heroic humanity pitted against hideous nature, turns up in several fin-de-siècle romances in addition to Wells's "The Man of the Year Million." Gabriel de Tarde, the French sociologist, left behind after his death the manuscript of a fascinating *Fragment d'histoire future* (*Fragment of Future History*, translated as *Underground Man*, 1905) in which a prosperous and united mankind is struck down at the peak of its glory by a kind of solar anemia. Little heat reaches earth from the sun, and a remnant of the human race flees underground to take advantage of the warmth near the planetary core, building a utopia that relies for its well-being on strict birth control.

The masterpiece of "last redoubt" stories is surely *The Night Land* (1912) by William Hope Hodgson. Primarily a writer of fantasy whose life was cut short on a battlefield of World War I, Hodgson avoided the supernatural almost entirely in this formidable work of science fiction. Even the few trappings of the conventional horror story that survive—mysterious forces of good and evil that have broken through "the Barrier of Life"—can be explained away as beings from another universe, although Hodgson supplies few clues regarding their identity. In any event, they hold one another in check, and most of the action of the novel consists of a straightforward battle between the men and women of a vast redoubt and the unimaginable harshness of nature in the endtime.

The setting of Hodgson's novel is several million years from now, when the sun no longer shines at all. The earth's surface has grown too cold to support life, but one hundred miles below the surface in a "valley" created by the cracking of the planet in an earlier disaster, the last human beings live in the Pyramid, a metal marvel of science eight miles high powered by a force known only as the "Earth-Current." The land around the Pyramid, the Night Land, is warmed by volcanic fire-holes. But its inhabitants are monsters. Some, like the Night Hounds, are entirely non-human, but the majority of creatures encountered by Hodgson's unnamed young hero are devolved human beings, "mixt and made monstrous or diverse by foul or foolish breeding . . . dread Monsters that did be both Man and Beast."[12] The hero must do battle with several kinds of these beast-men, who have in common only their brutish ferocity. For all practical purposes they are wild animals.

The labyrinth of the plot, and the convolutions of the quasi-archaic syntax used by Hodgson to suggest a distant age, need not trouble us here. Admiring *The Night Land* requires a specialized literary taste and a vulnerability to old-fashioned love stories that are combined in few readers, and fewer readers still of science fiction. But it is a unique work, informed by an imagination no less potent than that of Wells, and conveying an almost Wellsian message. Science, courage, and common effort will keep mankind alive even after the sun fails and earth has become a reasonable facsimile of hell.

Several years before publishing *The Night Land*, Hodgson reached the endtime in another major novel, *The House on the Borderland* (1908), in which the protagonist has a vision of the death of the sun. As the earth whitens with eternal snow, the sun turns darker and darker shades of red, growing colder all the while. The other stars die too, until nothing remains but two enormous central suns symbolizing the good and evil in the cosmos. Despite Wellsian touches purloined from *The Time Machine*, this earlier novel stands closer in technique and world view to Olaf Stapledon's *Star Maker* than to any work of Wells.

For historians of science, and its popularization, a fin-de-siècle literary relic of special interest is *La Fin du monde* (*The End of the World*, translated as *Omega: The Last Days of the World*, 1893), by Camille Flammarion, discussed above in "Round Trips to Doomsday."[13] There is no better informed story of the world's end through solar extinction than Flammarion's. The author was a professional astronomer and science writer. His *Popular Astronomy*, first

published in 1880, became one of the best-known books of its kind in
the Western world, and in *La Fin du monde* he presents a story of the
solar system ten million years from now that draws liberally on his
knowledge of nineteenth-century astronomy. Once again, mankind is
toppled just as it has gained complete mastery of itself and of nature.
Cold and drought drive it back to savagery except for two equatorial
cities of iron and glass, the last heroic redoubts of a doomed race,
situated in the dry beds of the former Pacific and Indian Oceans.

As astrophysicists shifted in the twentieth century to a quite
different theory of the sun's energy source from that of Helmholtz, and
as the new 100-inch telescope at Mount Wilson disclosed the existence
of other galaxies than our own, the probable amount of space and time
in the universe was enlarged beyond anything imagined in Flammarion's day. Not only did the remaining life predicted for the sun
increase by a factor of one thousand, but it became possible for the first
time to construct theoretical models of the history and future of the
entire universe on the basis of detailed knowledge of stellar and
galactic evolution through billions of years. Oddly, or perhaps not so
oddly, eschatological science fiction continued to present visions of the
end of all things, undaunted by the hugely expanded time-scale of the
new astronomy.

To stories of the death of the sun were soon added stories of the
death of the galaxy or the universe of galaxies. Many of these offer
cyclical concepts of universal collapse and resurrection, and like *La
Fin du monde* are discussed in "Round Trips to Doomsday." They
include Olaf Stapledon's *Star Maker*, James Blish's *The Triumph of
Time*, Brian Aldiss's *Galaxies like Grains of Sand*, Michael Moorcock's *The End of All Songs*, and George Zebrowski's *Macrolife*. All
are fundamentally hopeful fictions, of the heroic survival of man
through the eons and the continuation or rebirth of life in the next
cycle and even beyond. In one such novel, Poul Anderson's *Tau Zero*
(1970), the death and rebirth of the universe shrinks to the dimension
of a mere episode in the flight to safety of a man and his spaceship, a
flight that Joe de Bolt and John R. Pfeiffer call "a direct metaphor for
the myth of progress—advance or die."[14] The entropic disintegration
of the cosmos becomes just one more hurdle that the natural order
places in the way of negentropic man.

Entropy is a concept of many uses, a point further illustrated by
Pamela Zoline's often reprinted New Wave story, "The Heat Death of
the Universe" (1967), which mingles notes on entropy with glimpses of
the nervous breakdown of an embattled housewife. But in the realm of

purely apocalyptic fiction, the failure of earth's own sun remains a popular agency of disaster, as it was in the nineteenth century. One of the supremely imaginative works in this category is *Hothouse* (1962, in the United States as *The Long Afternoon of Earth*), Brian Aldiss's novel of life one billion years from now, when the sun has begun to enter its "red giant" stage, expanding and turning earth into a tropical nightmare. As in James Blish's "The Thing in the Attic," from *The Seedling Stars* (1957), the men of the future are a vastly altered race of agile creatures no bigger than monkeys, who live in trees. But in Blish, the tree folk are "Adapted Men," deliberately engineered by human scientists as part of a program to enable mankind to colonize alien worlds. In Aldiss, they are the product of devolution. Earth's changing climate and the rise of many deadly new varieties of plant and insect life have destroyed civilization. The devolved green-skinned descendants of *Homo sapiens* shelter in the branches of a banyan tree that covers a whole continent on the daylight side of the no longer rotating planet. Their simple matriarchal life calls to mind the Indians of the Amazon or the Papuans of New Guinea.

But existence is far more hazardous in Aldiss's future world than anywhere on earth today. Death is a daily event, inflicted chiefly by a fantastic array of carnivorous and poisonous jungle plants—the wiltmilts, the killerwillows, the bellyelms, the trappersnappers, and many others. The overheated earth "was no longer a place for mind. It was a place for growth, for vegetables . . . green in tooth and claw," full of "idiot hatred of all life but [their] own."[15] Human life has become as cheap as that of flies or ants today, and nearly every other mammalian species has long since met with extinction. "Over everything, indifferent begetter of all this carnage, shone the sun."[16]

As wary readers might have expected, Aldiss offers them a hero who rebels against the system and cuts loose from the tribe to seek better things. Accompanied by an adoring female, the young male Gren strikes out on his own. He enters into a symbiotic relationship with a mutated morel, the one species of plant life that has specialized in intelligence, albeit "the sharp and limited intelligence of the jungle."[17] The morel dazzles Gren with visions of restored greatness for humanity. Progress will resume, and men will be "like gods."

It is all a sinister swindle. The morel plans to use its human hosts to help establish a morel empire that will literally cover the whole earth, filling every hill and valley. Later in the story Gren encounters an intelligent dolphin who has enslaved three human beings and who frees him from the power of the morel in hopes of adding him to his retinue. Gren evades the dolphin's clutches, and the morel in turn seizes telepathic control of the dolphin, just as it had once controlled Gren. The combined knowledge of morel and dolphin yields a fuller understanding of what has happened to life on earth and what its future will be. The galactic fluxes that determine the cycles of stars, the morel reveals, also dominate those of life. As the sun has devolved, so have the biological orders. "All life is tending toward the mindless, the infinitesimal."[18] The sun will become a nova in a few more human generations, thereafter collapsing into a white dwarf, and earth will be seared clean of life. Using the dolphin as its host, the morel persuades a group of forest folk to accompany it on a voyage into outer space in the belly of a gigantic vegetable spider capable of interplanetary flight, to find a "good fresh place" among the stars.

Gren declines the morel's invitation to join its expedition. Nature is bringing matters to a close, and he will submit to its ways after all. "With a wonderful gladness in his heart, Gren looked down into the leafy depths of the forest."[19] He and his wife and child will go home, where they belong. He will leave to others the striving for glory in a latter-day cosmos. Be it ever so vicious, there's no place like home.

Hothouse is a curious amalgam of fables both for and against Darwin's nature. As much as in any work of speculative fiction ever written, nature figures as a ferocious killer of man. The sun, which has turned man into a diminutive savage, will soon incinerate him. Meanwhile, his life is menaced at every turn by sun-bred horrors of the vegetable kingdom, who have replaced him as lords and masters of the planet. At the same time, Gren's final decision to return to the forest ecology, together with the casting of the only highly intelligent beings—the morel and the dolphin—as shrewd amoral slave-masters, argues for an almost romantic acceptance of nature, warts and all. When it is no longer possible, in the appointed course of things, to continue the struggle, wisdom counsels acceptance. Those who contend that postwar British writers, like Aldiss, are especially fond of eschatological themes because World War II put an end to British world ascendancy, may wish to see in *Hothouse* a parable about the weariness of poor old Albion. Be this as it may, Brian Aldiss has written a strangely beautiful story about nature's power, man's limits, and earth's mortality.

3. Disorders of Heaven and Earth

What we have seen so far are chiefly entropic doomsdays, set at the end of earth's history, or at the close of cosmic time. Nature has, so to speak, worn out. Such is not always the case in stories of the world's end through natural causes. What should one make, for example, of stories of the sun that "goes nova" in the near future (disregarding, for the moment, the extreme unlikelihood of such an event, according to modern astrophysical theory)? Visions of the end of the world in a blaze of solar glory are common in short fiction, such as William Tenn's "The Custodian" (1953) and Edmond Hamilton's "Requiem" (1962). In both, mankind itself is not endangered, but has left for outer space ahead of the event, as it also does, much to the astonishment of would-be alien saviors, in Arthur C. Clarke's "Rescue Party" (1946). Such "novae" belong to another class of universal cataclysms, the sudden disasters that occur in modern times, as opposed to the predictable last stages of cosmic or solar evolution. Again, science is called in to provide rational explanations of the endtime. These disasters are further divisible into two sub-groups, the astronomical and the geological, although the line between them is often pretty fuzzy, and the difference matters little.

In a way, stories of this sort reflect a deeper pessimism about Mother Nature than those dealing with the longer term. Just as death in old age seems far less a tragedy than in youth, so the near-future world cataclysm gives nature a still more ruthless face than the endtimes of entropy. Consider Wells's "The Star" (1897), which draws a striking contrast between the everyday world of humanity, going about its essentially innocent business, and the random destructiveness of a rogue planet that invades the solar system, blunders into Neptune, burns white-hot from the force of the collision, and nearly wrecks the earth with heat, floods, storms, and other calamities as it hurtles by. The first scientist to foresee the catastrophe looks up at the star, then still far away,

> as one might look into the eyes of a brave enemy. "You may kill me," he said after a silence. "But I can hold you—and all the universe for that matter—in the grip of this little brain. I would not change. Even now."[20]

Man's mind is defiant, even if his body is helpless against the immense brute force of the cosmos. In a more tender vein, Alfred Coppel shows the selfless love of a father for his daughters as solar flares threaten earth in "Last Night of Summer" (1954), and Richard Matheson describes the mutually forgiving love of a rebellious son and his mother on the eve of the world's destruction by an intruding star in "The Last Day" (1953).

But the sudden celestial calamity often gives scope for Promethean heroism, as in Clarke's "Rescue Party." The theme of sur-

vival against great odds has always been a stock-in-trade of adventure
fiction of all kinds, and it seldom works better than in the imaginary
confrontations of men with the heavens themselves. A representative
American story from the earlier days of science fiction is *The Second
Deluge* (1912) by Garrett P. Serviss. One of the founders of the
American Astronomical Society and the author of popular books and
articles on astronomy, Serviss approached life in the "can-do" spirit of
the Progressive Era, joining enthusiasm for science and technology
with an elitist social reformism similar to Wells's. His sequel to *The
War of the Worlds*, in which no less a personage than Thomas Alva
Edison enables mankind to carry the war to the enemy's home planet,
was published in 1898 as *Edison's Conquest of Mars*. *The Second
Deluge*, another novel of technological derring-do, was inspired by the
visit of Halley's Comet in 1910. Here, the menace comes not from
Martians but from a "spiral nebula" full of water that dumps six miles
of rain on the planet, drowning even Mount Everest. The scientific
Noah who rescues a remnant of mankind in his metal ark is Cosmo
Versál, an independently wealthy genius and an irascible realist. He
alone correctly foresees the coming doom, and he alone takes rational
steps to survive it. Scientists, "the true leaders . . . trained in the right
method," constitute the largest single group of individuals handpicked
by Cosmo for his ark.[21] An upthrust of dry land in Colorado becomes
the base of a manly new America, supplied with atomic energy by the
invention of one of Cosmo's protégés and purified by a program of
systematic eugenics taught by Cosmo himself. Despite the worst that
nature could do, the new race of mankind will be "far superior, in
every respect, to the old world that was drowned."[22]

American-style heroics are also the order of the day in the best-
known stories of cosmic disaster from the 1930s, Edwin Balmer and
Philip Wylie's *When Worlds Collide* (1933) and its sequel *After Worlds
Collide* (1934); and in the most persuasive of "comet" novels, *Lucifer's Hammer* (1977), by Larry Niven and Jerry Pournelle, in which the
forces of science and reason win their armageddon against cannibalistic Luddite fanatics in what remains of California after the head of a
comet wipes out most of civilization. J. T. McIntosh settles a hardy
remnant of mankind on Mars as an upsurge of solar activity renders the
earth uninhabitable in *One in Three Hundred* (1954). Celtic heroism
wins the laurels in Fred and Geoffrey Hoyle's *The Inferno* (1973),
when only the Scottish Highlands and a few other far northern areas
weather the cooking of the planet by a tremendous explosion at the
center of the galaxy. The Hoyles give mankind added assistance from a

mysterious super-being (not God), who reduces earth's temperature
in the nick of time before all life dies. But the unmistakable hero of the
story is a Gaelic-speaking Scottish physicist. He undergoes a kind of
racial reversion to Highland clan chieftain when civilization disintegrates, but he also retains many of its values in confrontations with less
humane rivals.

Tougher still in many ways are the heroes of the novels of
Edmund Cooper, an Englishman with working-class experience who is
the despair of liberal critics and feminists of all stripes, but a powerful
writer nonetheless, and an unflinching spokesman for some of the
most characteristic ideals of modern Western civilization. His defense
of modernity receives its fullest expression in *The Cloud Walker*
(1973), set in a distant future after ruinous world wars, but for his
perspectives on man's place in nature, a better text is *All Fools' Day*
(1966). The catastrophe in *All Fools' Day* is not of man's doing. In the
summer of 1971, a new kind of sunspot makes its appearance, emitting
a hitherto unknown variety of radiation ominously named after the last
letter of the Greek alphabet. The "Omega" rays produce only one
serious effect: people of normal emotional and mental health feel an
irresistible compulsion to commit suicide. As the radiation intensifies
through the 1970s, the suicide rate increases correspondingly, until
three billion people have died at their own hands. In the British Isles,
only one hundred and fifty thousand inhabitants remain out of fifty
million, and all of these are "emotionally disturbed—the cranks, the
misfits, the fanatics, the obsessionals, the geniuses, the idiots, the
harmless eccentrics, the homicidal maniacs, the saints and sinners
extraordinary who had never found peace or happiness or understanding in an ordinary world."[23] They call themselves the "transies," short
for "transnormals." Everywhere on earth, it is All Fools' Day. And
everywhere on earth, the sudden demographic collapse and the insta-
bility of the survivors have put an end to civil society.

Cooper sets his story first in London and then in Norfolk, where
his hero, an advertising executive and poet manqué, finds a safe haven
in a cottage on a small island. It is now 1981, and England is a jungle,
ruled by packs of dogs and rats, by herds of wild pigs, and by bands of
madmen. The scenes of gang rape, mass murder, and animal attack are
as terrifying as any in science fiction, topped off by a remarkably
graphic account of a forest battle between pigs and rats witnessed by
the hero from a tree. There is also a vivid scene in the British Museum,
where the library has been "converted into a vast cosmopolis of nests
for vermin." The hero expresses surprise "at how much of history

could be eaten—and probably not only by insects and animals. But then, he reflected grimly, life was essentially cannibalistic."[24]

Salvation follows. The former advertising executive lives to collect a group of the most humane survivors who repair to Cornwall, transform it into an easily defended base of operations, and from their Cornish stronghold slowly advance eastward, conquering England county by county. The transies grow old. Their sane, normal children begin to build a new civilization on foundations of science and reason. In July, 2011, the hero dies just after dawn with happy memories of his beloved. "It was a fine summer morning, promising a long warm day."[25]

Cooper's message is straightforward. Without the firm governing voice of reason, man cannot prevent his natural impulses from turning him into a murderous lunatic. Without the interference of man, the natural world of plants and animals swiftly becomes a slaughterhouse. Even man's best friend, the dog, degenerates into a deadly killer as soon as he no longer feels the leash around his neck. As for the sun, the arbitrary assassin of nearly the whole human race, what else can one expect of the universe?

Needless to say, not all writers who complain about the hostility of nature share Cooper's faith in man's power to restore order when nature runs amok. In R. C. Sherriff's *The Hopkins Manuscript* (1939), mankind survives the fall of the moon to earth despite widespread devastation, only to destroy itself in wars over the mineral rights to the lunar debris that now fills half the Atlantic Ocean. Still other scenarios find nature guilty of pointless violence but emphasize man's selfishness, cruelty, and heightened estrangement from his fellows under the pressure of calamity: notably, the cycle of four great eschatological novels by J. G. Ballard, *The Wind from Nowhere* (1962), *The Drowned World* (1962), *The Drought* (1965), and *The Crystal World* (1966). In each of the Ballard novels except *The Drought*, the ostensible cause of the catastrophe is astrophysical, but the author's main concern is with man himself, and in particular with what he calls the "death of affect." The heroes of his endtimes are monsters of *apatheia* who survey bloody nature and her victims with indifference until they become willing victims themselves. But their surrenders are not meant to be taken at face value; each is a metaphor of psychic change too far below waking consciousness for realistic description. In all of Ballard's work, as David Pringle concludes, "nature is essentially alien to man."[26]

The remaining group of natural disasters in the literature of doomsday that deserves notice in this section is the geological: ends of civilization or the world brought about by convulsions of the earth itself. Such ends are the oldest of all, going back to the myth of the Flood preserved in the *Epic of Gilgamesh* and in Genesis. Worldwide floods are relatively common in science fiction, with earthquakes, vulcanism, droughts, and ice ages rounding out the list. Again, catastrophe may be used to help argue the case for a cyclical view of history, for heroic humanism, or for tragic or absurdist pessimism, with nature in each instance cast as the bludgeoning destroyer, huge and implacable.

Some of the better examples of cyclicism in tales of geological disaster are discussed in "Round Trips to Doomsday." Among these are Jules Verne's posthumously published story of cycles of world flooding, *L'Éternel Adam*, and M. P. Shiel's *The Purple Cloud*, in which the agency of destruction is a lethal gas vented into the atmosphere by the eruption of a volcano. S. Fowler Wright hints at a cyclical view of world history in his novels *Deluge* (1928) and *Dawn* (1929), and James Blish offers a more explicitly cyclical history of the future involving successive ice ages in *Midsummer Century* (1972).

For uncomplicated heroism, in a plot that may have been filched from *The Purple Cloud*, nothing in early science fiction outstrips George Allan England's interminable saga of manly struggle against nature, *Darkness and Dawn* (1914). Also noteworthy, if lower-keyed, are John Christopher's novel of Londoners valiantly coping with a new Ice Age in *The World in Winter* (1962), his scenario of global destruction through earthquakes in *A Wrinkle in the Skin* (1965), and such recent stories as *Ice!* (1978) by Arnold Federbush and *The Sixth Winter* (1979) by Douglas Orgill and John Gribbin. In *The World in Winter* and other narratives of a second Pleistocene epoch, the heroes are tough new varieties of the human type, men and women who draw on racial memories or on Arctic folk wisdom to create simpler cultures capable of surviving in a fiercely hostile world.

But success is not always assured in geological doomsdays, any more than in those produced by events in outer space. J.-H. Rosny's hero Targ in *La Mort de la terre* (*The Death of the Earth*, 1912) wages an unremitting war against the great drought that dooms humanity after millennia of progress. One by one, earth's settlements have accepted the "irresistible will" of the planet, and have submitted without complaint to euthanasia. When the last community agrees on a plan for voluntary phased euthanasia, Targ and his wife and sister alone refuse to cooperate. They flee to a small oasis, where Targ has located enough water to keep them alive for two years. But in the end all efforts fail. Targ's wife and children are killed in an earthquake that engulfs their oasis, his sister takes poison, and Targ is left alone, the last man. Still spurning euthanasia, he allows himself to be devoured by the strange ferromagnets, the living rusts of the desert that are destined to replace mankind as the next lords of creation. No matter how great man's power once was, earth is incomparably greater. Earth has spoken, as so many times before in geological history, and a new age begins—without man.

Rosny's view of inanimate nature as a pitiless juggernaut is also that of our final exhibit in evidence, his British contemporary Arthur Conan Doyle in a noval of the same period, *The Poison Belt* (1913). Here the disaster is astronomical, but the mood is the same. Doyle's scientist-hero Professor Challenger compares earth to a bunch of grapes "covered by some infinitesimal but noxious bacillus"—i.e., mankind. When the planet passes through a belt of deadly ether, as Challenger predicts will shortly occur, it will be like a bunch of grapes passing "through a disinfecting medium." The ring of a telephone interrupts his lucubrations.

"There is one of our bacilli squeaking for help," said he, with a grim smile. "They are beginning to realize that their continued existence is not really one of the necessities of the Universe."[27]

In the imagination of secular eschatology, when the endtime arrives from natural causes it is not a judgment, and its agonies are not a punishment. Nature is not divine. Against her man stands alone, David against Goliath, winner or loser depending on his will to survive, or dumb luck.

4. Tooth, Claw, and Tentacle

Some of the afflictions promised for the endtime by St. John, it may be recalled, bear the likeness of animate nature. Death is brought by the Fourth Horseman in the form of "pestilence and wild beasts." The angel of the fifth apocalyptic trumpet lets loose giant locusts with the tails of scorpions, and the angel of the sixth trumpet summons horses that breathe fire, smoke, and sulphur, killing one-third of mankind. The Satan of the last days is described as "a great red dragon," an endtime metamorphosis of the serpent who tempted Eve. In the thirteenth chapter of Revelation, the dragon confers its power on a "beast" with ten horns, seven heads, the body of a leopard, and the feet of a bear, the infamous "Beast of the Apocalypse," who conquers the world and rules it for forty-two terrible months.

In St. John, the monsters that bring death and destruction to mankind are supernatural beings, symbols of divine wrath. But much of their frightfulness stems from their resemblance to the real monsters with whom we share the planet, the poisonous reptiles, stinging insects, fanged carnivores, and other creatures who mean us no good, and who—in secular versions of Revelation—are perfectly capable of challenging man's hegemony, or even threatening his existence. Although not as numerous as stories of cosmic and geological doom, those that imagine diaster through the doings of life-forms other than *Homo sapiens* furnish a significant variation on the theme of world's ends attributable to nature. They take on still more importance if we include, as we must, the endtimes involving extraterrestrial beings. In science fiction, as in science, "alien" species belong as much to nature as any variety of earthborn life.

All but a handful of stories of biological disasters, whether caused by terrestrial or extraterrestrial organisms, take their inspiration from the view of nature expounded by Charles Darwin and his various successors and popularizers. Like T. H. Huxley in his essays on evolution and ethics, they contend that no matter how far man may drive back the jungle in his dealings with his fellow man, he remains in a state of war with nature, and she with him. The literature of the biological doomsday brims with references to extinct species, contests for food and living space, mutations that upset the ecological balance, mindless struggle in the rain forest, the anthill, the ocean deeps, the microscopic world—wherever life is found and its suffering is disclosed by the patient biologist. Instead of the juggernaut, nature appears in tales of biological disaster as the mother of sharks and tigers and tentacled horrors from Mars. She is no longer quite so vast or indifferent, but she is much more obviously hostile, and much less obviously maternal.

This chapter opened with a discussion of one such tale, J. T. McIntosh's *The Fittest*, in which mutated animals sever all of civilization's vital links in a few years. As the title suggests, the world view of the novel is throughly Darwinian. Even in stories centered on other kinds of catastrophe, menaces from animate nature contribute materially to the predicament of terminal man. Among just those already mentioned, one thinks of the hounds and ape-men of *The Nightland*, the killer plants of *Hothouse*, the dogs and rats of *All Fools' Day*, the wolves of *The Sixth Winter*. But there are stories aplenty, like *The Fittest*, that see animate nature as the principal agency of man's destruction in the endtime.

One classic situation in eschatological fiction, with many Biblical resonances, is the pestilence that runs wild and wipes out all or most of the human race. The first purely secular novel of the world's end, *The Last Man* (1826) by Mary Shelley, may have been inspired in part by Grainville's *Le Dernier homme* and Byron's "Darkness," but the catastrophe by which Shelley reduces mankind to one survivor is not astronomical. Thinking perhaps of the epidemic of cholera that was heading toward Europe from India in the 1820s, as well as the Black Death of the fourteenth century, she imagines a plague spreading westward from Turkey into Greece. Eventually it engulfs the whole world, until only one Englishman is left. The novel is full of melancholy reflections on the puniness of man in the face of a nature that is herself exhausted and cranky in her dotage. Plague is also the killer in Thomas Hood's cynical narrative poem "The Last Man" (1826) and in Edgar Allan Poe's Gothic horror tale, "The Masque of the Red Death" (1842).

But these early stories of worldwide pestilence lack the clear focus of later examples, inasmuch as the natural causes of disease were not yet known in the first half of the nineteenth century. The microbiological discoveries of Pasteur and Koch did not occur until the second half. Joined to the theory of evolution by natural selection, a product of the same period, they enabled writers to interpret disease as just another instance of nature's feral offspring hard at work attacking and devouring their appointed victims, not unlike the consumption of lambs by wolves. By the turn of the century, world-destroying plagues were an established part of the repertoire of the scientific romancer. Jack London's "The Scarlet Plague" (1912) strikes down all but a few hundred members of the human race, through the action of a germ so virulent that no bacteriologist lives long enough to prepare a serum against it. Van Tassel Sutphen's *The Doomsman* (1906) describes a neo-medieval New York of the twenty-first century after a plague known as "The Terror" takes only a few days to decimate mankind in 1925.

Of more recent stories, it goes without saying that the most important is George R. Stewart's *Earth Abides* (1949), a persistently popular reworking of "The Scarlet Plague." Again, the pestilence spreads too swiftly to contain. "No one was sure in what part of the

world it had originated; aided by airplane travel, it had sprung up
almost simultaneously in every center of civilization, outrunning all
attempts at quarantine."²⁸ There is even a chance that the virus had
escaped from "some laboratory of bacteriological warfare." No one
knows. In any event, most of humanity dies. A few individuals survive
because of natural immunity, but as in the Jack London story, they
quickly revert to savagery. Stewart takes an austerely ecological view
of the tragedy, prefacing his narrative with a meditation on nature's
penchant for writing off whole species:

> As for man, there is little reason to think that he can in the long run
> escape the fate of other creatures, and if there is a biological law of flux
> and reflux, his situation is now a highly perilous one. During ten thousand
> years his numbers have been on the upgrade in spite of wars, pestilences,
> and famines. This increase in population has become more and more
> rapid. Biologically, man has for too long a time been rolling an uninter-
> rupted run of sevens.²⁹

In *Earth Abides*, the next roll is snake eyes. By the end, its protagonist—a former graduate student of ecology—has given up all hope of
reviving civilization among his Neolithic descendants. Known as the
"Last American," he discontinues the school lessons he has given for
many years and teaches the youngsters of the tribe a more valuable
skill: how to make bows and arrows.

Micro-organic disaster may also occur in the form of blights that
ignore man and the other animals but deprive them of the plant life on
which they all depend for sustenance. J. J. Connington (nom-de-
plume of the Belfast chemist Alfred Walter Stewart) produced such a
scenario in *Nordenholt's Million* (1923). Here the evil-doer is a mutated denitrifying bacterium, which originates—by a nice, if improbable, twist of literary irony—when a fireball of lightning strikes a
specimen dish in the study of a London science writer named Wother-
spoon who is surely an irreverent caricature of H. G. Wells. The new
bacterial strain takes root in Regent's Park, then quickly annexes the
rest of London, spreads throughout England, and eventually conquers
the planet. By breaking down all nitrogenous material in the soil, the
mutant converts it into loose sterile sand in which plants cannot grow.
The prognosis for mankind is death by starvation within the year.

From this point on, *Nordenholt's Million* becomes the story of the
titanic efforts of one man, the platinum tycoon Nordenholt, to beat
nature at her own game by ruthlessly seizing power and mobilizing the
best talents of the British nation in the Clyde Valley for a crash

program of bacteriological research and mass production of nitrogenous material. All remaining food supplies are rounded up to keep the Clyde Valley workers alive. On Nordenholt's orders the rest of the country, after sabotage of its communications and transport facilities, is abandoned to starvation. Forty-five million men, women, and children die. But it is far better to let them die, Nordenholt argues, than to prolong their lives for a short while and in the process lose mankind's last chance for racial survival. Men similar to Nordenholt pursue similar policies in Japan and the United States, but elsewhere in the world death and chaos are universal. "All that had once been arable land became a desert strewn with the bones of men."[30]

Connington gives his hero ample opportunity to lecture on his philosophy of life, a philosophy of the purest Darwinism, supplemented by technocratic fascism. To compete and succeed in the real world, and above all in the world of the new bacterium, men must stop their "gabble about Democracy" and submit their affairs to scientific management. Life is struggle. Just as in lower nature, victory goes to the strong and the organized. "Of course," Nordenholt tells his chief lieutenant, "the brute is the basis. A wolf-pack will give you a microcosm of a nation: family life, struggles between wolf and wolf for a living, co-operation against an external enemy or prey."[31] Civilization softens the struggle to some degree, but it does not abrogate the responsibility to take whatever measures are needed to ensure survival in an unsentimental cosmos.

The same "lifeboat ethics," in Garrett Hardin's phrase,[32] permeate *The Death of Grass* (1956, in the United States as *No Blade of Grass*), an effective story of blight, famine, and the survival of the strong by John Christopher. *The Death of Grass* avoids the technocracy of Connington's novel, but its view of nature, and of nature's laws as they apply to man, does not differ all that much. A virus that unselectively kills all grasses, including wheat and rice, causes worldwide hunger and the breakdown of public order. Christopher's protagonist, a London engineer, leads a band of armed survivors through a lawless England to his brother's farm in the hills of Westmorland. They kill remorselessly in self-defense as they go, and in the denouement the engineer is forced to shoot his own brother to save his group. There is no place for squeamishness or charity in the new order. "Nature was wiping a cloth across the slate of human history, leaving it empty for the pathetic scrawls of those few who, here and there over the face of the globe, would survive."[33]

Tales of assault by the creatures of the macro-organic world, such as McIntosh's *The Fittest*, add little to the picture of life presented by Stewart, Connington, and Christopher, except perhaps the enhancement of the horror of it all, since the attackers now are creatures that man can see, often creatures with eyes and limbs and brains. In the McIntosh story, the progeny of common household pets have become man's relentless enemies, revealing in Mother Nature the traitor as well as the savage. Other examples are H. G. Wells's story "The Empire of the Ants" (1905), Arthur C. Clarke's "The Awakening" (1951), Daphne Du Maurier's "The Birds" (1952), and Arthur Herzog's *The Swarm* (1974). In *The Day of the Triffids* (1951) by John Wyndham, a giant mobile plant is the implacable enemy. Olaf Stapledon's *Darkness and the Light* (1942) shows mankind falling before armies of overgrown rats, and in a singular episode of the same author's *Last Men in London* (1932), earth's first high civilization is ruthlessly exterminated by hordes of shaggy beasts: with the ingenious twist that the fallen civilization had been created by lemurs, and the shaggy beasts are our own ancestors.

The worst nightmares of all involve murderous attacks on *Homo sapiens* by intelligent beings from other planets. Dumb brutes or barely animate viruses have only instinct, and the laws of biochemistry, to guide them. Aliens, whose level of development is usually "higher" than man's, can be held to stricter account. When even they prove ferocious, treating mankind as a dangerous rival, an irritating pest, or a source of slave labor or food, they show Mother Nature at her most purposefully malign.

Such is clearly the view of nature in Wells's *The War of the Worlds* (1898), perhaps his best novel, and one in which his biological *Weltanschauung* figures prominently. Despite superior technology and obvious sophistication as social animals, Wells's Martians are not humanitarians. They believe that "life is an incessant struggle for existence." Because their own world has grown too harsh to support life, these beings, with "intellects vast and cool and unsympathetic," have determined to make earth their own. Just as mankind itself has wrought "ruthless and utter destruction . . . not only upon animals, such as the vanished bison and the dodo, but upon its own inferior races"—a reference to the Tasmanians, who died out in the 1870s—so the Martians propose to clear their new home of the vermin that infest its surface.[34] The war of the worlds is, unexpectedly, won by earth. But the victory is entirely a matter of jungle economics. The Martians are

attacked and destroyed by earth's microbes, an order of life unknown
and apparently unsuspected on Mars, and one against which they have
no line of defense.

The theme of alien invasion pioneered by Wells has attracted
hundreds of writers and film-makers since *The War of the Worlds*.
Some of the worthier successors to Wells's story are John Wyndham's
The Kraken Wakes (1953), Thomas M. Disch's *The Genocides* (1965),
and Keith Roberts's *The Furies* (1966). Wyndham and Roberts allow
man to win, after much loss of life, but Disch requires his obliteration.
In *The Genocides* the unseen aliens whose machines convert earth into
a farm for the raising of skyscraper-tall food plants deal with man as
man himself would deal with garden pests. The helpless hero is dis-
mayed at the ease of the aliens' victory. "What was worse, what he
could not endure was the suspicion that it all meant nothing, that the
process of their annihilation was something quite mechanical: that
mankind's destroyers were not, in other words, fighting a war but
merely spraying the garden."[35] His suspicion turns out to be correct.
The reader's only indication of what the aliens think of mankind is
contained in a report to their headquarters, describing the "incinera-
tion of the artifact" known as Duluth-Superior, and the unfortunate
escape from its flaming ruins of some 200 to 340 of the "large animals"
who had constructed it.[36] Duluth is the last such "artifact" on earth.
Now that it has been properly levelled and sown, most of the aliens'
work is done. The insignificant remnant of mammalian fugitives will be
tracked down and torched by robot exterminators.

In the routinely racist consciousness of writers who worked before
the middle of the twentieth century, yet another kind of "alien"
menace was furnished by men of color, viewed more as a perverse
force of nature than as fellow human beings. Wells's passing reference
in *The War of the Worlds* to the Tasmanians, harried to extinction "in
spite of their human likeness,"[37] is a mild instance of such racism. Less
mild is the world's end fiction, especially in the period 1890–1914,
featuring apocalyptic race wars. White civilization comes under attack
by yellow, brown, or black men, formidable because of their great
numbers, diabolical cunning, reckless disregard for human life, or
whatever. Good, if horrendous, examples of race war in science fiction
are the novels of M. P. Shiel on the subject of the Yellow Peril. In the
first, *The Yellow Danger* (1898), a fiendish Chinese-Japanese doctor,
filled with lust for a white woman who spurns him, engineers a world
war that climaxes in an assault by screaming yellow hordes, four
hundred million strong, on the European mainland. Shiel describes

the Chinese as inhumanly sadistic, swarming over their white victims like waves of rats. "It is impossible for the vilest European," he notes, "to conceive the dark and hideous instincts of the Chinese race."[38]

George Allan England furnishes a comparable picture of Afro-Americans in his *Darkness and Dawn* (1914); and in the original Buck Rogers stories by Philip Francis Nowlan, collected as *Armageddon 2419 A.D.* (1928–29), the villains are "Han Mongolians," a yellow people from the interior of Asia who are deservedly slaughtered at the end just as if they had been "tigers or snakes."[39] The characterization of the Hans matches the stereotypical cruel Chinaman of Shiel and other anti-Chinese literature of the time, although Nowlan adds the hypothesis that their blood may have been tainted by breeding with extraterrestrial humanoids thought to have landed in inner Asia late in the twentieth century. In any event, whether literally or only figuratively from another world, non-whites often seem not to belong to the human race, in the imagination of early writers of science fiction. They must be included among the forces of animate nature threatening mankind with disaster in apocalyptic fiction.

5. Natural Means and Human Ends

One considerable story of an uprising of the forces of nature against man's rule has so far escaped our attention. In Karel Čapek's satirical masterpiece *War with the Newts* (1936), the themes of struggle with nature, race war, and the end of the world are intertwined with astute political and social criticism that raises questions about the underlying intentions of writers of eschatological fiction. As satire, Čapek's novel comes packaged with clear warnings that it must not be taken literally. But to what extent is nature the true antagonist of mankind in any fiction of doomsday through natural causes? Even if the author himself intends nothing more than depiction of the war between man and nature, does his story bear within it other meanings?

War with the Newts, at least, has all the layers of symbology that any professional archeologist of literature could wish for. Čapek's figures of evil, giant black salamanders from the waters of an island near Sumatra, first appear in the novel as biological curiosities, living fossils who have recently undergone rapid evolution. They prove to be educable and even learn to speak. Conscripted as slaves to dive for pearls, they breed prolifically. Uses for their labor multiply as well. Soon, they far outnumber mankind, occupying all the world's coastal waters. Advancing from slaves to proletarians to masters of their own

militarily superior but fundamentally antlike civilization, by the
novel's end they have begun demolition operations along the coast-
lines designed to increase their living space. Men will be confined to
highland reservations where they will work for the newts.

We cannot take the time here to delve into all the delicious details
of Čapek's story, but it is clear that the newts are symbols of every
force in modern history that stands opposed to authentic human
culture. They are Martian invaders, mutant monsters, enslaved savages, sullen factory workers, mass-men, Morlocks, soulless technocrats, and finally Nazis—but always the "other," the dehumanized
self, much like the victims of the epidemic of rhinocerotism in the play
by Ionesco. Animate nature furnishes the primary symbol of alienation, but the problem extends far beyond nature, into the very heart of
the human condition and the course of world history.

It is worth our while, at this point, to step back from the question
of man versus nature, and take note, however briefly, of other levels of
meaning in eschatological fiction. There can be no doubt of a sense of
estrangement from nature in modern thought, which the internal
development of both science and philosophy since Kant helps to
explain. But as Isaac Asimov points out in *A Choice of Catastrophes*,
there is actually very little in modern scientific thought to fill a reasonable man with acute fear of doomsday.[40] The end of cosmic time is far
away, the chance of a great world-smashing accident is remote, and
giant spiders are not really about to devour Philadelphia. Why, then,
so many tales of natural catastrophe?

One answer, much too easy an answer, is that the tale of natural
catastrophe is a cheap thrill, a form of escapism that does not cost us
the feelings of guilt often stirred by visions of future wars or man-made
ecological disasters. This explanation has even generated its own
apocalyptic story, Robert Silverberg's "When We Went to See the
End of the World" (1972), in which jaded time travellers visit the
distant end of the natural world in search of diversion, ignoring the
collapse of society that is taking place right under their noses. No
doubt a great many run-of-the-mill fictions of the world's end by
natural causes are simply entertainment, on the same level as a
haunted house in Disneyland or a Godzilla movie. But the most
mindless commercial art still has its complexities of appeal and effect,
not always known to its creators. In any case not all apocalyptic fictions
are run-of-the-mill.

Another answer to the question of the abundance of tales of
natural catastrophe is that visions of catastrophe meet a spectrum of

psychological needs of writers and readers alike that no other imaginary events can quite fill. This answer is certainly true, if not the whole truth. The end of the world enables us, for example, to project in our imaginations a time when all our enemies, all the sources of our current distress and feelings of powerlessness, are removed, and we have survived. Such a situation is not exactly depressing. On the contrary, it may provide enormous satisfaction. Moreover, the satisfaction is much the same regardless of the cause of the catastrophe. By this reckoning, the author's choice of catastrophes is almost random, an observation borne out by the fair number of writers, such as John Wyndham, Brian Aldiss, Edmund Cooper, James Blish, and Fritz Leiber, who move freely back and forth between stories of natural and of man-made catastrophes, but who have the same things to say in each. This point is especially cogent in considering the work of J. G. Ballard. The catastrophes in the stories he published down to the mid-1960s are of natural origin, and since then man-made, but his world view and psychological insights have changed little; the typical Ballardian anti-hero keeps on mutilating himself in the same way, and for the same dark reasons.

A behavioral interpretation of doomsday literature, to be complete, must add the understanding that the world-ending disaster is quite often a metaphor for internal conflicts. Just as the demons of mythology are ways of expressing awareness of the "evil" in ourselves, so the various ways of ending the world attributed to Mother Nature in apocalyptic fiction may symbolize destructive impulses within the self: the death-wish in all its homicidal and suicidal forms. Ballard is unintelligible without resort to this line of interpretation, and there are several other equally obvious writers—M. P. Shiel in *The Purple Cloud*, Bernard Wolfe in *Limbo*, Gore Vidal in *Messiah* and *Kalki*, and so forth. But perhaps all writers of eschatological fiction, consciously or unconsciously, are calling our attention to the enemy within, to the forces that contrive private doomsdays in the muck of the id.

Then again, the naturally produced world's end may be a metaphor for an anticipated social apocalypse, a radical change in the public order of things. Throughout the history of revolutionary thought, not excluding the Book of Revelation, prophets of utopia have foreseen a future in three stages—steep decline, catastrophe, and salvation. In science fiction, one can argue that dystopian stories like Aldous Huxley's *Brave New World* or John Brunner's *The Sheep Look Up* refer to the first stage of the messianic paradigm, whereas fictions

of the world's end refer to the second, the fiery catastrophe that will
usher in the happier times beyond. Even if the fictional world's end is
literally terminal, aborting the paradigm, the reader can always interpret such pessimism as an awful warning, rather than a prediction of
things actually to come; no alternative paradigm is intended. But our
point once again is simply that in the use of doomsday fiction as
metaphor for revolutionary social change, it makes little difference
whether the catastrophe originates with nature or with the acts of men.
Its function is to destroy the old world and to make possible the new.
Any sufficiently tremendous earth-cracking event will do.

In dealing with writers who supply explicit views of post-
catastrophe utopias or at least substantially improved social orders,
this interpretative strategy is difficult to fault. The fact that improved
societies often turn up near the end of stories of natural catastrophe, as
well as near the end of stories of man-made catastrophes, speaks for
itself. Among the works discussed in earlier sections that catch sight of
a better world are Tarde's *Underground Man*, Serviss's *The Second
Deluge*, Connington's *Nordenholt's Million*, and Cooper's *All Fools'
Day*. But the majority of our sample narratives fail to go this far. What
most of them do have in common is a thorough awareness of the
vulnerability of civilization, and the ease with which its structures
disintegrate in the face of disaster. In nearly every scenario of the end
of the world through natural causes, as through man-made causes,
attention centers less on the catastrophe itself, whatever it may be,
than on the way it succeeds in unravelling the threads of the social
order.

There is also one aspect of civilizational crisis that stories of
natural catastrophe illuminate especially well. Part of the crisis of
modernity is the erosion of the systems of belief and value that once
helped to integrate Western civilization and now lie, for many of us, in
ruins. Stories of man-made catastrophes continue the ancient tradition
of prophetic warning, by which sinful man is reminded of his disobedi-
ence and the wrath to come that his wrong-doing has earned. But to
the extent that tales of disaster through natural causes do pointedly
refer to the natural order, they refer also to a belief in the underlying
harmony of man, nature, and God that no longer exists in the secularized consciousness of modern man. In such tales, nature is not a
symbol of divinity, or a garden for man to tend, or a cosmos proclaim-
ing the coherence of creation, or even a storehouse of punishments
provisioned by God to keep wayward man in line. In a universe with no
known transcendental purpose or sanction, nature simply exists, in-

different to man, capable by the grinding operation of its laws of wiping him out in the wink of an eye, or in the fullness of time. As for God, the alleged creator of this obscene wilderness, there is nothing at all to say. Secular man does not believe in such a thing as God, who rarely appears or even rates a veiled allusion in eschatological fiction. The secular universe is a theater of absurdity and rebellion: the absurdity of man in his fatherless void, and the rebellion of nature against the stewardship of disinherited man.

We exaggerate. The old faith persists in some quarters, as can be seen even in the microcosm of apocalyptic literature. Although most writers of doomsday stories belong to secularism, novels of the end-time such as Robert Hugh Benson's *Lord of the World* and C. S. Lewis's *That Hideous Strength* witness to the survival of traditional Christian consciousness. Other writers have turned to mystical or pantheist world views that preserve much of the essence of the old transcendental faith. The apocalyptic canon of Olaf Stapledon, Aldous Huxley, and Doris Lessing shows how much (or how little?) can be done along these lines without sacrifice of artistic integrity. The popularity of what we have called the messianic paradigm of future history—the "happy ending" so common in doomsday literature— also betrays the influence of traditional belief, even when the future anticipated is thoroughly secular in content.

Nevertheless, the case for the natural disaster in speculative literature as evidence of the agonies of secularization and the sense of estrangement from being itself of a predominant type of modern mind, is too strong to dismiss. The case grows stronger still when we note that the tale of natural disaster has been chiefly a British and European product. There are plenty of American examples, but only because science fiction of every sort is churned out in such prodigious quantities in the United States. The ratio of natural to man-made disasters in American fiction is significantly lower than in fiction produced across the Atlantic.[41] Since unbelief has always been deeper, more wide-spread, and more belligerent in Europe than in America, this is precisely what we should expect if a positive correlation did exist between secularization and the literature of natural disaster.

Now and then, a writer of eschatological fiction has commented explicitly about the correlation. The best examples are stories cast in the form of parables, such as Brian Aldiss's "Heresies of the Huge God" (1966) and J. G. Ballard's "The Drowned Giant" (1965). The genius of Ballard's story is that it transforms the death of God into a natural disaster, a narrative of divine putrefaction worthy of comparison with the episode of the Madman in Nietzsche's *Joyful Wisdom*. Ballard has recently dealt even more explicitly with the theme in a superbly ironic story, "The Life and Death of God" (1976). But such matters are usually better left for the reader to discover on his own.

In still one more Ballard story, "The Voice of Time" (1960), the end of the universe is addressed with a sweet, resigned bleakness that converts the death of God, and God's nature, into a tearless farewell. It can also help us with the envoi of this chapter. Ballard imagines that living things will not have to wait for the end of the universe to die: when stars reach a certain point in their decay, the biological kingdoms supported by them fall asleep. On earth at the time of the story, the "narcoma syndrome" is spreading inexorably. Victims stay awake a little less each day, until they go to sleep forever. But the universe is not silent. Not quite. A radio telescope receives signals from various parts of the cosmos, signals counting down the years to the extinction of each star. "These are the voices of time," the astronomer tells his friend, "and they're all saying goodbye to you."[42]

One thinks again of Nietzsche's Madman, comparing the news of the death of God to the light that arrives from distant stars. Both take a long time to reach earth. The world view of "The Voices of Time" is probably still less credible to the average earthling than the Apocalypse of the Book of Revelation. But Ballard and all his many fellow exponents of secular eschatology are doing their part to reduce St. John from prophet of God's word to just another science fiction writer.

Notes
Selected Bibliography
Index

Notes

1: The Remaking of Zero: Beginning at the End

1. Ray Bradbury, "The Highway," reprinted in *The Illustrated Man* (Garden City: Doubleday, 1951), p. 62.
2. Ray Bradbury, *The Martian Chronicles* (Garden City: Doubleday, 1950). The symbolic burning of artifacts of the old world is related to the Adamic mythology of the frontier which Bradbury explores throughout *The Martian Chronicles*, and thus it is not surprising that a likely source for "The Million-Year Picnic" is Nathaniel Hawthrone's 1844 story "Earth's Holocaust," about an immense, apocalyptic bonfire meant to cleanse the earth of "the weight of dead men's thought." Bradbury anthologized the Hawthorne story in his 1956 collection *The Circus of Dr. Lao and Other Improbable Stories*.
3. Mircea Eliade, *Myth and Reality*, trans. by Willard R. Trask (New York: Harper Torchbooks, 1968), p. 76.
4. Norman Cohn, *The Pursuit of the Millennium* (New York: Oxford University Press, 1957).
5. Eliade, p. 30.
6. J. G. Ballard, "Cataclysms and Dooms," in *The Visual Encyclopedia of Science Fiction*, ed. Brian Ash (New York: Harmony Books, 1977), p. 130.
7. George R. Stewart, *Earth Abides* (New York: Ace, n.d. [1949]), p. 122. Subsequent references to this edition will be by page number in the text.
8. Eliade, p. 72.
9. See Bruce Gillespie, "*The Long Loud Silence*," in *Survey of Science Fiction Literature*, ed. Frank N. Magill (Englewood Cliffs, N.J.: Salem Press, 1979), III, 1241.
10. Harlan Ellison, "A Boy and His Dog," reprinted in *The Beast That Shouted Love at the Heart of the World* (New York: New American Library, 1969), p. 254.
11. M. P. Shiel, *The Purple Cloud* (New York: Paperback Library, 1963 [1901]), p. 13.

12. Cohn, p. 308.
13. John Bowen, *After the Rain* (New York: Ballantine, 1959), p. 124.
14. Alfred Coppel, *Dark December* (Greenwich, Conn.: Fawcett, 1960),
    p. 191.
15. Coppel, p. 197.
16. Coppel, p. 196.
17. Bowen, p. 75.
18. Willis E. McNelly, "*Earth Abides*," in *Survey of Science Fiction Litera-
    ture*, ed. Frank N. Magill (Englewood Cliffs, N.J.: Salem Press, 1979),
    II, 690.

3: Ambiguous Apocalypse: Transcendental Versions of the End

1. Rainer Maria Rilke, *Tagebücher aus der Frühzeit* (Leipzig, 1942), p. 71,
   quoted in Erich Heller, *The Disinherited Mind* (New York: Meridian,
   1959), p. 162.
2. Frederik Polak, *The Image of the Future*, trans. and abr. Elise Boulding
   (Amsterdam: Elsevier; San Francisco: Jossey-Bass, 1973), pp. 222–30.
   See also his "Utopia and Cultural Renewal" in *Utopias and Utopian
   Thought*, ed. Frank E. Manuel (1966; rpt. Boston: Beacon Press, 1967),
   pp. 290–92.
3. "A true myth is one which, within the universe of a certain culture (living
   or dead), expresses richly, and often perhaps tragically, the highest
   admirations possible within that culture." Olaf Stapledon, "Preface to
   English Edition," *Last and First Men* (1930; rpt. with *Star Maker*, New
   York: Dover, 1968), p. 9.
4. Mircea Eliade, *Two Tales of the Occult*, trans. William Ames Coates (New
   York: Herder and Herder, 1970), pp. xii–xiii. On fantastic literture generally, see the review essay by Theodore Ziolkowski, "Otherworlds: Fantasy and the Fantastic," *Sewanee Review* 86 (Winter 1978): 121–29.
5. Brian Stableford, "Religion," *The Science Fiction Encyclopedia*, ed.
   Peter Nicholls (Garden City: Doubleday/Dolphin, 1979), p. 493.
6. Polak, *The Image of the Future*, p. 229.
7. M. H. Abrams, *Natural Supernaturalism: Tradition and Revolution in
   Romantic Literature* (New York: Norton, 1971), pp. 65–70; Thomas
   Carlyle, *Sartor Resartus* (1836; rpt. London: Everyman's Library, 1908,
   1959), Bk. III, ch. viii. See also Hélène Tuzet, "Cosmic Images," *Dictio-
   nary of the History of Ideas*, ed. Philip P. Wiener (New York: Scribner's,
   1973), I:513–23.
8. The terms are those of, respectively, Robert Scholes, *Structural Fabula-
   tion* (Notre Dame, Ind.: University of Notre Dame Press, 1975); R. D.
   Mullen, "Supernatural, Pseudonatural, and Sociocultural Fantasy," *Science-Fiction Studies* 5 (1978): 291; Darko Suvin, *Metamorphoses of Science Fiction* (New Haven: Yale University Press, 1979), ch. 4; Alexei and

Cory Panshin, "Metaphor, Analogy, Symbol and Myth," *Fantastic* 21 (February 1972): 96; and S. C. Fredericks, "Problems of Fantasy," *Science-Fiction Studies* 5 (1978): 33–44. I have not found persuasive the efforts of Suvin (pp. 8–9, 22–27, 64–69) and Robert M. Philmus, "Science Fiction: From Its Beginning to 1870," in *Anatomy of Wonder*, ed. Neil Barron (New York: Bowker, 1976), pp. 3–16, to develop "scientific cognition" into a criterion for differentiating science fiction from apocalyptic fiction and metaphysical fantasy. Philmus, however, does show awareness of the relativity of science as a concept.

9. Suvin, *Metamorphoses of Science Fiction*, p. viii.

10. Donald A. Wollheim, *The Universe Makers: Science Fiction Today* (New York: Harper and Row, 1971), p. 44.

11. Brian M. Stableford, "Science Fiction and the Image of the Future," *Foundation* No. 14 (1978): 31.

12. C. G. Jung. *Flying Saucers: A Modern Myth of Things Seen in the Skies* (1958), trans. R. F. C. Hull (Princeton: Princeton University Press, 1978), p. 16 (also in his *Collected Works*, Vol. 10); Nigel Calder, *Spaceships of the Mind* (New York: Viking, 1978). Jung offers brief psychological analyses of two science fiction novels of eschatological transcendence, Fred Hoyle's *The Black Cloud* (1957) and John Wyndham's *The Midwich Cuckoos* (1957) (pp. 120–27). A UFO novel of considerable originality that is based to some extent on Jung and avoids the "technological angel" cliché of much science fiction is Ian Watson's *Miracle Visitors* (1978). The *deus ex machina* device has its purportedly non-fictional equivalent in speculations about ancient astronauts, e.g., *Chariots of the Gods?*, *The Spaceships of Ezekiel*, and *God Drives a Flying Saucer*.

13. The earliest descriptions of science fiction as contemporary apocalyptic that I have found (but I have not made a systematic survey) are two essays originally published in 1953: William Atheling, Jr. (James Blish), "Cathedrals in Space," reprinted in his *The Issue at Hand* (Chicago: Advent, 1964), p. 54, and Gerald Heard, "Science Fiction, Morals, and Religion," in *Modern Science Fiction: Its Meaning and Its Future*, ed. Reginald Bretnor (New York: Coward-McCann, 1953), p. 255.

14. The most recent comprehensive definition of apocalypse as a genre is by John J. Collins in *Apocalypse: The Morphology of a Genre*, ed. John J. Collins (Semeia, 14; Missoula, Mont.: Scholars Press, 1979), p. 9: "'Apocalypse' is a genre of revelatory literature with a narrative framework, in which a revelation is mediated by an otherworldly being to a human recipient, disclosing a transcendent reality which is both temporal, insofar as it envisages eschatological salvation, and spatial, insofar as it involves another, supernatural world." The definition is based on the analysis by Collins and his colleagues of all surviving examples of literary apocalypses from the Eastern Mediterranean from 250 B.C.E. to 300 C.E. (Jewish, Early Christian, Gnostic, Greek and Latin, Rabbinic, and Persian). Personal salvation is characteristic of all apocalyptic but is beyond

the scope of my discussion; cosmic salvation or renewal, however, is not universally present—some apocalypses discuss only personal salvation, others show only the destruction of the world. Historically, of course, the Book of Revelation, which does include cosmic renewal, has been the most potent influence on Western apocalyptic and serves as the prototype for the literature analyzed in David Ketterer's important book, *New Worlds for Old: The Apocalyptic Imagination, Science Fiction, and American Literature* (Garden City: Doubleday Anchor, 1974). Eschatological transcendence in speculative literature can, however, be ambiguous, cynical, or negative, as this essay will demonstrate.

15. The most useful previous discussions of eschatological transcendence in speculative fiction, in addition to Ketterer's *New Worlds for Old*, are Jack Williamson and David Ketterer, "Apocalypse," in *Science Fiction: Contemporary Mythology*, ed. Patricia Warrick, Martin Harry Greenberg, and Joseph Olander (New York: Harper and Row, 1978), pp. 435–41, and the articles by Brian Stableford and Peter Nicholls on "Conceptual Breakthrough," "Cosmology," "Devolution," "End of the World," "Eschatology," "Evolution," "Far Future," "Religion," and "Superman" in *The Science Fiction Encyclopedia*, ed. Peter Nicholls (Garden City: Doubleday/Dolphin, 1979). Transcendence in speculative fiction covers far more than the end of the world. A useful survey is Tom Woodman, "Science Fiction, Religion and Transcendence," in *Science Fiction: A Critical Guide*, ed. Patrick Parrinder (London and New York: Longman, 1979), pp. 110–30. Alexei and Cory Panshin, "The Search for Mystery (1957–1968)," *Fantastic* 22 (April 1973), 94–113, 130, and Stableford's previously cited "Science Fiction and the Image of the Future" both offer provocative insights.

16. H. P. Owen, "Eschatology," *Encyclopedia of Philosophy*, ed. Paul Edwards (New York: Macmillan/Free Press, 1967), 3:48–49.

17. On this see Brian Stableford, "Eschatology," *The Science Fiction Encyclopedia*, pp. 199–200.

18. Franklin L. Baumer's 1954 essay, "Twentieth-Century Version of the Apocalypse," reprinted in *European Intellectual History Since Darwin and Marx*, ed. W. Warren Wagar (New York: Harper Torchbooks, 1966), pp. 110–34, and Nathan Scott's " 'New Heav'ns, New Earth'—The Landscape of Contemporary Apocalypse," *Journal of Religion* 53 (1973): 1–35, together provide a comprehensive survey of modern apocalyptic attitudes. The authors reflect the prevailing moods at the time of publication: postwar "crisis thinking" (Baumer), countercultural antinomianism (Scott).

19. B. A. Gendreau, "Transcendence," *New Catholic Encyclopedia* (New York: McGraw-Hill, 1967), XIV:233–35, is helpful in differentiating the various technical meanings. Secular uses are treated by William A. Johnson, *The Search for Transcendence* (New York: Harper and Row, 1974), which is as its subtitle indicates "a theological analysis of nontheological

attempts to define transcendence." His primary cases in point are Charles Reich, Herbert Marcuse, R. D. Laing, Ernst Bloch, and C. G. Jung.

20. Arthur C. Clarke, *Report on Planet Three and Other Speculations* (1972; rpt. New York: Signet, 1973), p. 130. (The variants are mine, not Clarke's.) Eric Rabkin has called my attention to a significant qualification to which Clarke alludes only hurriedly: the technology is indistinguishable from magic only to those who do not understand the technology. Clarke's own example of Edison confronted by the laser does not seem apt.

21. On Clarke, the essays by Robert Plank, David N. Samuelson, and John Huntington in *Arthur C. Clarke*, ed. Joseph D. Olander and Martin Harry Greenberg (New York: Taplinger, 1977) are especially helpful, although in sharp disagreement with one another. Samuelson points out (p. 233, n. 15) that the first part of *Childhood's End* was published in 1950 as a novelette with the title "Guardian Angels."

22. Robert Hugh Benson, *Lord of the World* (1907; rpt. New York: Arno Press, 1975), pp. 351–52.

23. H. G. Wells, *The Complete Short Stories of H. G. Wells* (London: Ernest Benn; New York: St. Martin's Press, 21st printing, 1970), pp. 109–14.

24. H. P. Lovecraft, "The Call of Cthulhu" (written 1926, published 1928), in his *The Dunwich Horror and Others* (Sauk City, Wis.: Arkham House, 1963), p. 130.

25. H. P. Lovecraft, "Nyarlathotep," in his *The Doom That Came to Sarnath and Other Stories*, ed. Lin Carter (New York: Ballantine, 1971), p. 57. On Nyarlathotep, see L. Sprague de Camp, *Lovecraft: A Biography* (Garden City: Doubleday, 1975), pp. 138–39; Lin Carter, *Lovecraft: A Look Behind the "Cthulhu Mythos"* (New York: Ballantine, 1972), pp. 17–19; and George Wetzel, "The Cthulhu Mythos: A Study," in *Howard Phillips Lovecraft: Memoirs, Critiques, and Bibliographies*, ed. George Wetzel (North Tonawanda, N.Y.: SSR Publications, 1955), pp. 18–27, esp. 20–21.

26. Camille Flammarion, *Omega: The Last Days of the World*, trans. not given (French, 1893; English, 1894; rpt. New York: Arno Press, 1975), p. 286.

27. The story is found most conveniently in Charles L. Harness, *The Rose* (New York: Berkley Medallion, 1969), pp. 102–42.

28. Theodore Sturgeon, *More Than Human* (New York: Ballantine, 7th printing, 1972), p. 188.

29. Dan Morgan, *The Several Minds* (New York: Avon, 1969), pp. 116–17; the second in his four-novel New Minds series. Becky, it should be noted, is a telepath; Jerry, a well-meaning journalist, is not.

30. H. G. Wells, "The Man of the Year Million" (1897 text) in *H. G. Wells: Journalism and Prophecy 1893–1946*, ed. W. Warren Wagar (Boston: Houghton Mifflin, 1964), pp. 3–9; see also the summary and discussion in *H. G. Wells: Early Writings in Science and Science Fiction*, ed. Robert M.

Philmus and David Y. Hughes (Berkeley and Los Angeles: University of California Press, 1975), pp. 150–51, 237. On *The Time Machine*, see Alex Eisenstein, "*The Time Machine* and the End of Man," *Science-Fiction Studies* 3 (1976): 161–65. On devolution in general, see Peter Nicholls, "Devolution," *The Science Fiction Encyclopedia*, pp. 166–67, and the thematic 02.15.1, "The Monstrosity of Evolution," in *The Visual Encyclopedia of Science Fiction*, ed. Brian Ash (New York: Harmony Books, 1977), pp. 191–94.

31. Karel Čapek, *R.U.R.*, trans. Paul Selver and Nigel Playfair, in *A Treasury of the Theatre*, ed. John Gassner, rev. ed. (New York: Simon and Schuster, 1950), p. 433 (Epilogue); John W. Campbell, "The Last Evolution," in *The Best of John W. Campbell*, ed. Lester del Rey (New York: Ballantine, 1976), pp. 1–21. On cyborgs, see *Human-Machines: An Anthology of Stories about Cyborgs*, ed. Thomas N. Scortia and George Zebrowski (New York: Vintage, 1975), esp. pp. xiii–xxv.

32. On the concept of synchronicity, see C. G. Jung, *Synchronicity: An Acausal Connecting Principle* (1952, 1955), trans. R. F. C. Hull (Princeton: Princeton University Press, 1973) (also in *Collected Works*, Vol. 8).

33. Stapledon, *Last and First Men*, p. 13.

34. Wells, *Complete Short Stories*, pp. 594, 603–4.

35. Sir Arthur Conan Doyle, *The Poison Belt*, (1913; New York: Macmillan, 1964; rpt. New York: Berkley Medallion, 1966), pp. 40, 43, 77.

36. Robert Silverberg, "Introduction" (1978) to *Born with the Dead* (1974; rpt. New York: Berkley Medallion, 1979), p. xi.

37. Arthur C. Clarke, *Childhood's End* (New York: Ballantine, 22nd printing, 1972), p. 208.

38. See Theodore Ziolkowski, *Fictional Transfigurations of Jesus* (Princeton: Princeton University Press, 1972), pp. 250–56.

39. Abrams, *Natural Supernaturalism*, p. 56; see also pp. 25–28.

40. Flammarion, *Omega*, p. 287.

41. Clarke, *Childhood's End*, pp. 29–30, 135–37.

42. Carlyle, *Sartor Resartus*, Bk. III, ch. viii, p. 194.

4: *Round Trips to Doomsday*

1. Mircea Eliade, "Preface," in Paul Vulliaud, *La Fin du monde* (Paris: Payot, 1952), p. 6. See also Eliade, *The Myth of the Eternal Return*, trans. Willard R. Trask (New York: Pantheon, 1954).

2. David Ketterer, *New Worlds for Old: The Apocalyptic Imagination, Science Fiction, and American Literature* (Garden City: Doubleday, 1974), p. 14.

3. Krzysztof Pomian, "The Secular Evolution of the Concept of Cycles," in *Review* 2 (Spring 1979): 573–74.

4. Thucydides, *History of the Peloponnesian War*, trans. Rex Warner (Baltimore: Penguin, 1954), p. 24.

5. One may argue that all fiction is cyclical, in the sense that it presents the rounds of life and death, analogies drawn from history, or cycles of hubris and nemesis. In the same vein, Frank Kermode labels much of modern fiction "eschatological" and John R. May labels it "apocalyptic." See Kermode, *The Sense of an Ending: Studies in the Theory of Fiction* (New York: Oxford University Press, 1967); and May, *Toward a New Earth: Apocalypse in the American Novel* (Notre Dame, Ind.: University of Notre Dame Press, 1972). Literary criticism too often reduces to semantic gaming of this doubtful sort. In the present essay we play no such tricks. Our concern is only with cyclicism as a conception of the shape of world history.

6. Niccolò Machiavelli, *History of Florence and of the Affairs of Italy* (Washington: Dunne, 1901 [1532]), p. 204.

7. See W. Warren Wagar, *Good Tidings: The Belief in Progress from Darwin to Marcuse* (Bloomington: Indiana University Press, 1972).

8. M. H. Abrams, *Natural Supernaturalism: Tradition and Revolution in Romantic Literature* (New York: Norton, 1971), pp. 180–81. Grace E. Cairns comes closer to Hegel's own arcane language in characterizing his view of history as "One Grand Macrocosmic Dialectical Cycle in which the Infinite Spirit posits itself as abstract Infinite; dialectically this immediately gives rise to its negation, the whole infinitude of finite particulars of the concrete world; and the negation of the negation (synthesis) which is the concrete infinite (Absolute Whole-Idea)." Cairns, *Philosophies of History: Meeting of East and West in Cycle-Pattern Theories of History* (New York: Philosophical Library, 1962), p. 287.

9. See Jacob Burckhardt, *Force and Freedom: Reflections on History*, trans. Mary D. Hottinger, ed. James Hastings Nichols (New York: Pantheon, 1943 [1905]).

10. See Hans J. Schoeps, *Vorläufer Spenglers: Studien zum Geschichtspessimismus im 19. Jahrhundert* (Leiden: Brill, 1953), and Wagar, pp. 163–67.

11. For a convenient introduction to Spengler's thought, consult H. Stuart Hughes, *Oswald Spengler* (New York: Scribner's, 1962).

12. See Pitirim A. Sorokin, *Social Philosophies of an Age of Crisis* (Boston: Beacon, 1950), and Wagar, pp. 199–203.

13. See, for example, Abrams, pp. 313–16.

14. Walter M. Miller, Jr., *A Canticle for Leibowitz* (Philadelphia: Lippincott, 1960), p. 255. Emphasis Miller's.

15. Ibid., p. 273.

16. Robert Scholes and Eric S. Rabkin, *Science Fiction: History, Science, Vision* (New York: Oxford University Press, 1977), pp. 225–26.

17. Miller, *A Canticle for Leibowitz*, p. 235.

18. René Barjavel, *The Ice People*, trans. Charles Lam Markmann (New York: Pyramid, 1973), p. 208.

19. Larry Niven, *The Magic Goes Away* (New York: Ace, 1978), p. 171.

20. Camille Flammarion, *La Fin du monde* (Paris: Ernest Flammarion, 1917 [1893]). See especially ch. 6, "La croyance à la fin du monde à travers les

âges," pp. 171–215. Available in English as *Omega: The Last Days of the World* (New York: Arno, 1974).

21. Flammarion, *La Fin du monde*, p. 246.
22. Omégar and Eva, as opposed to Grainville's Omégare and Syderie. For the latter, see J.-B. Cousin de Grainville, *Le Dernier homme* (Geneva: Slatkine, 1976). Available in an 1806 English translation as *The Last Man; or, Omegarus and Syderia, a Romance in Futurity* (New York: Arno, 1978).
23. Flammarion, *La Fin du monde*, p. 402.
24. Ibid.
25. For Huxley on the end of the world, see his "Evolution and Ethics" (1893), in T. H. Huxley and Julian Huxley, *Touchstone for Ethics, 1893–1943* (New York: Harper and Row, 1947), pp. 93–94.
26. Jules Verne, "L'Eternel Adam," in *Hier et demain: Contes et nouvelles* (Paris: Hetzel, 1910), p. 263.
27. See Bernard Bergonzi, *The Early H. G. Wells: A Study of the Scientific Romances* (Manchester: Manchester University Press, 1961), especially ch. 1, "H. G. Wells and the *Fin de Siècle*."
28. George R. Stewart, *Earth Abides* (Boston: Houghton Mifflin, 1949), p. 373.
29. Richard D. Mullen, "Blish, van Vogt, and the Uses of Spengler," *Riverside Quarterly* 3 (August 1968): 172–86. A revised version, with sympathetic notes by James Blish himself, appears as the Afterword, "The Earthmanist Culture: *Cities in Flight* as a Spenglerian History," in Blish, *Cities in Flight* (New York: Avon, 1970), pp. 597–607. See also Blish's discussion of Spengler in William Atheling, Jr. [James Blish], *The Issue at Hand* (Chicago: Advent, 1964), pp. 60–61.
30. Blish, *Cities in Flight*, pp. 82, 208, and 515.
31. Ibid., p. 596. See also Blish's other novels, *The Seedling Stars* (1959) and *Midsummer Century* (1972), both with cyclical messages, and the Spenglerian and Toynbean magazine stories discussed in Paul Carter, *The Creation of Tomorrow: Fifty Years of Magazine Science Fiction* (New York: Columbia University Press, 1977), pp. 221–27 and 245–55. Of special interest is the Jack Williamson story "Breakdown" (1942), which appeared in *Astounding Science-Fiction* just two years after L. Sprague de Camp published a factual article on Spengler, Toynbee, and other cyclical prophets in the same illustrious pulp. Carter, pp. 223–26.
32. James Thurber, *The Last Flower: A Parable in Pictures* (New York: Harper and Row, 1971 [1939]), no pagination.
33. Keith Roberts, *The Chalk Giants* (New York: Berkley, 1976 [1974]), pp. 135, 137, 211, and 216.
34. Recall Etienne Gilson's shrewd complaint that Teilhard did not write theology, but rather "theology-fiction." Quoted in Jacques Maritain, *The Peasant of the Garonne*, trans. Michael Cuddihy and Elizabeth Hughes (New York: Holt, 1968), p. 119.

35. Thomas D. Clareson, "Many Futures, Many Worlds," in *Many Futures, Many Worlds: Theme and Form in Science Fiction*, ed. Thomas D. Clareson (Ohio: Kent State University Press, 1977), p. 19.
36. Olaf Stapledon, *Last and First men* (New York: Dover, 1968 [1930]), p. 233.
37. Olaf Stapledon, *Last Men in London* (London: Methuen, 1978 [1932]), p. 127. The lemurs play for Stapledon the part taken by the pacifist dogs in Simak's *City*.
38. Brian Aldiss, *Galaxies like Grains of Sand* (New York: Signet, 1960), p. 144.
39. Michael Moorcock, *An Alien Heat* (New York: Harper and Row, 1972), p. 11.
40. Michael Moorcock, "Introduction," in Moorcock, *Dying for Tommorrow* [British title, *Moorcock's Book of Martyrs*] (New York: Daw, 1976), p. 8. In addition to *An Alien Heat*, the novels in Moorcock's *Dancers* trilogy are *The Hollow Lands* (1974) and *The End of All Songs* (1976). See also his story of the revival of technological civilization after a nuclear holocaust, *The Ice Schooner* (1969).
41. George Zebrowski, *Macrolife* (New York: Harper and Row, 1979), especially pp. 241–81. Cf. Isaac Asimov's gemlike short story "The Last Question" (1956), in Asimov, *Nine Tomorrows* (New York: Fawcett, n.d. [1959]), pp. 170–83. In a class by itself stands Asimov's *Foundation Trilogy* (1951–53), a work both clearly cyclicist in the spirit of Spengler and Toynbee and progressivist in the spirit of Wells. What it lacks is anything more than a weakly realized image of disaster. Asimov's galactic empire crumbles, but its decline (inspired by Asimov's reading of Gibbon) is more Byzantine than Roman.

6: The Rebellion of Nature

1. J. T. McIntosh, *The Fittest* (Garden City: Doubleday, 1955), p. 134.
2. Ibid., p. 19.
3. Ibid., p. 174.
4. Ibid., p. 48.
5. Ibid., p. 19.
6. T. H. Huxley, in T. H. Huxley and Julian Huxley, *Touchstone for Ethics, 1893–1943* (New York: Harper and Row, 1947), p. 67.
7. Bertrand Russell, in *Mysticism and Logic* (New York: Norton, 1929), pp. 47–48 and 56–57.
8. See A. J. Sambrook, "A Romantic Theme: The Last Man," *Forum for Modern Language Studies* 2 (January 1966): 25–33.
9. Anatole France, *Le Jardin d'Épicure* (Paris: Calmann-Levy, 1907), pp. 26–27.
10. H. G. Wells, *Men Like Gods*, in *The Works of H. G. Wells, Atlantic Edition* (London: Unwin, 1924–27), 28: 107.

11. See W. Warren Wagar, *H. G. Wells and the World State* (New Haven: Yale University Press, 1961), pp. 65–76.
12. William Hope Hodgson, *The Night Land* (London: Nash, 1912), p. 521.
13. See pp. 87–89.
14. Joe De Bolt and John R. Pfeiffer in *Anatomy of Wonder: Science Fiction*, ed. Neil Barron (New York: Bowker, 1976), p. 132.
15. Brian Aldiss, *The Long Afternoon of Earth* (New York: Signet, 1962), pp. 5, 44, and 71.
16. Ibid., p. 43.
17. Ibid., p. 69.
18. Ibid., p. 191.
19. Ibid., p. 192.
20. H. G. Wells, "The Star," in *The Short Stories of H. G. Wells* (London: Ernest Benn, 1927), p. 648.
21. Garrett P. Serviss, *The Second Deluge* (New York: McBride, Nast, 1912), p. 76.
22. Ibid., p. 397.
23. Edmund Cooper, *All Fools' Day* (London: Hodder and Stoughton, 1966), p. 21.
24. Ibid., p. 47.
25. Ibid., p. 192.
26. David Pringle, in *J. G. Ballard: The First Twenty Years*, ed. James Goddard and David Pringle (Hayes, Middlesex: Bran's Head, 1976), p. 51.
27. Sir Arthur Conan Doyle, *The Poison Belt*, in Doyle, *The Professor Challenger Stories* (London: Murray, 1952), p. 240.
28. George R. Stewart, *Earth Abides* (Boston: Houghton Mifflin, 1949), p. 15.
29. Ibid., p. 9.
30. J. J. Connington, *Nordenholt's Million* (London: Ernest Benn, 1923), p. 223.
31. Ibid., pp. 189 and 190.
32. See Garrett Hardin, "Living on a Lifeboat," *Bioscience* 24 (October 1974): 561–68; and also Hardin, *The Limits of Altruism: An Ecologist's View of Survival* (Bloomington: Indiana University Press, 1977).
33. John Christopher, *No Blade of Grass* (New York: Avon, 1967), p. 124.
34. H. G. Wells, *The War of the Worlds*, in Wells, *Seven Famous Novels* (New York: Knopf, 1934), pp. 265–66.
35. Thomas M. Disch, *The Genocides* (New York: Berkley, 1965), pp. 70–71.
36. Ibid., pp. 31–32.
37. Wells, *The War of the Worlds*, p. 266.
38. M. P. Shiel, *The Yellow Danger* (London: Grant Richards, 1898), p. 109.
39. Philip Francis Nowlan, "The Airlords of Han" [1929], *Amazing Stories* 36 (May, 1962): 134.

40. See Isaac Asimov, *A Choice of Catastrophes: The Disasters That Threaten Our World* (New York: Simon and Schuster, 1979).
41. In the two hundred and fifty works inventoried by this writer, the ratio of natural to man-made disasters in American fiction is approximately one to two, and in British and European fiction, one to one.
42. J. G. Ballard, "The Voices of Time," in *The Best Short Stories of J. G. Ballard* (New York: Holt, Rinehart and Winston, 1978), p. 93.

Selected Bibliography

Fiction

Aldiss, Brian, *Greybeard*. New York: Harcourt, 1964.
——. *The Long Afternoon of Earth*. New York: New American Library, 1962.
Anderson, Poul. *Tau Zero*. New York: Doubleday, 1970.
Ballard, J. G. *The Crystal World*. New York: Avon, 1966.
——. *The Drowned World*. New York: Penguin, 1962.
——. *The Wind from Nowhere*. New York: Penguin, 1962.
Balmer, Edwin, and Philip Wylie. *After Worlds Collide*. New York: Warner, 1933.
——. *When Worlds Collide*. Darley, Pa.: Arden Library, 1933.
Blish, James. *Black Easter*. Garden City, N.Y.: Doubleday, 1968.
——. *Cities in Flight*. New York: Avon, 1970.
——. *The Day After Judgment*. Garden City, N.Y.: Doubleday, 1970.
——. *The Triumph of Time*. New York: Avon, 1958.
Brackett, Leigh. *The Long Tomorrow*. New York: Ballantine, 1955.
Čapek, Karel, *War with the Newts*. London: George Allen & Unwin, 1937.
Christopher, John (Youd, Samuel Christopher). *No Blade of Grass*. New York: Avon, 1956.
Clarke, Arthur C. *Childhood's End*. New York: Houghton Mifflin, 1953.
——. *2001: A Space Odyssey*. New York: New American Library, 1968.
Cooper, Edmund. *Seed of Light*. Atlantic Highlands, N.J.: Hutchinson, 1959.
Crichton, Michael, *The Andromeda Strain*. New York: Knopf, 1969.
Delany, Samuel R. *The Einstein Intersection*. New York: Ace, 1967.
Dick, Philip K. *Dr. Bloodmoney; or How We Got ALONG AFTER the Bomb*. New York: Ace, 1965.
——. *The Three Stigmata of Palmer Eldrich*. New York: Doubleday, 1965.
Donnelly, Ignatius. *Caesar's Column*. Chicago: F. J. Schultze, 1890.
Doyle, Arthur Conan. *The Poison Belt*. New York: Macmillan, 1913.
England, George A. *Darkness and Dawn*. Westport, Conn.: Hyperion Conn., 1914.

Flammarion, Camille. *Omega: The Last Days of the World (La Fin du Monde)*. New York: Cosmopolitan Pub., 1894.

Frank, Pat. *Alas, Babylon*. New York: Lippincott, 1959.

Harrison, Harry. *Make Room! Make Room!* New York: Berkley, 1966.

Hilton, James. *Lost Horizon*. New York: Morrow, 1933.

Le Guin, Ursula K. *The Lathe of Heaven*. New York: Scribner's, 1971.

London, Jack. *The Scarlet Plague*. New York: Paul R. Reynolds, 1912.

Marle, Robert. *Malevil*. New York: Warner, 1974.

Miller, Walter, Jr. *A Canticle for Leibowitz*. New York: Lippincott, 1959.

Norton, Andre. *Star Man's Son 2250 A.D.* New York: Fawcett, 1952.

Pangborn, Edgar. *Davy*. New York: St. Martin's, 1964.

Percy, Walker. *Love in the Ruins*. New York: Avon, 1971.

Roshwald, Mordecai. *Level 7*. New York: New American Library, 1959.

Shelley, Mary Wollstonecraft. *The Last Man*. London: Colburn, 1826.

Shiel, M. P. *The Purple Cloud*. Cutehoque, N.Y.: Buccaneer, 1901.

Shute, Nevil (Norway, Nevil Shute). *On The Beach*. New York: Ballantine, 1957.

Silverberg, Robert. *Nightwings*. New York: Avon, 1969.

Simak, Clifford D. *City*. New York: Ace, 1952.

Stapledon, Olaf. *Last and First Men*. London: Methuen, 1930.

———. *Star Maker*. London: Methuen, 1937.

Stewart, George R. *Earth Abides*. Los Altos, Calif.: Hermes, 1949.

Tucker, Wilson. *The Long Loud Silence*. New York: Clark, Irwin and Co., 1952.

Vance, Jack. *The Dying Earth*. New York: Pocket Books, 1962.

Varley, John. *The Ophiuchi Hotline*. New York: Dell, 1977.

Vonnegut, Kurt, Jr. *Cat's Cradle*. New York: Delacorte, 1963.

———. *The Sirens of Titan*. New York: Dell, 1959.

Weinbaum, Stanley G. *The Black Flame*. Reading Pa.: Fantasy Press, 1948.

Wells, H. G. *The Time Machine*. Bridgeport, Conn.: Airmount, 1895.

———. *The War of the Worlds*. Garden City, N.Y.: Doubleday, 1897.

Wilhelm, Kate. *Where Late the Sweet Birds Sang*. New York: Pocket Books, 1976.

Williamson, Jack. *Darker Than You Think*. New York: Fantasy Press, 1948.

Wyndham, John (Harris, John Beynon). *Re-Birth*. New York: Ballantine, 1955.

———. *The Kraken Wakes*. New York: Collins, 1953.

Nonfiction

I. Biblical

Lehman, Strauss. *The End of This Present World*, Grand Rapids, Mich.: Zondervan, 1967.

Lindsey, Hal. *The Late Great Planet Earth*. Grand Rapids, Mich.: Zondervan, 1976.

Simpson, Douglas J. *The Apocalypse.* Nashville: Randall House, 1975.
Wilkerson, David. *The End Times New Testament.* Old Tappan, N.J.: Chosen Books, 1975.

II. Literature

Aldiss, Brian. *Billion Year Spree: The True History of Science Fiction.* Garden City: Doubleday, 1973.
Amis, Kingsley. *New Maps of Hell.* London: Four Square Books, 1963.
Berger, Harold L. *Science Fiction and the New Dark Age.* Bowling Green, Ohio: Bowling Green University Popular Press, 1976.
Hillegas, Mark R. "Dystopian SF: New Index to the Human Situation." *New Mexico Quarterly.* 31 (1961): 238–49.
―――. *The Future as Nightmare: H. G. Wells and the Anti-Utopians.* New York: Oxford University Press, 1967.
Kermode, Frank. *The Sense of an Ending: Studies in the Theory of Fiction.* New York: Oxford University Press, 1967.
Ketterer, David. *New Worlds for Old: The Apocalyptic Imagination, Science Fiction, and American Literature.* Bloomington, Ind.: Indiana University Press, 1974.
Levin, G. "Swinburne's End of the World Fantasy." *Literature and Psychology* 24 (1974): 109–14.
May, John R. *Toward a New Earth: Apocalypse in the American Novel.* Notre Dame, Ind.: Notre Dame University Press, 1972.
Percy, Walker. "Notes for a Novel about the End of the World." *Katallagete* 3 (Fall, 1970): 5–12.
Simpson, J. "World Upside Down Shall Be: A Note on the Folklore of Doomsday." *Journal of American Folklore* 91 (January, 1978): 559–67.
Walsh, Chad. *From Utopia to Nightmare.* New York: Harper and Row, 1962.
Warrick, Patricia, Martin Harry Greenberg, and Joseph D. Olander, eds. *Science Fiction: Contemporary Mythology.* New York: Harper and Row, 1978.
Wollheim, Donald. *The Universe Makers.* New York: Harper and Row, 1971.
Woodcock, George. "Utopias in Negative." *Sewanee Review* 64 (1956): 81–97.

III. Philosophy and Religious Thought

Altizer, Thomas J. J. "Imagination and Apocalypse." *Soundings* 43 (1970): 398–412.
Boulding, Kenneth E. *The Meaning of the 20th Century.* New York: Harper and Row, 1964.
Clarke, I. F. "End of the World Is at Hand." *Futures* 7 (April, 1975): 157–62.
Cohn, Norman, *The Pursuit of the Millennium.* New York: Oxford University Press, 1957.
Davidson, James West. *Logic of Millennial Thought.* New Haven: Yale University Press, 1977.

de Chardin, Teilhard. *The Phenomenon of Man.* New York: Harper and Row, 1959.
———. *The Future of Man.* New York: Harper and Row, 1964.
Hayes, R. "Utopia: SF, Doomsday." *Contemporary Religion* 230 (April, 1977): 201–5.
Mussner, Franz. *Christ and the End of the World.* Notre Dame, Ind.: Notre Dame University Press, 1965.
Sanford, Charles L. *The Quest for Paradise: Europe and the American Moral Imagination.* Urbana, Ill.: University of Illinois Press, 1961.
Tuveson, Ernest Lee. *Millennium and Utopia: A Study in the Background of the Idea of Progress.* New York: Harper and Row, 1964.
Wink, Walter. "Apocalypse in Our Time." *Katallagete* 3 (Fall, 1970): 13–18.

IV. Science

Cohen, Daniel. *How the World Will End.* New York: McGraw-Hill, 1973.
Dennis, Geoffrey Pomeroy. *The End of the World.* London: Eyre and Spottiswoode, 1930.
Heuer, Kenneth. *The End of the World: A Scientific Inquiry.* New York: Rinehart, 1953.
McCabe, Joseph, *The End of the World.* London: G. Routledge, 1920.
Meyer, Max Wilhelm. *The End of the World.* Chicago: C. H. Kerr. 1905.
Morris, Richard. *The End of the World.* Garden City, N.Y.: Anchor Press, 1980.
Motz, Lloyd. *The Universe: Its Beginning and End.* New York: Scribner's, 1975.

V. Social Science

Cottle, Thomas and Stephen L. Klineberg. *The Present of Things Future: Explorations of Time in Human Experience.* New York: The Free Press, 1974.
Greisman, H. C. "Marketing the Millennium." *Political Society* 4 (1974): 511–24.
Gunnell, John G. *Political Philosophy and Time.* Middletown, Conn.: Wesleyan University Press, 1968.
Heilbroner, Robert L. *The Future as History.* New York: Harper and Row, 1959.
Leon-Portilla, Miguel. *Time and Reality in the Thought of the Maya.* Boston: Beacon Press, 1968.
Pocock, J. G. A. *Politics, Language, and Time.* New York: Atheneum, 1973.
Yaker, Henri, Humphry Osmond, and Frances Cheek. *The Future of Time: Man's Temporal Environment.* Garden City, N.Y.: Doubleday, 1971.

Index

Ballard, J. G., 4, 169; *The Crystal World*, 158; *The Drought*, 158; "The Drowned Giant," 171–72; *The Drowned World*, 158; "The Life and Death of God," 172; "The Voice of Time," 172; *Wind from Nowhere*, 158
Balmer, Edwin: and Philip Wylie, *After Worlds Collide*, 10, 15, 156; and Philip Wylie, *When Worlds Collide*, 9, 15–16, 156
Barjavel, René, 74; *La Nuit des Temps*, 85–86; *Le Diable l'emporte*, 89; *Ravage*, 9
Bates, Harry, "Alas, All Thinking!," 114
"Bathe Your Bearings in Blood!" *See* Simak, Clifford D.
"Battle of Dorking, The." *See* Chesney, Sir George
Bell, Neil, *The Gas War of 1940*, 122
Bellamy, Edward, *Looking Backward*, 103
"Bell-Tower, The." *See* Melville, Herman
Benson, Robert Hugh, *Lord of the World*, 59–60, 67, 171
Beresford, John, "A Negligible Experiment," 99–100
Bergson, Henri, 93
Berossus, 75
Bester, Alfred, "Adam and No Eve," 122–23
Bickerton, A. W., 144
"Big Flash, The." *See* Spinrad, Norman
"Big Space Fuck, The." *See* Vonnegut, Kurt
"Big Trip Up Yonder, The" ("Tomorrow and Tomorrow and Tomorrow"). *See* Vonnegut, Kurt
Billion Days of Earth, A. See Piserchia, Doris
Bingen, Hildegarde, 47
"Birds, The." *See* Du Maurier, Daphne

Black Death, The. See Dalton, M.
Black, Ladbroke, *The Poison War*, 122
Black Lamb and Grey Falcon. See West, Dame Rebecca
Blake, William, 142
Blish, James, 74, 169; *A Case of Conscience*, 68, 90; "Cathedrals in Space," 125; *Cities in Flight*, 90–91; *Doctor Mirabilis*, 90; *Earthman, Come Home*, 90; *Midsummer Century*, 159; *The Seedling Stars*, 153; "Surface Tension," x; "The Thing in the Attic," 153; *The Triumph of Time*, 152; "We All Die Naked," 129; and Norman L. Knight, *A Torrent of Faces*, 128
Bloch, Robert: "It Happened Tomorrow," 115; *Strange Eons*, 61
"Book of the Machines," *See* Butler, Samuel
Bowen, John, *After the Rain*, 9, 14, 15
"Boy and His Dog, A." *See* Ellison, Harlan
Brackett, Leigh, 10; *The Long Tomorrow*, 5, 15
Bradbury, Ray, 142; "The Highway," 1–3, 19; *The Martian Chronicles*, viii, 3
Brainrack. See Pedler, Kit
Brave New World. See Huxley, Aldous
Breuer, Miles J.: "The Gostak and the Doshes," 123; *Paradise and Iron*, 116, 119
Briefing for a Descent into Hell. See Lessing, Doris
Brunner, John: *The Sheep Look Up*, 169; *The Shockwave Rider*, 130; *Stand on Zanzibar*, 50, 128, 130
Brunngraber, Rudolf, 50
Burckhardt, Jacob, 79
Burgess, Anthony, *A Clockwork Orange*, 23

Torrent of Faces, A. See Blish,
James
"To Walk With Thunder." *See*
McLaughlin, Dean
Toynbee, Arnold J., *A Study of
History*, 80
Tragedy of Man, The, 22
*Treatise on General Sociology.
See* Pareto, Vilfredo
Triumph of Time, The. See Blish,
James
Tucker, Wilson, 10; *The Long
Loud Silence,* 7–8, 9, 10, 123
Tung, Lee, *The Wind Obeys
Lama Toru,* 128
*Twenty Thousand Leagues under
the Sea. See* Verne, Jules
Twenty Years at Hull House. See
Addams, Jane
"Twilight." *See* Campbell, John
W., Jr.
2001: A Space Odyssey. See
Clarke, Arthur C.

"Uncanny, The." *See* Jentsch,
Ernst
Underground Man. See de Tarde,
Gabriel
Undying Fire, The. See Wells,
H. G.
"United Planets." *See* Reynolds,
Mach
Unthinkable. See Sibson, Francis
Updike, John, 48–49

Verne, Jules, 88–89; *L'Eternel
Adam,* 159; *Twenty Thousand
Leagues under the Sea,* 85
Vico, Giovanni Battista, 79; *New
Science,* 78
Vidal, Gore: *Kalki,* 91, 169; *Mes-
siah,* 67–68, 169
"Voice of Time, The." *See* Bal-
lard, J. G.
Voltaire, *Candide,* 142–43
Vonnegut, Kurt: "The Big Space
Fuck," 132; "The Big Trip Up
Yonder ("Tomorrow and
Tomorrow and Tomorrow"),

128; *Cat's Cradle,* 133–34; *God
Bless You, Mr. Rosewater,* 134;
Mother Night, 134; *Slaughter-
house-Five,* 134
*Voyages: Scenarios for a Ship
Called Earth,* 131
Vril Staff, The, 106
Vulcan's Hammer. See Dick,
Philip K.

War in the Air, The. See Wells,
H. G.
"Warlock" series. *See* Niven,
Larry
War of the Worlds, The. See
Wells, H. G.
"War That Will End War, The."
See Wells, H. G.
War with the Newts. See Čapek,
Karel
"We All Die Naked." *See* Blish,
James
Wells, H. G., 28, 93, 137, 142,
151, 163; *All Aboard for Ar-
arat,* 100; *Back to Methuselah,*
63; "The Empire of the Ants,"
165; *The History of Mr. Polly,*
95; *Kipps,* 95; "The Man of the
Year Million," 63, 114, 149–50;
M. Brittling Sees It Through,
121; *Men Like Gods,* 150;
Mind at the End of Its Tether,
150; *A Modern Utopia,* 109;
The Salvaging of Civilization,
121; "The Star," xi, 155; *The
Story of the Last Trump,* 65,
66; *The Time Machine,* 63, 64,
87, 89, 109, 145, 149, 151; *The
Undying Fire,* 100; *The War in
the Air,* 120–21; *The War of the
Worlds,* ix, xiii, 73, 156, 165–
66; "The War That Will End
War," 121; *When the Sleeper
Wakes,* 105–6; *The World Set
Free,* 121
Welt im Chaos. See Wessels,
Dieter
"Weltuntergang." *See* Soyfer,
Jura